9/05

Farewell,
My Only One

Farewell, My Only One

Antoine Audouard

Translated from the French by
Euan Cameron

Houghton Mifflin Company

BOSTON · NEW YORK · 2004

First published in Great Britain by Canongate Books Ltd., 2004

For information about permission to reproduce selections
from this book, write to Permissions, Houghton Mifflin Company,
215 Park Avenue South, New York, New York 10003.

Visit our Web site: www.houghtonmifflinbooks.com.

Library of Congress Cataloging-in-Publication Data
Audouard, Antoine.
[Adieu, mon unique. English]
Farewell, my only one / Antoine Audouard ; translated
from the French by Euan Cameron.
p. cm.
ISBN 0-618-15286-5
I. Cameron, Euan. II. Title.
PQ2661.U326A6613 2004
843'.914—dc22 2004047273

Book design by Melissa Lotfy

Printed in the United States of America

QUM 10 9 8 7 6 5 4 3 2 1

To my children
Marie, Alexandre, Hélène, and Ulysse

In memory of
Véronica Quaglio
and Jean-Dominique Bauby

and to Susanna,
my Only One

*He who acquires wisdom, acquires grief;
and a heart that understands cuts like
rust in the bones.*

BISHOP POSSIDIUS,
Life of St Augustine

Prologue

T ODAY, during Matins, one of our brothers fainted. The
sound of his head striking the stone echoed over the
abbey while we were singing Yahweh has sent me to
bind up hearts that are broken, to proclaim liberty to captives.
I, too, was feeling weary and a fever was spreading waves of icy
heat over my limbs and throughout my body.

As two lay brothers led Brother Guy away, we let the peace of
the psalm sink into us. I did not weep; my sorrow was lighter than
my burden. Even when we heard Guy's cries as we crossed the
Close, no head turned and we sang, with one voice, one heart.

In spite of the cold, more than one of us was sweating beneath his cowl.

As we made our way from the church back to the priory of
Saint John, the wailing abated. The light of the full moon bathed
us, as we lay in our bunks, in the colour of cemeteries. Then we
heard them: they were no longer the wrathful cries of a thousand devils fighting for possession of a soul, but the sobs of a
humble man suffering, as we all do.

I prayed for you, Guy, my brother. But I was thinking of
myself.

✦　✦　✦

As I was leaving the chapterhouse this morning after Terce, I asked the prior for news of Brother Guy.

The prior said nothing; I was on the point of repeating my question when he gestured with his hand in the direction of the well. Guy was standing there alone, looking much calmer. A golden light flickered about his fair hair and shone on his shoulders — he was not someone who belonged to our age of stones and rain, but to some ancient book, a prophecy come true. I went over to him and, when he saw me, his eyes glazed with a look of unspoken supplication. I smiled at him.

'Did you feel as though you were not alone last night?' I asked.

He swept his hand over his face as he sometimes does when chasing away flies and phantoms.

'I see wonderful things,' he murmured in that low, tremulous voice which seemed to belong to someone much older.

The sun had just passed over the nave of our church, the air was full of a promise that would not be fulfilled, and yet there was still some of that joy within me too. I smiled.

'Not so much arrogance, little brother. I'm telling you, you're not alone.' I lay my hand on his shoulder and squeezed it. This gesture, with which Abelard used to subdue me, was now mine. But I would not use it to control or constrain.

I returned to the *scriptorium* while Guy continued to gaze up at the sky.

The prior found me with the quill of my pen crushed against my scroll of parchment and my head cradled in my elbow. He glanced at the fire burning in the hearth.

'All this heat and no one to enjoy it,' he muttered without any bitterness.

He's a peaceful and seemingly good man who will become abbot as long as no bishop meddles. His nose, eyes and mouth are all squashed untidily over his flat face, and yet there is something truly gentle about this ugliness. One of his legs is stiff, which always makes him look as if he is running, even when he walks.

'Are you copying?'

I nodded. He asked nothing else. He really must not find out what is concealed beneath my reserved bearing, my stern, scholarly face and my hours of study.

He went out without saying another word.

I penned a few more words — the last. I tightened the sheepskin leather straps that hold the parchment together. I rolled it up inside the rough cloth bag which I slipped beneath my cowl. I stood up and my bones creaked like an old boat.

I knew what I still had to do, I knew every detail of what had to be done up to the moment of my death, and even after.

That evening, after Vespers, I would speak to that innocent, Guy. I would trust him with my secret.

In the midst of the silent night there is no silence. The monks snore, the monks talk and cry out, the monks wrestle with angels and with devils, the monks wail over their childhood nightmares. Only a storm can quieten them and, unfortunately, storms do not occur every night.

My body felt as light as my soul and I wandered about among my brethren as if I were haunting them. I knew where Brother Guy's bunk was; my hand brushed lightly against him and he opened his eyes. 'Come, my brother, my friend, the time has come.' He got up and followed me.

We went down into the Close and left the priory by the east door. We walked in the moonlight, which flooded the abbey in a grey light. There, where as a young clerk I had watched the carpenters erect a wooden ceiling, the stone cupolas rose up like so many skies.

Guy, who was behind me, asked no questions — when I approached the altar and knelt down, he merely shivered slightly.

In the nave, at the height of a man's arm, almost at the southern corner of the transept, there was a stone that I knew had never been securely fixed. But when I touched it with my hand it did not budge.

Guy heard the cry of surprise that escaped from my lips; he saw me pushing, grumbling and perspiring. I turned to him with tears in my eyes.

Without saying a word, he too attacked the side of the stone with his hands and his fingernails, both of us scraping away at it together, cutting our fingers and scratching our skin, our flesh mingling with the limestone.

The stone did not shift. It was not enough to believe in miracles. When we stopped, out of breath, Brother Guy wiped his hands over his face and on his cowl. We gasped and collapsed on top of one another.

'Do you see?' he asked eventually in his low voice.

I didn't see. He pointed to a cavity, to a length of stone that we had been unable to loosen — one of those putlogs into which scaffolding beams had been placed during the course of construction.

With my hands I indicated the size of the cavity that Guy had discovered. I ran my fingers over the contours and at the same time I thought of it as the Jerusalem that awaited me in my dreams.

In one quick gesture, I took the bag with the scrolls from around my neck and I placed it where it was meant to fit, in this recess where no one would ever find it. No one? I looked at the simpleton, the fool. He helped me replace the stone: he took the dust mixed with blood from the ground and swallowed it. He wiped his lips. No one? The simpleton, the fool would hold his tongue. And if he did talk, nobody would listen to him.

I was weak and unsteady on my legs.

And this is how the monks would find us when the first rays from the east light up the altar — an old man dying in the arms of a child with eyes that are too bright.

Part I

Nothing for the Journey

1

Take nothing for the journey: neither staff,
nor haversack, nor bread, nor money; and
let none of you take a spare tunic.

LUKE 9:3

I T WAS on a frozen mud road in France, one day in the winter
of 1116, when Louis VI was king and Stephen de Garlande
his chancellor, when Galon was Bishop of Paris and Paschal
II our most Holy Father. It was a time of commonplace woes. I
was twenty years old but I had seen more than my share of full
moons.

My father fought at Hastings against the Normans. It had left
him with a real horror of conflict and a good deal of respect for
his new king — as my Christian name, William, indicates. When,
as a child, I used to dream of tournaments, he was exceedingly
persistent in forcing me to study. He handed me over to teachers
who knew nothing, and I was beaten for getting the better of
them. For months I stopped listening and was tempted to feign
stupidity.

Every Latin translation was drummed into me; to avoid further toil I had secretly learned a little Greek. My father would
not allow me to duel, even with a wooden sword, even with
children who were less robust than me. As far as knowledge of

7

weapons was concerned, I escaped with a few scratches from bushes. Under stormy skies, I confronted springs and the shadows of oak trees.

I would not be a knight.

My only friend was called Stephen. He was an errant priest who sometimes shared the bed of one of our servants. He told me about the world and encouraged me to seek God on my own. He said with a smile that there was nothing more terrible and more beautiful than man.

It was he who told me the secret of my birth—my illegitimacy —and in doing so he did me a great favour as well as much harm. The habit of telling the truth at an early age in a world full of lies is a weapon as well as a hindrance. I continued to respect the person I called my mother, a pale woman with cold hands who never gave me a name, thereby hoping no doubt that I would cease to exist. She did not touch me or so much as glance at me. Not being noticed by those one wants to be noticed by teaches you more about life than do ferulas and beatings—you learn to know that you are not loved, unless by chance or accident.

I would not be a father.

When everyone is desperately trying to make his presence felt and to leave some trace of himself, it is soothing to the soul to make of one's absence a cloak for all seasons. It was my own way of *fleeing to the absolute on one's own*—and without delay.

I would be anybody. Or rather, with the secret and limitless pride which made a difference that only I was aware of: nobody.

Father Stephen used to tell me that the Ulysses of a thousand wiles and the heinous Ulysses were actually the same man and, by extension, all men. He knew the animals and the stars, the courses of rivers and the composition of the love potion from which Tristan had drunk. He told me love stories and he would say (though in a low voice) that at certain hours of the night, in rivers and forests, in churches and solitary places, Love was at one with woman and with God. As regards religion, he had a preference for superstition and accounts of miracles; he even used to say that these were the only things he believed in. He didn't care for the great mysteries.

Knowing his tastes, peasants and poor monks from our part of the countryside would come and relate their stories, telling him about swarms of devils and armies of angels, of voices from heaven. He collected them in a little book and I sometimes helped him fold the pages.

We roamed along our English lanes, and my feet felt the softness of our hills and our hump-backed bridges. He took me to our squat country churches to see the ancient relics: the sword which a certain lord, upon his return from the wars, had sunk into a stone as he made a vow never again to resort to violence; the face of a prostitute that had been carved into the wood of the cross when she vowed to sin no more. Furthermore, he had strong hands with which he soothed pain, and he had the rare ability to be patient and say nothing when people spent too long recounting their tribulations to him.

When I was twelve years old, he was discovered dead, his legs broken, his eyelids sewn shut. Such violence and mystery were not in keeping with this good man who was not in the least corrupt, and whose only crime had been to love the warmth of a woman's body too much.

I would not be a priest.

All I was good for was living in my dreams.

At the age of sixteen I told my father that I needed a horse and wanted to see the world. He gave me several gold sovereigns which were stolen from me after just a few days . . . *Take nothing for the journey: neither staff, nor haversack, nor bread, nor money; and let none of you take a spare tunic* . . . I was seasick on board a ship, imagining they were abducting me to sell me as a slave to some Moors (such nightmares afflict you on pitch-black nights when your heart is down). I crossed France without stopping, and I studied in Rome with a monk who knew Augustine by heart. I remember the bewildering melancholy that seized me when I heard him say these words: *My childhood died a long time ago, but I, I live* . . . I witnessed a sect of Pythagoreans who ate nothing but grass and met at night to talk in low voices about the true significance of numbers.

Although my father hadn't given me a horse, I found some along the way, as well as dogs, unicorns and all sorts of wondrous animals that I recognised, but whose names I didn't know. I spent a year in Salerno with a woman physician who tended bishops and princes from all over Europe. We travelled by boat and slept on a blue island with white rocks where only birds and snakes lived. She showed me her gifts and invited me to share them. She gave me a golden chain which some minor king had bestowed on her. When I told her that I was leaving, a sad expression came over her brown eyes (she had brown skin, too, from which I used to lick the salt, and those eyes would close, and there was a rumbling sound in her rising breast when I entered her, and afterwards, resting and perspiring, I would see that sweet smile that made her whole body unwind, and mine as well). Then she recited these ancient and very simple lines, which made me want to look away:

> *Go and be happy, for nothing lasts.*
> *But always remember how much I have loved you.*

I went.

I wore out my arse on ships' benches, on horses' saddles. I had some leather shoes that turned up at the ends and made children in villages laugh — women's shoes! — and I walked barefoot over sharp stones.

I scoured the earth. I knew the shores as well as the open sea. I knew how light the air and the heart feel when you reach the summit.

I read few books, remembering that Socrates mistrusted them but that words are our only means of learning. I liked the rigid expressions on the faces of men who believed that they knew all things, and I liked to frequent taverns and drink a light white wine that simplified all thought.

I travelled through Spain, to Cordoba, where I acquired a little Arabic and some Hebrew, as well as new names for God: Elohim, Allah the Merciful, the terror of the Infidels. I discovered that there were other holy books, and no doubt still more across the seas and beyond the mountains.

In order to eat, I served others and took unexpected pleasure in allowing myself to be mistreated. And I taught and I sang; I could play the rote, as well as the three-holed eastern flute, the sound of which made children mill around me, clapping their hands and asking for more. I also picked fruit and corrected Latin verbs with rather more gentleness than had been used on me. When I arrived in a remote place where men spoke with pebbles in their mouths and disliked strangers, I took out my flute; then I sketched the walls of a house, an oak tree and a church on a tablet. In this way people realised that I came from a place where there was a house, God and trees. Their expressions grew less impenetrable and I was given bread and goat's milk, and sometimes a glass of a wine thick as blood, which I had to drink with a smile.

Others spoke to me readily. You don't need to try too hard to blot out people's memories of you: you just have to ignore the first question they ask. They are so full of themselves and so certain that they are unique that they then open their hearts freely and allow their bellies to be tickled passively, like dogs. On some evenings, it makes you want to scream. But the soul does not reap its rewards until the last.

I learned of my father's death when I was in Venice, gazing at the lagoon and contemplating boarding a ship and, contrary to his wishes, going to war at last. For I was sick of all these new experiences the world offered, all these universe builders. I wanted to watch my face as my tears fell in the green water. I caught a brief glimpse of myself with perfect clarity; and then my features disintegrated in the little waves, and what I had learned about myself sank for ever.

My headaches as well as my sorrows deserted me.

I went to visit my father's grave and, without knowing why, planted a tree a few feet away. It was a comfort for me to see that I was looked upon as a stranger in my own village too. To make of the whole world a place of exile, to be at home everywhere.

I re-embarked on a quiet ship full of pilgrims, who sang as they made their way to Sainte-Foy de Conques.

I grazed my hands pulling on their oars and hoisting their sails. We sang to the glory of God and even to the beauty of women. At sea, when the moon is full in the dark sky, all routes become one: at the whim of the wind, the soul submits.

They were not seeking miracles or begging favours. Others might build churches; at the risk of their lives, these people were offering their songs to the glory of God.

They never volunteered the notion that I might join them; in a moment of vanity which was probably the result of seasickness, I think this secretly upset me.

I left them on the sandy shore, lifting their gowns above their white ankles to avoid the sea, hopping about like frogs and laughing like children.

As I departed along a path that passed behind the dunes before disappearing into the woods, tears were streaming down my cheeks. I wasn't even sad. It was simply that I knew I could never participate in the happiness of others; I would be the one who arrives too early or leaves too late, the one who is not called or who, when invited, wakes up in the middle of the night knowing that the party is over.

2

I ARRIVED AT Fontevrault abbey having followed the course of the Loire. Some devout but prudent pilgrims had advised me against the place: the order was the creation of a lunatic. His heart aflame with promises, Robert of Arbrissel ventured into brothels to make his conversions and slept naked among the nuns, who were virgins or young widows. The worst part of it, they would tell me, was not so much that there was a priory for men and another for women within the same walls —which in itself was the source of terrible scandals—but that on the instructions of the founder, the head of the order was a woman.

I liked this touch of lunacy which accorded secretly with my own madness. I also needed to stop for a while and share the company of humans.

Fontevrault was in disarray: while on a visit to the priory at Orsan, Robert had been taken ill. In the panic that ensued, the abbess, Petronilla, had gone to be with him. On the return journey, Robert's body fell victim to all kinds of greed and envy— from peasants and nobles alike, who wanted to cut out his heart and put it in a shrine so as to attract God's blessing on their wretched church and some revenue from pilgrimages.

Thanks to my fine handwriting, I had succeeded in obtaining

employment from the *armarius*, Brother Andrew, whose scribe had just died. The old man was writing the story of Robert's life in order that he should be made a saint.

Days passed and we waited for news from a messenger or a traveller. All we had were rumours: his body had drifted away on the current, like that of Moses, or had been carried off on a chariot of fire. Brother Andrew shook his head: the life of a saint — a genuine one — was not founded on such nonsense.

The doors of the abbey opened and a hymn could be heard; outside, an unruly crowd clustered around. It was he, it was Robert who had come back to die on his own land, surrounded by his little brothers and sisters.

'Hurry up,' Brother Andrew grumbled at me, 'you'll see, there won't be any room left in the church.'

He sighed as he watched the smoke rising from the great cones on the kitchen roofs. We hadn't even had time to eat. I supported him, pushed him forward, dragging him and crying out: 'Make way! Make way!'

Petronilla came at the head, walking beside the bower of branches on which Robert lay. He had been carried along byways and floated down rivers by a succession of men and women who took it in turns so that his soul did not escape during a moment of inattention. Behind the abbess came some important figures: his friend Geoffrey of Vendôme, Archbishop Léger of Bourges and a host of priests and monks who grieved for him as forsaken lovers do.

'Is he dead or alive?' asked Brother Andrew. 'Tell me; I can't see anything.'

Robert's withered hands were folded over his cilice and his eyes were closed. And yet it seemed to me that breath still filled his lungs and that a little blood flowed through his cheeks.

'I don't know,' I told Andrew.

The procession halted at the entry to the nave; far off, a lifetime away, the choir gleamed. The monks and religious did not pause for a moment: they took their places near the altar, while the poor gathered together at the back of the church. Many had to remain outside for lack of space.

Two men walked down the central aisle, moving at the same pace, but so dissimilar that it was as if they had come from separate worlds: the one dark, the other pale in appearance; the one strong and handsome, rather like a bear, the other younger, with a face that was already haggard, and with sparse hair and hollow cheeks, looking as if he were returning from travels that had subjugated all wolfish desires.

Petronilla advanced towards them. Andrew caught my sleeve.

'Bernard of Fontaines,' he whispered. 'He's just left the abbey of Cîteaux to found a monastery at Clairvaux, in a valley infested with wild beasts.'

'The tall one?'

'No, the other one. His name is Peter Abelard. He thinks he's the greatest philosopher in the world.'

I could see him from the corner of my eye as a slight smile raised the wrinkles in his face on which everything was always plainly written.

'They loathe one another,' muttered Andrew, not displeased.

'Do they know each other?'

'They don't need to in order to hate each other. Anyway, watch...'

With a sign to the lay brethren, Petronilla gave the order for the litter to be lifted and carried up to the altar. Bernard and Peter stepped aside. She stood beside Robert and took his hands, placing one over the other.

My gaze was fixed on Peter Abelard. He was a cleric with an unkempt tonsure, bushy eyebrows and a nose that was too large; he had lively, laughing eyes that were very dark and which moved from irony to anger at the merest impulse.

Without turning round, Bernard went to close the double doors.

'He's young but tiresome,' Andrew declared with a hint of respect. 'Apparently he forced his entire family to take the veil, and he has threatened hell-fire on those women who do not submit.'

Petronilla presented the cross to Robert and his lips remained closed, as did his eyes, while on his chest there was a flutter of motion so weak it could have been that of a bird. There was general weeping, and tears on every face.

When the light from the east shone on Robert of Arbrissel's countenance and he opened his eyes, a murmur could be heard. His lips moved as if to speak, but no sound emerged, no prayer, no plea to the Lord. All that could be seen in his expression was an infinite distress; his eyelids flickered.

Bernard approached; monks and nuns knelt. We put our hands together to recite the 'Our Father' as the sun gradually lit up each fold of Robert's shroud.

When we rose to our feet, Peter Abelard had opened the doors behind which the paupers and whores had gathered; they too were on their knees and from their lips the words of the same prayer were uttered.

Bernard stood up and walked over to the master of studies; he was holding his stomach as if it was burning him and his eyes were feverish.

'. . . in the dust and in the mud,' said Robert of Arbrissel.

'What is he saying?' Andrew asked, but I did not reply, being prevented from doing so by furious voices telling us to hush.

> *From the depths of my distress, I cry to you*
> *Merciful God, hear my plea*
> *And do not look upon the extent of my sins*
> *So that justice may be accomplished,*
> *Merciful God.*

The women continued singing the *Pie Deus* as long as they could. When they stopped, all that could be heard was the groan that slipped from Robert's throat.

When there was no longer any echo, it meant he was dead.

✦   ✦   ✦

Brother Andrew and I were walking around the cloister.

'I don't feel like writing,' he said.

'You have to finish . . .'

'A prayer is needed.'

'You'll compose a fine one for him.'

He turned towards me, his forehead etched with lines that might have been made by a stylet, his face the colour of old wax.

'You already know too much for your age.'

'I'll keep it to myself, if you want.'

I felt overcome with an inexplicable pride. We clerks are not honoured, our shoulders are never dubbed by a sword, and our glory is a song that is passed from lip to lip without anyone knowing who wrote it. When Brother Andrew hired me, at the point at which his copyist had stopped, I simply wrote the epitaph for my confrere who had been summoned to oblivion. *Anno Gracie M° CXVI, obiit Ademarus; successit Wilhelmus . . .*

'What troubles me,' Andrew continued, 'is that I'm not sure I'm creating a saint.'

'Why?'

'To begin with, he's the son of a priest. That hasn't bothered anyone for centuries, but the times are changing. And then he spent a long time in the outside world . . .'

'He's not the first!'

'He used to visit brothels . . .'

'. . . to convert lost souls!'

'He knew a woman, several perhaps.'

'Augustine was no better.'

'Look at Bernard of Fontaines . . . I've read that he claimed to have driven away a woman, who crept into his bed to keep herself warm, as if she were the devil . . .'

'You're joking! As Jerome would say, *he shall walk upon burning coals and his feet shall not be burned.* But very well . . . if that's what he's really like, he will become a saint. Become his biographer!'

He gave me a sideways glance and saw me smile.

17

'A biographer of saints . . . What a life! I'm too old,' he said. 'Robert will be my last. And he really does frighten me.'

We took shelter in the *scriptorium* and Andrew said nothing while I took out the implements, the tablets for the draft, the parchment and goose quill. He paced to and fro around me, gradually immersing himself in the gilded legend of the last days of Robert of Arbrissel. His features lit up.

'We should have killed him before now,' he said at last.

'Why do that?'

'This endless slow death, it's already taken too long, people won't like it. And the groaning at the end . . . too sad, a suspicion of paganism, traces of doubt, not enough light. The Virgin Mary's missing. We can do better! Come on!'

He warmed himself by the fireplace, the only one in the abbey. Light from the flames was flickering about his face.

Suddenly we heard the sound of voices coming from the north gallery of the Close. We glanced at one another. Andrew sighed. I laid down my pen.

Bernard and Peter Abelard were alone with Petronilla in the chapter room.

'The words,' thundered Abelard, 'did you hear the words that came from his mouth?'

'I heard the will of Our Lord,' Bernard said softly.

'There were over three hundred of us in the abbey and the Lord spoke to you alone?'

'Keep your arguments for your students, brother, as well as your logic . . .'

'"In the dust and in the mud." Isn't that what he said?'

Abelard shifted his gaze and gestures from Bernard to Petronilla. He didn't understand. He was used to being able to convince people in a flash, with a word; but God's reed was a resilient athlete.

Petronilla looked away. A simple and more human sorrow afflicted her. So many people wanted Robert to have his tombstone beside the altar and she was weary of the constant struggle. Then . . .

'We shall bury him in the church,' she said finally, not daring to look at Abelard.

He conceded defeat while Bernard raised his open hands to heaven.

'May God's will be done, brother.'

The two men glared at one another and neither gave way — the dark eyes of the philosopher versus the light, transparent, intense gaze of the Abbot of Clairvaux.

'Take care,' Abelard said eventually in a muted voice, 'not to confuse your own will with His.'

'What can I do if He speaks to me,' said Bernard with his steely sweetness, 'and if I hear Him?'

The lay brothers heaved up the stone to create the space that awaited Robert.

Still more wretches arrived on foot, their hose, or the rags that were wrapped around their feet, torn to shreds along the stony pathways; lords on horseback, bishops, Jews, people from Montsoreau, from Bourgueil, from Tours, even from Orléans; the roads bore their tears, and the Loire had become the river of grief.

Christ's champion was dead.

I could scarcely remain standing during Mass.

In front of the church, Bernard of Fontaines was preaching abnegation of the world, love of solitude and the beauty of the deserts. He was speaking about his vale of Absinthe, about Clairvaux. Five or six young men, noblemen with childlike eyes, stood beside him: they truly believed that honey can be tapped from rocks. They would follow him shortly.

Abelard left on his own.

As Robert's coffin sank slowly into the ground, I left the abbey like a thief stealing relics. I felt very weak and very small.

I forbade myself to imagine Brother Andrew's expression when he discovered I was missing. His old hand would have to complete the life of a saint who was not and never would be holy.

Once outside the walls, I left the priory of St John quickly. The merchants were already offering single hairs from Robert's head or the sandal that first set foot on the soil of Fontevrault. I risked being noticed in the crowd if my face wasn't streaming with real tears: I fled in the direction of the Vienne, towards Candes—and thence to the Loire. I needed paths that widened into roads, streams that became torrents and rivers.

Dusk had already fallen, and at the church of St Martin the bells were ringing out the canonical hours. I would not be singing the office. I walked along narrow lanes in the lengthening shadows. I found a husk of bread, drank water from the stream and breathed the air of the birds.

I did not know why I walked up that hill and why my legs were no longer painful.

When I reached the top, the figure of a horseman almost sent me tumbling to the bottom.

It was Peter Abelard, swathed in his cloak, with his dark skin and clothing, his black eyes and his face darkened by the furrow on his brow, surveying the landscape and watching this little man climbing towards him.

He dismounted, tethered his horse and sat down in front of it. He smiled and hailed me with a finger.

'So, you're not with God's flock?'

'No.'

'Then what are you doing? Were you following me?'

'I think so.'

His chest heaved with laughter. His warm voice enveloped me. I felt drunk without having touched any wine. He opened his hand to me.

'Let us sit down and talk.'

At first we did not speak. The moon cast silver beams over the stream. The breath of his horse warmed me.

'Were you really following me?'

'I was following you or I was fleeing, it depends . . .'

'Do you know who I am?'

'A master.'

'What do you want from a master?'

'Nothing, really.'

'And yet you were following me. You should do what I do, friend: kill your masters.'

As the fires began to glow and the air grew cool, I didn't ever want to leave this weary man who spoke like Jesus. I envied the solitude that weighed him down. I was ashamed of the words I wanted to utter as he stretched out his heavy body and tightened his horse's saddle. He wrapped himself in his cloak.

'You'll have to make your own way, but you'll know the reason why.'

'And if I don't want to make my own way?'

He did not reply. The shadow of his horse disappeared into the moonlit landscape. My heart was thumping.

I had found him, this master whom I did not seek.

3

I APPROACHED the town in crab-like fashion. My feet were hurting me badly and my coat was too big for me.

Just as I was reaching the top of a hill, a group of horsemen rode past, spattering me with earth. I heard them shouting: it was a prince returning home, accompanied by jangling soldiers and groaning prisoners; surrounded by his trusty barons, he was sure to have hung the wicked and made the poor seethe.

Once the ground had stopped shaking and the dirt had fallen off me, I realised I was in the town: I had stumbled over a pig.

Houses came into view and with them men, choked with fear and worry, traces of hope still glistening on their faces, running about as if they were drunk. It had not rained for three weeks. People walked with their mouths hanging open.

Sparkling silver and gold, the Seine could be seen from the slopes of the hill, together with its sandy little islands where supplicants sought refuge in troubled times. At dawn, a light rose from behind the pallid sun and a slight breeze skimmed the fronts of the squat houses; it slipped through openings, arches and windows, bringing with it an unjustified optimism despite the drought.

I had seen other towns, with vast clusters of wood and stone, that seemed to follow a divine plan. But here, in spite of forests of church towers that loomed up like masts, a very human madness prevailed, a filthy but marvellous confusion in which ruins and new buildings, areas of grovelling wretchedness and huge tracts of vines, all the havoc and enthusiasm of a new dawn, existed side by side without there being any clear line to distinguish them. It was as if a fire or an army of looters had ravaged the town, while at the same time and without stopping work, amid the noise and the streams of blood, builders and joiners, painters and stonemasons, working collectively and without guidance had, through some mysterious communal impulse, constructed new dwellings for the pleasure of the grandees or the glory of Christ. There were new bell towers complete with their bronze fittings, broken spires, ruined steeples, collapsed walls, scaffolding that seemed to reach to the sky, from which the walls of an apse could be seen soaring up, or the broken arches of a nave. As I was standing there speechless, admiring the layers of this miraculous disaster, a little man with a tonsured head tugged at my coat.

'Have you a sou, friend?'

I turned out my pockets.

'Nothing. Where are we?'

'The church is known as Notre-Dame-des-Champs. That big farm and that wine-press you see down there were the Roman baths. They make wine there now. Are you a pilgrim?'

'If you like . . .'

In disbelief he scratched the wound that adorned his skull like an insect.

'What are you looking for here?'

'I wander around towns in search of masters . . .'

'This is a town with too many masters,' he sniggered.

'And you, are you a prince among thieves, or a thief among princes?'

He stared at me, intrigued.

'Both, I imagine. I survive. I follow my master and shall not be yours. Come with me.'

23

Some men had gathered around us, all looking alike in their rough, frequently patched-up robes: there is only one way of being poor. He turned towards me.

'We are joining the procession. From afar we shall see Bishop Galon and God knows what relics that are being carried to Notre-Dame. Secretly, it is said that we are praying for rain . . . But shhh! . . . that smacks of paganism. So, will you come?'

The little man was ugly and had the agility of a devil, but sometimes his face opened out into an innocent smile; a group of people was gathering around him — they were gesticulating and shouting, and I, who had spoken so many languages, no longer understood any. When they all began moving, I followed, just doing my best not to fall.

We stumbled along the slopes of the Mount Sainte-Geneviève and, after trampling through rows of vines, we re-joined the body of the procession at Saint-Julien-le-Pauvre.

Below the Petit Pont, in the arches, the windmills had stopped turning. A few bathers were waving their arms around and the water came bursting through in gushes — silt-laden water that could no longer rid itself of impurities, scraps of fish and remains of animals, in the flow of the river.

In order to see, you had to stand on tiptoe and contort yourself; grubby children had climbed up onto the shoulders of men whose backs were as large as a double harness.

The sounds of men shouting and the noises of animals combined in unison as they waited in exasperation. The dry heat affected the throat; I looked at the dust rising from the ground, thrown up by thousands of footsteps. I was thirsty.

In the distance the quays along the Grève and the market were at a standstill since all the townspeople were at prayer in the streets or in the shade of walls. On the other side of the island, if you twisted your neck to the south and towards the Mount Sainte-Geneviève, the eye could follow the undulating wave of churches and vines, gardens and ruins; and beyond the sea of hats and bonnets fifty feet ahead, just at the level of the small castle by the Petit Pont, I could see the tall figure of the bishop with his stooped shoulders.

In his mitre, with its representations of the miracles of the saints, and his white silk cloak, embroidered with threads of silver and gold, he looked like an angel sent on earth by Our Lord to announce the good news.

Just in front of the bishop, the deacons were carrying shrines containing relics that were being taken to Notre-Dame: one of St Denis's fingers, St Geneviève's heart and—directly from Jerusalem—a nail from the True Cross bearing the actual dried blood of Jesus Christ on it.

In front of me was a girl in a blue coat wearing a golden flower in her hair, the nape of whose neck disappeared the moment I came a little too close. The few paces that separated us constituted an entire journey: she was there, she was not there, she returned, she was gone.

When I saw the flower fall from her hair, I hurled myself among the forest of legs to pick it up. I don't know how I didn't fall, or how I found the energy to rise to my feet again and rush onwards. I opened my hand: a few crushed petals.

As we left the Rue Saint-Christophe, we emerged onto the square, among the ruins of the old cathedral of Saint-Étienne. Over there, opposite the porch of the Last Judgement, framed by saints and doctors of the Church, Bishop Galon was waving his arms about, his words coming and going on the stiff wind. 'Kneel down! Kneel down!' people were crying, while I remained standing—I was searching for the girl I'd lost. The flower was falling apart in my clenched fist.

The bishop went into the church, the crowd surged forward again, and the throng was unbelievably dense, picking me up and setting me down like a castaway in the midst of strangers, who all wanted to touch those shrines, and to kiss them.

The church was just a droning crush of men who were trying

to climb up onto the plain columns and hold onto the leaves and birds on the chapiters. Those who continued to come in knocked over the pews as well as their companions.

When I got my breath back, the girl was there before me and I was within touching distance of her shoulder. Next, she disappeared into the swarm of men and I charged forward, crying out, bumping into people and hurting myself. She was on the ground, a flower in blue, being trampled. Trying to protect her head, she had scratched her hand, and there were drops of blood on her fair hair. I knelt down to grasp her arm.

The light of her pale blue eyes.

'Come on,' I begged her, 'you must get up or else you'll die.'

I don't know what she heard but her arms clasped my neck. I lifted her up and I forced my way through, heedless of the blows and protests.

I am not strong. I have never carried a woman.

We passed the porch, making our way against the flow of the crowd that continued to jostle and push. We managed to escape to the far side of the baptistery and alongside the wall of the Close. When I put her down I suddenly had no more breath left and had to sit down beside her, my chest burning like a furnace. We remained where we were for a few moments, covered in dust and sweat, desperately trying to take our minds off the terrifying scene that almost smothered us. It was she who spoke first.

'Thank you.'

'I had your flower . . .'

She looked at me, her blue eyes questioning. I opened my hand. She saw the flower—what remained of it, a patch of yellow on my palm. She looked at me and smiled.

'Did you snatch me away from the tumult just to give me this?'

Behind the exhaustion there was sweetness in her voice. As she stood up, I wanted to take her arm to help her. She rejected my offer with a smile. A body so distant that is so close . . . She licked the blood from her hands.

'I would have died . . .'

She said that without any particular emotion, more as if in surprise.

'Just consider that I don't like flowers being trampled upon . . .'

'Tell me your name. My uncle would be angry if my rescuer had no name . . .'

'William.'

'I shall not forget you, William.'

She walked through the archway at the entrance to the Close and disappeared.

I wanted to call her; I said nothing. I didn't know her name.

When I returned to the square it was still just as packed.

I felt a drop of water on my forehead, another on my neck. Rain was falling over the Seine and a murmur rose up from the throats of the pilgrims.

A babble burst from their lips—a prayer, an offering of thanks. When I became caught up in the crush—those who were trying to get in still wanted to come in, while those who were inside now wanted to get out—I had the feeling that a mountain was falling on top of me.

I fainted.

4

WHILE I was unconscious, I found myself dreaming that I was at the very top of that hill on which the entire city had been revealed to me, teeming with animal life and shimmering with fierce energy. My spirit hovered above men's houses and time enfolded me and carried me away. The absolute freedom I revelled in gave me a pleasant sense of well-being. I was rudely awoken by a slap.

I wept, all of a sudden aware of a pain in my back, a pain in my balls, a pain in my ribs, and feeling that the earth was cold and the world unjust.

'Are you dead or alive?' enquired a voice belonging to the realm of shadows.

I sat up, still groaning and blinking, and brushed my hand over my mouth and cheeks. A lantern was swinging above my reeling head.

A powerful hand, as broad as a saddle, raised me to my feet. I found myself face to face with a dark countenance over which the lantern cast a ghostly light.

'What are you doing there?' he growled.

'How about you?'

'I see a poor wretch lying on the ground. What would you do

if you were me? Would you strip him bare before kicking him to death?'

I laughed along with him. The full moon lit up the ruined tower of the cathedral of Saint-Étienne and to my left I could make out the dark mass of Saint-Jean-le-Rond and the walls of Notre-Dame Close. Apart from the odd cry in the night, everyone was asleep in the Hôtel-Dieu. It was the time when only madmen, stray beasts, and the dying are to be heard. Restless souls could be glimpsed, furtively hurrying by.

He placed his hand in mine; this fierce grip which had crushed necks and abducted women could be gentle.

'My name is Arnold,' he said, suddenly affable, 'and I come from Brescia, in Italy, land of the unworthy popes.'

'And I am William, who set off from Oxford and journeyed through many a town and country in order to learn and to watch others quarrel.'

'Are you thirsty, William?'

He gave me no time to reply. We walked past the Grand Pont and crossed the deserted Grève. The rain had stopped. There was no longer a breath of air; the heat rose up our legs; the stench of rotten fish tickled our nostrils. In a tavern hidden away at the bottom of an alleyway in the Monceau Saint-Gervais, I drank strong ale with my new-found friend.

He spoke in the natural way a child does, without fear or restraint. He had been brought up in a spirit of anger against those in power, which was rekindled whenever he witnessed injustice, malice or folly. He loathed oppression and he believed that God wished men to be free. He asked me what I was searching for in Paris. I demurred.

'My master,' I said eventually in a low voice, staring into my glass of ale.

'What do you mean?'

I repeated what I had just said, looking into his dark eyes.

'My master, I tell you.'

He struck the wooden bench on which he was sitting and his face lit up.

'Friend,' he said, enunciating his words, 'I am your salvation. I have just the master you need—the only master I can abide myself—and to speak truthfully the only master there is around here.'

'I know,' I said. 'Peter Abelard.'

'How do you know of him?'

I told the story of my wanderings, about Brother Andrew, about Fontevrault and its women. Arnold gazed at me wide-eyed, as if I had come from another planet. I also told him that I knew nothing about Abelard—apart from the power of his mind and the solitude he kept. That made him laugh. Solitude? The philosopher could not take a step on the Île de la Cité without crowds surrounding him. He was the greatest philosopher of his age, a man who could clench a stone in his hands and make it ooze with syllogisms, a man who spoke of the unity of the divine trinity in daring analogies, who caused the brave to tremble and cowards to flee.

'When he speaks,' said Arnold, 'it's as if Aristotle and Plato were re-embodied in this one man so that mysteries crumble and reason triumphs. With him, you feel prompted to go where no man has been before, due to ignorance and fear especially, and you realise that it is not wrong to understand everything we believe in. He's a man who opens doors, and if he can't open them he overcomes them . . . He speaks the languages of others better than any other master—and that's why everyone fears him, hates him and refuses to confront him. Have you heard about how he destroyed William of Champeaux, and held old Anselm of Laon up to ridicule?'

'No.'

'It was as wonderful as Jesus in the Temple . . .'

There was a look of childlike emotion in his eyes.

'You love him, don't you?'

'You will love him.'

After that we spoke about the sins we had committed, our cowardly acts, our derelictions of duty, about Cordoba and Rome, about Jerusalem where we would soon be going; he and I had both seen soldiers of Christ returning from that place, their hands bloodied and laden with gold, their eyes still wild from having seen the face of Yahweh—and not that of his Angel. I told him what he wanted to hear about my past. He made me laugh with his gesticulations. We were happy in one another's company and we didn't want to part. After the beer came the wine, a light wine from the Orléans region, which flowed down the corners of our lips as though we were drinking it from the vine itself, and which made us sing psalms.

Arnold had climbed up onto the table and was dancing with all the dexterity of a bear, singing Italian songs. He was denouncing all hypocrites and liars and claiming to settle his accounts in private with God.

He wanted us to perform a raucous dance together, but I was feeling as heavy as an oak door, I could scarcely keep my eyes open and I believed I was participating in some new Bible, at the mercy of the curses of a drunken Jeremiah.

That night, once Arnold had at last succumbed to silence, he hauled me over streams and across gardens; we encountered shadows which could have been those of lost animals, or could have been creatures that return to the city when it's dark and which tremble with fear at every noise, every glimmer of light and every breath of wind.

We arrived at what he informed me was an inn, where students, poor pilgrims, vagabonds and brigands all slept together, waiting for sunrise, at the time of the Lendit fair. It was a large wooden house behind the Saint-Lazare leper hospital.

'Don't worry about anything,' he whispered as I was about to fall asleep on a straw mattress that smelled of corpses, 'you only get woken up by prayers and the dead.'

That night I slept like a man who has found himself, a free man. A soft voice was whispering in my ear that she would not forget me.

I was woken by the sound of groaning. It was the death-rattle of a dying man not far away from me, a man among a heap of others, some of whom were asleep and resembled corpses, while others were shivering and covering their ears, if that could be called being alive. It mattered little to me: dawn had come; I was eager for the city. I had travelled too much to have to wait long for my first morning among the streets, the smell of stables and rubbish, and the yellow sunlight on the stone. I shook Arnold's elbow, and he had barely given a grunt before he was on his feet. *Be ready!* says the Apostle. He was.

'Let's go,' I said in a low voice. 'Come.'

He looked down his beard at me, as if contemplating a new breed of animal and rubbed his eyes with his fists as if he wanted to force them back into their sockets and down into his body. My Arnold, my luster for life, how I loved this simple gesture of yours and how nostalgic I felt at the same time at the thought of losing you! And then he grunted:

'Stranger, you're crazier than a madman . . . And believe me I've seen a few, unless I'm crazy myself, that is . . .'

I began to laugh softly, so as not to disturb the dead, while we pretended to tidy our mattresses, thumping them like large, clumsy children.

A candle was still burning, lending those who were alive the same waxen pallor as the dead and concealing them among the living. Shadowy figures came and went, dispensing unction, whispering consolation and empty promises in the ears of the sick. Arnold crossed himself and avoided them as if they were the devil. Beneath the archway at the entrance, an elderly monk dressed in black gazed at us as though we were ghosts.

Down the length of the broad street that leads down to the Seine, shopkeepers were waking up. Along the route from Saint-

Denis to the Cité, on the days of the great pilgrimages, from all over Europe there came a procession of the wise and the sick, clerks, or simply men who have hope in their hearts. And when the insane arrive in a drove, bleating like sheep, there are fortunately thieves and shopkeepers to reassure the righteous man and put life back on course again.

'Look, look!' said Arnold as if he were inviting me to share in a drink, extending his arms towards the horizon.

Jewish and Lombard moneychangers were checking their balances and poring over their books. Butchers were returning, heavy footed, from the Grève abattoirs, covered in blood and bearing carcasses around their necks; dealers from Flanders and Lorraine were spreading out their cloths, letting the material run through their fingers; cobblers were kneading leather for sandals, while saddlers weighed down by saddles were inching forward like horses that were too small.

Everywhere there were hordes of men disappearing beneath their baskets; Italians, Moors and men in turbans whose eyes gleamed in the early morning darkness were unpacking goods whose names alone transported you to distant climes: the finest woollen items from Syria, leathers from Phoenicia or Cordoba, spices and wines from Greece, streams of silks, powders with which to colour the days, pieces of steel you could use to stab someone through the heart, little animals made of gold and ivory that looked as if they might come to life if you breathed on them correctly, amulets and spells to induce love, or death, parchments and magical rings — that morning the whole world had decided to set out its treasures, its baubles, its most incomparable arts as well as the most grotesque creations of man.

Arnold was filled with wonderment. He conversed in every language, he gesticulated, he spoke to tight-lipped Blacks, to melancholy Saracens, to conjurors who with a wave of their hands could make doves carrying small silver coins appear, to elderly dwarf women who could walk upon their hands and who had nothing to sell but a single sandal; he talked to loiterers who were preparing their wiles and their ruses. He juggled with the jugglers; he tumbled better than the tumblers. Oh, the fibs he told and the people he took up with and later dropped!—and I just followed behind, happy merely to be in the shadow of the showman.

People confided in him, they told him packs of lies, they suggested all sorts of deals, and he made light of everything, making promises in turn, leaving behind cries and jokes, songs and little gold pebbles as his pledge.

Walking at a different pace to us were the water-sellers, the swine and the soldiers. A frisky horse had unseated its rider and there were cries of 'Watch out!' Children wearing ill-fitting shoes went about on their own, begging for a coin, a sou, or twice as much, with varying degrees of impudence. Servants who were so well dressed that it was hard to imagine how their masters might be attired were, with a wave of the hand, claiming the very best objects, which would then disappear immediately. Beneath tents that were being unfolded men would arrive sweating under the weight of blocks of ice; they were inviting us to drink—certainly it was already hot enough. There were fragrances in the air that gave you a longing for life, a life of cravings, a craving to travel and to be sick. The sky was empty, blue and without hope, and all these people were already perspiring.

By the time we reached the Île de la Cité the day had well and truly dawned, a day of burning heat that would not end without miracles or without crimes.

There were vines and fruit trees: the bishop's garden was very much the garden of the Lord. The apse of the church had also fallen into ruin. We sat down beneath a plum tree and ate ripe black plums whose juices dripped from our fingers.

'This evening, after Vespers, we'll go and see the master,' said Arnold in a delightfully solemn tone.

I didn't reply. I let myself be lulled by the breeze that wafted through the trees and caused leaves and fruit to rustle and sway. Between the branches of a cherry tree I could see flat barges making their way down the Seine; the haulers were standing, their hands shading their eyes, their muscles tensed; the sounds of the cries and the stampede reached us in muffled bursts. Under the Grand Pont, the waters of the Seine were low and sluggish. We shall not be driven out of paradise: nobody would dream of finding us here.

Arnold continued to daydream as he thought of his hero.

'You know, in the evening he'll stay and drink and sing with us . . . He says that his poems are worth more than his philosophy.'

I smiled. I thought of the girl I'd rescued. I opened the palm of my hand and inhaled her lingering fragrance. Arnold looked at me, taken aback.

We left the garden, crossed the square and went down to the river bank in silence. Arnold bent down and cupped some river water in his large palm. It remained in the hollow of his hand, and he swirled it round as if it contained a secret or a treasure, or as if a spirit would emerge from it. Then, suddenly, he called to me:

'William! William!'

He snapped his fingers shut and opened them again; his hand looked like a fish drying in the sun. His expression was serious, like that of children; afterwards, he shook his hand and burst out laughing. He moved in circles around me, dancing some strange dance:

'William! William!'

It must be the most wonderful and funniest thing in the world to dance while you wait for it to rain. Once he had twirled me round and round, he stopped and placed his hands on my shoulders.

'William, promise me you'll be my friend.'

He misunderstood my silence.

'Don't you want to?'

'I don't want to hurt my friend. And what kind of friend is it who will soon leave?'

'You'll stay.'

I ought to have laughed at his confidence, but it warmed my heart.

5

I saw her first, at the entrance to the Close, just as I was arriving with Arnold. She was walking in silence with a servant, a woman with skin as black as coal. She was wearing that blue cloak which had first caught my eye—and I was not surprised to admit that I fell in love with her before I had really set eyes on her. Arnold caught me looking at her and gave me a slap.

'Heloise,' he said. 'So you already know Canon Fulbert's beautiful niece, do you?'

'I scarcely knew her before I was clasping her to me. You see how close we are . . .'

He gazed at me, eyebrows raised, before dragging me onwards. As we made our way through the streets of the Close with its houses built of wood and stone, amid the atmosphere of calm that was such a change after the excitement and chaos of the rest of the Île de la Cité, Heloise's name buried itself within my heart.

Arnold told me that Master Peter Abelard's lesson was held in a house which Archdeacon Stephen had lent to the chapterhouse in return for a promise that at every full moon a Mass for his soul would be served by two canons at the chapel of Saint-Aignan.

We caught up with a short man with fair, close-cut hair whose blue eyes shone with kindness.

'William, allow me to introduce Peter the Child—the Child,' said Arnold enthusiastically. 'William has traversed Europe from east to west and north to south in search of a master the equal to ours . . .'

'And Arnold has convinced me that I'm now here for good,' I said, laughing.

'I admire Abelard and his philosophy, but I have only one master,' said the Child as he turned to Arnold.

Arnold raised his arms heavenwards, 'So, too, do I, Child most wise. I, too, am subject to Our Lord . . .'

The Child gave a reassuring smile and they began to talk about what was going on in town. The subject of their discussion meant nothing to me, nor did the names: Senlis, Garlande, Galon, Gerbert . . . I heard tell of hatred that could lead to murder, of the brutality that motivates men's emotions, be it in the name of God, or the name of the king.

As we drew near to the school, other small groups attached themselves to ours: the sons of Breton lords, the lame, the crippled bastard offspring of bishops, absconding novices and simonious priests—and even humble students intent on learning. The desire for knowledge is never expressed in silence: they were bawling.

We entered the cavernous room, a former warehouse where a smell of spices still lingered; those who had arrived first were seated on benches, while others were placed wherever they could fit; the shortest climbed up onto the shoulders of the stronger ones. In the middle of the circle, you could see the master's back. He was wearing a black linen gown (later he told me how he had organised his wardrobe once and for all: a linen gown if the weather was warm, a woolen one if it was cold, and black whatever the weather or the season).

He raised his hand and there was silence; at last he turned round and I could feel his gaze settle on me, as if I was the only one he was going to address. Even though this impression was doubtless shared by everybody in the room, the conviction that it was true wafted over me like a strong, sweet liqueur. I wanted to be loyal to this man even if he asked nothing of me. I wanted him to recognise me and to like me.

'God,' he began, gently drawing out the word, 'can he do other than what he does?'

He waited for the silence to be broken by a few murmurings.

'God made it rain yesterday,' he continued with a smile, 'despite Bishop Galon.'

Laughter filled the room. Arnold nudged me with his elbow.

'. . . But could God have wished for it not to rain? Could he have wished for something to happen that did not happen? Or for something not to happen that did happen? Or again that it should have happened differently—fine rain instead of a downpour?'

The grey light of day seeped through the arches of the gallery that opened onto the street, and some torches had been lit. Faces were illuminated by the quivering light of the flames; there were expressions ranging from admiration to fear—and even, in certain cases, hatred.

'Well, my friends! Is it to be the blind leading the blind? Or will one among you enlighten us?'

Some voices were raised, invoking the Evangelists, Augustine, Origen or Boethius. He listened, approving or rejecting with a nod or a look. Then he called a halt to the proceedings. His eyes were gleaming with mischievousness.

'At this stage there's no need for all these eminent authorities, for you must know that I am talking to you under their guidance . . .'

He raised his eyes heavenwards, as an acrobat might, adopting an anxious and immediately contrite expression.

'To take a different tack, all that we require is a little care and some grammar . . . What did I actually say that alarmed you so? Firstly, I asked whether God *could* before asking whether he *would*. What are we talking about, in fact, his will or his power? For if it's to do with his will, I have made a statement that must have struck you as obvious and made you want to strip me of my clothing for being a bad master and a false prophet . . . What kind of God would it be who did not want to do what he wishes, or did other than he wishes? He would not even be Plato's demiurge, who has the excuse of not being God . . . But if, then, we are discussing his power, we're going to have to know the meaning of words: for the very fact that God is capable and has the power to do everything is what defines Him. Do we not call him the Omnipotent? And in the Trinity, if the Holy Spirit is wisdom and Jesus Christ is goodness, then God is power. So who is this all-powerful being who is incapable? It could not be God. But perhaps, albeit slightly against our wishes, we should go back to the preceding notion: could he wish something to be better than it is and yet isn't? Or else for something to take place at a different time to when it does take place? Before—if that were in his power? Or afterwards? But then it is his infinite goodness that causes us to doubt. How are we to understand a God who does not wish for everything to be for the best? And thus, my friends, the matter of a little rain has led us to confront an awesome question . . . If, during this period of heat that parched our throats and made most of you drink too much beer, God did not want it to rain, then he has no Goodness—and yet he has; if he wanted it but was unable to create it, then he has no Power—yet he has; and if he neither wanted it nor could create it, then—I scarcely dare whisper it—then he doesn't exist—yet he does. Is there in this room a mind filled with the Spirit who, through logic or dialectic, *involucrum* or *integumentum*, can help us out of this quandary in which, if we persist, we have the choice between the anguish of aporia and excommunication followed by eternal damnation?'

Those who had come with wax tablets were scribbling away furiously, sitting cross-legged or else standing and using the backs of those in front of them. My ears were buzzing and

I felt as if my mind were not progressing quickly enough.

Outside, the storm was now raging and we could hear the rain pattering down on the cobbled lanes of the Close; as the mud rose, everyone from priests to beggars sought shelter. Inside, a volley of questions and answers rang out. One man had been following the teachings of Hugues at Saint-Victor and was setting his traps; another remembered St Jerome; Master Peter skilfully steered his path in the direction that he had chosen from the start.

'Did you see? Did you hear!' Arnold whispered.

Abelard was now conducting a discussion with a fanatical nominalist who was trying to make him say that, since three names had been assigned to God in the Trinity, there were therefore three Gods; then a monk in a white habit asked him anxiously if he had really said that we have to be doubtful of everything, even God.

He stood his ground, grew impatient, counter-attacked; he harassed his adversaries, wore them down and took them on at their own game. He waxed and waned, he made them laugh. He was a master of words as well as a master of silence.

At the end (once he had established that since God is able to do anything, he only does what is right, in other words what is), there was a sigh of relief, and as the first of the students left the room it was as if a magic circle were traced round him. Not that Arnold knew anything about magic; he took my arm and dragged me forward.

'Master Peter! I have a wrangler here with me . . .'

The master looked at me: there was a little perspiration on his brow and weariness in his eyes. He was panting softly, rather like a wrestler, and there was a smile on his face. I noticed the silver brooch, depicting a wonderfully graceful lamb, that buttoned his cloak.

'I know him, your wrangler . . .'

I could see the lines that ran across his forehead and furrowed his cheeks, like scars from the thrusts of swords that he had suffered in his jousting with words.

'I came, as you see . . .'

He smiled. His eyes peered into mine: serious, intense and with that dancing light in them.

'I was expecting you,' he said, taking me by the arm. 'Come with us—we're going for a drink.'

I followed him out into the street, where a noisy, happy little group had clustered around him, trying to catch his attention. The young lady, Heloise was returning alone.

'I'll catch you up!' I called to Arnold.

I walked behind her along the streets of the Close as far as her door where an angel was keeping watch.

'Your name is Heloise.'

She turned round and smiled—her pale blue eyes misted over in the rain.

'I said that I wouldn't forget you.'

'You left without telling me your name.'

'You must believe me, William. I take my promises seriously, as well as my follies.'

'I do believe you.'

It was as if an invisible veil that separated me from her made me shy and almost stupid. I had known women; I had never known a woman like her. I told her that Peter Abelard was my master.

'What is he teaching at the moment? Logic, the Categories? Or is it what he blasphemously calls "Theology"?'

There was a touch of irony in her voice and she spoke with the familiarity of an equal. I mumbled. The lesson that I had just attended was still whirling around in my head.

'He speaks powerfully and he looks upon others as if they ought only to exist in the shade of his sunlight.'

Heloise's face was hidden in the large hood of her blue cloak. She had the insubstantiality of a dream—and she knew how to show herself off while concealing herself better. I was standing very close to her, like a miserable wretch, and I had a burning desire to speak to her, to tell her how I felt: the lure of a woman, my friend, can undo you and tear you to pieces.

'Are you going to let me into my own house or does my uncle have to come and do battle with you?'

'Will you come to a lesson with me?'

'Wait and see,' she said as she pushed open the door, her sad eyes laughing.

The rain had stopped. I ran, light-footed, holding my gown in both hands as I danced my way through the puddles.

Leaving the paved Close, I could not avoid the mud in the square. In the distance, near the Jewish quarter, I could see the philosopher and his friends. I ran and caught up with them.

Peter Abelard moved forward as if he were the only person present, chatting to people here and there.

'Did you see?' whispered Arnold. 'Even the animals turn away from him.'

I looked at him to see whether he was being funny; his expression was serious. He really does believe that he has met Jesus; after all, it's no different from what happened to the apostles. All we lack are one or two miraculous cures.

They were jostling each other with their elbows and speaking too loudly. There was a certainty about the knowledge these young men had and therefore a confidence that was naïve, pretentious and touching.

Peter the Child, the man with the chubby face, was quieter than the others. He wore the black habit of the monks from Cluny. He said that his prior sent him to Paris last winter to keep up with what was being discussed at the Schools.

'And what have you discovered?'

'I listen and I learn; everything is beneficial to those who wish to sing the praise of God.'

'Why do they call you Child?'

'Because as a child, I collected miracles. I continue to do so.'

He smiled. There was honesty in his blue eyes; a virtuousness that concealed further virtues still. I can decipher faces.

Behind the synagogue, in the heart of the maze of alleyways in the Jewish quarter, the group entered a tavern at the sign of Vulcan and a man who was actually very ugly welcomed Abelard.

'I am your servant Samuel, Lord, here to serve you.'

'That's enough, Samuel, your prophecies will lead you to blasphemy.'

The inn-keeper dragged his almost dead leg as if it belonged to someone else and yet he moved about with remarkable agility. His large hands protruded from short, powerful arms and he had the shoulders of a wrestler.

We passed through a curtain and entered Vulcan's forge: it was a curious, warlike cavern in which everything was painted dark red and the walls were decorated with shields, lances and swords.

Abelard presided at the head of the table; opposite him was Peter the Child. Then came Simeon the doctor, Robert le Roux and Cervelle, a small, slender man who spoke in a high-pitched voice. Immediately next to me was Christian, a fair-haired young prophet, bearded and hirsute like a Norman.

Arnold was helping Samuel to bring the ale and he set the goblets on the table — a thick brown, mossy liquid like milk from Sainte-Mère-du-Houblon, as warm as a fire, as a woman.

'Where does he come from?' Christian asked Arnold, pointing his finger at me.

'I was born in England, at the court of a rather violent prince, near a landscape of damp hills . . . And I've come from Fontevrault, where I've relinquished my duties as a copyist . . .'

Christian swept a slender hand through his blond hair.

'I knew it, I knew we were brothers! I, too, copy bibles at the abbey of Saint-Germain-des-Prés. And since the monks are pleased with my delicate handiwork, I show them something of the art I learned in Northumberland, and I lay aside my pens and bring out my paintbrushes, my gold fluid, my pots of purple or saffron . . .'

'What do you paint for them?'

'Images that dwell within them day and night . . . Holy virgins wearing sky-blue mantles . . . but also fiendish animals coupling, worse than griffins and monsters . . .'

'I should very much like to see them . . .'

Christian just smiled.

'William!' called Abelard.

I got up from the end of my bench. He gestured to me to come forward and, in spite of the swearing, I made my way among the students, being careful not to spill the ale in their goblets.

When Peter Abelard smiles, the lines on his cheeks widen and his dark eyes sparkle. And yet, even in that moment of abandon, I could not fail to notice the flicker of anxiety that glistened beneath his gaze.

'Do you want me to call you Master?'

'Call me whatever you wish, I don't mind . . . With some people I insist, who knows why . . . From those who pay me, all I expect is their money . . . From those disciples who are dear to me I ask nothing—whether they call me Peter, or friend, or nothing at all.'

'Disciples?'

'*Discere*—to learn and nothing more. I don't walk upon the waters, I haven't founded the church which is already there, we won't all go about en masse curing the sick and preaching the gospel. If you wish, I shall awaken you to reason and I shall help you to search not for the truth, but the things that resemble it, and with which you can live and face the world.'

'Where did you obtain all your learning?'

'I was aware of books all too quickly and they became a part of me without my learning them. Unable to discuss matters with my brothers any longer, I set off debating all over Brittany, Normandy and France. I searched for Origen or Boethius, Socrates and Augustine. Above all, I searched for Jerome, to whom I've been strangely attracted ever since I first read his letters . . . But masters great or small—I had none. Everywhere I went I came across nothing but old priests who repeated what old priests used to say, droning on and waving their arms about in the air, and explaining Genesis with an inspiration that they thought was divine but which was nothing but the same thing rehashed over and over again: "*In the beginning, God created the heavens and the earth*. What does holy scripture tell us? That God first created the heavens, then the earth . . ." You don't say . . . ! I wanted to beat them with my fists, but instead I beat them with words, to their great shame and humiliation. Having worn out all these false masters I became a master myself. Occasionally, I regret not being a knight like my brothers Gérard and Yves, and not having been a crusader; but there's a fire in me that even the destruction of Antioch and the massacre of all the infidels would not quench. William?'

He laid his hand on my arm and squeezed it gently. His cloak trailed at his feet; beads of sweat dripped down from his chin onto the powerful neck that rose up from his tunic.

'William, do you hear me?'

I nodded without replying.

'I wasn't joking when I said I was expecting you. Will you stay with me? Will you go to war with me?'

'War!'

He was one of those men who was able to trap you with a glance and whose thunderous speech could caress you; when he took your hand, you wanted to be his friend and brother, and you wanted him to talk to you privately, from his heart. You couldn't imagine what a peculiar honour it was to serve him.

'That may seem a strange word to use—and I grant you that we won't have to take down from the walls the trophies that Samuel has had forged at the Vulcan . . . But we shall have to fight, nevertheless! Don't rely on today's lesson, don't be taken in by the appearance of outward calm! That priest with the modest expression who questioned me about the Trinity, he hates me! And that shifty monk who doubts whether reason can serve revelation, he loathes me too! And even the person who pretends to admire me, who imbibes my words during my discourse on Ezekiel and calls me "Master" and pays me twice the amount, he also hates me! I've upset too many people to be left in peace for long . . . And then I'm not sure I like peace . . .'

'War, how funny . . .'

Peter Abelard didn't care for people being funny.

'There are the enemies whom I know and there are those more powerful ones whom I do not yet know . . . There are all those who do not like the fact that as a man I speak to other men about all manner of things, including God.'

'I do like your war, Peter, it's a war that's worth fighting and losing. I'll fight it with you, if you wish.'

'Look at our army,' he smiled. 'Doesn't it cut a proud figure? Look at them getting drunk so as to give themselves courage on the eve of fierce battles. William, I want to ask you something else.'

'Tell me.'

'Why did you pursue Heloise?'

'Pursue her?'

He burst out laughing.

'Pursue? Pursue?' he repeated, mimicking me as if it was the funniest thing in the world. 'Yes, pursued,' he roared. 'I saw you, you were pursuing . . .'

'I noticed her yesterday, during the procession. I snatched her away from the crowd, which was crushing her. I saw her once more, before the lesson and again, on leaving.'

'Three times. You must have thought it was a sign . . .'

'Probably.'

'They say she's a scholar . . .'

'Is that what is said?'

'He irks me with his questions. They do say that and they're certainly wrong because she's never followed the teachings of a real philosopher.'

'Perhaps she will come now . . .'

'Now that you've pursued her? I leave her to you, she's no beauty!'

I had been holding my breath during his questions. His last remark released me. I gestured to Arnold to get up and I joined him; I caught fair-haired Christian's expression and made a clumsy attempt to wave goodbye. He called out something which I did not hear.

The street was alive. It was never completely dark at night; and even in daylight one came across bewildering or alarming nocturnal scenes. Over there, children were begging for food from those who had less than them; here, there were old women volunteering younger ones — their daughters, they said — for one-night marriages that meant the girls had to be stitched up again next morning. A virgin's blood had a certain value or else was worth nothing, it all depended. You could hear the sound of the horses, made dangerous and magnificent by the darkness, as their hooves hammered the ground and echoed over the cobblestones; there were pigs which, since they never slept, might trip you up at the corners of alleyways and which squealed horribly when they were struck. A man holding a torch and walking at a blind man's pace was muttering psalms to himself taken from an unauthorised bible. Suddenly silent, we were walking in the direction of the Close, which was where our house was, feeling as ill as our sick brethren.

At the end of the boards of the Mivrai, we crossed the Place de Grève. The market stalls were closed but the stench of rotting fish and meat turned our stomachs. Now that the downpour had stopped, the heat was beginning to rise up from the ground.

I thought, with a kind of terror, I think that I am in love but I don't know what it is to love and I think I am in love for the first time. It's enough to make me want to laugh, to laugh until I choke. Arnold takes me in his arms; he clasps me and lets me go, clasps me, then lets me go. He doesn't ask anything.

6

Fiet amor verus,
Qui modo falsus erat.
Love that once was false will become true.

OVID, The Art of Loving 8:2

A
RNOLD AND I had left Saint-Lazare for the mouth of
the Bièvre: there was a priory house there belonging to
Cluny that had been put under the gentle jurisdiction of
Peter the Child, and his only duty as far as the abbey was concerned was to send back reports on the follies of the Parisian
masters.

The house particularly welcomed those pupils of Peter
Abelard who were rather more than pupils, those who did not
pay, those whom he used to take drinking, those who would
desert him like all the others when times changed.

Without Abelard saying as much, perhaps without his even
being aware of it, I felt that we were enjoying the benefits of a
discretionary benevolence that allowed him both to teach in the
Close and to be startlingly unconstrained in the words he used.

I used to enjoy spending time in the warehouse that opened
onto the street, storage rooms in which a stone sculptor kept
his statues while waiting for them to be painted. If I wished to
be on my own, I would sometimes go and sleep there, clinging

with one hand to St Sebastian's arrows, the keys of St Peter or St Augustine's book, dreaming or having nightmares while surrounded by actual biblical characters.

Amid all this sanctity there were a few profane subjects. Having spent so much time among statues, my hands had cupped the drooping breasts of a statue of Niobe mourning her children and seeking consolation. But here as elsewhere it was not wise to form attachments: no sooner had you confided in a prophet or an angel, or entrusted your fate to a king, than the following day he was sent into exile in some church or other.

At night, among this gathering, I seemed to see imperceptible movements which I tried to catch with one eye, but which always eluded me. Did these stone people touch one another or make love once the creatures of flesh and blood had at last left them in peace? It appeared unlikely — only the spirit still illuminated their lives. Clasped in Niobe's arms, however, I did feel that with a few centuries' patience she might have been mine.

Peter's friends had accepted me from the moment I joined them; this may have been kind-heartedness, but it might also have been casualness; I believe it was simply that the master had chosen me and that there was nothing more to be said.

Arnold spoke to me about his dreams: I feared for his purity which would later be his downfall, and I was alarmed by what he remembered from the lessons — not logic or reason, but fire to enflame his fury. I noticed that he was often in conflict with Cervelle, that ageless boy with the ugly but intelligent face, who used his mind to put an acceptable distance between himself and the world. Cervelle never spoke of what he believed in, he never admitted that he was frightened or in love; of all of us, he was the only one whose mind was sufficiently agile to drive Abelard into entrenched positions on rare occasions. Christian had a luminous faith and sweetness about him; although he lived an angelic life, he did not believe that the body was the enemy of the soul.

Peter the Child was wholly good.

When the master asked me to stay behind, the others with-drew without saying anything. After the lesson he took me with him and we would wander off to the Isle of Jews or the Isle of Cows and laze about together on a sandbank. During the night he dictated his notes for future treatises and tried new arguments or fresh analogies on me; I would reply and encourage him, timidly to begin with, then with increasing boldness. Watching the assurance with which, in front of everyone, he subsequently developed what we had attempted by trial and error, I felt a pride in my heart at having been singled out.

One day, Cervelle, with his customary irony—sardonic and ungenerous, but always fair—began calling me John. When, pretending not to mind, I asked him why, he sniggered:

'Are you not the disciple whom Jesus loved?'

'I must have her,' said Abelard slowly, separating each word.

Tears, which I immediately held back, welled up in my eyes.

'William, I need her,' he repeated as if in a dream—and there was no need for him to utter her name. I knew.

Heloise had sometimes come to listen to him. As far as I knew, they had not exchanged more than three words.

A sort of routine had become established between her and me that I found impossible to break: we would walk together a little at the end of the lesson before she disappeared, giving the excuse that she could not keep her uncle, the canon, waiting. Whenever I was with her, the words that I had promised myself I would say the previous night vanished, and I was left speechless as a mule.

She told me about her life in snatches: she described her vast childhood home, at Montmorency, surrounded by vineyards, and the gut-wrenching pain she experienced when as a girl she was sent away to board with the nuns at Argenteuil. She remem-bered that on the morning of her death, her mother, Hersende, had put a flower in her hair: in the evening the flower was no longer there. She spoke of Dido, of Cornelia, and of the heroines whose destinies rent her heart and seemed, without her understanding why, to conjure up her own fate. Her Latin was elegant and classical—images sprang forth effortlessly from her lips. She had chosen her friends: she could express the music of Virgil or the almost vulgar enthusiasm of Catullus, the elegance of Horace, the sadness of Ovid. She did not speak about Abelard—and I never questioned her.

'It's unreasonable,' I eventually said to my master.

'You're talking about reason?'

A strange paralysis gripped my heart and mind and made me incapable of uttering simple words. This object you're playing with, just as you do with the Categories of Aristotle, has for the past fortnight been the blood pumping through my veins, the air that I breathe . . . This woman, whom you want to take away from me and who does not belong to me is, nevertheless, mine . . . You are my master in all matters, you know what I know better than I do myself, but you are taking away what you have given me, and worse still—you are stifling me, crushing me, draining my life away . . .

I had said nothing. Only that wretched remark 'It's unreasonable', which made no sense at all and, more to the point—as I knew only too well already—would only provoke him.

It was only later that I became aware of everything that silence signified—and that ultimately my fate, my wretchedness and perhaps my good fortune were contained there in their entirety.

I did not see Heloise in the days that followed. I did not know what to expect, what to fear. If she went away, I would be protected from my master's unbearable threat; if she came no more, my love would be fixed in an absence, in a dream. And yet, of course, as I waited for her, I retained neither much logic, nor much grammar.

We were a noisy group, happy but chaotic, and after our lesson we never tired of continuing to argue and discuss things as we crossed the square in front of the cathedral, jostling some of the shopkeepers as we turned into the Jewish quarter before passing the Petit Pont, where some new masters had already installed themselves, attracting the curious with strange syllogisms.

With Arnold, I instigated rebellious tactics to eliminate the transgressions of this base world; with Christian, I spoke about Heloise — not, God forbid, my silent passion, but about the curious attachment the master had developed for this girl whom he did not consider beautiful.

'He will have her,' said Christian fatalistically. 'We must just pray that she doesn't cut his hair while he's asleep.'

I did not laugh. He noticed it.

When the others went to bed the three of us often stayed up late discussing our hopes and our fears; we still drank the thick, tepid ale — or else that bitter Étampes wine which went down without one noticing. That was when we were all excellent friends.

One night, when Arnold had finally fallen asleep, stretched out like a bearskin rug in front of the fire, Christian and I went for a walk among the statues. We were drunk of course. More than ever, it seemed to me that we were in the midst of a forest of stone, two figures who could have been struck motionless and dumb at a wave of the hand — that was how Christian would become a prophet and I an apostle.

For a long time he made me talk about my wanderings and about the people I had come across — the wise men and the warriors, those who were born under a magic constellation, those who had come back from the world of the dead. I told him about Courtly Love and the tournaments, the perfumes of Spain, and about waiting for the Lady.

'Do you still want to know what I do?'

'I'm no longer so sure.'

'You're right. It's best kept a secret. I don't know it myself.'

He looked at me solemnly.

'All sorts of people dwell within me and sometimes, when I've finished drawing an initial, I feel furious that the universe is not mine so that I can celebrate the glory of God and the greatness of man.'

'Nothing more?'

He pummelled me with his fists and we could not stop laughing.

'Come on now,' he said when we had calmed down, 'close your eyes and trust your little brother Christian!'

He slipped off my gown and my tunic and he placed his hands on my bare shoulders.

'What are you doing?'

'Don't be frightened,' he whispered, 'I've actually been to Sodom, but it was as an angel . . .'

'Can I open my eyes now?'

'If you promise me you won't be afraid.'

I wasn't frightened. I was simply shivering because of the cold. By the light of a candle he laid out his colours, his quills and his brushes. I watched him, eyes riveted, as he prepared this pagan ritual.

'Now turn round, you're not allowed to see.'

When his quill touched me, light as a wing, I had a dreadful desire to laugh, but I controlled myself.

'Don't move. Remember you're a stone now; you've got to keep still.'

I obeyed. I almost managed to forget the sensation, by turns unpleasant and gentle, of being licked by an army of insects. My breathing became so soft that I could have been dead, imagining myself sent to heaven, with my feet in the air, among the army of saints who decorate a row on the arches of those curved porticos you see everywhere at the entrance to churches. Or could I be a monster, crushed beneath some foot? At the Last Judgement, I would be both vice and virtue.

'Very good, William.'

His voice came to me from another world. He probably talked

like that to the pages of his books. Then he began circling round me, a joyful faun, a dancing priest, and I no longer found it difficult pretending to be still. With my feet firmly planted on the ground, I didn't know where my breath had gone and it would have needed a thrust from a sword to bring me back to life.

'Now you can look. But be sure to move very slowly. Don't forget you were a stone.'

My heavy head slumped forward: the tip of my breast was an initial letter painted in gold, and across the whole of my chest I could see letters of a language which, from upside down, looked as if it belonged to a race of barbarians. I looked particularly at the images that hung down me: at my sides, which were covered by intertwining foliage in which a squirrel or an egret was hiding; at my neck, from which the column of a temple of Solomon rose up; and the base of my stomach, where a woman swathed in veils was offering herself upon a bed with sky-blue sheets studded with gold stars. Her lips were the colour of blood.

'Do you recognise her?'

'*I am dark but comely* . . . If I have the Song of Songs on my belly, what have you painted on my back? The Apocalypse?'

He was putting away his materials.

'Don't try to look. There's nothing evil there, but I've hidden a little secret patch, on your own body, so that you may remember that even the body can't teach you everything. One day you will be allowed to know, but not before I tell you.'

Although he was speaking a little ironically, there could be no doubting his seriousness. I moved so that I could see my page move, prompted by the invisible hand that was my body, my muscles, my breathing, my own heartbeat. *I am black, but comely, O daughters of Jerusalem* . . . He snuffed out the candle with his fingers. Dawn came. I picked up my tunic and I got dressed: the Song of Songs disappeared in the folds of my gown.

'It's very strange, my friend, to be a book written by you and whose last words are still secret . . .'

'Every book is like a pilgrimage or a man's life: the reward comes at the end.'

The street itself, at daybreak, where I stretched my legs among the cats, was a book in the process of being written; the street was a line that snaked between the houses, gardens and vines, along which my flaxen-haired friend, with his rainbow fingers and ink-stained nails, walked beneath a stormy sky.

'I am weary,' said Abelard, 'and I am old: I shall soon be forty.'

'The acme! The *floruit*!'

'You may mock. The time that a generation of men has passed, I have spent in arguing. As far back as I remember, when I was at my first school, in Nantes, I was no taller than a box hedge and I was arguing with my first masters about Latin declensions . . . Along the entire length of the Loire, at Angers, at Saumur, then at Loches with that devil Roscelin, and at Laon with old Anselm, I was still arguing . . .'

'You'll die arguing.'

He struck the table.

'Indeed, I will not!'

Two or three days had passed since his confession—if that is what that soldier's demand for booty can be called. I avoided his lectures and held my breath. I knew very well that the miracle of Heloise's absence would not last.

He picked himself up again and grew more mellow.

'Seriously, William, don't you think it's time for me to take a woman?'

'Do you want to get married?'

'Me? You must be joking! It would wreck my reputation, undermine my career, preclude my . . .'

'You see.'

'But taking a woman is not the same as getting married. Taking a woman is . . .'

'What about her? What will be left of her once you've taken her?'

'She will be educated and the most perfect of women.'

'And ruined for ever, you know very well.'

'She will go back to the convent. What else can she hope for? She has nothing but her beauty . . .'

'I thought you didn't find her beautiful!'

'Everyone makes mistakes. Nothing, I said, apart from her beauty and her mind. In other words, nothing. And who do you think she would have after me? The king's butler?'

There was so much quiet and cheerful scepticism about him and, as always, such perfection of reasoning, that it bordered on innocence. Confronted with this paradox, my heart swelled: I was so happy under his guidance that in spite of myself he was persuading me to share his beliefs, and in so doing to become the instrument of my own suffering. But I had no idea what lay behind this: seeing only my own loss, I was growing blind to his.

His eyes had not left me—they were plunged deep into my turbulent heart and they were indifferent to what they saw there. It hurt me to see her leave even though she had never been mine; it hurt me to have hung my hopes on a few words which she may not even have uttered. And yet I felt dizzy at the thought of being involved with a man who was wiser and knew more than I did, but who above all *desired* in a way that I thought I was incapable of.

'Find her for me,' he said at last.

Squeezing me gently on the shoulder, he got up and left without waiting for my reply. I remained where I was, feeling subdued, gazing at the fire.

7

I KNEW THAT Heloise's uncle said Mass every Friday evening at the chapel of Saint-Julien, where the apse opens out at the far end of the Close, above the Seine, as if suspended between sky, stone and water. People said it was the very place where the saint's boat had landed, with the leper aboard, and that sometimes Jesus returned at night in the guise of a beggar to contemplate men and to grieve over the fact that they were not better. Over the years the rock had subsided and the nave was inclining: if it tilted any further it would end up slipping into the Seine, dragging along the saints, the just and those who were not.

With its unusual nave, its low vault, the paucity of light and that very humble way it had of suggesting that men should huddle together, it was a chapel dating from the time of the first Christians—not one of those splendid vessels such as Cluny, not the great mountain that was being built at Chartres—but a simple boat that listed while the disciples doubted and Jesus slept; you could weep all alone in there and no one would hear you apart from the God of the humble and the afflicted, the God of the wretched whom one entreats in a low voice.

I stood in the darkness listening to Mass, allowing the spirits of generations past, who had been born and had died here, to permeate through me, mingling in my memory the prayers of both the dead and the living.

Fulbert's words—he's a heavy, plump man whose eyes, which are as blue as those of his niece, express unexpected anxiety—droned away inside my head without my being able to understand what they meant; I was lost in the song of a crow that had come to seek shelter, in the sounds that came up from the river, and in the buffeting wind, which made the haulers groan and pull all the harder; I was that beggar who waits but who will receive nothing.

Heloise was listening to her uncle, her head bowed as if he were Paul the apostle, her blue cloak thrown over her shoulders. Her pure, slightly husky voice rose to sing a psalm—yet again that Song of Songs which the awesome Crusaders of the True Faith had never stopped intoning.

> *Behold, you are beautiful, my love;*
> *behold you are beautiful;*
> *your eyes are doves.*
> *Behold, you are beautiful, my beloved,*
> *Truly lovely.*
> *Our couch is green.*

Heloise turned towards me, recognising me. I had grown pale, so striking was her beauty, and it was with some difficulty that I became accustomed to her very soft, oval-shaped face, her eyes that gleamed with intelligence and tenderness, an expression that I knew to be animated, alert, and possibly amused, should there be anything to laugh about, but which I could also imagine gripped in the concentration of study.

The Mass was over.

Heloise took her uncle's arm graciously and the stout man smiled—the smile of a large, fat, good, ruddy-faced man, who eats pork and drinks good wine every day—and the top of his skull shone.

I was wearing a golden-yellow tunic and a velvet cloak of the same colour, embroidered with wild flowers, red, white, and yellow too. I looked like a vision of spring in autumn. I drew near. He glanced at me with a kindly but anxious look.

'I am sent by my master Peter Abelard, philosopher, theologian, master of the Notre-Dame school . . .' I said to Fulbert, trying not to look at Heloise.

'I know who Peter Abelard is,' replied Fulbert respectfully.

'Most important of all, this is the man who saved my life, Uncle,' said Heloise.

'So it's you!'

'. . . author of a treatise on the Trinity and the divine unity, former master of the schools of Sainte-Geneviève, of Melun, of Créteil, pupil of William of Champeaux and Anselm of Laon . . .'

Heloise looked puzzled. I tried not to catch her eye. We left the church through the crypt situated in the north arm of the church: the west door was open to the breezes from the river.

As I explained my business (and it was another me, speaking with ease and conviction, while I, huddled up at the pit of my heart, felt nothing but shame), the canon led me through the narrow streets of the Close to his house. By the time we reached his front door I had still not understood whether he was flattered, worried, or tempted . . . He spoke to me about what was happening in Paris, about the Comte de Meulan's raid, the finances of the chapterhouse, the archdeacon's ambitions, Garlande's mischief, about the importance of the school and a dispute about a prebend. Whenever I returned to the subject in hand, he avoided me with the agility of a juggler.

Even though she was walking behind us, I could sense Heloise's eyes staring at me. Finally, just as we were shuffling about outside her door, I could hold back no longer.

'What shall I tell my master?'

'You will tell him that his proposal does me more honour than I can say.'

'But what else?'

'You will tell your master,' Heloise's calm voice intervened, 'that my uncle's house is full and that there is no price — for all his prestige and attributes — that can be paid for the favour he is asking.'

'Heloise!'

'You will tell your master to make his own requests, instead of sending a poor student . . .'

'Heloise!'

The canon turned pink, almost choking.

'You will tell your master,' he broke in, 'that I willingly accept and that my niece's lessons can begin tomorrow. You will tell him that I insist he should have total freedom to teach as he thinks fit and that his methods shall be mine. You will tell him that if his knowledge has to be taught by strokes of a cane, then he can cane her! You will tell him that I want her to be the most educated and most perfect woman in this kingdom and that I will give up my own prebend and my place in the chapterhouse for that . . .'

'But your niece is opposed to this . . .'

'I have spoken!'

'But your house is full . . .'

He gestured impatiently. Heloise pushed open the door of the house and shut it violently in our faces.

'She doesn't want to,' I said.

'She will want to.'

I left him to his reveries, convinced that his niece was going to be given lessons by Aristotle. My legs scarcely carried me; I set off on my way, however, taking grim pleasure in pursuing my task to the end.

She caught me by surprise just as I was walking past the baptistery of Saint-Jean-le-Rond, at the very spot where we had spoken the first time. She was dressed in black and a dove was flying about above her head.

'Why did you do that?'

'He asked me to.'

'Are you more base than I thought?'

'More stupid, anyway.'

'William, I don't understand . . .'

'Honestly, I don't know why I've always preferred asking questions to replying to them . . . I remember that Adam's real troubles began when Yahweh asked him: "Where are you?"'

I made this last remark with as much frivolity as I could muster. She gazed at me for a moment. There was more surprise than pain in her eyes. My heart was beating as if it would break. I think that if she had asked me one more question, the dyke would have given way. Her gaze scanned the cathedral square, which was once more crowded with stallholders and bogus masters, then returned to me.

'William, I don't know who you are or what you want. You saved my life and that's enough for me. Now I want your promise.'

'My promise . . .'

'Your promise that you will me do me no harm,' she said at last, with forced self-assurance. 'And your promise that you will not leave me either.'

'I will stay with you.'

Then I began mumbling with emotion and I shot off like an arrow, leaving her lost for words.

'Where are you, fool?' I kept saying to myself as I staggered around. Like Adam, I could do nothing but reply: 'Lord, I was frightened and I hid.'

'Were you successful?'

I had calmed my restless heart by going to pray in the little church of Saint-Julien-le-Pauvre. Peter the Child's house was now quiet and I had found the master resting on a bed of leaves, his eyes closed; the lines that ran across his cheeks and his forehead had almost vanished.

'Well, are you going to tell me?'

I knew very well that my silence would not exhaust his patience, but I was finding it hard to speak.

'Tell me if she loves me.'

'I don't know whether she does. Her uncle certainly does.'

'He's a bit of a simpleton, isn't he? That's what Garlande told me.'

He hardly ever mentioned the name of his protector, the archdeacon who had become Louis VI's chancellor and was aiming still higher.

'He loves his niece and there's something rather crafty and obstinate about his stupidity that makes him less simple-minded than the others.'

'Don't be so subtle, you're wearying me. What did he say about my proposal, is he pleased, does he want to accept?'

'He wants you to cane her to make her understand . . . He knows that philosophers never know what time it is and he realises that lessons will sometimes have to take place at night.'

'It's worthy of the trap Jacob played on Esau. And what about her, what did she say?'

'She doesn't want to.'

'Why?'

'You must ask her.'

'It doesn't matter. She will want to. You must speak to her.'

She will want . . . First Fulbert, now Peter . . . She'll want: men who make decisions over women's heads. I could bear it no longer. I punched the bench on which I was sitting.

'You must speak to her yourself.'

'Calm down. Very well, you're right, I'll speak to her. But the thing is . . .'

'What?'

'The fact is, I don't know. These are things I've never spoken about.'

I could not prevent myself bursting out laughing.

'Don't make fun of me . . . What do I know about women? My

mother Lucy, my sister Denise, the classical heroines, Dinah, the daughter of Jephthah . . .'

'Do I know any more than you do? Let your heart speak!'

I needed, moreover, to lend him *my* heart, to feed him the phrases that came to my lips.

'William, I don't know what my heart is.'

He said this in all seriousness, calmly, like a man who had never thought about the matter and who was getting ready to tackle it in the way one confronted universals.

'All you have to do is compose a song.'

'A song?'

'*Petrus habet Heloïssam.* That would be amusing.'

A feeling of gloomy irony gripped my insides. *Petrus habet Heloïssam.* Sing, you ass—or remain silent for ever. Sing—and know your own heart. He stood up and started to chant.

'*Petrus habet . . . Petrus habet . . .*'

I walked over to the steps that ran down to our garden. His eyes were closed and he was preoccupied.

'William, don't leave!'

'What is it now?'

'Do I irritate you?'

'Haven't I done enough for you today?'

And against my own inclinations, haven't I done enough . . . and against hers . . . He was going through these motions once again, and I was beginning to know this sort of behaviour rather well: first of all he would let his dark eyes gaze into mine as if he had never seen me before, as if he were discovering me for the first time, looking at me admiringly, as though I were some wonder of nature; the dark eyes of innocence, the trusting eyes of a friend. Then he would come up to me and put his hand on my shoulder, a powerful hand that was gentle and insistent. His gaze would not leave me until he felt that I was weakening, that my anger had subsided and that he had control of my confused feelings. Only then did he speak.

'William, my friend, I think you are my only friend.'

I sighed. I wanted to believe him: it was good to be the only friend of the greatest philosopher in the world.

'What I am telling you, I cannot tell anyone else. Believe me: my enemies would not imagine how innocent I am . . . My spirit wanders freely in the world of the mind—it is king at the Court of Kings. But my body is that of a bear who leaves his cave and discovers the light of the sun, the curious human dance, the snares along the roads. I stand erect and I fight with my paws, I look fearsome and in a moment of panic I can probably wound or kill; but my heart is filled with apprehension and terror. Are you still willing to help me?'

He released my shoulder and he stared into the fireplace where nothing was burning. He was close to tears and his fervour was winning me over. I was no longer frightened to be with him and I was no longer angry. *Petrus habet Heloïssam*. Peter had chosen Heloise, Peter loved Heloise without knowing her and without knowing how to love: may she be his.

8

N O S O O N E R had Christian, who was out of breath, and Arnold warned me than I rushed over. We had been squelching about in the pools of mud in which a few blackened beams, chests that had been broken open, and trestles without tables were still immersed, and where men seated on their now useless buckets were staring numbly at the houses.

Peter was alone, on his knees, his head covered with ashes that were still warm, in the midst of the ruins of the Cloister of Notre-Dame school.

'What's he doing?' asked Christian.

'He's in a fury,' said Arnold.

Peter raised his head at our approach and sat up straight.

'The school is no more,' he said with a forced cheerfulness.

'You didn't burn with it,' said Christian. 'If there's still a master, there's still a school . . .'

'How did it happen?' asked Arnold.

He gestured vaguely.

'A warehouse where they store wheat . . . as far as I know . . .'

'Where will you teach?'

'I don't know, William. In the ruins of the cathedral, at Samuel's house, on the Petit Pont . . . Or I'll make my way back up to the Mount Sainte-Geneviève, that will make me feel young again and it will wear you out . . .'

We were now in the cathedral square. We came across students, canons, soldiers. They looked at Peter and turned away again after a moment's hesitation. He was walking more slowly than usual; his body seemed heavy and his expression was inscrutable. As Peter the Child came towards us, he leant over towards me.

'I feel tired,' he whispered. 'I've no more strength. Tell them that I'll go on alone.'

'Don't do that. Resist.'

He stared at me for a moment. He hesitated.

Behind the Child came the master's little army, his soldiers of misfortune, each of them looking distraught. We embraced one another. Abelard stood to one side.

'They're trying to kill him,' muttered Arnold with ill-contained anger.

'He'll kill himself on his own,' croaked Cervelle.

'You're getting on my nerves.'

'Calm down, Arnold,' said the Child. 'Cervelle's quite right. There's something about him that makes him his own worst enemy and more dangerous than all his enemies put together.'

The bells of Saint-Germain rang out first; then, further away, towards the south, those of Sainte-Geneviève and Notre-Dame, just within earshot, and then, from every corner of the city, came those of Saint-Victor, Saint-Pierre-aux-Boeufs, Saint-Serge and Saint-Bacchus, Saint-Jacques, and finally, Saint-Julien, the weakest voice of all.

'Come!'

Abelard looked at us, a fresh smile on his lips.

'Come on, children!'

And without further ado, he set off firmly in the direction of the Petit Pont.

✦   ✦   ✦

Over the following days, while Peter Abelard, with my help, was preparing to move into Fulbert's house and spending his nights dreaming of ravishing the canon's niece Heloise, with whom I was secretly in love, a strange spectacle could be seen from the banks of the Île de la Cité.

At the port of Saint-Landry, instead of eggs and spices being loaded aboard, the master and his disciples were embarking. There he stood, surrounded by other boats, preaching and commenting on parables with astonishing images and expounding on paradoxes with a skill that was disconcerting. Occasionally a swell caused the smaller boats to toss about; the vessels had been lent by the new corporation of merchant watermen, who wanted to encourage the continuity of the progress of knowledge and—but this was very much secondary—please the itinerant scholar's powerful protector, Stephen de Garlande.

Bishop Gerbert, who had succeeded Galon and did not care for Peter, had nonetheless promised him a new school, in one of his outhouses, behind the cathedral. In his gardens there were trees that produced rare essences as well as an olive tree from the Mount of Olives. Ill-intentioned gossips used to say that in this way, within hearing distance of the Pope's representative, Abelard would be more restrained in his audacity and his blasphemous comparisons. In the meantime, his lessons given on the waters gained him a reputation which went largely beyond clerical circles. From one of the bridges, from the boards of Mibrai, from the shores of the island, people would often call out to us: 'Disciples! Would you walk on the water with Jesus?' But though they made fun, there was respect too, as if these simple folk knew that lessons given on water are finer than those given on land.

Yes, nothing could have done more for Peter Abelard's renown than this inland navigation. Not since the Normans, three centuries earlier, had Paris experienced such an invasion; every morning new vessels could be seen joining the fleet of logic. Words were passed from boat to boat and they changed meaning at the whim of the lapping waves. Over the broad arm of the Seine, amid the sandbanks and the barges, the sound mingled with that of the offshore wind, the disorderly waves and the gulls.

Later on, when the legend and the curse of Peter Abelard had begun to take root, it was said that his lessons delivered on the water had been the result of his being banned from teaching on *terra firma*. But for us, discovering the world in the ebb and flow of the river, these early autumn days were wonderful. *Blessed are you who sow beside the waters . . .*

On the morning of the third day, Heloise came, bringing with her birds that chirped as they chased each other above the bishop's garden.

My legs were heavy from bad dreams and drinking too much. I longed to say 'I love you' once more to this woman who did not love me. I forgot: I had never said anything to her; my lips had been sealed, so as to make sure she didn't hear me.

She looked at me and waved as she walked quietly by, but she didn't stop; I was sitting sifting soil between my fingers, a fistful of soil that I let run from one hand to another until nothing but a little dust was left. When I'd finished, I started again. The master was alone, a few feet away, beneath the olive tree. He was reading a book— *Timaeus*, I think—which he had been talking to us about for several days, comparing the Soul of the World with the Holy Spirit. *The earth was without form and void, and darkness was upon the face of the deep; and the Spirit of God was moving over the face of the waters*. He saw her and sprang to his feet.

They exchange words with one another, but I do not hear them—the humming in my ears. There are others who are closer to them, but I do not see them—the veil that covers my eyes. I could stir myself, but I am motionless, apart from the movement of my hands which, ceaselessly, vainly, sift the soil. Now I can see: they are alone.

It's a solitude that my body remembers: the solitude of

lovers. It's a solitude that I would know even if I had not experienced it: a solitude that can drive one to despair if one is on one's own. You speak to me and I alone hear you. I speak to you and you alone understand me. What I know, you already knew. What you begin, I finish. Have you noticed how beautiful the world is? Do you know how to float off into the sky? Do you want to walk, to talk, to be silent? They speak, they smile. They are silent, they smile. The sun rises over the vineyards of Bercy and the Seine shimmers with golden reflections—my hand would not caress your body any better than this.

'Did you see?'

It was Christian who was pulling me by the sleeve. I wanted to say 'I know'—but the words didn't pass my lips.

'Come.'

He took me by the arm but I didn't want to move. I wanted to stay like that, for ever, suffering just a few feet away from them.

One by one they drifted away: Peter the Child, Cervelle and Simeon, Célestin, Gilbert, Geoffrey of Chartres, even Arnold, who had not understood quite what was going on, but whom Christian dragged along with him.

Heloise and Abelard didn't see me: whether I was present or absent was unimportant. The garden sloped gently down to the shore: they walked side by side, gracefully, without touching. I was aware of Heloise's gracefulness. Abelard's was something new, something stranger; his black linen gown seemed more delicate, his waist was thinner, his bear-like gait more nimble.

That day, all but one of the boats would remain empty.

9

H E CAME to the priory with her and we spent the evening laughing and singing. Our queen with the bright,
shining face was not to be outdone. She loved being
the only woman amongst all these men who for the most part
had not known any and were discovering the mystery in her
eyes. Arnold had lit a fire in the hearth because it had been cold.
Late in the evening, we saw their hands searching for one another, as well as the looks they exchanged, which were evidence
of an intimacy in which we had had no part to play. My friends
left the room one after the other to return to the dormitory
which was on the second floor. I did not want to leave — and silence set in. The bell of Saint-Victor chimed: I had lost track of
time, I think it was for the vigil.

> Go forth, O daughters of Zion,
> and behold King Solomon,
> with the crown with which his mother crowned him
> on the day of his wedding,
> on the day of his gladness of heart.

I began to laugh to myself and they looked at me. I glanced
and saw the dying embers; I was dying with them — *on the day of*

his gladness of heart. I desired your death, Solomon Abelard, I want you to be accursed and to die in pain.

I went up to bed with the others.

I thought that I had got over it all, but the night was still long. I could not sleep. I kept my eyes open: the crackle of the fire, the breathing of men in the night hours, the world at prayer. I was alone. Alone: in a sense.

I could hear them.

Softly spoken words, stifled laughter, silences . . . the rustle of material, the creaking of the wood . . . My God, why are they making love here, a few feet away from me? Why continue to crush me and trample me, as if I had done harm? I know I have blasphemed with words, but You are my witness that I have sinned very little — the lowliest priest is a hundred times worse than me. My God, remember your servant Job and do not allow him to fall into the hands of Satan, be merciful . . .

I rose and went down the first few steps of the staircase, and in a low voice, like that of a supplicant, I said: 'Peter . . .' Nothing had changed; our friends were all asleep, and I was the only wretch to share in their fornication without being a part of it. I wanted to escape and join my beloved statues, but it meant going past them — he inside her, in her warmth and her tenderness, each of them lost in the other's desire, each of them trying unsuccessfully to muffle any noise.

Heloise was smiling, her eyes closed, lost in a world which I would not enter. Would I not touch her? It was as well. Did she not love me? That was as well, too.

But I still loved her.

I felt very much alive as I walked out into the night. Heloise's shadow was alongside me and would not leave. She bathed beside me in the Bièvre stream and she laughed as she caught moonfish with her hands. She stripped off her surcoat, her gown and her blouse as women do in eastern fairy tales — a dance in which the naked flesh is never revealed because one veil always conceals another.

Sing, my love, sing of your new love for the greatest philosopher in the world! Sing of the astonishment coursing through both your bodies as the master's disciples leave the house and, eyes dull with sleep, join me beside the river.

They are silent, there is nothing to say, nothing to do, except eat the grapes that Christian had picked from the vineyard at Saint-Victor, to spit out the coarse skin and let the juice dribble down our chins.

Sing, my love, sing of your so potent love which will live fearlessly for all too brief a time! Sing of the joys that are so short-lived, sing of what is obvious but inexplicable! You are alone now and you are saying things to each other which none can hear and none can understand while he, stroking you gently with his large hands, is reawakening your body and you are surprised to discover that you desire that pain — what am I saying? — that you are calling out for it, demanding it.

You two seem to have been waiting for so long — and yet, when terror was my mistress, I alone knew what it was about your skin, your eyes, the murmurs of your hearts . . .

The bells chimed for Matins, then Prime: the dawn clothed us without covering us. It was cold, as beggars and the poor can attest every night God grants to them. Arnold had fallen asleep against my shoulder — a giant who can drift off fearlessly into sleep. Christian stretched.

'Do you think we can go back?'

'I feel like some bread.'

The nearest bakery was by the Laas enclosure: we waited there happily like scrawny cats as the heat burned our limbs. A child with his eyes full of sleep was talking in a strange language to his fingers as if they were visitors charged with a mission.

'Where has the canon gone?' asked Arnold.

'To Chartres, on pilgrimage.'

74

'I hope for his sake that he didn't place himself under the protection of the Virgin.'

Christian began to laugh, then Arnold, and finally me. We laughed till the tears came and we had to stop.

'The Virgin,' said Christian, hiccupping.

We set off, still laughing, juggling the burning hot bread in our hands. A group of nuns looked at us disapprovingly.

'It's not particularly funny,' I said eventually.

Arnold's expression was always cheerful, but a cloud had already come over Christian's face. The air reverberated with the sounds of the world awakening. Men were stretching and saying their prayers, others were opening their eyes to their hunger. How to go on living and hoping for one more day? The earth, newly drenched by the dew, gave off scents of the forest as well as the sewers of the city; by a curious effect of the dawn light, Notre-Dame seemed to be emerging like the mist from the ruins of Saint-Etienne.

'Who would believe that the folly of wise men is more foolish than that of other men?' said Christian eventually.

'The folly of love—isn't that what others call wisdom?'

'No doubt. If he didn't have so many enemies . . .'

'His friends are more powerful than his enemies,' said Arnold.

'You know very well that he'll be on his own at the end,' Christian muttered.

'That's not true,' said Arnold somewhat pompously. 'I'll be there, wherever I am.'

Christian grimaced in disbelief, perhaps a mite contemptuous. Arnold looked at him menacingly, a hand was raised, a punch was thrown. I had to shout at them to stop.

'That'll do!'

They glared at each other, this French lion and this Italian bee, with such hostility that it made me—and very soon them too—want to smile. We all embraced.

'Are we going to wait by this door all day?' Arnold asked.

'No, open it,' said Christian.

'You do it.'

Arnold demurred.

'What did the Child say?' he asked.

'Don't you know? He was summoned to Vézelay. The prior died and they want to elect him.'

'Our Peter, the Child who loves miracles?'

'The very same. I don't think we can go on calling him the Child . . .'

Arnold shrugged as he pushed open the front door. We followed him, climbing the stairs in silence. We found Peter Abelard alone, standing by the ashes in the hearth. The back of his powerful, rigid neck did not move. His black linen robe was crumpled like a sack. He did not look at us.

'Peter?'

I spoke in a low voice—almost as if I didn't want him to hear.

'Peter?'

He did not stir.

'Peter?'

'Love—and do as thou wouldst.'

It was his voice—so deep that we scarcely recognised it—not the voice of the master but that of a man who has discovered an unknown country within himself.

'I often wondered what that really meant . . .'

He turned towards us at last. Tears were flowing down the two vertical folds of his cheeks. His face had grown old. We had never seen him weep.

'So that's what it was . . .'

10

IS EXPRESSION changed over the course of the days. Tense, non-communicative and worn, he gradually relaxed and you could see expressions of a fleeting sweetness that were not at all like him. The songs of birds could be heard in his logical progressions.

The bishop had soon put a stop to the scandal caused by the lectures on the water. Not since Jesus himself had anyone dared take himself for Jesus in this way: they weren't going to get involved in that business again, with all its complications! While waiting for a room to become available in its premises, the school had been moved to the far end of the Close, to the house of a canon who, after suffering terribly, had just died.

The devil would come to collect you a little earlier than expected and the dying might be overcome with convulsions and start uttering incoherent words as the flames burst from their mouths and their bodies began to burn. If they hadn't made a full and sincere confession before dying, all that would remain of them was a pile of bones amongst ashes at the moment that their souls were cast into the depths of hell-fire; but if you prayed to Christ, intercession through the Father was certain, all your troubles were ended, a marvellous light came over your face and death came peacefully. This belief, which was more reliable than astronomy and geometry, was taught to me by Peter the Child, and before him by Andrew, and before him by my friend the priest—it was a belief that was as old as mankind.

The chapterhouse must surely have allocated these quarters to us out of spite: they were less than half the size of the previous school (whose walls were already filled to bursting), and they could only house a small number of those who wished to hear the master. Some of them spent the night outside the door to be sure of hearing him the following morning.

I have said that he had changed. Not everybody may have noticed this: he still had that freedom of expression that took your breath away, and that lack of patience with stupidity that so delighted us. '*Stultus*,' he would mutter under his breath—nowadays there was less anger and less aggression, but an irony that was just as wounding.

Rumours quickly spread about his moving into Canon Fulbert's house, but no more attention was paid to them than to any other news, and probably less than to the latest reports of skirmishes between Gerbert and the Chancellor, Stephen de Garlande. Men of God between themselves . . .

Heloise no longer came to the lectures and nobody saw them together, by day or by night. The canon told everybody at the chapterhouse that he had Aristotle living at his home, which was irritating though not surprising, for Fulbert loved to boast. Thus it was that Peter Abelard let his relationship be known in his own inimitable way.

On Monday, he used the following sentence as an example of grammar: 'Peter loves his ladyfriend.' On Tuesday, he followed this with: 'Peter's wife is his ladyfriend.' On Wednesday, expounding on property and accident in Aristotle's *Categories*—or Boethius's commentaries on them, to be precise—he happened to remark: 'Peter's ladyfriend has blue eyes.' And so it continued: by the end of the week the whole of the Île de la Cité was buzzing with the curious news that the man whom everyone believed had chosen chastity for ever was in love.

As was bound to happen, the only person not to know what was going on was Heloise's uncle, who strolled about the Close with a cheerful expression while people muttered behind his back.

By chance, or it may have been a portent, it was at this time that the figure of Bernard of Clairvaux, with his hollow cheeks and his gleaming eyes, could be seen in Paris, newly emerged from his fearful valley of Absinthe. He came to Paris as if to Babylon, frothing at the lips, the pain in his belly newly awakened as though he had been eating worms and burning embers. He was not seen preaching at schools or on the bridges: he was too wary of those stout fellows who, taught by the masters, walked about the streets of the city passionately proclaiming the merits of a reason, which he suspected served God only in order to destroy him.

I went to listen to him: he preached his sermons in a small church on the road to Saint-Denis, near Saint-Martin-des-Champs. I felt very isolated as the flow of light and anger poured from his lips. The time is nigh, he said in a low voice, the time is nigh. Remember: *by your hard and impenitent heart you are storing up wrath for yourself.* Oh, how hateful is this city where it is impossible not to see sinfulness! Where at night it is not the silence of the Close that reigns but the pantings of fornication, the cries and vomiting of a return to debauchery . . . *Men whose hearts are filled with every injustice, with perversion; with cupidity, with malice; radiating nothing but envy, murder, quarrelling, treachery, cruelty; slanderers, detractors, enemies of God, insulters, the arrogant, the braggarts, those who play with evil . . .* Oh, that promise of the love of Christ, which alone can save us! His gilded words recalled the God of love and the God of vengeance, the God of mercy and the one who wielded the sword. Was he Isaiah or Paul himself when he hammered out: *I will destroy the wisdom of the wise, and the cleverness of the clever I will thwart?* As for me, in a sweat and my legs quaking, I believed I had heard war declared on Peter Abelard.

I tried to discuss it with my master. All he did was laugh.

'The Abbot of Clairvaux?' he said sarcastically. 'Is he in Paris? He won't stay here unless he wishes to die here. Let him preach that *the desire of flesh is death* and go back peacefully to his solitude.'

After that came the songs: they were sung from one end of Paris to the other, from the Île de la Cité to the left bank and up to the Mount Sainte-Geneviève; they sped along the bridges and into the countryside, as far as Chaillot. They put the name of Heloise on every lip—as well as her smile, her modesty, her lowered gaze, her learning. There was little difference—the breadth of a leaf, the passing of a season—between these songs and the laments that Peter would compose later on. This gaiety was brief and endangered and it therefore had a marvellous, unique lightness.

At the priory ill feeling began to stir, fuelled by hatreds that were older than us and which resurfaced without our understanding them. Peter the Child had left, Abelard was in love, and we were orphans. How much longer would the priory survive, how much longer would I wander about at night among my brothers the apostles or the kings of Judah?

Arnold was suspicious of Roux, Christian of Simeon—and everyone loathed Cervelle. I was also the subject of a vague and foolish jealousy between my two friends, Arnold and Christian. It was an appalling litany. I could not stand their pointless quarrels and I blocked my ears. True, I missed the Child's smile and his kindliness. His God was the just, merciful and gentle one, and not the one who allowed the sins of the fathers to be visited on their children, those of brother upon brother . . . He saw us as being better than we were; and wasn't this because we were better than we ourselves believed we were? But we would not realise this until later, when we understood that there was no traitor among us, just blind men at the height of noonday, thirsty and groping our way.

At night we did not sleep much and we found ourselves caught up in whispered conversations; in the morning we prayed again, in no particular sequence, in the chapel that Peter the Child had allotted to us just before he disappeared. What a curious troupe of servants of the Lord we were, last-minute helpers —unless that minute had already passed . . .

Christian's book was beginning to fade on my body.

One morning, for the first time, there was silence during one of Peter Abelard's lessons. He was commenting on the Epistle to the Romans when a student asked him a straightforward question, prompted by a classical debate brought about by a theme of Jerome's that was contested somewhat insincerely by Augustine.

He said nothing.

For a few moments we thought this was a tactic and that he was turning the words over in his mind, waiting to come out with one of those bits of nonsense at which he was so adept and which delighted the class.

Then I realised that it was nothing of the sort: his eyes were blank. He had forgotten. *Jerome, fourth letter to Eustochius, second paragraph . . . Augustine, second book of 'The City of God', chapter XIX* . . . A number of us knew this and we didn't dare look at one another. What need had I to whisper it to him? He knew all this by heart and he always amazed us by the speed with which he could make the link between the texts, the exegesis and the commentaries, and bring out their inconsistencies and resolve them like a magician, or else leave them unresolved before explaining the rules by which he himself, addressing the mystery in all humility, intended to remove the obstacles. In all humility . . .

He stood with his hands on his stool. He did not move. *He was small.* The longer the silence went on, the mumbling grew louder: one by one, the students came to realise that the master had had a lapse of memory or did not know. There were murmurings of incredulity and embarrassed laughter. Then, at last, he raised his hand and reached it out over the assembled gathering, and calm was restored, a fragile, nervous calm.

'I'll explain all that tomorrow,' he said in a monotone, his face pale, drained of blood.

For a few seconds, the audience hesitated: there could have been a commotion, a riot . . . But the master's friends acted quickly: each of them ushered the others towards the exit, muttering 'Tomorrow, tomorrow, he's tired . . .'

I waited for him in the street and we walked away together in silence; we left the Close, crossed the bishop's garden, behind the church on the farthest point of the island, and went down to the Seine along a path that wound its way among the saplings— Gerbert had had them planted to mark his taking up his duties. When we are all dead, they will be fine oak trees.

He sat down on the bank. One never wearied of watching the play of light over the Seine, the boats, the windmills that turn between the arches of the Grand Pont; here you felt you were aboard a ship towing the city on its great voyage through Time, and on blustery days the wind clawed at your face.

'I don't want to give any more lessons.'

'You astonish me.'

'I'm fed up with these idiots . . . and my desires lie elsewhere.'

'We were aware of your desires . . .'

He smiled wearily.

'You were aware, were you? I long for songs. You don't know what sort of woman this woman is. With her, I never know whether I'm asleep or awake; I don't know whether I'm breathing or not unless my breath is mingled with hers; if I close my eyes I start up for fear of losing the thought of her in my mind; and when I'm with her I laugh like a child whom she has to gag at night so that I don't wake up her fool of an uncle and all his household. And do you know what?'

'Tell me.'

'I beat her. I really do beat her as he asked you. She cries out in genuine pain and I imagine him smiling happily, convinced that my blows are bringing her all the knowledge in the world. And that makes us come, come all the more.'

I didn't want to laugh. I didn't want to imagine Peter Abelard touching Heloise, stroking her and hurting her, bringing her to orgasm and reaching a climax with her. And yet . . .

'When he goes out, since the old servant is half deaf and blind (and in any case I console her with good doses of philosophy), we christen every corner and room in the house.'

'That's enough, Peter . . .'

'Why?'

I didn't answer, I never do answer—and he never listens to my replies . . .

He put his arm round my shoulder.

'You're like a brother to me,' he murmured, 'more of a brother, surely, than my blood brothers, the knights and the monks . . . As for the others, I have to restrain myself from constantly calling them fools, those idiots . . . You're the only one who understands me.'

My heart was thumping and I felt sad. I was his brother when he needed me and a stranger when I embarrassed him; all the same, I preferred being his brother.

'You realise that I'll leave the school soon.'

'Leave the school? Not be a master anymore?'

'Well, yes . . . I'll leave this one just as I left the others.'

'So where will you go?'

'Who knows? To England, to your country, or else to Italy, to Spain, to Toledo to find out about those Arabs you mentioned and who know Greek better than us . . .'

'I know those countries, Peter. There is no school worthy of you.'

'I'll join a monastery—Vézelay perhaps, I've been invited there by the Child, or to Cluny. There are times when I think solitude would suit me.'

'Solitude—with monks who would hate you.'

He looked genuinely surprised.

'Why should they hate me?'

'You ask for it . . . But that's beside the point: you love this city too much. And what's more . . . you'd make a very bad monk!'

A mischievous expression came over him.

'At least people would talk about me!'

'Whatever you do, people will talk about you. So . . .'

'William, would you take over from me?'

The question took my breath away. He pressed the point.

'I'll speak to Garlande about you . . . The bishop will not stand against him—the king himself can't refuse him anything.'

William of Oxford, master of the Notre-Dame schools! That sounded good, but it also sounded wrong: an illusion I could not believe in myself.

'We'll discuss it again. Is that a promise?'

'That's right, we'll discuss it.'

'Will you help me?'

What did he want? To send Fulbert away on some distant pilgrimage, no doubt, or else obtain a few more funds to get rid of the maidservant or to pay for some pleasure . . . Whenever I close my eyes, I have this image that I try to banish but which comes back to me all the same: they're half naked and are running after one another, he catches her, they embrace, fall to the ground and grapple with each other furiously.

'Will you help me?'

He could not be unaware of the disaster that was coming. Neither could Heloise, anymore than I or anyone else could. The ignorance in which Uncle Fulbert so charmingly cloaked himself was merely misfortune slumbering as it stocked up with bitterness and venom.

The stone was the colour of the sun and the cries died down in the evening. My master had again taken me by the shoulder and we were both swaying together like two men who had drunk too much. In the garden, a deacon noticed us and set off at a run.

✦ ✦ ✦

'Germain,' he said, 'do you remember?'

It was a white-robed monk, surrounded by other white-robed monks, who was yelling a little bit louder than the others as all the while semi-naked men were breaking down our door. When he told me his name, he simply let his hood slip from his head and I could see his scar, the black insect that dwelt on his skull. He sniggered.

'You were looking for a master and you found one: a master of baseness and lies, a master of deceit and an enemy of God!'

'You weren't such a good monk, as I remember . . .'

'I've found my way.'

As if it were a trophy, he showed me the little wooden cross that hung round his neck.

'Bernard of Clairvaux? Do you know the man?'

'The prophet?'

'Shake off your stiff neck, wicked son of Israel! It is he who speaks the true word of Christ.'

'Is it he who ordered you to destroy our house?'

The men showed no emotion as they laid waste. Heads, arms, keys and books, all made of stone, were being tossed through the arches. I watched as the friends of my nights were smashed: Michael and Gabriel with their broken arms, Joseph and Benjamin, the brothers who would now no longer run away, and the winged monsters, the musicians and the millers, the weighers of souls, knights and peasants—all corpses among which the passers-by threw their rubbish, and the animals defecated.

Germain looked at me as I watched—and at Christian who had joined me, and Arnold, and all the others. All of a sudden we saw a man running, waving his arms about, and stopping in the midst of the shattered debris. He opened his mouth, but no sound came forth; he wrung his hands and gazed at us alternately, the white-robed monks, the clerks, the henchmen, without uttering a word. Gently, like a pauper, he lay down among the stones and began to groan.

'Who is it?' asked Arnold.

No one answered, but we all knew: it was the sculptor, the man who had created all this from nothing. I turned to Germain.

'It's not his fault,' I said hopelessly.

'You always want to save others. But nobody can save anyone else—only the grace of Our Lord.'

'He was also searching for that, for grace . . .'

'Grace! Don't make me laugh! In God's house there are no images, no statues, no gold and no incense. There's the stone, the light and the men who pray. Of you, all that will remain . . .'

He blew between his fingers as if to say: 'Just that.' Arnold made to grab him by the collar, but I stopped him. A terrible surge of violence beat at my temples and coursed through my hands.

'Let me teach him . . .' begged Arnold.

'No.'

I looked at Germain.

'You will call off your soldiers of God. You will stop this now, you vermin. Now.'

My voice was quaking.

'And you will help that man up and bring him back to us. Straight away.'

'You'll regret this,' he muttered—but with a wave of his hand he put a stop to the violence.

He picked up the sculptor, who was covered in stone dust and almost lifeless, and he threw him at my feet. As his men withdrew, he stood alone in front of us. He raised his finger and pointed at Christian, at Arnold, at Simeon, at me.

'Die,' he said. 'You, you, you and you. Die, all of you. Perish in hell with him.'

He drew his hood back over his head and turned his back on us. It began to rain, a cold, icy rain.

One by one they left the house on the Bièvre, driven by fear and the onset of winter. One of them went back to his monastery, another to his estate, a third became a priest, while someone

86

else went on a pilgrimage to Jerusalem. Even my dear Arnold, my battler, my tender-hearted giant, set off for Italy promising revolutions such as had never been seen before.

I had taken in the sculptor and given him my bed. I slept on the floor alongside him and fed him on beef broth. I discovered that his name was Gislebert and that he was tall, thin and silent. One morning, I found that he was no longer there.

It fell to me—and to Christian—to close the door that led to the priory.

I walked around one last time amongst the shattered statuary and put a saint's broken sword in my pocket.

'Where will you go?' asked Christian as we were leaving.

I looked at him without saying anything. I had not thought about it.

'To Saint-Victor?'

'To old Champeaux? You're mad, he'd kill you. Come with me to Saint-Germain. They use as many copyists as a priest does hosts.'

'I'm not sure if that's what I want.'

'You don't need to be sure. All you need do is follow me.'

I followed him.

Snow had fallen over Paris, an early snow that covered our footsteps and shrouded the fields, vineyards and church steeples. The street vendors were not sure whether to set up their stalls that morning. A papermaker was comparing the whiteness of sheets with that of the ground before folding them.

'Are you still suffering?'

He had asked this out of the blue, just as he might have enquired about an old leg wound. I hesitated.

'Well . . . no . . .'

'No?'

'Yes . . .'

'But?'

'No.'

His laughter was muffled by the snow and we played at tag

like children. Yes. No. If not, perhaps. If not on another occasion, another life. I left Christian to make his way towards Saint-Germain while I slipped away into the cluster of cattle and carts to cross the Petit Pont and return to the Île de la Cité and the Close.

I had never been inside Fulbert's house—a house built of wood and stone, the façade of which was adorned with that figure, now my friend, of an angel with curly hair: an Heloise come from heaven.

As if it were an oversight, she was wearing a blue hair-band the colour of her eyes, as well as a bracelet of the same shade on her arm, so slender beneath her tunic. She was alone with her elderly servant, the one with a Saracen's complexion, who left as I entered. Cheerfully, she led me to an upstairs room where there was a fire burning with blue and green flames. Double-arched windows opened onto the street below, allowing the rare winter light to filter through the parchment blinds.

'Well?'

'I'm going to Saint-Germain.'

'You're leaving him too!'

There was such vivaciousness in her response that it gave me a start.

'Aren't you going to ask me why I'm leaving?'

'Why are you leaving?'

I did not speak. After all, what did going to Saint-Germain matter? It was so near, yet so far; so far, and yet so near . . . I told her so, speaking clumsily and finding it hard to restrain the anger which was making me so annoyed with myself.

'What's the matter?' she asked at last, with a sudden gentleness.

'I don't think I want to talk to you.'

'When will you want to?'

'When you're no longer there to listen to me.'

'Do it straight away then, because I don't understand what you're saying. Come on now, William, stop this sighing . . .'

I took as big a breath as I could.

'Tell me . . . Tell me what to do with a love that is like the moon in daylight when the sun is shining . . . that is like an autumn day once summer has come . . . Heloise, I am unable to rid myself of the sense of unfairness that makes me wake up at night whenever I consider how fate has allowed me to find you at the very moment I was losing you . . .'

She raised her hand. I held it back.

'If you really want me to talk, I don't want you to speak. I want you to understand—for once, but only once—the strange feeling I am experiencing at the moment. I love you. You do not love me. I say this in modesty and without hope and all I ask of you in return is not to answer me with words which I, in my own way, know better than you yourself . . . Yes, those words that in dreams I have placed on your lips, you must leave them with me and I won't even embarrass you with my silence. Just let me whisper that I love you forever, my love; I promise that I won't grieve, that I won't disturb you, that I won't throw myself on my knees to beg a pittance of you—the breath of your lips on my face, the touch of one of your fingers, *Time is all I beg, mere time, a respite* . . . I give you thanks for enabling me to experience this—it may not last forever, it may take flight tomorrow because I am a human being, and a man among humans, and because it is only today that I am sure of the purity of my commitment.'

'Stay with me,' she said all of a sudden.

She had taken the velvet bracelet from her arm and was fingering it.

'What do you mean?'

'I don't know myself, but I understand a little better when I hear you speak: it gives me the impression that I am speaking rather than you . . . You mustn't think I am ignoring what is in your heart, it's just that the discovery of my own feelings is taking me on such a distant journey and it rocks my small boat so violently . . . *She burns, the unhappy Dido* . . . At times this love I have for him overwhelms me and it's as if I need nothing else; and sometimes I have a feeling of terrible loneliness, a sense of exile that has already taken root within me.'

'I shall be the friend you desire — if this is what you wish. Present when you have need of me. Absent when I may not be required. I shall be the like the angel at your doorway. I shall whisper the words you need when your burden is too heavy. And when you say "I love you", it will be as if I were saying it.'

She took my hand.

'I love him. I'm frightened. Will you stay with me, now?'

One word remained on the tip of my lips — the word 'always', which brought tears to my eyes. That eternity which we search for on earth and find only in Heaven . . . I opened my arms and she snuggled up to me. The restlessness in my heart was soothed. It was a moment of peace, without a trace of sadness; there is some good to be derived from hopelessness. My hand ruffled through her hair, dishevelling it and continued running through it like a comb: this motion, and this motion alone, could have gone on for hours — nothing further ensued.

'Well?'

Fulbert's plump figure stood at the doorway. She turned her still distressed face towards him; the blood had drained from mine. He could not see me against the sunlight. Heloise rose suddenly, ran over to him and hugged him warmly.

'I wasn't feeling well, Uncle.'

I too stood up. He unlocked his arms from the embrace and walked towards me with a fierce look on his face.

'Who are you?'

'Don't you remember?'

I tried to sound as casual as possible but I was a little short of breath.

'Uncle,' Heloise interrupted cheerfully, 'he's William, the man who rescued me, Master Peter's pupil.'

'What's he doing in this house?'

'Master Peter isn't able to give me my lesson today. He sent him to inform me of this and to give me some work to do.'

Fulbert relented. The magic name had its effect: Master Peter.

'Would you care for some wine? It's wine from his part of the country, the region around Nantes, which his father Berengar, the knight who took holy orders, sent to us . . . It's called *berligou* or *berlingot*, I can't remember. A wine to warm the cockles of your heart. So, will you have some?'

He did not wait for me to answer and snapped his fingers. The maid with the dark complexion came in with two crystal goblets in her hands.

'I shall leave you,' Heloise said merrily, 'you have things to discuss.'

She disappeared downstairs without giving him time to reply. He turned to me.

'To Peter Abelard! He's a master who will be remembered,' said Fulbert, raising his glass.

I joined in with all the enthusiasm I could muster.

'Tell me about his lessons,' he said, clicking his tongue. 'Heloise doesn't tell me much. She prefers to keep them to herself.'

'He's a master who's exacting and wonderful!'

The canon's red face beamed; he rolled the words around his lips: 'exacting and wonderful'. Oh! How fine that sounds!

'He knows the value of each word in every language of the world—and whether that is a thing.'

'Hmm, hmm, whether that is a thing . . . That's splendid. William?'

He poured himself some more wine and his face was gleaming.

'William, tell me the truth.'

'Certainly.'

'She's clever, isn't she?'

'Very.'

'I'm going to tell you a secret: I want her to be even more clever. I want—may God forgive me—I want her to arouse jealousy and for everyone to say: "That's Heloise, she's the most accomplished and cleverest woman in the world. She's Canon Fulbert's niece."'

There were tears in his eyes and I envied him his simple faith and trust in his niece's qualities.

'Do you see, people won't any longer say: Fulbert, like the Bishop of Chartres? They'll say: Fulbert, like the Canon of Notre-Dame. When she goes back to Argenteuil, she will teach the nuns all manner of wisdom and philosophy. That of Christ, I mean — well, that which the Lord allows.'

'Is there any other?' I asked.

'William?'

I looked at him in profound and sincere innocence.

'Do you take me for an idiot?'

'But how can you think . . .'

'I'm asking you a question. I may be foolish and somewhat vain, but I'm not totally deaf; I believe that in the chapterhouse, in the Close, and among the students who think they are masters, they are whispering that . . .'

I stopped him with a firm wave of my hand.

'No, I don't think you are an idiot.'

'Good. You see, either you are wrong or else they're right. I am an idiot, a *simpleton*, but no one should take advantage of me, and it's wrong to make me unhappy.'

'Who would want to . . .'

'Come on now, William, come on. I've put my fate in your hands — or rather in your master's. I've put more trust in you than I do in my own life. Can I say more than that?'

I stammered and stepped backwards towards the staircase, and almost fell.

'Don't fall over, my friend. And don't take her in your arms again, even if she's not feeling well. I don't know what would become of me if I grew really foolish. And I don't want to know.'

11

I TOO, started giving private lessons. The entire city had taken up philosophy, and not just courtiers and the gentry, but also money lenders and even prostitutes and butchers, who wanted their children to be able to distinguish between the obscure sophisms listed by Aristotle. I demonstrated the existence of God by expounding to the dull-witted on the subtleties of the argument between Anselm, Lanfranc and Gaunilon; in a relaxed moment I found myself wandering in the garden of the negative theology of Denys—above all, I enjoyed playing Socrates as I made my way through a shower of questions.

I stayed on the Mount Sainte-Geneviève, at the home of a man from the Vendée—a parchment maker by profession—who never stopped smiling and who rented me a room for a few centimes and the promise that his son—a large, graceless boy who hated being taught—would be a doctor of the church before long.

Abelard had begun teaching again, but he had sunk into a routine that brought with it murmurings, protests and even brawls. His skill and his memory usually enabled him to extricate himself from dangerous situations. But what had happened to the imagination and the thirst for discovery that had made him famous? No one now came to his lectures tingling at the thought of the daring propositions they were about to hear. I tried to speak to him on several occasions, but he kept his distance, not even giving me the opportunity to open my mouth. 'You bore me,' was the only response I had if I mentioned the name of Fulbert.

Finally, one morning he did not come.

It had never happened before, and the host of students remained nonplussed for a few moments before they dispersed. Most of them set off in a group towards the Petit Pont: it was not the time of year for frolicking about in the water or sunbathing. The Seine was frozen.

A small group of them went down to the river bank — one brave fellow launched forth, then another, and thus, one by one, from the bridge you could see logicians and theologians going through the motions of their dance without their dancing master, waving their arms and legs about meaninglessly, slipping, tumbling around and yelling like children.

That evening, as I was studying by candlelight, there was a knocking at my door, which gave me a start. I didn't dare speak too loudly.

'Who's there?' I whispered, pressing my face to the door. The knocking grew louder.

'Is that you, William?'

I recognised his voice. I gathered my breath before opening. 'Well?' he asked.

His hair was dishevelled and his black woollen gown was crumpled; in particular, there was a glint of confusion in his eyes that I had not seen before.

'Aren't you going to ask me to sit down?'

I pointed to the bench which I had been using to study; with a glance he spurned it and stretched out on my bed, his hands behind his neck. I waited.

'Mars and Venus were caught unawares by the blacksmith,' he said with a sigh at last, a trace of amusement in his voice.

At first I said nothing; I looked at him, this extraordinary man, who was still incredulous at the affront done to his philosophy.

'And then?'

'And then what?'

He sat up, gazing at me with his dark eyes in which intelligence would never die.

'I'm here, am I not?'

He had been driven out in the middle of the night, half naked (for the furious canon had scarcely given him time to slip on his tunic!) and told to collect his books by the following morning or else they would all be thrown into the Seine. Fulbert had locked up Heloise—Heloise who was silent and did not cry, and who refused to answer him and refused to say whether she had been taken against her will.

Abelard had that look of surprise on his face, which I saw later during the disastrous periods of his life, as if his suffering belonged to someone else.

'How could he . . .'

'You wouldn't listen to me . . .'

I could not help making this pointless remark. He did not allude to it.

'What can I do? How can I see her? Will he talk?'

'He, talk? He'll keep quiet, naturally. He wants to avoid the scandal which would sully his reputation just as much as yours.'

'No doubt. But I want to see her, William, touch her, hold her in my arms, as I've done every night for so many nights . . .'

'In your dreams, don't you understand! You must give her up.'

'You don't know me.'

He was standing up and smiling now—smiling and shivering simultaneously, as if he was about to take revenge for his helplessness upon me.

'I will not leave her. She is mine . . .'

'Peter, Peter . . .'

'What's wrong? What's the matter with you all? I tell you she's mine. Don't you believe me?'

'I believe you. But it's not her I'm talking about.'

'Talk about whatever you want, I won't listen to you! I'm leaving.'

I prevented him going to the door. My heart was beating as if I was lovesick.

'Peter, Peter . . .'

'But stop repeating "Peter, Peter . . ." as if you want to build a church upon me! I need her, you must understand, nothing else matters to me. Will you help me?'

I did not reply. I did not look at him; the cold air brought the pure sound of Matins being sung, and it clutched at my heart-strings. Finally, I turned towards him. The expression in his eyes had softened and at last it was me, his friend, that he was looking at.

'William?'

'Yes, Peter.'

'Thank you . . . And William?'

'What?'

'Thank you again.'

He lay his hand over his heart.

Canon Fulbert's door was closed throughout the day. The Saracen woman accepted my money, but she would not open the door any wider; gesticulating, she told me to come back later. Later was never the right time.

I found him at last, while he was alone at prayer in the little chapel above the Seine. I knelt down beside him and began to recite the same prayers, trying to coordinate my breathing with his. He finished, made the sign of the cross and rose without giving any indication that he recognised or disdained my presence. I followed him. He crossed the Close as if intending to make his way to the square in front of Notre-Dame; suddenly he stopped opposite Stephen de Garlande's house, the only one in the Close to boast a tower. He turned and pointed his finger at me.

'You have betrayed me,' he said.

I was taken aback by the gentleness of his voice. I had imagined he would be angrier; it mattered little — I wanted to find out what he meant.

'You're mistaken. It's he who has betrayed me. He insults you as a guest; his offence to me is to a friend . . .'

He was silent. I felt moved at the sight of his red face.

'I am humiliated,' he said with a sob, 'humiliated to the core of my being. And her silence . . .'

I knew that I had succeeded. It was not a question of whether or not he believed me: he wanted to talk, to open his heart. I took his arm and he allowed himself to be led; we entered the little chapel of Saint-Aignan.

'She says nothing. I implore her to speak from dawn till dusk, I hit her, I entreat her, I weep, I argue: she continues to say nothing. I leave her on her own, I come back, I storm, I cajole: still she says nothing. Her silence is worse than spitting in my face. He's taking from me the child I have brought up, the young girl I have watched grow up and blossom, the woman who would have been one of the paragons of Christianity. Her silence wrenches my heart, William, and I don't know what to do . . .'

I waited as he kept on weeping, wretchedly, messily. He snuffled and wiped his nose with his sleeve. He was both ridiculous and magnificent, a touching sight. He loved her.

'Will you speak to her yourself?' he asked.

'If you wish . . .'

'Tell her that her uncle loves her and forgives her, no matter what he may have said or whatever she may have done. Tell her that I'm an ass and a swine — tell her that never again will Jephthah sacrifice his daughter. Tell her that I don't believe, I cannot believe and never will believe in her crime. Tell her that if she stops seeing this . . . trickster, this knave of hearts . . .'

He choked and was unable to control his rising voice.

'If she gives him up,' he stammered—but he couldn't go on.

He continued to cry, his tears running even more freely if that were possible, and I almost wept with him, and for him, and for her, and for myself . . .

'If she gives him up I'll give her, I'll give her . . .'

He didn't know what he was saying. He'd do this. He'd do that. He raised his hands towards the altar in prayer, the words consisting of moans and sobs and childish spluttering. His plump fingers were shaking.

'Come.'

He sat up stiffly and looked at me with red eyes.

'Come, let's go . . .'

He followed me, docile and dignified, crushed by sorrow and anger that erupted in gasps in the absence of words.

When she saw me, Heloise looked momentarily delighted. Her eyes shone and, either through naïveté or presumption, I could have believed that it was me she was happy to see.

'How is he?'

She blushed and began again.

'Forgive me, William . . . I haven't spoken to anyone for so many days and I was worrying about him because I didn't know.'

'He's staying with me in a small house on the Mount Sainte-Geneviève. He doesn't sleep, he doesn't study, his thoughts are solely of you. When he writes, it's your name that his pen traces on the parchment.'

'Is he really not studying? Tell him that for me he is the master and that the master always studies, even when the tempest rages, even in exile. Tell him that and give him . . .'

She opened the chest beside her bed and took out a small book which she clasped tightly in her hands.

'. . . give him this as a token of my love.'

If it should happen that some particle of dust should fall on the bosom of your beloved, let your fingers remove it; if there is no dust, remove that which is not there all the same . . . Oh, the sage advice of Ovid and the lovers who have read it and followed it to the letter, caressing each other at one moment, fondling a breast the next, and placing themselves under the exacting ferula of the god Love . . . In the margins of each page all I could see were their interwoven names, or sometimes just their initials; they had exchanged pens and spent many a grammar lesson spelling out each other's names, as if the constant repetition of the letters carried with it all possible magic and happiness.

Her bosom rose and fell, and a few drops of perspiration glistened on her lip; her cheeks were rosy, the shawl that covered her shoulders had slipped down, displaying her neck as well . . . I have knowledge of you, my love, my silent desire is my knowledge. She opened her hands to give me the book and I could see scars on her right palm. I took her hand.

'Are you wounded?'

She smiled.

'A love wound, my friend . . . We held a stone in our clasped hands—a piece of pink quartz—the corners of which we tried to blunt in amorous combat. It was the corners that had the better of us—he licked my hand, and I licked his, as we groaned about the pain we had done to one another, whilst begging each other to do it again . . .'

Her eyes were still dreaming about it all.

'William, I'll tell you my secret and you must promise not to say anything about it—even to him.'

'I promise you.'

'I'm expecting his child.'

'I can't not tell him.'

'You promised.'

'Then you must free me from my promise . . .'

She placed her delicate, injured hands over her belly. She was happy. She did not know where life was leading her, but it was a beautiful, exceptional life. She belonged to him. *You are the only master of my body as of my soul.*

'What will you do?'

'What will he want?'

What would happen tomorrow was a matter that concerned a God who had suspended his judgement; what would happen tomorrow was the will of he whom she would always obey. It didn't take much logic to persuade her that, in order to express his will, he had to know . . .

I closed the door quietly behind me, promising her that I would come back the following day, and every day. I feared Fulbert so I tip-toed down the stairs. He was sitting by the fire, his head nodding. I held my breath as I walked past. The dark-skinned servant gazed at me reproachfully, perhaps threateningly.

Grey sky and grey stone — in the streets of the Close I could breathe at last.

'Do you know how women become pregnant?' I asked.

'Do I know . . .'

His face froze. We were sitting in his room, adjacent to mine, which the smiling Vendean, glad to have this gathering of philosophers in his home, had rented to him. He was surrounded by his manuscripts and we were trying to make our way through the confusion of the Fathers of the Church.

'You're teasing me.'

'Do I look as if I'm teasing?'

'It's not possible. My career will be over if this is discovered . . .'

How calmly he said that! My career . . . This is the same man I saw bemoaning the setbacks of love, the man who took refuge at my home, begging me to be his messenger; the man who, only a few minutes ago, was shaking as he asked me whether she remembered his name.

He came and sat down on the chest where he had begun to sort out those of his books which were still neatly bound. He was fingering his copy of *Ars amatoria*.

'Do you love her?'

He stared at me with the scornful expression that he reserved in his lectures for those of dull intelligence. *Stultus* . . .

'As well and as badly as I know how to love.'

'I shouldn't have asked you that, Peter, because you take it wrongly . . . But let it pass. *Love her and do as thou wouldst.* Do you hear me? *Do as thou wouldst with her.*'

'It's God speaking, not a man.'

He said that without any real surprise, with a slight curiosity —like a logician who has discovered a new paradox and who mulls it over in his mind, calmly considering it.

'I'm talking about your love and hers, about the right it gives you, about the limitless possibilities that it opens up for you.'

'I don't know what lies behind my desire . . . I don't know what this child is. I can't see it, I don't understand it, and the threat of its existence is a disaster as far as my life is concerned.'

'*What thou wouldst.*'

'I would not.'

He leapt up, his dark eyes taking their revenge on me for this enigma that had inflicted itself on his life and which no instrument of rhetoric or dialectic, however powerful, however subtle, was able to divulge. Then his expression softened: the terror that caused him to breathe fire became a more humble prayer. One I could understand. It was my turn to be unwilling.

'No.'

'Speak to her, I ask you to do this.'

'I will not speak to her and my friendship for you is such that I will not even tell her that the idea of this crime was born in your mind.'

'A child, William . . . What shall I do?'

No sooner had he made me angry than I had to smile. He

asked this question in such a childlike way. Did I know any better than he? Could I tell him that people abandon children without that tug at the heartstrings, that feeling I knew so well.

'What do people do with children? They live—and that's all there is to it.'

'Come, let's go out.'

After days of snow and cold, a blackish mud was seeping down the streets of the Mount. The sky was grey, striated with leaden strips. Instinctively, our steps led towards the Pont, the lively centre of our old Cité. Street sellers were setting up their boards; jugglers were blowing on their hands to warm them. The frosty façade of the Hôtel-Dieu smelled of death. We moved on and plunged into the alleys behind the Jewish quarter.

In a stall, we allowed a woman with gentle hands to cut our hair.

On Sunday, it occurred to Abelard to go to Mass with Heloise —he went to Mass only when he was forced to do so, giving the excuse, if he was asked, that he served God through his studies. It was a promise they had made to one another, he told me casually, a diversion. I read it as a darker, more mysterious commitment. I delved no further: I could not go on adding to my own daily exhaustion the priestly duty of knowing more about their love than they did themselves.

Fulbert's tears had given way to a profound dejection, a sort of indifference. I should do what I considered right. I considered it right to deceive him and to go on deceiving him, adding fabrication to insult. And yet I did not feel guilty: doing what one has to do is never a pleasure and it does not always achieve peace of mind. So it was that I deceived him once more—fabricating a yearning for prayer (a flicker of hope shone in his tear-swollen eyes at the mention of this word) as an excuse for taking Heloise to a Mass that was a lovers' tryst.

On the appointed Sunday, I found myself next to Heloise in

the front pew of the cathedral, facing Bishop Gerbert who was celebrating Mass, and if I turned my head I could see Peter Abelard, pretending he was praying, in one of the side-chapels of the nave.

It would have been expecting too much of me to be beside her and not to feel distressed—in that state of *ataraxia* beloved of the Stoics; but I coped fairly well now in concealing my trembling heart and maintaining an expression of serenity which could pass for that of a wise man. Yes, words sometimes rose to my lips and it was like a bad habit which one keeps on trying to give up, an illness from which one is never cured, yet you learn to live with it. I said nothing, I didn't even whisper.

How beautiful you were! What with your absolute modesty and that virginal blue cloak which you wore over your shoulders, it was like watching Eve in that fleeting second when you shot a glance at him. Yet there was a note of restraint in this surrender, a nobility, an awareness in this triumph, a premonition of sorrow in this joy that nothing could tarnish.

You greeted me with a gracious inclination of the head when we met at the entrance to the church, beneath the tympanum depicting Christ in majesty, girdled by the lion and the eagle, the bull and the lamb. I suddenly realised as we were making our way down the centre of the aisle why he had asked me to walk slowly, as if in a procession.

It was a wedding—his own so to speak—which he was attending as if in the guise of a thief, a beggar, a forsaken lover for whom all that will soon remain will be his prayers and his passion.

I was overcome with pity as well as anger: was it not my role that he was now stealing from me yet again? Then, with your arm in mine, my love, enveloped in the scent of your skin, in the pale light of your gleaming eyes, I forgot all that.

Later, in the grey dawn of their marriage, and later still, at the time of their forced nuptials with God, when she approached the altar, weeping beneath her black mourning veil, I would blush as I remembered the day when she went through the sanctification of her union with me—who meant nothing to her—while the man she loved observed her from the shadows.

The following night, we had to escape.

Part II

The Assembly of the Lord

12

He whose testicles are crushed or whose
male member is cut off shall not enter the
assembly of the Lord.

DEUTERONOMY 23:1

WE RODE for an entire day and night, we rode until we and our horses were exhausted and could cope no more. Every stage of the journey awakened memories of schools at which the master had debated; we were in no mood for lessons, however, even if they were those of his past.

Abelard was heavy and felt stiff, so we had to stop frequently to let him catch his breath. While he rested on his knees in the shade of an oak tree, Heloise laid her hands over his head and he closed his eyes, pretending to sleep. He groaned as he got to his feet, asking whether it would soon be over.

It had been his idea to disguise Heloise as a nun, wearing the habit but not the veil, her already round belly concealed beneath the folds of an ample cowl and wrapped in a blanket. I did not approve of this and she felt ill-at-ease: occasionally we laughed nervously, but even the impious know that they should not provoke God with impunity.

We were fleeing. We never travelled on the king's highways, opting instead for narrow pathways where branches flicked our faces and where foxes and wolves made their homes. We spent the first night in one of those dense forests, on a bed of leaves, expecting to be robbed or devoured at any moment.

The sight of the River Loire gave us renewed confidence; we were leaving France and we no longer thought, every time the ground shook with the beat of horses' hooves, that we were about to be seized, tethered and thrown into a damp prison. Fulbert and the entire chapterhouse, the bishop and the king himself, no longer seemed such formidable figures. Abelard recovered, his features relaxed and his face took on a youthfulness that I had not seen in him for a long time. Whether we walked or rode, in the daytime or at night, Heloise moved with the same gracefulness; her belly became rounded like the Virgin Mary's. When she looked up there was a boldness in her gaze, an absence of fear that I envied.

We grew accustomed to encountering brigands and did not give them a second thought; we also chanced upon fugitive monks, penniless pilgrims and tradesmen. Like them, we were there *for a reason*. Like them, we had an aim, a hope, a secret; and like them we experienced great uncertainty—another way of being alive.

We no longer avoided the hamlets and villages. Beneath the porches of churches built of stone and wood my friends sang and children would come up to them. On market days we collected a few coins. A well-armed knight asked us who we were and with unconscious bravado we told him the truth. He burst out laughing and hoped we would escape the Pope, his legates and his bishops.

The weather grew warmer and in the mornings the woods were filled with the light of spring; through a gap in the forest of elm trees we caught sight of a glittering river. So we tethered our horses, removed our shoes, and we ate bread and cheese as we watched the sparkling water flow past—a spectacle that has always silenced philosophers.

'Soon you will see my Brittany.'

My Brittany . . . The way he said that! I had never thought of him as a Breton knight, journeying over the moorlands, brandishing lances, riding through magical forests to bring back secrets unknown to man.

'Soon you will see my homeland, my rivers—the Saint-Guèze and the Sèvre—drink my wine and breathe the sea air mingled with the scent of the marshlands . . .'

'At your pleasure, most powerful sire . . .'

There was a gentleness in Heloise's irony which would enable him to endure insults. He turned to her and smiled, and he put his hand on her breast. She let him have his way.

'Before he took holy orders,' he said proudly, 'my father served the Duke of Brittany, Alain Fergent. As a child, I remember him taking me to see the tapestries that William the Conqueror had had embroidered, at Bayeux . . .'

I interrupted him.

'Now there's someone I do not admire . . . It's because of those accursed Normans that I was condemned to a wandering life, serving a clerk on the run and a bogus nun. I'm not at all happy . . .'

They both laughed. Abelard put his arm round my shoulder —that affectionate gesture that made me dependent on him and which sometimes made me feel a little genuine affection.

'Without you, William . . .'

'Without me?'

We were covered in dust and the sun was warm. He undressed her with the motions of a lover, as if I was not there—unless, on the other hand, this was done for my sake. The crumpled habit lay on the grass, as did the white linen gown, and her white body too. He did not remove his black tunic when he picked her up and took her in his arms; he stepped circumspectly into the muddy water and bathed her as if he were baptising her, and as he rolled her in his arms, with her hair fanning out and her nipples hardening, her body bobbed up and down in the waters; a smile on her lips, she did not cry out, she said nothing, she was captive; in silence, my throat parched, I yearned for her. Then he lay her down on the bank, wrapped in his cloak, and he caressed her and warmed her as he murmured words I could not hear.

In the evening, we found ourselves a few leagues from Fontevrault; before we even reached the hospice they were clasping each other as if they were about to be separated forever.

'You're not really thinking of stopping here?' I asked.

'Why not?'

'We're both known here . . .'

'So much the better! Must we travel any further?'

It was agreed that Heloise would arrive on her own, and Peter, with me, one hour later. Angarde was dead, Petronilla was travelling, and Robert of Arbrissel had been laid to rest in the very place he did not want to be buried. The place where we had witnessed all that passion—and the first confrontation between Peter Abelard and Bernard of Clairvaux—seemed different. News of the death of the founder now attracted crowds of pilgrims, who all gathered in the abbey, in front of his tomb, after Mass. The saint who would never be a saint (rendering the tireless efforts of my friend Brother Andrew useless and almost laughable) attracted people even crazier than him, who considered a horsehair shirt too soft a garment and preferred to cover it with scraps of metal, and even nails, so that their skin became a wound that would never heal. They believed that God's wheat would grow from their blood spilt on the stones.

Peter Abelard was greeted with fear and respect; people muttered behind his back. He was invited to the chapterhouse, while I stood waiting for him, reflecting on the silhouettes of the women I had noticed in the Close and pondering indulgently on the devil within us, that is to say in him, in me . . .

He emerged from the chapterhouse with a smile on his lips.

'What was on the menu for the day?'

He gave me a half-smile, a look of delight in his dark eyes for once.

'Abstinence.'

I burst out with wild laughter that I could not suppress and he laughed with me, beating his thighs.

'And you preached abstinence to them?'

'You wouldn't want me to preach lechery to them!'

The *armarius* was a young man with a long face and hair that was already a yellowish grey. The tip of his nose was red and he wiped it with his fingers. I asked him what had become of Brother Andrew.

'Dead,' he mumbled in an unprepossessing voice, without raising his eyes from his book.

'I guessed as much,' I said angrily, 'otherwise you would not look so sad.'

He put down his stylet.

'They found him lifeless, laid out on Robert's actual tomb, at Prime.'

'And his *Life*?'

'What do you mean?'

'It's what he was writing—Robert's biography. What's your name?'

'Berengar.'

'Berengar, Brother Andrew did not die without having completed his life of the founder of your order. Look for it and find it.'

Berengar stared at me for a few seconds before plunging his head back towards his manuscript, without replying.

That night, Peter rose from his bed. God alone knows where his rendezvous was—beneath the fireplaces of the deserted kitchens, in the refectory, or perhaps further away in the forest, beside the stream. I stayed awake, waiting for him, sharing with him the power of that desire which respected nothing but itself.

At dawn, after Matins, we set off on the road again.

Denise wept as she clasped him to her. Standing two paces behind them, Heloise smiled as she held her belly. The stream narrowed into a bend and the waters roared as they forced a passage among the flat stones.

'Let me go, dearest sister,' said Peter with a laugh, trying to release himself from her embrace, 'let me go so that I can tell you what I've been doing . . .'

'Don't worry,' she said, 'I'm well aware.'

Denise released him and came over to us. She embraced Heloise, then she took my hands in hers. This woman whose face, tanned by the fresh air, was still young had hair that had turned grey from grieving; in her eyes and in her mouth there was a goodness and a sweetness that would never fade.

'Come,' she said, taking our hands. 'You must show them the house.'

The house on the banks of the stream was a place where people had been happy. The children who ran about here were, without realising it, retracing the footsteps of children who had been born before them. It was rather strange to think that it was beside this narrow stream, frequently hidden by the trees, that the wielder of words had grown up.

We were in a manor house that retained the intimacy of the peasant dwelling which, a few generations previously, its owners must have known, when they would have slept cheek by jowl, trying to find a position closer to the fireplace, unconcerned by others' groans and bad dreams. Peter bade us sit down by the hearth.

'This is it,' he said simply.

I looked at Heloise. Her eyes were shining as if he had introduced her to a world beyond her heart's desire. This was it . . . This was where the battles had taken place, and the tournaments, where heads had been brought back on the tips of lances, where many a Christian knight, many a man with the strength of two had passed by, believing he could accomplish what had never been achieved; this was where you heard women's muffled laughter, where a man's voice told stories in the darkness where they slept—and where a child, his eyes closed, would hear enough to fill the dreams of centuries.

'Where are the men?' I asked Peter. 'I know your father's dead, but what about your brothers and your brother-in-law . . . ?'

'Making a name for themselves. But it's my name that will make them famous . . .'

Denise came to sit down with us and poured us a goblet of a white wine that made one want to sing the moment it caressed the palate.

'So you love her, my old Peter,' she said with a smile.

He looked at her with feigned severity. At home, in Brittany, the master of the Notre-Dame schools was still called 'my old Peter'.

When evening fell, he wanted to burn Heloise's nun's habit. She reproached him for this pointless sacrilege and, taken aback, he abandoned his plan. Then, weary though we were, he took us on a walk along his stream; after the oaks and the elms came the ripening vines with their golden promise, and always that heady smell of the sea. At a bend in the path we came upon the rear of the château that belonged to Daniel, the lord of Le Pallet, with its powerful keep and its chapel, almost humble by comparison, where his ancestors were buried. His parents' tomb was in the cemetery below.

He prayed.

Next, we crossed over the road that intersected the town and climbed down a fairly steep slope; another few yards and the stream flowed into the Sèvre.

'Come on! Come on!' he started shouting, waving his arms around and dancing about like a child. 'Come and see!'

I gave my arm to Heloise who was walking slowly in the high grass. He was standing erect, like an oak tree. At this juncture the stream was as wide as a river and many a peasant, many a son of an impoverished squire, had dreamed of journeys, watching it flow past. In the west, beyond Nantes, the sun was setting. He held out his arm in the opposite direction.

'That's where I set off.'

After two days spent rushing about the fields and the woods, he grew impatient — and with it came that groundless optimism that crept over him as quickly as did despondency.

At midnight he took us to a tower that stood alone in the middle of the vines, the remains of a priory never used by the monks of Vertou. The full moon tinted the clouds orange, like lingering strips of sunset. Several feet above the still sleeping earth, having avoided the snares of a crumbling staircase, we were now closer to the sky. He perched astride the ruined wall, joyfully straddling both time and the night.

'Heloise,' he said enthusiastically, 'I've found it.'

She had stayed behind with me on the top step; she was shivering in the chill breeze, breathing in the aroma of the mingled waters — river, sea and marshland.

'What have you found, my love?'

'The end of our troubles, peace with your uncle, a calm life for you, and for me . . .'

'All at once?'

'Everything. Even William will agree with me. And you know what he's like, he treats me very harshly.'

'Enough! We place ourselves in your power, master.'

'Let us be married.'

For a moment nothing happened and Heloise's dishevelled hair still floated over her shoulders and mine; then she pushed me away and raced down the steps, not taking any of the precautions we had taken coming up. She dashed over the rubble at the foot of the tower and sped off into the vines. When he noticed, Peter pushed me aside. I followed him.

He didn't call out to her: all I could hear was his breath, which soon grew hoarse, and my own; occasionally I caught sight of his faint shadow at the far end of a row of vines. Were it not for the sudden way in which she had disappeared, you would think it was a game.

Peter soon gave up the chase; he sat down beside the small wood that adjoined the Saint-Guèze stream. His expression was like that of a scolded child.

'What did I say?'

'Let us be married.'

'Is that so terrible?'

'I don't want to.'

She had sprung up out of nowhere, like an elf, and she stood before us.

'I don't want to, do you understand?' she repeated firmly.

I was as surprised as Peter. He wanted to get to his feet, but she stopped him with a movement of her hand.

'My master will allow me to speak without stirring. My master will allow his lady to tell him, just once, that she does not want to. And having heard me, my master will do as he wishes.'

She spoke quickly, in a firm, assured voice; her two hands were clasped round her shoulders as if she were trying to protect her body from the cold, or from some impropriety. She quoted St Paul, of course, she quoted St Jerome, she summoned Seneca to her aid, and Socrates, and Cicero, who was unable to devote himself simultaneously to a wife and to philosophy. She built him up the better to demean herself: he was the philosopher of Christ and of mankind, whereas she was one of those women who only brought trouble and humiliation upon themselves. Let God be her witness—she had only ever wanted the best, the finest and the grandest for him. And now he wanted to share domestic chores? Did he intend thereby to appease her uncle by this trickery? It would be a dangerous illusion.

I listened as he did, struck by her passion and her skill, and captivated by the paradox that in depicting herself as short and ugly she had never appeared so tall and beautiful. It seemed to me that the allusions to the Ancients and the trail of Biblical figures, and the cruel anecdotes, concealed a more secret and more demanding plea, but one which her hidden pride and her excessive humility did not allow her to reveal.

In the end, it grew extremely cold. Peter stood up and took her in his arms, first loosening her hands which were clasped round his neck. She let herself go to him; the debater had no need to argue, or the logician to reason. A smile and a soothing hand were all the man needed.

I led the way. When we reached the stream — and the grey, jagged outline of the manor house in the moonlight — there was not a sound to be heard apart from their murmuring voices.

I settled down to sleep beside the embers and, like a wet dog, I began to feel warm, while cooing sounds of 'I love you' rose up behind me.

13

I SET OFF for Paris on my own.

Strange that I no longer felt the lightness of my young age, strange that my knowledge weighed down upon my shoulders heavier than any baggage.

It is not fear (dying by the wayside is a possibility which we cope with easily) that makes your footsteps heavier, nor the weariness that causes you to lie down beneath an oak tree after a few leagues. You left on horseback, you are returning on foot; the shadows that have pursued you are still with you.

Now it is night-time: their love envelops you and your past illusions make you smile. Their love is bigger than you, incomprehensible and magnificent; it's he to whom you must give precedence, rather than the petty temptation to imagine yourself as the master. The words are not yours, nor are the sudden gestures—any more than the wind that scatters the dust behind the horses, any more than the rain and the mist, the creation of the sun, the moon's smile and all those things, be they human or natural, endowed with substance or not, which make up the world we know and blindly try to understand and make sense of.

That is the world you must serve, William, there is nothing else you can do.

With every new dawn, my steps grew stronger.

✦ ✦ ✦

'So how's the parchment going?' I asked.

The Vendean lay down his piece of chalk and the smile on his lips screwed up into a little pout.

'No one wants to read in this cursed city—but if it's something to write on they're after, well, they fall over each other for it! Look at this: vellum ordered by men sent by the chancellor himself! I imagine it's for a treaty, a charter or a disposition. I dream of such things as I ply my lath or my piece of chalk, and I say a little prayer for those animals on whose backs, through my efforts, history will be written.'

'The parchment maker as philosopher . . . Are you going to open a school too?'

'No, I'm joking. It must be your presence here. You see, my real problem is finding respectable young men to prepare the hides, watch over the baths, and do the rubbing and scraping . . . in short, to learn the business. By the way, where did you go? And your peripatetic friend?'

I made some vague gesture with my hand. His kindly smile returned.

'Of course, it's none of my business; it's only that several people were asking after you both. Not all of them wished you well, to judge by their faces . . . It's probably a good thing that I didn't know where you were. Do you want to have a beer? It's beginning to get hot.'

I declined and did my best to slip away without annoying him.

'William? Is someone sleeping in your room?'

'You're asking me? You're the one who ought to know . . .'

'He was sitting waiting for you outside your door.'

'And you let in everyone who waits by my door?'

The Vendean's smile vanished for a second.

'He had a sad expression.'

This was how I came to find the young stone-cutter stretched out on my bed, wrapped up in a green overcoat, his hands joined over his stomach, rather like a recumbent statue. He got up as I entered—a thin, narrow face, long hair stiff with dust and filth, a neck like a heron's. It was hard to believe that this man with such feeble muscles could summon up the strength necessary to sculpt those powerful figures.

'I was waiting for you,' he said.

'Gislebert . . .'

'You remember my name . . .'

I mainly remembered how distressed he was and how I had held him close when everything had been smashed and he was crying like a child.

He showed the palms of his hands and gestured impatiently.

'I'm going now.'

'I thought you were waiting for me.'

'I wanted to thank you. I've done that.'

'Thank me for being the cause of everything of yours being destroyed?'

'Everything of mine? I don't know. I reckon that everything of mine is still mine as long as it is within me. But you're right— as long as I don't use my tools I won't know.'

'Where are you off to?'

'I'm going where squires and lords have need of me, where portals are being built, and I'm going to carve angel musicians and monsters with claws where no man can go and see them, for the glory of God alone . . . At night, I see Christ rising from the dead; and in the daytime he is in my hands.'

'Do you want to stay another night?'

'Waiting for you?'

'Resting, you great ass.'

'Resting? I've rested enough, I reckon. I'll show you something instead.'

I knew what I had to do and, of course, I didn't feel I needed to hurry; what Gislebert had to show me—whatever it was— was a welcome distraction.

At nightfall he opened the chests in which Peter's and my manuscripts were kept. He held them up to me, asking me to tell him what each contained; he made me laugh when he shook

Aristotle's *Logic* against his ear as if he was going to make stars or sounds spring out of them.

'So you don't know anything about rhetoric?'

'Does this animal shit like you and me?'

A gleam in his green eyes made me realise that only a blind man could really consider him ignorant. The Soul of the World arose naturally from the fountain of his hands. I was reminded of Christian: so distant, yet so similar.

He suddenly jumped up.

'Where is there a Mass?'

'Vespers was over a long time ago. Why do you need a Mass?'

'I need Mass every day. Otherwise I'll die.'

We set off and found a haven in the service being conducted by the monks at Sainte-Geneviève. My friend's face lit up at the Offertory: there was no need for a learned discussion to reach a conclusion about the Real Presence. He lived it daily.

He led me through streets and fields, through artisans' alleyways and vineyards. He pointed out churches to me by climbing up their façades and onto their pillars and buttresses as if it was a game. Perched up on a capital or a tympanum, he called out to me: 'Well, are you coming?' Tracing the stonework with his finger, he described for me the figures of Eve and the angels of the annunciation. Because he insisted, I climbed up, I accompanied him on top of the roof of Saint-Julien, the smallest church of them all, and I noticed a bush growing there.

'The tree of life,' he murmured.

'Help me, I'm falling.'

'You're not falling, you're flying.'

He just laughed and it was impossible to feel really frightened with him. Late into the night—and until dawn, once we had returned to my room on the Mount—he told me about his life and his dreams and how, one day, his name would be found on the tympanum of a cathedral.

I all but forgot about Fulbert and my mission.

+ + +

I imagined the astonishment of the Normans, two and half centuries earlier, on discovering this city that was as beautiful as a ship from the high seas that has sailed up a river and has moored itself in the corolla of gently sloping hills; in this early spring light, how blasphemous their desire to burn and pillage must have seemed to them! And yet the call for blood, the rasp of fire and the clash of weapons were inevitable—and delectable.

I walked along the embankment hoping I would not reach the small castle on the Petit Pont; on the bridge I prayed I would not have to enter the Jewish quarter and emerge in the cathedral square. The heart of the city is tiny, the churches are numerous, the door always open, and the crowd is dense.

'William!'

I heard the voice at the same moment as a hand grabbed me.

'Christian. I was thinking of you . . .'

'Walking in the opposite direction?'

'Your monks frighten me and I don't want to do any more copying.'

'There I am talking to you like an abandoned whore. Come on, let's have a drink and you can tell me . . .'

I held my breath and hesitated.

'You don't want to? Now I'm getting cross.'

'You won't be cross if I tell you that I'm going to see Fulbert on behalf of Master Peter Abelard . . . We'll have a drink after-wards, if I'm still alive!'

'Apparently he was overcome with grief and almost died after our hero absconded with his niece!'

'Does he know I have anything to do with it?'

'I don't know. I hope not for your sake. The whole town is talking of nothing else—a matter for rejoicing or for complaint, depending on whether it's a monk or a student you're talking to . . . Do you need me?'

'Just come with me as far as his front door. I need courage.'

On the way, as we passed by the Close wall, I told him of my astonishing meeting with Gislebert and about how I believed—

although it was probably in a dream — that I had climbed up a church wall.

The angel on Fulbert's door lay smashed on the ground. I turned towards Christian, who gave a shrug of helplessness.

'Courage, brother . . .'

I sighed as I went through the door.

The house was swathed in darkness, as if for a funeral. The dark-skinned servant looked blankly as I came in, then turned and walked away. It could have been to go to the market or else to alert her master. I felt as if I had walked into a coffin; a few hours in this place and you would begin to feel as if you yourself were dead.

Then I spotted him. He was sitting on a bench, in front of an extinguished fire, his head in his hands. When he looked up at me, I noticed that his ruddy face had become ashen. He gazed at me in astonishment for a long time.

'My friend,' he whispered, 'my poor friend . . .'

I clasped him to me — an unhappy child, weeping and muttering words of vengeance as he called upon a deaf God. Once he had calmed down, I began to trot out my latest falsehood.

'A message has reached me from the man who was my master and whom we shall call "the traitor". My first instinct was to throw it in the fire, but I considered my friendship for you and your loss. He says that she is alive and in good health and that you should not worry about her . . .'

'It's the serpent saying that!'

'He says that the pain he caused you by seducing her, even violating her, under your roof grieves him terribly and that he is contriving to find a way to repair this wrong.'

'The swine talks of reparation! Will he just give her back to me?'

'He says that a powerful feeling for each other binds them together and that furthermore . . .'

'Furthermore?'

'That she is about to give birth.'

Fulbert's stupefaction brought back the colour to his face. I could see that he contemplated his misfortune in all its aspects but he had not considered this particular one.

'But what a cur, what a monster . . .'

'He therefore says that he suggests, given these circumstances, that the only reparation possible, worthy of you and of her is . . .'

'To hell with him!'

'That they marry.'

Fulbert put down the poker he was playing with.

'That they marry,' he repeated in a blank voice.

He looked away.

'Show me that letter,' he said to me sharply.

'I've burnt it.'

'I don't believe you.'

My virtue thus offended, I protested loudly. If this was how he was going to behave, I had no alternative but to leave the house. Fulbert, albeit with an unaccustomed reticence that I took to be the calm that follows rage, quickly laid down his arms.

'Very well—you know that I believe you. It's just that it's . . . dreadful. It's sensible, but dreadful all the same.'

I let his words hang in the air.

'He makes only one condition.'

'Because on top of that he's laying down conditions . . .' he muttered with bitter irony.

'It's that the marriage must remain secret.'

'I don't understand.'

'It's a part of his letter which I myself . . .'

'He's only had minor orders conferred on him. He can . . .'

'Yes, but he's . . .'

'He can get married. Without any doubt he can. Of course he'd have to give up . . .'

'He's . . . Well, he believes he is, he says he is . . . and everyone thinks he is ... the greatest philosopher in the world ...'

'And we know that he's nothing but a cur. But it matters little.'

'Philosopher and theologian, master of schools, a career that can take him ...'

'Far.'

I could scarcely believe it, but there was a semblance of a smile on Fulbert's face.

'I understand,' he said. 'I understand him.'

'Then you understand him better than I do ...'

'But of course! It's logical. Dreadful, but ... logical. Which comes as no surprise to anyone. How could a humble canon of Notre-Dame de Paris, who for the trifling reason that he wanted to protect his only niece, threaten the career of such an illustrious creature? Aristotle wants your niece. What's that you say? Aristotle has your niece and he is doing you the honour of marrying her in secret. Our joy will therefore be in secret too.'

'Do you accept?'

'Tell me, you student of the devilries of the mind, whether a simple fellow like a canon is correct in his reasoning. Tell me whether, in order to be rid of my anguish and my sadness, I have any choice in the kind of dishonour that shall be mine ... To know—but in secret—that my honour is restored ... that's a satisfaction that will go a long way towards achieving its aim ... To know—but with strict instructions not to tell a living soul—that, contrary to appearances, I am not the Fulbert people laugh up their sleeve at, the canon with horns, the cuckolded uncle ... the knowledge of it would, in the long run, certainly make me intelligent. To know that I'm quite wrong to be miserable would make me happy in my tearful state and would cure my foolish bitterness ...'

'The marriage could not be kept secret ... It's madness on his part ...'

'But who's saying that that is what matters to me? The secret, my honour ...'

'But you are!'

'Do you remember my question?'

I pouted and shrugged.

'You see, even now, even here, you take me for a cretin. I'll tell you this, William: everything is wrecked and none of this is getting us anywhere, everything is destroyed and I am gazing upon the smoking ruins . . . And you, you talk to me of my honour, which has been trampled on by these rogues, these false priests, these great minds who parade up and down the bridges and the market-places . . . What effect do you think this has on a wretched old man? Go on, go and find your master . . .'

'It's not . . .'

'Go and find your master, in Paris or in hell, and tell him I accept. And also, William . . .'

'Yes?'

'Never set foot in this house again. But, William . . .'

'But?'

'Let that be a secret between us, of course.'

I could still hear his voice on the staircase.

'William! Do you hear me?'

'Yes.'

'Remember you're a shite.'

Neither Christian's wisdom nor Samuel's wine could console me. It's true that swine were foraging about in our path, causing us to stumble, and that it was dangerous; it's true that it stank and that the whorehouses were wretched, with those dark-eyed women who didn't say a word and just lay down and opened their legs. Not even a false promise, not even a tiny fib! And the diseases! And the new bridge that was promised us and which never came! What a city!

I had a temperature and I wanted to sleep far away from Paris, to wake up speaking to the birds, with a dog's tongue licking my face.

I felt ashamed of myself every time I thought about what had happened—not so much because of what I had done, but for having been unmasked. *Blessed are the pure in heart!* Christian and Gislebert took me off drinking—and in my drunken stupor and self-pity I had the good fortune to see them become the spitting image of one another. They were laughing kind-heartedly and I laughed until I realised they were laughing at me. And after threatening them, I then started to laugh too.

'William, you're a villain,' Christian said.

'William, cover your face,' added Gislebert.

As the night wore on, our drunkenness blended—and promises were exchanged. They both slept in my bed and I slept alone in Peter's. When I left at dawn, with a heavy head, they were both asleep with a smile on their lips and Christian's blond angel head nestled in Gislebert's bony shoulder.

I took good care of myself as I made speed for Brittany.

Spring caught up with me as I reached the banks of the Loire, that wide and sluggish river of life with its little islands where a hermit can watch the boats pass by as he hides beneath the trees, hoping that someone will notice him, cast him a crust of bread and ask for his blessing. I hurried on, eating just enough to continue on my way—some bread made of black bran that was heavy in the stomach, and some fruit—and stretching out on the ground, wrapped in my overcoat, whenever I felt weary. I came across travellers—processions of beggars, trusting pilgrims, and merchants on their way to a fair, at Orléans—and I had the good sense to make out that I was dumb. Finding me more destitute than they, the poor creatures unleashed a torrent of words (since I could not speak, I could hardly point out that I was not deaf), heaping contempt on me because they could not rob me.

A few leagues from Le Pallet, I caught sight of the castle and began to run, overcome with an irrational anxiety. At the bend in the river, Denise was waiting for me.

14

HELOISE'S cries were met with calls of 'Come on, come on' from Denise, followed by gentler words, 'Breathe my dove, breathe my pretty sweetness, breathe for Heaven's sake', and her hand on her perspiring brow. God knows, I had no idea what was going on beneath that sheet and wished I could have been elsewhere, sitting with Peter beside the stream and tossing pebbles, rather than being assistant midwife, for I was hardly the sort of man intended for such tasks.

Then a louder cry than the others took my breath away and I realised I was going to have to work.

'Go and get some water, hurry,' ordered Denise.

I felt foolish standing alone, next to the cauldron, which hung from a tripod in the chimney-place. It was terribly heavy and I didn't want to burn myself.

'Can you manage?'

I almost screamed as I grabbed the handle and spilt the pan, several drops of water scalding my feet. Having half submerged the room, I limped over to the tub. I poured the water, and as I did so, I could not help looking over to the bed. In a fleeting glance, I observed in terror a world of blood and torn flesh from which Denise's hands, which were covered with indescribable substances, were removing a red and violet bundle, which was moving about like a chicken with its throat being slit. That was what life was.

'Hold it,' said Denise, 'I must look after her.'

Before I had time to say no, the baby had been placed in my rigid arms.

'Where is he? How is he?' murmured Heloise in a tired voice, as she tried to sit up.

'He's beautiful, my dear, don't worry,' Denise told Heloise in a soothing voice, bustling about as she cleaned her up. 'And you, don't just stand there, bathe him!'

'In the water?'

'What a great oaf he is! In the water, of course, not in the cesspool! I'll be with you after I've said a quick prayer.'

With my hand cradling his head, and holding him with the other as best I could, I bent over to bathe him, trying not even to look at the white snake that hung from the middle of his stomach. At the moment his body entered the water, he relaxed and opened his eyes.

He seemed to smile at me.

'Now, William, go and find Peter for me and tell him he's the father of a fine baby boy.'

Denise took him from my arms and—it was a curious sensation—I felt myself dispossessed, vaguely jealous. She dried him with a cloth and then rubbed him gently with salt and herbs. After that, she laid him on his mother's belly.

'Hold him,' she said, 'he's your own flesh and blood.'

Heloise laughed and cried, and tears suddenly welled up in my eyes. Denise saw me.

'You're not there when you're needed and there when you're not,' she said, not meaning to be unkind. 'Now go and look for him, I beg you.'

Night had fallen and the stars were beginning to shine; it was a moonless night. Peter was stretched out naked on the flat rocks.

'You've got a son!' I exclaimed.

He splashed himself, heaved his heavy, powerful body out of the water, and then wrapped his overcoat round him to dry himself.

'Should I be happy?'

He was, but he didn't know it.

'Fulbert accepts your offer.'

'That, too, makes me happy. Did you tell Heloise?'

'She was . . . busy?'

He burst out laughing.

'Let's go and see the boy. What shall we call him?'

'He's your son!'

'I remember a night such as this, many years ago. I was thirteen years old and my father had sent me to study at a priory near Saumur, and I already knew more Latin than all the monks put together—and more logic. I was dreadfully bored and I was infuriated by these teachers who taught me nothing. Yes, I realise, you know the story! One night, the prior came and woke me, but it was not to say prayers. I don't know why this man persisted in treating me with affection despite my protestations and my constant quarrels with my so-called teachers. He led me to an open clearing and made me look at an eclipse of the moon with the aid of a strange apparatus. When I asked him what it was, he simply made me promise, before he replied, to remember that I had not known and that it was he who had taught it me.'

'What was it called?'

'Astrolabe.'

'You want to call your son Astrolabe? Can you imagine yourself saying: "Astrolabe, take up your tablets and your stylet and go and finish the second decad of Titus Livius"?'

'Why not? It would make a change from Guibert, Yves, Hildebert or Baudri . . . Baudri . . . that would make them laugh . . .'

We returned to the house, which was bathed in soft candle-light. Heloise was dressed in white and she was resting; beside her, in his little crib, lay the child who had smiled at me, wrapped up in his swaddling clothes.

'His name will be Peter,' said Denise in a low voice.

'I rather think his name will be Astrolabe.'

'Astrolabe? Is that his idea?'

'Let's not go on about it,' said Abelard, gazing at his child, but careful not to touch him. 'We'll call him Peter Astrolabe and say no more about it.'

I took him gently in my arms, under the watchful eye of Denise.

'You'll wake him up,' moaned Abelard.

'No, I won't. Come.'

We went out into the blackness of the night; woken immediately by the cold, the baby opened his eyes and started to cry.

'You see,' Abelard said to me irritably.

'But won't you just touch him?'

He glanced at the child again.

'I don't think so,' he said. 'Not now . . .'

'Then speak to him . . .'

Abelard hesitated for a moment. Then he began speaking in a low voice—an old trick used by orators to engage the attention of a noisy room. I was furious: his son had scarcely been born and he was treating him like a pupil.

'Look at the sky, my son, look at the movements of the celestial bodies paying homage to Earth . . .'

The baby stopped crying.

'. . . look at the one moving spirit that impels the world and impels our minds . . .'

Denise took the child from my arms.

'You're mad,' she said.

'What harm can there be in listening to the breath of the Soul of the World?'

'What good?'

She cradled the child, who was now asleep again.

'We shall leave tomorrow,' said Peter.

Denise reacted with a start.

'With her? In that case you really are crazy!'

'With her. Do you expect me to marry William?'

'Does she know?'

'She soon will.'

I was beginning to know him sufficiently to gauge the anxiety that lay behind this bravado. At night, he slept beside her and swathed her in affection. Until dawn, I could hear their mingling voices, those lovers' whispers that I had already been privy to, that I had let sweep over me like a river, when they called each other by secret pet names.

I awoke in the daylight, under the glare of a powerfully built wet-nurse who was feeding the baby. Heloise was standing and gazing at her child, her morning sky eyes filled with love and, already, with sadness.

'We're leaving,' she said in a dull voice.

'Let me speak to him.'

'I don't want you to speak to him. I want to do what he tells me.'

'Where is he?'

She nodded towards the stream.

'Let me hold him,' she said to the nurse, who obediently took the child off her breast and passed him to her.

'I love you,' she said, her eyes filled with tears, while the child also cried from hunger, 'I love you.'

I could not bear this unhappiness and could not look her in the face — the pain gripped my whole body. I ran into the woods and wept with her, but far from her.

Our way was sad and few words were spoken. The weather was stormy and we pulled up our hoods, without seeking shelter and without slackening the pace of our horses. Peter went in front, on his own, and I stayed behind with Heloise, who was inconsolable. I looked at her constantly and her grief affected me as well, and behind that grief — to my surprise and confusion — lay desire, but also compassion.

Once night had fallen, we slept either at inns or at monastery hospices, or outside, in the woods, if there was nothing nearby. Then I would make a fire and the master would sit silently, as did his two pupils, watching the flames and listening to the noises of animals close by and the howling of the wind.

One night when he was in a deep sleep (and the clouds had parted, the moon was climbing the heavens and it was impossible for me not to think of the astrolabe), she came and lay down beside me. Her arm entwined with mine and her head rested softly on my shoulder. You ask a great deal of me, my love, but don't worry, I thought to myself, I find there is an abundance in my heart that I never suspected and my only pleasure is that you can delve into it without even having to question me with a look.

'I love him so much, William . . . If anyone has to be blamed for deserting our son, I reproach myself and not him . . .'

'And yet . . .'

'I know. As an example I cite those subjugated wives and diabolical women throughout scripture and literature. Do you think he believes me? I don't even believe myself: you have no idea how proud my love is. I was proud of my knowledge and my knowledge has been humbled. All I am proud of now is being his, being what he wants, despite him and despite myself. I am proud to be his servant, I glory in being his mistress and I would be his whore were he to ask me, happy in another's arms as long as I could see joy in his eyes. What does it matter to me if I wear embroidered cloth, add spices to my soup, or tell the whole of Paris that I am the wife of the master . . . He has remembered some foolish remarks about Xanthippe and Socrates that I made in my tirade against marriage. It's fortunate that he has not understood the madness within me: I loathe this marriage which will destroy our love — I know this with a tragic certainty, it's obvious — and yet already, in order to please him, I have to be my own worst enemy. In the end I shall be left alone with that love.'

'I'll be there.'

My voice quavered and she held my arm a little tighter.

'I know, William, I know you are my friend and his. I know you won't desert us. And yet, ultimately, we shall be alone all the same.'

She fell asleep against me, but when I awoke she was with him. I watched them, surrendered one to the other, and told myself that until loneliness befell them, I would be the one who was alone.

It was a curious spectacle, this dawn marriage, in a small church high above the Seine, at which each of us kept our feelings, our words and even our glances to ourselves. The priest mumbled his phrases, and the witnesses wished they could have been somewhere else.

A few of us had come with Peter — Christian, Gislebert, even Master Ives, the parchment maker, with his latest apprentice, a shy, solemn fellow from the Creuse who kept turning around as if he was being pursued by an army of devils invisible to all but him.

As they walked up to the altar, Fulbert held Heloise so roughly that the knuckles of his fingers were white. His face was its normal red complexion again, but there was none of that geniality, none of that cheerful foolishness that used to delight Peter. Heloise was pale as a ghost. They did not look at each other. Peter Abelard walked behind them, alone as usual, enormous in his black linen gown. When they reached the priest, Fulbert finally released Heloise and shrank back on to a bench with an elderly lady — sister? cousin? — who took no notice of him. Abelard now stood beside Heloise, but instead of that overwhelming, almost embarrassing intimacy which I had witnessed, it was as if a wall were separating them.

The voice of a child or a young girl rose up from the darkness and the words were heart-rending.

Let not my glory create any obstacle to your own
If you prefer to put my life before your soul.

All I could see was the curved nape of Heloise's neck.

There would be no celebration, no banquet at which we could drink, or sing, or weep—there would be no dances in which to forget oneself, or buffoons to recall the bridegroom's achievements, or minstrels to entertain the gathering with stories from the past.

There would be the echo of that voice born in darkness— *What else, what more shall we say? What tears, what cries shall we utter?*

There would be the sadness of this endless dawn, and the sorrows of those creatures who, one by one, were drawing closer to still more sorrow.

15

YES, we walk alone, like blind men in the heat of the midday sun, burning our hands on the stones, stumbling over animals, slipping up in streams, discovering the impossible geography of other people's faces by reaching for their noses and their eyes — and letting ourselves be bitten in return.

There are days when the hurly-burly of everyday life is the only truth, when the words we utter with our mouths, our invocations and our prayers, are like the grunting of pigs, the barking of dogs. Everything around us — and which we have created with great difficulty, with much inventiveness, with great pretensions to piety — our proud chimneys, our church steeples, our bronze bells, all our logic and fine feelings, they're all a bad joke. We proudly call ourselves dwarfs perched on giants' shoulders: we drag ourselves along the ground, ghastly lepers whom we would turn away from in horror were we to see ourselves in a mirror.

We lie down like trees crashing to the ground, and if our chests still heave, they are raised up by a wind born before us: the power of creation is that of disorder, of chaos. In the story of the world, all around me, I hear the restless brothers urging me to prepare myself for the Judgement. Be ready, they say, keep the candle lit . . . But our story is probably already written, and we read it with the clumsiness of children discovering the alphabet. The flood is imminent, and none of us is called Noah.

I often got up in the middle of the night and, without making a sound, I put on my tunic and surcoat, hose and cloak, and, like a thief of men's souls, I walked to the top of the Mount to look at and feel the city. I was neither king nor master and I had no difficulty—unlike Robert of Arbrissel—in burying myself in the mud: nothingness was good for me, it soothed my restless heart. I then gazed upon my city, as one might gaze at a much loved woman who is about to go away, and yet whose sleep is lit with a smile of happiness. (I remembered Salerno and the harm I did you, you whom I called my love, and other names too, you who gave me your body to feast upon and made me promise never to harm you. I remembered that suffering does not diminish with time, and that the pain we have received and have inflicted become one and the same emotion, which gnaws at our hearts, and that we long to return to our loved one to whisper sweet nothings—just for those little gestures that do not change anyhing but mean we are together once more, as we were when the pain did not hurt, as when we were dazzled just to look at one another—no regrets, no remorse. Too many forces are constricting us for us even to dream of a destiny other than our own, life falls apart as it unravels and there is nothing we can say to the other person, nothing we can do, *we do not enter the same river twice*. To ask forgiveness is absurd, so we go on living and it is in this breath, as death approaches—with all the devils hissing in our ears and tugging at our limbs, their racket deafening the sweet music of the angels playing their rebecks and lutes—when we have no strength left and no one to talk to, that the light suddenly dawns, we had known it for ages: my God, it was so simple . . .) My eyes grew wide and I could see: the delicate lights of the city danced, her flares, her candles, her lovers' glances; her night birds flying, her shouting and singing, her foul stenches; the night-watchman passing with his roll-call of the dead (*Awake, ye who sleep, pray to God for the departed!*), the trading at all hours, let the Matins bells ring! The crushed wheat, the moulded clay, water-sellers, wafer-sellers, knife grinders and vendors of blood, let the Lauds bells ring! Desperate profiteers who would even sell separate parts of their bodies, bright-eyed children who came to the city with hunger in their bellies and hope in their hearts, and ended up with a bucket and shovel in their hands, emptying heaps of rubbish from in between houses, and tossing it in the river.

Alone, a man was squatting against a church wall, and as he pissed, he juggled a few balls in the air and whistled an old tune; he winked at me and I passed on by.

When the Prime bells rang, I was reborn.

On the other side of the hill, I walked down to the village of Saint-Marcel, and from there in the direction of Saint-Médard, where the little houses and the patches of vines and fruit trees were clustered around the monasteries. I could hear the blend of their voices chanting the first psalms of David. I was jealous of this peace and this safety. Did I say I had no regrets? One regret tore at my heart: why was I not with them, in the choir, singing my trust in God? Why could I not be that persecuted just man who cries out and appeals for vengeance, why was my voice not linked to theirs in prayer, why could I not subjugate myself by joining an order that would bring peace to my soul? Always this solitude, this having to be strong and putting reason above all else—almost above faith—this harsh and stupid habit of wanting to be a man, a real one . . . And behind it, this dreadful sadness, soon to become acedia—as much a mortal sin as lust.

By following the Bièvre, I arrived at the Seine, as the torments of the night gave way to the tumult of the day. I was happy to be jostled, almost knocked over by the horses and the heavily laden mules. Some Victorines were leaving the house in which we were living: that was good. I walked along the banks on my own: calm down, you're alive. You're not better than anyone else, not worse. You try honestly to follow their injunction: *know thyself*.

Then, ambling slowly along, I wended my way through the flow of men and animals making their way to the Cité, laden with all the riches and all the rubbish in the world, its hopes and its crimes, and I walked back up to my room on the slopes of the Mount.

I still continued to act as messenger: through cajolery and a few coins, I'd persuaded the sad Saracen woman who worked for Fulbert to betray him; she passed on Peter's message to his mistress and handed me those Heloise had written. We met to do business at the Pallu market, where letters and coins were exchanged beneath crusts of bread.

A curious thing, which bothered me and now amuses me: Peter paid me. The students gave him money for his talks and he gave it to me to keep quiet. It occurred to me to refuse, but I dismissed the notion. I told myself: I was neither worse nor better than anyone else.

I no longer felt embarrassed reading their love letters. I didn't know why, but Peter gave me the strange seal—the merged heads of a man and a woman—with which he closed his letters; Heloise sent hers open, as if she wanted the whole world to know about her. Their promises, their wretched quarrels and their secret trysts had become the stuff of my dreams—and sometimes my waking hours: I once happened to follow them from afar, when they thought no one was looking. They were at the steam baths, near the new market at Champeaux, a place one does not enter lightly. What did it matter to me . . . And yet I waited in hiding for them until the evening: they were smiling as they left and were running around like young people.

Master Peter Abelard had rediscovered a new energy, and his students had done so simultaneously. I didn't know where he found the time to study, but once again new images flowed from his lips: he used his seal to talk about the Trinity — and the scales fell from one's eyes, one's ears were opened, men knew . . . Never before had so many students come — and from all over the kingdom and beyond, from all over Europe. This married man was having an affair with his wife — could any lovers' game have been more appropriate to arouse his blood, mind and senses?

In the evening, he wanted to tell me all about it and I tried to prevent him with timid words: I already knew far more than I wanted to know. But his triumph was too great and for Peter Abelard there could be no real triumph without words: he fucked her in the vineyard that belonged to Saint-Victor ('Can you imagine, if old William of Champeaux knew!'); he fucked her in her uncle's garden while he was at Mass and she was feigning illness; he even fucked her in the street, in a doorway, hidden by an ox; fucked her beneath a cart; fucked her in front of a young clerk who was frenziedly tossing himself off; fucked her against the door of the convent of Saint-Éloi to commemorate the expulsion of the nuns there for immoral behaviour; fucked her beneath one of the arches of the Grand Pont; fucked her beneath an arch of the Petit Pont; fucked her in a baker's oven and in a mill; fucked her in a money changer's shop in exchange for a livre minted in Paris; fucked her at Samuel's house on a table where their love-making caused all the pots and goblets to crash to the floor; fucked her in the Close, just after the lesson — she was adept at cleverly disguising herself, particularly as a boy, and that's how he liked to take her — also as a nun of course, as he had done ever since the journey from Le Pallet, and he liked to reach orgasm calling her 'my nun' and 'my canoness', and her shyness and protests excited him because he knew that they concealed further audacity and new initiatives, the mere thought of which caused him to wake with a jolt during his lust-obsessed nights.

One evening when Peter had given her instructions to get Fulbert drunk, having cuddled her uncle as she used to when she was his adored little niece, he went to the house in the Close, went up to her bedroom and took her more roughly than ever—and he had to smother her cries with his hand—he even had to gag her, using his tunic as a cloth. 'Naked and silent, and wrapped in my woollen cloak, I wanted her more than ever, I wanted to clasp her till I could crush her . . . I picked her up and took her in my arms, she was quivering with cold and fear, like a forest animal, I laid her down on the chest on which she puts out her clothes, and I took her again, and her gag was so tight that I almost had to resort to violence to enable her tightly pressed lips to at last release a few moans . . .'

Fulbert's voice in the middle of the night made their blood run cold. Peter had taken off her gag and she had barely caught her breath when his voice boomed out and drew closer and he was already knocking at the door. 'Did I call out, Uncle? It must have been a bad dream . . . Go back to bed and I'll try to sleep . . .' For a long time afterwards, their hearts beat and they laughed as they came together again, promising each other all sorts of unprecedented pleasures, and gambling on defying the world as if tomorrow did not exist.

My heart was thumping as I listened: they were there before me, naked, chasing one another, dancing about, wrestling, making love . . . I was the silent, inert partner of their frolics, an animal with nocturnal vision, whose yellow eyes shine in the darkness and observe every pore of skin, every drop of pleasure.

It brought about near-impotence.

In order to distract me from my melancholy state, Christian wanted to take me to the taverns, public baths or brothels on the right bank, where there are women newly arrived from the Levant who are very adept at caring for men in my condition. I stubbornly refused, for I preferred to stay on my own, staring after the shadows left by my master and his friend, and waiting for him to return and talk to me. Christian had painted a gate on my wall, and on either side of it a masked man and woman were making a sign or an invitation to one another, against a background in which the foliage and friezes formed a labyrinth in which I could lose myself, either in candlelight or in the light of dawn. Pretending that I was protecting it, I had hung a linen curtain, the colour of rose of Tyre, on the wall.

Rumours of their marriage spread, fuelled by Fulbert, his friends, and the canons of the chapter of Notre-Dame, and denied vigorously by Abelard and Heloise. It was an absurd struggle into which Peter waded passionately, sustained by sentiments that were as mediocre as Heloise's were noble. In any case, one might as well deny that the Grand Pont had been rebuilt in stone, deny that King Louis VI had built a round tower at his palace, deny that the Lendit fair took place at Saint-Denis — deny as much as you want and the time will always come when you won't be bothered to deny any more.

That moment was approaching.

To begin with, Fulbert had locked up his niece and it was said that she didn't even leave her room for meals. Shut up in the Close, the life of a recluse awaited her. Then came the first relaxations of discipline: the rest was due to my collusion with the servant woman. People now said that nothing could cure the canon of his moroseness and that he sometimes burst into terrible furies when he would beat her, striking her with all his strength because she had enjoyed the blows inflicted on her by the monster.

Peter brought her with him one evening, breathless and dishevelled. I had not seen her for several weeks and it seemed to me that behind the even greater nobility of her bearing there was a quality of panic about her expression that had not been there before: her efforts to be responsible for herself while still belonging to him were exhausting her. Her features were drawn, her cheeks were hollow.

'We'll have to put a stop to this,' he said, looking at me.

Heloise came to embrace me, and she remained clasped to me, her breast heaving with a choking sob.

'He beats her, he torments us, he does not keep his word. He had promised secrecy, yet news of our marriage is all over the town . . .'

Peter's face was pale and he was convulsed with a violent anger. I concealed a snigger at his mention of disloyalty and keeping one's word.

'It's too much for him, Peter.'

'You're on his side?'

'You know whose side I'm on.'

'It's a war, do you understand. And you have to know whom you're with and whom you serve!'

His eyes were bulging out of their sockets and I felt desperately worried. And yet I was paralysed and it was impossible for me to stand up to him or make him retract his childish words. I made a faint gesture of dismay, and turned towards Heloise, who was looking at the ground.

'Have I not served you well, Peter?'

'Indeed. But now is the moment of judgement.'

'What do you want to do?'

He turned to Heloise.

'We have to shock him, deal him a blow from which he will not recover and which will pacify him for good!'

'Poison him?'

'No!'

A howl burst from Heloise's throat in reaction to this word which had escaped unconsciously from my lips. Peter softened his voice.

'I didn't say that. It was William . . .'

'I'm sorry, Heloise. What I said was absurd and I never meant to say it.'

'Do you understand, Peter? I'm ready to betray him and to do so over and again for love of you, and may God be my only judge . . . I am ready to live with his shame and his beatings . . .'

Peter grew agitated and interrupted her.

'But it's not that! Who's talking about killing anyone? All I want is for you to go away for a while. I want to make him realise that his foolish words can turn against him and that it is I who . . .'

'And that you hold me in your power.'

There was a sadness in her voice—but no bitterness. She stated the fact calmly.

'You could put it like that.'

'But I want it like that . . .'

He did not pick up the imperceptible irony.

'You will enter Argenteuil. You will take the habit, but not the veil.'

'Peter,' I interrupted, 'you don't enter a convent for "a while". One is a novice . . . or a nun. And it's for ever.'

'You can be a . . . a boarder.'

Silence descended on us. He hesitated over that final word. The blood-coloured veil I imagined in his mind—and the pallor of Heloise, who said nothing. His hands shook. She looked at him and he became agitated, then he recovered.

'But what's the matter with both of you? What does that mean, "for ever"? It means nothing to a man like me, who has the bishop, the chancellor—the king himself, in other words—in my pocket. I only have to snap my fingers and you—you can come in—you—you can go—you—you must leave Paris . . . Do you understand, I know them all! I do as I please!'

He shouted these last words. I suddenly felt very calm. I no longer heard his voice ranting and raging. I was among the noises of the still crowded street, where a cart laden with barrels had overturned and where men were rushing around, puffing and panting, uttering insults that warned of disaster, where horses were whinnying and there was much shouting, much futility . . .

'If God himself were speaking—I mean addressing me face to face—I don't know whether I'd hear him. But if you speak, I will listen to you; say the word, and I will do it.'

There was no longer any trace of irony in Heloise's voice.

✦ ✦ ✦

143

During the nights that followed, I pondered on what seemed to me more a matter of desertion than self-denial — and I blamed myself fairly frequently for having been weak with him. Beneath the summer moon, the right words would come to me as I gulped down a cooling breeze.

A year had already passed, and I — the wanderer who had always lived freely, and who, even when begging for bread, had always maintained a proud demeanour — found myself controlled by this master who was crushing all that was purest and most beautiful to me.

I wept with fury, shedding tears over her and myself, my willpower obliterated, my strength and my confidence shattered. That voice which knew how to seduce and to threaten, those powerful hands which drew very real images in the air, those dark and fiery eyes which in a single flash could express both affection and vengeance followed me, haunted me and made of me the child I could never have been, who preferred to succumb and give way to another's absurd violence.

My emotions no longer belonged to me — what I had read of the sages meant nothing to me. If Cicero and Seneca themselves could have sent me signals, my confusion would not have been any the less. He made fun of it and exploited it, pretending to toy with the tempestuous winds and still reach port; a child too, a Bacchus who would end up torn apart by the horses he had unleashed.

So he abducted his wife in order to put her in a convent.

They spoke about it in the City, even in royal circles, I was told, where there was curiosity, amusement, scandal. As for Fulbert, he rushed around the Close, beside himself with grief; Peter whispered secretly that the uncle, not content with holding her prisoner, used to beat her to avenge himself for some affront or other — he was pleased that this terrible brutality had been brought to an end.

Fulbert went to see Bishop Gerbert and asked for justice to be done to this treacherous and reprehensible perverter. But the bishop was still close to Garlande—the archdeacon who had become chancellor—and Garlande protected Peter. The bishop was therefore not present when Fulbert arrived—and neither was the dean, the new archdeacon. Fulbert was received by a young cantor who tried to soothe him with the kind, well-intoned words that cantors know how to use. But here was a creature who was screaming, threatening to appeal to the Pope and to convene a council which would make them all tremble: hypocrites, simonists, Nicolaitans (and he had the names of those who paid concubines or prostitutes, and those dignitaries in the very highest places, and everything would become known and people would be very surprised!), for they were all liars. And word would get around about the handsome payments they received! He called upon the most holy Gregory, on Benedict, on Augustine, on Jerome, on Paul—and on Jesus himself. With tears in his eyes, he said that such injustice had not been inflicted on any man since Job; he cried out that vengeance would be more terrible than any punishment.

The wretched cantor preached in vain—with words that were increasingly less effective—that wrath was a poor counsellor and that he must wait for the dean or the bishop. He timidly suggested that one was nevertheless dealing with the man in charge of the Notre-Dame school, and with that Fulbert was unleashed: since when had people been afraid of a master of schools, the most minor of clerics, and in this case a master who ought more appropriately to be called a master of rape and deceit, who was fit only to receive the punishment of the Sodomites? He had scarcely paused to gather his breath than he began spluttering again, shouting and weeping at the same time, and creating an appalling scene, faced with which the panic-stricken cantor eventually started to make his retreat.

The bishop knew his chapterhouse and his Fulbert. He had him taken to his apartments and made him wait there for an hour or two; when Fulbert's rage had turned to torpor, Gerbert came in wearing his full bishop's apparel—crosier, mitre and stole—as if he was about the celebrate the Easter Mass.

'I am told,' he began in a gentle voice, 'that you have been creating a disturbance ...'

Exhausted, Fulbert admitted defeat without further struggle: all he dared request was that the abbess of the convent at Argenteuil be asked as to whether his niece had given her consent. Gerbert agreed magnanimously and sent the weary and drained canon away with a tap on his head.

During this time, apparently unaware of the turmoil he had caused, Peter Abelard went on pursuing the delights of his affair: he who probably thought that he would save his soul more easily by disguising his wife as a nun, had transformed her, dare I say it, into a truly bogus nun, and had worked out in his mind some extraordinary stratagems for taking her away and disappearing with her.

With even more pride than in all the previous episodes, he told me how he had crept into the convent enclosure (by bribing the gatekeeper and forcing his way past a few terrified novices) and, as the office was being sung, as the sweet voices of the nuns rose up from the church, he had taken her in the empty refectory under the eye—and almost as if with the blessing—of the Holy Virgin Mary.

'You can't imagine what it's like to reach a climax surrounded by sanctity! It's a rarer and more subtle pleasure! And her own tears, the way she hit me when she rebuked me—because I had to force her slightly, you see—and her own pleasure, and our fear (when the moment before, stimulated by my audacity and my words, she had promised to deliver up to me a young nun who was a virgin, who used to wake up in the night moaning with desire, and who she later heard weeping to herself) when we realised that the singing had stopped and that we were going to be discovered ...'

He ran off and made his escape, the blood thumping at his

temples, understanding at last what the devil meant and that temptation was not just a little word that you utter accidentally: he wanted more.

He suggested taking me to some establishment on the right bank that he knew about, where he had been with her. Straight away, the image, both alluring and repelling, came to my mind of the steam baths, and the memory of my childish spying.

'There are women of every colour there,' he said, 'of every shape, and men who are women, unless it's the other way round . . . It's as hot there as hell must be.'

'Enough.'

He looked at me, surprised and slightly contemptuous. What was wrong with me? What was this sudden prudery, this virginal timidity? I took a breath before telling him in a voice initially unsure of itself, but which grew in assurance because he did not interrupt me, what I thought of his mad escapades. When I'd finished, this extraordinary man remained silent and then simply said:

'You're right.'

Never had he earned so much money; in addition to the payment he had succeeded in obtaining from the chapter, a great many students paid him. We were still lodging at the Vendean's house, but he had hired himself a servant, a sad creature who answered to the name of Christian des Quatre Routes (where these four roads led to, I was never able to discover) and whom we called simply Quatre-Routes.

'Quatre-Routes!'

The sad fellow appeared. Peter took out his goose quill, his ink well and a sheet of vellum. The man waited absent-mindedly, with a heavy brow. Peter wrote a few words, dried the page, then folded and sealed it.

'You will take this to Canon Fulbert.'

'Will there be a reply?'

'Wait and see,' said Peter somewhat curtly.

Quatre-Routes went off without another word.

'I don't like the fact that your servant does not care for you.'

'He likes to serve, that's enough.'

'It wouldn't be enough for me. What did you say to Fulbert?'

'I'm proposing peace.'

'What sort of peace?'

'The only possible kind: resuming our previous lives.'

I shook my head.

'You're crazy. He'll never accept.'

'He has no choice. What's more, he's humiliated . . .'

'Precisely. Believe me, I know the virtues of humiliation and self-abasement better than a monk who follows the Rule of St Benedict step by step . . . But there . . .'

'Well?'

'He suffers too much.'

He came and sat down beside me on the edge of the bed. There was a pleasant smell of mint and verbena: our wealth allowed us a new bunch of fresh leaves every day. Through the window we could see the sun setting on an endless summer day. He had recovered from his euphoria and was reflecting on things with a moderation and honesty that would have been incomprehensible to anyone who had heard him unleashing his deranged ideas a few minutes earlier.

'I know that I'm crazy and that it is the Devil who is inciting me; and I know very well that there is only one way, that of Our Lord Jesus Christ. Merely invoking his name, I find peace again, and I feel the breath of his forgiveness on my stiff neck; I come late, Lord, out of breath perhaps, perhaps too late, but my heart is humble and I commit my sins to you . . .'

He interrupted himself.

'Do you believe me?'

I looked at him in amazement. He seemed so composed, so sincere, as if in prayer—it was impossible not to believe him! He laughed before he sighed.

'You believed me, eh? Not for nothing does God's athlete call me the "juggler". You see, I'm as good at contrition as I am at commenting on Ezekiel. But you can believe me with confidence: I also believe myself. The problem is that I also believed myself just now and this very afternoon, in the refectory—and even now I cannot be sure of my shame, so great was my pleasure and so greatly do I yearn for more. For years I have been so sensible, William, and so chaste, so absurdly chaste! No doubt, if I had behaved as others have—like all those priests who mutter about me, like all those false apostles—taking a serving woman here, a prostitute there, I would not be dazzled quite so naïvely by the seductions of the crime I am committing. But there we are: I have come to sin through the main door. Ah! Enough of this nonsense—I know I have to stop all this, I know there must be peace. But which kind?'

'There's only one . . .'

'Do you think so? Do you remember my old quarrels with William of Champeaux and our furious arguments about words and things?'

'Of course I remember!'

'What fun we had . . . And you should have seen the old boy's face!'

'That doesn't tell me which kind of peace.'

'Yes it does: there is no peace. Just look at William: I've crushed him, ripped off his helmet, smashed his coat of mail, so that he had to leave the battlefield, and yet back he comes, protected on all sides, setting up a school—what am I saying, an order—and going about pleading poverty (the poor fellow's only a bishop!) and speaking ill of me everywhere . . .'

'There you go again!'

He nudged me.

'No, I'm having fun, that's all. But I still think there's no peace. There's only that old chivalry: jousting, banners, confrontation, conquest! Look at Jerusalem, look at Antioch, look at our noble lords: they knock down walls, they burn the infidels, they skewer children, they put soldiers to the sword, they set fire to homes, they bring back the True Cross . . . That's hard and serious work! But to have to sort out all those frantic people who would slit one another's throats for a bit of power, to have to become involved with Byzantine diplomacy, to spy in order to discover the next piece of treachery . . . How tedious!'

'Do you want a different sort of woman?'

'I never weary of subduing her. And believe me, she does not give in without a hard struggle!'

'She's yours, Peter, she says it often enough. Could you not simply love her?'

Night had fallen fully. He did not answer me. He stood up and stretched.

'It's late, let's get some sleep. Quatre-Routes has not come back.'

'Perhaps there was no reply.'

'Then he must be hanging around in a tavern.'

'I thought that one of his many virtues was that he only drank water . . .'

'It's a problem partaking of the Mystery of Creation, and it's enormously dangerous to make analogies about the Mystery of the Trinity, or the Incarnation. As for the mystery of each human being, let's agree it's beyond us.'

He was already in his bedroom. I fell asleep immediately on my bed, without undressing; when I awoke, I could see through the curtain that his candle was still burning. He lay naked on his bed, fast asleep, like a powerful, drunken, happy, victorious bear.

I snuffed out the candle.

There would be no peace.

16

I SCREAMED before I woke up.

A powerful hand was clamped to my mouth, and other hands were grabbing my arms, holding them apart and tying me to the bed. A gag had been stuffed in my mouth and a blindfold put over my eyes before I could utter a word. I wanted to be sick, I was half suffocating and was thrashing about desperately.

'Calm down,' said a voice that was familiar, 'calm down at once.'

I ceased my futile struggle. I was still in a panic and it felt as if a stone had been placed on my throat. The man came and sat down beside me. From Peter's bedroom I could hear blows being struck and the sound of fighting. The man leaned over me. He breathed into my ear for a second before he whispered:

'If you keep quiet, you're going to see . . .'

I knew this voice, but fear had closed a door in my memory.

'. . . but what you'll see won't please you.'

He snatched the blindfold from my eyes: all I could discern to begin with was a sea of light and, in the middle of it, the blade of a knife. It was an enormous chopping knife in which my panic seemed to be reflected. Only then did I cast my eyes at the man who was holding it.

'You have to have friends,' said Germain with a smile. 'And you have to know how to keep your promises.'

He stood up; the knife hung from his hand—he let it gleam in the rising sun before putting it down on my chest of drawers.

'Now I'm going to take off your gag. If you cry out, you'll regret it. But I'm sure that a man like you will want to do all he can to display the ancient virtue of moral strength by keeping silent during his suffering. Although . . .'

My spirit stubbornly refused to stand the strain; I was unable to calm my beating heart; albeit unwillingly, I had become the hero of one of those Passion plays that are enacted outside churches. I could not even take pleasure in the fact that my cross was a bed with a good straw mattress.

'You have to be very strong to let yourselves be so very care-less. You and your master think you're very strong, but you're nothing but a pair of clumsy and wicked children.'

'Are you no longer a monk?'

'No airs and graces, Jesus! You know all about vows of stability, don't you? Monks or canons, clerks or peasants, whether clothed or not, here, there . . . Haven't we reached the moment of Judgement for the simple travellers of this world who pray while they wait for the next . . .'

He jumped up suddenly and grabbed his knife.

'Haven't we all got our stations to pause at along the way before we reach the end? *Obiunt Germanus, Petrus, Wilhelminus* . . . and our names won't be inscribed on any roll of the dead. It will all be clear when our time comes. And God knows, many things can happen before we die. Eh, William?'

The groan came from the next room—a muffled groan that didn't sound like Peter's voice, but which could only be his.

'You're beginning to understand, you fool, you stiff-neck, you people who are too slow to submit. Do you know it took an

Arab scholar to make me aware of the beauties of the knife. Until then I only had a limited, mundane notion of this implement—I thought that it was used to cut meat and to defend oneself in dark places. But this Arab (all praise to this priceless friend! Many fine and important things shall come to us from these Arabs, I promise you!) showed me some fascinating innovations. Imagine, for example, if I wanted—God forbid—to cut off your ears ... Neatly, of course: we're among Christians, and we would not wish to suffer the indignity of being filthier than the Arabs. You see, I wouldn't start doing it in any old way: you have to go from top to bottom. Watch carefully.'

He made the gesture several times, watching me until he was satisfied with the effect he had had.

'Beautiful, isn't it? Now, your nose. Quite something, your nose! What would you bet? Top to bottom, in the same way? No, no, a practical, intelligent boy like you will have guessed already: it's from bottom to top. You see?'

He repeated this latest manoeuvre, thrusting in a circular motion, like a sword.

'Do you like it? These craftsmen knew a thing or two: an ancient technique put to sensible use! Every movement must be elegant and restrained, you see, because they all have their purpose. But we've still got a long way to go: we've only just reached the interesting part. And that, well ...'

He snapped his fingers. The two men were masked and were wearing aprons and blood-stained gloves.

'Do you know what my two friends' occupation is? A fine job —and a useful one. There's no guild yet, but there will be, because it deserves one. Of course, it doesn't quite have the nobility of some professions, but it's an indispensable activity, and to learn it requires strength, determination and a sense of opportunity. It's not a job for a *beginner*, you see. Experience is respected —you understand. But I'm chatting on and you're dying to find out. Do you know what they do, or don't you? Well: they're pig gelders. Pig gelders!'

He began to laugh, and he went on laughing so much he almost choked.

'And as everyone knows, castrating a pig or a man . . . Right . . .'

One of the two men took out a thin cord from his pocket. He snapped his fingers several times. He came towards me.

I felt as if my chest was going burst and I began desperately trying to move around, but in vain. While one of them held my legs I could feel myself being stripped and as my body emptied itself through every extremity, I sobbed and shook like a frog; every inch of my body was overwhelmed by fear and humiliation and I believe I begged forgiveness in a shameful way. The masked man—his powerful hands calm and precise—tied my scrotum neither too tightly, nor too loosely.

'We'll do exactly the same as we did with the other one,' said Germain, 'but I'll be the one holding the knife. Do you remember? You have to have friends. And you have to keep your promises.'

There was a commotion on the stairs and people were shouting: the two men looked at Germain and shoved him out of the way; he dropped his knife, then made as if to pick it up, but already there were knocks on the door (and I wept, unable to stop, and I pissed myself and shouted as I heard Peter's groans, which stopped and started again, stopped and started, and my lips stammered out incoherent words—'Oh terror! terror!'—could that be called a prayer?) and Germain let out a cry of fury, picked up his knife, opened the door and, taking everyone by surprise, tore down the stairs. I can say nothing about the scuffle that followed: I lost consciousness.

Neither rage nor tears meant anything when you awoke to your shame. You were alive: that's all you could say about yourself. In the turbulence that surrounded you, in the midst of cries and questions, you could not distinguish friendly faces from those of strangers. All familiarity had vanished: every human face bore the features of a wolf. In your bewilderment, the only refuge you could find was to be alone by the well, letting water flow over your face and your neck, as if you were being newly baptised.

Your body was reeling: you felt cold when everyone else was perspiring; your cheeks and one of your hands shook slightly; you stood alone staring at the door to the beyond that was painted on your wall (in the confusion, the curtain had fallen down, and it lay strewn over the floor like a rag that no one could be bothered to remove), from Terce to Sext, from Sext to Nones, Vespers and Compline. The door opened and you entered a world where only fear and the devil — which amount to the same thing — reigned. With closed lips you prayed to those you knew: the Father, the Son, the Holy Spirit. You knelt down and you asked that this stain be cleansed from you.

The moment you closed your eyes, the roar of Judgement descended upon you and you swore that you would never sleep again; naturally, exhaustion took over and you sank into a slumber before waking up with a start. You made involuntary movements: you kept touching your thigh — you could still feel those hands that had violated you and that string that was tied to you, and you were not really sure whether that knife was used or not.

A eunuch in spirit — the Bible tells you. Is that what you are now?

Christian said that you were lucky, and you looked at him in amazement. You kept repeating to yourself: 'I am whole, I am alive' — something within you has been shattered and is still being crushed. You forced yourself to smile — who would understand your anger when the fate of your master was so much worse than your own? — and for the first time the words escaped from your lips: 'Yes. I was lucky.' It gave you a strange feeling to talk about yourself in the first person.

Secretly, you were glad that the moment when you saw Peter was constantly delayed. Gislebert, whom you imagined to be alone, did something that did not tear you apart. He did not talk to you but he looked at you like a brother: then, very gently, so as not to alarm you, he reached out his hand to your face and stroked your cheek. For the first time, you could close your eyes without being afraid.

Two doctors came to examine you and you refused to allow yourself to be touched, and then a crowd of people—clerks, students, women, the bishop himself, and Garlande—started asking you questions, but you had the impression that your answers were not very important. How many men? Two. Why do you say two? You were sure that if you said 'three'—if you merely mentioned the name of Germain, your nightmare would begin again. (You suddenly saw him clearly: in this dream, you were one of the prisoners whom the bastard, Thomas de Marle, had suspended from a wire attached to the testicles. He laughed and twisted your neck as he spoke to you—this way, he said, some part of you is being yanked for each one of us.)

The Vendean came to see you, his face grey from sorrow and shame. It was that wretch of a servant, that Quatre-Routes, who had let them in and had overpowered him. What could he have done, alone among his folios? And I believed him, I soothed him and I thanked him. A hint of a smile returned to his lips and his eyes.

'Are you sure?' he entreated me. 'It was a terrible disgrace all the same . . .'

Christian spent a long time with you, and through him words became acceptable again. He was gentle, but not complacent—a man and a friend. With him you could weep to your heart's content and recall your own failure without breaking down again. A smile flickered in his wise prophet's face.

'This is how we are,' he said, 'and it is good to be reminded of it sometimes. No paths to humility can be bad.'

He told me that all over the city people were shedding tears—the kind of uncomprehending astonishment they display after disasters, the stupefaction of an emotion that affects each and every one. Strangers (even if nobody was a complete stranger in our small town) looked at one another, shouted at one another, embraced each other and grieved over what had happened. Sometimes a sign was enough, sometimes a few words—there was both anger and tears. Those who sang his songs, those who loathed him, a man who knew the man who made his sandals, the man who made the cloth for his coat, the man who looked after the toll-gate on the Petit Pont, the man who kept the pool at Sainte-Geneviève where his fish were caught, the man who bound his books, a man whose brother was taught by him, the man who made the flour for his bread, and all their brothers, wives and daughters, and their servants: it was a city whimpering, a lament that never stopped, a cry of endless regret.

Nobody talked about me and that was for the best—they scarcely knew that there had been a man in the room next to him and that he too almost . . . In the days that followed there would be lamentations, poems, letters, candles lit outside the school—and even a degree of mockery, such as the new delicacy that sellers of sweetmeats had christened 'Peter's balls'—but today there was only that whispering and those exchanged glances, that astonishment, that rare moment when one person's grief was everyone's grief.

I spent the days that followed in a fog through which only muffled noises from the outside world reached me. Peter, who had barely recovered, wrote of his humiliation and anger to the bishop, the king, and even the pope.

I slept. I wanted to sleep in spite of the nightmares and the howls that woke me. It seemed to me that talking and confronting the world—my friends, even—were ordeals that I would not survive. Every visit required me to behave as a man—and I couldn't be sure that I still was one, knowing how precarious the dividing line was. I remembered that I had laughed when I read the story of that monk who, when the time came for prayers, and despite his desire to be good, snatched hold of his genitals and shook them frantically, all the while weeping with shame and confusion. I would no longer make fun of this man—my brother.

Fortunately, when they came back, my friends Christian and Gislebert did not listen to me. As for the others, I was aware of their solicitude even if their questions, once civilities were over, were all directed at Abelard. But there we were on familiar ground. For the past two years, I had become accustomed to the fact that people did not address themselves to me to know what I wanted or thought, but to find out his latest comment, his latest logical discovery, his latest invention, his latest folly, or whether it was true that he had met the prior of Saint-Victor or the abbot of Cîteaux.

I had therefore developed a personality which was not so much mine as his. I knew how to be him as well, if not better, than he did, and to step aside when he appeared and all eyes were turned on him. Many a lesson had I begun, when his studies or his love life had detained him, only to fall silent when his tall figure approached and, with a laugh, he would ask them how many would follow me were I to open my own school. I blushed, and rather than hear the outcome, I preferred to assure him that there was no other school than his and that it was now up to him to rectify the errors I had made.

The habit of being someone else other than oneself makes us experience their torments as if they were ours and to forget our own misfortunes in order to experience theirs all the more deeply.

Alone and abandoned, I called upon God in a feeble, resigned way. I had seldom prayed to him recently and there were few men I could turn to. They filled me with disgust: their hands that I no longer wished to touch, their foul embraces, the lies that tarnished every word they uttered. This habit of being someone else had also protected me from everything, and the evidence of other people's mediocrity struck me as too heavy a burden to bear. Yes, ultimately the farce was a sad one and I laughed no longer. I ventured your name, Lord, with closed lips at first, but then they quivered with the mumblings of an old man, before opening out into real words, songs even, which rolled from under my tongue and rose up to you. I spoke to you of my humiliation, and I walked up the steps one by one, recognising and bemoaning my shame, knowing that you were the only one who could understand it, and then I entered into this light which I knew was good, which I knew you had intended for me, and I knew that none of this suffering was in vain.

The words of my first prayers had seemed to belong to some foreign and barbarous tongue, but as I repeated them they took on a new strength and tears welled up in my eyes without shame or self-consciousness—my tears of pity had turned into tears of love, and I ought to praise You for having brought about this change and for having granted me your grace in the depths of my unworthiness.

I was terrified when I saw him. What I had experienced virtually alone, while I was mumbling my prayers (I stayed in my bedroom or I went to a church, to Saint-Serge and Saint-Bacchus, or else I went down to the Cité and took refuge in Saint-Julien, in the church that abuts the Seine, or Saint-Denis-de-la-Chatre, at the end of the Grand Pont), now suddenly confronted me in all its wretched grandeur.

Peter had at first been taken to Garlande's house (I never saw these powerful people, and although he was not one of them, he claimed to be on friendly terms with them and knew all about the mad things they did; he spoke to me about their love of power and money with an amusement that made me admire him, because he could have been like them but didn't allow himself to be so, whereas we simple folk had no other choice but the pride of the humble, the pride in defeat that always leaves us by the wayside, trying in vain to protect ourselves from the burning sun and the tons of dust kicked up by their horses' hooves), then later—by an irony of fate—to the house of a canon, a street away from where Fulbert lived, where the door was always closed and where rubbish piled up almost every morning.

I found him at his school, alone. He took me in his arms and his tears mingled with mine. Then I noticed the book he was reading: it was a simple psalter, of the kind you learn to read at the monastery schools.

'I am very much to blame,' he said, 'and my entire philosophy is now in a psalm . . .'

> *Lord, rebuke me not in thy anger,*
> *Nor chasten me in thy wrath!*
> *For thy arrows have sunk into me,*
> *And thy hand has come down on me,*
> *There is no soundness in my flesh*
> *Because of thy indignation . . .*

I said nothing. Nothing in his face or his body had visibly altered: neither his heavy appearance, dressed in a black gown, nor the burden upon his shoulders, as he repeated the psalm after me:

> *For I am ready to fall,*
> *And my pain is ever with me.*
> *I confess my iniquity,*
> *I am sorry for my sin . . .*
> *Do not forsake, O Lord!*
> *O my God, be not far from me.*

A sob died in his throat, then he caught his breath again. He raised his bushy eyebrows—he was about to ask a question. The moment passed and his expression clouded over.

'I must see her,' he said.

We went to Argenteuil to wait for her.

The convent was surrounded by fields, woods and vineyards in which the grape harvest had begun, with the tightly packed little town built around it. The nun at the gate recognised Abelard, and I think she even gave him a knowing smile. His own expression remained impassive. While we were waiting in the refectory of the hospice, he began to talk to me about the treatise he was writing on the unity of the Holy Trinity, in which he passionately rebutted those who refused to explain the mysteries; he also wanted to put the final touches to his book on logic (after all the troubles his system had brought me, it was the least I could expect); he also wanted to make further progress on a project he had been working on secretly for a long time, which he referred to jokingly as *Yes and No*.

To stave off the boredom of waiting, and because he had once again dragged me into the world of his dreams and made me the privileged partner of his mad reasoning, I followed him.

'I've noticed,' he told me in a confiding tone, 'that there are contradictions and insurmountable problems to be found in Paul, in the founders of the church, in the Acts, even in the Gospels, and I am applying methods of doubt and reason to them . . .'

I felt a shiver run through me.

'You mean you are casting doubt on the Gospels?'

'No, no, you ass, I am simply developing the advice of Jerome and applying it to them, and the terms I am using are no different than those used by Anselm of Canterbury—and let me say that his "proof" of the existence of God is worse than anything I could have said . . . After all, these texts were written by men, copied and re-copied—errors and contradictions could have crept in . . . I am only determining the method that should be used to resolve all of this, correcting errors and re-establishing the authority, one and indivisible, of the divine word. But the moment you talk of human reason to certain false disciples, they get terribly upset . . .'

The smile had come back to his face. A few days earlier I had seen him reading a psalm about divine surrender with tears in his eyes and could imagine him leading a cloistered life of silence, meditating quietly on his fate and praying for divine mercy—and I didn't even dare to contemplate his wound, about which he said nothing. Now here he was gaily holding forth, his confidence returned, his voice low to begin with and then barely audible—perhaps he was hoping to attract a small gathering.

It was lunch time. A crowd of paupers and pilgrims, travellers and sick people, in search of food, comfort and a prayer, had begun to flock into the refectory. There was the sound of shuffling, of benches being moved, of grace being muttered; an old, worn-out voice was already clamouring for wine, and there were all these wretched of the earth, people who survived as best they could, not caring about some analogical audacities spoken by a now wandering philosopher.

'Peter, William . . .'

It was the voice of Heloise. Pale and dressed all in black, she laid her hands on our shoulders. She looked tired: she had not slept. The prioress was with her, silent and stern of aspect despite her relative youth. With her eyes she ordered us to rise.

To my surprise, we left the guest buildings and entered the convent proper. The prioress led us into the Close, opened the *armarium* for us, and—another surprise—left us. I sensed that arrangements had been made.

At first, there was nothing but silence between us. Peter's eyes were only on her, while she was doing her best to share herself between him and me. And then he wrung his hands, his expression clouded over and the tears started to flow. They stood opposite one another, as on that first day, beside the Seine, by the boats—since then so much water has flowed past, so much love and, already, so much suffering.

Now they no longer noticed me: not yet touching one another, they mourned their grandeur and their wretchedness, their rise and their fall.

Once so confident and self-assured, he looked like an old man, and his body moved heavily like a block of stone, his heart racked by sorrow and suffering; a moan convulsed her entire body, her breast heaved, her fingers writhed in anguish and every breath became a sob.

I, too, wept with them, affected more and more by a grief so immense that it encompassed my own.

'To you,' she said in a scarcely audible voice, 'I was obedient to you in shame and misfortune, as much as I was when we sang together with joy . . .'

'Obedient to God,' he said more firmly, interrupting her with his hand, 'both of us obedient to the justice of God, brother and sister in Christ . . .'

She stared at him.

'Justice?' she repeated. 'You pay—we pay this barbarous price and you call a dirty trick carried out to satisfy an old man's pride the "justice of God"?'

'Fallen from the height of my pride, humiliated when I had lied, punished when I had sinned . . .'

'And it was when you made amends for your crime that you were punished?'

'You know very well that untruthfulness involved deceit, too —and that the lie was mine and not yours.'

She half choked as she began to cry again.

'I didn't want to!' she cried. 'It was you who made me.'

'I know . . .'

'All I wanted was to love you and be yours—and even doing everything you wanted was not enough. What greater love do you require, my love? A love that subjects God's will to yours? A love that makes me—even more than the wife of Augustus— your servant, your whore . . .'

Now he took her in his arms and I could see the tears flowing down the furrows of his face—she used to run her finger along those once dry rivulets which she called his 'riddles'—equally inconsolable and unable to stem the tide of emotions that he had sworn he would stifle. All he could do was to continue repeating 'I know' in a faint voice, as if he were asking her forgiveness. She suddenly recovered herself.

'I would never accept,' she cried, 'never, do you hear?'

He looked at her without saying anything. What could he say?

'I will love you even if you don't want me to love you—and

I'm not talking about my uncle, the chapterhouse, the bishop, the king and the pope with his curia. You can treat my love as if it were nothing and the more you trample on it the more it will be mine. *My secret rests with me?* That is my secret, and I shall cry it out with my eyes, my mouth and my hands! You ask me to consider that fair? Fair! Anyone would think you were relieved! Was it I who was the *thorn in your flesh*, and are you now, at last, going to agree with St Paul? Was it you—forgive me, William— who a few days ago violated me in the refectory and would have done so again in the church itself had I not bitten you? Your road to Damascus passed along the banks of the Grève, where the pig gelders dwell . . .'

'That's enough,' said Peter.

'I shall not be silenced. Would you like me to praise the Lord with you, for me to sing of his infinite mercy? Don't worry, I'm going, I'm leaving . . . *In my absence I shall bind myself to you with black flames and when cold death* . . .'

'Enough, I say.'

'. . . *shall have separated my soul from my body, my shade will be with you everywhere.*'

'Heloise, I want you to stop.'

'And I want nothing, my love, nothing but a word you do not utter . . .'

'Well?'

Her arms fell back beside her body, and her anger subsided. Overcome with despondency, she sniffed and wiped her eyes. Even in her wretched state it was impossible for her to be ugly.

'I love you,' I said.

'What?'

'That word is love—"I love you"—does one have to be the greatest philosopher in the world to understand that?'

He looked at us in turn.

'You speak to me of that, all of you,' he said in a low, hissing voice, full of cold anger, 'with a vigour that has deserted me for ever. Haven't I paid enough?'

'Is it love that you have paid?'

'I've paid with my desire and my cowardice and my lies . . .'

'I ask your forgiveness, Peter.'

He looked at her in astonishment.

'Are you asking me for forgiveness? But I'm the one who . . .'

'If you cannot love me, can you not at least forgive me?'

'But I love you!'

The words slipped from his lips involuntarily, at the very moment that the prioress entered the *armarium*. Her face was impassive.

'It's time for Vespers, Sister.'

Heloise did not take her eyes off Peter. He rose, and motioned to me.

'We shall return tomorrow,' he said.

'Tomorrow,' she repeated, with an entreating glance at the prioress.

'Tomorrow,' the nun said, after a pause and a sigh.

We went back the following day and the opening scene was played over again: the nun at the gate with her enigmatic smile, the refectory, the paupers, the prioress. But this time Peter was silent, and whereas before my time had been spent listening to his torrent of words and his plans, on this occasion there was just time itself, with its noises and its tedium.

Heloise was waiting for us in the *armarium*. She lay down her book.

'I never received my forgiveness,' she said with a slight smile.

'I forgive you, even though there's nothing to forgive.'

'Thank you.'

She bowed her head graciously.

'And now?'

Contrary to all logic, there was a trace of hope in a life to be lived in her question. Knowing what Peter was about to say to her, I was tempted to remove myself.

'We had wanted to live human life to the full,' said Peter, enunciating his syllables, 'and we have lived it, oh how we've

lived it—nobody can say we haven't drunk its milk and eaten of
its fruits—we still have the pulp on our lips and the taste in our
mouths . . . And that—my wife, my love—is our situation. We
have only one way out . . .'

She stared at him intently.

'I'm not frightened.'

'I know. We can still live a life in God—by taking our vows.'

'I'm not frightened.'

'I know.'

(I could not help hearing a silent, heartrending cry: may I not
live? But it was mine, not his—for Heloise's cries belonged to
him, as well as her silences.)

'I've spoken to the abbess. You will take the veil tomorrow.'

'And you?'

'In a few days' time.'

'Where?'

'At Saint-Denis.'

We had discussed the place at length—and particularly his
being tempted to join Peter the Child at Cluny, where he had
become the prior after he left Vézelay. But Abelard did not want
to leave Paris—he had fought too hard to sacrifice the position
and renown he had acquired there and even if he was renouncing everything else, he was not renouncing that—and Saint-
Denis was the abbey of the kings. For the time being, it was not
this that bothered Heloise.

'Me before you? Don't you trust me? Are you frightened that
I'll escape, that I'll go back to worldly life again?'

'You and I was what I said.'

'But you've arranged for me to do it before you.'

She spoke in a soft voice, without any anger, as if curious
about the strangeness of things. Even if Peter denied it, he and I
knew very well that she was right: the arrangement concealed a
fear.

'You're injuring me,' she said in the same tone of voice,
'you're injuring me more than you've ever injured me . . .'

He made as if to stop her. She pacified him.

'Don't worry, just listen to me. You're hurting me more at this moment than you have done with any of your other demands; and you alone know (as do I in my heart, each night when I pine for every minute of our love, when even our shameful and depraved acts are pleasures that I yearn for and moan over) how far I was prepared to stoop for you . . . It's as if we were already separated and you were rejecting me . . .'

'Heloise . . .'

'How beautifully you celebrated my name! You placed it on everyone's lips and you excited the jealousy of women, of serving girls and queens! They cared not a jot for your philosophy, I can tell you, and you didn't arouse them with your universal truths; but they knew who you were and my name was on their lips. Is that what you do with this beloved name? Has it become hateful to you in so short a time? You'll miss it, you know, and may God not judge me as harshly as he judges you, now . . .'

'Heloise, I know—do you think I'm accusing you?'

'Oh, no. And of what? Though guilty, I am quite innocent . . . Will you be with me tomorrow?'

'Yes.'

She breathed more calmly and the anger that had almost consumed her subsided. There was only a sadness that carried her away from him, and from me.

'My heart is not with me, but with you, and if it is not with you, it is nowhere . . .'

(At night, when I'm unable to sleep, I repeat these words, inscribed in my heart's memory alongside the most ancient wisdom: *my heart is not with me . . .*)

'. . . and if you are with me when I take leave of myself, I shall not be alone.'

'I shall be there.'

When they embraced, I left the room; I don't know why, when I had seen and heard everything, when I was aware of the groans that issued involuntarily from their bodies when they made love, but I suddenly found myself confronted with an intimacy that disturbed me. Perhaps I was also beginning to suspect — somewhat belatedly — that it is too great a burden for one person to know everything about other people's lives.

The prioress came out of the chapterhouse and when she saw me, she started to approach me. We both came to a halt and were standing like two statues. I remembered Gislebert's strange army, and my nightly walks. Thus do life's whims assign us to different roles. Eventually, I walked over to her.

'This isn't a chapter from the Rule that you've just read,' I said with a smile, 'but I'm grateful to you.'

'I suffered because of a man,' she said simply — and she smiled too.

I found Peter at the front door. A boy with green eyes, whose small dog never left his side, brought us our horses. Peter gave him two coins.

'You've made a mistake, Master, there's one too many.'

Peter gave him a third coin. The boy tossed it in his hand, making it glitter in the sunlight, and set off towards the stables singing.

We didn't speak as we rode. Just as we were drawing near to the gate next to Saint-Denis-de-la-Chatre, he turned to me:

'What about you?' he asked.

'Me?'

'Where are you going now?'

I let go of my reins in order to gesture — with a circular motion of my arms — at the stars; but I didn't answer. I had not considered what I would do. Just as I thought I was leaving their troubles behind me, here I was caught up in them again, although a life in which I could not be constantly with one or other of them, alive to their joys or their sufferings, would have struck me as worthless, impossible even. And yet, in the time it would take to say a few prayers and make a vow, they would soon be separated for ever, each in their enclosed order, singing to the glory of a God who had treated them so savagely. So, what about me?

'I don't think they'll be prepared to have me at Argenteuil . . .'

He could not be bothered to laugh.

'I've spoken about you to Abbot Adam.'

'I see you've arranged everything for each of us.'

I had tried—but, I fear, in vain—to keep my voice calm and free of any aggression.

'Do as thou wouldst.'

I accompanied him as far as the bishop's house. At a time when the king was working towards the consolidation of his power by making alliances and striking a blow against unruly vassals, the bishop was busy making repairs to his house. There were workers everywhere in his apartments and there wasn't a single corner where they weren't busy building or decorating, sculpting or painting.

Gerbert was as stockily built as Abelard, and about the same age, but he had the plumpness and dancer's elegance of a man who visited Rome frequently. He had put on his stole and was holding his crozier. Standing beside his throne, tonsured, and wearing a red surcoat, with a heavy gold chain around his neck, was the monster whom Bernard of Clairvaux had already denounced, Abelard's friend Stephen de Garlande who, together with his brothers, held the key posts in the kingdom. His nose was so long that it produced a shadow on his thick, almost violet lips; he had the fine hands of a musician and a strangler. Last of all, in the background, there was a smaller man I didn't know.

'His Holiness the Pope is dead,' said the bishop.

'Again!'

The ironic exclamation came from Garlande, 'You haven't convened us to elect a new one, have you? After all, we're all men of God in this room . . .'

The bishop took no notice; he knew that Garlande, an adulterous archdeacon and perhaps a sodomite, who was obsessed with money, had once wanted his position and had schemed in brutal fashion to achieve his purpose; he could not have forgotten that after his defeat he had used his influence to favour his own ends and that his choice was not necessarily—in Yves de Chartres' opinion—one of unimpeachable purity. To make matters worse, Garlande had become the principal adviser of a king who was still young and weak, yet forceful and decisive, who had an exalted notion of his responsibility, but felt threatened on all sides.

'My friends,' said the bishop, 'on behalf of our dear and respected master of schools, the attack on whose person has deeply upset all of us, the blame for whose spilled blood falls upon us, and whose shame is ours as much as his, I wanted to . . .'

Garlande made a gesture of impatience.

'. . . I wanted to show how resolutely we have been following his business and how, apart from the sincere feelings it induces in us . . .'

'You're not going to cry?' Garlande intervened. 'Your tears will finish us off! So, in short, you have nothing to say.'

'If you would let my lord bishop finish . . .' said the small man without moving, and with such shyness that it was impossible to read into it any lack of respect.

'Who's this?' asked Garlande, without looking at him and addressing himself to the bishop, as if he were speaking about a chest of drawers or a crust of bread.

'A young adviser to Abbot Adam of Saint-Denis. He was extremely successful in some tricky assignments—even those involving Rome.'

'What's his name?'

'Suger.'

'But I know you! You were at the Estrée school with His Majesty.'

'I had that honour, when I was still very insignificant and he was already very important.'

'I am much affected by this reunion,' said Abelard, 'but I thought that the crime committed against me was what these important characters were concerned with ...'

'I was saying,' Gerbert continued, clearing his throat, 'that we have suspended Canon Fulbert from his prebend and from all duties at the chapterhouse.'

'Suspended him?'

'Furthermore, we are actively pursuing the perpetrators of the ...'

The bishop, visibly embarrassed, searched for his words, looking up at his portrait of Pope Paschal II — unless it was that of his successor, Gelasius — and even at Garlande.

'... the attack.'

'Have you questioned Fulbert? Do you know who the people involved were? I mean — are you actively looking or are you ...'

'You doubt the bishop, my dear Peter,' said Garlande, bowing towards the prelate. 'I know that doubting is your profession — reasonable doubt — but how can you doubt that he is not actively — very actively — looking? Do you expect to know the results of his activity instantly? My Lord?'

The bishop blushed.

'As I was saying, we are hopeful ...'

'You see, hopeful.'

'... I mean we are assured, we are virtually certain ...'

The bishop fell silent; his hands were raised, his face flushed.

'While My Lord the Bishop was actively searching for these criminals,' said Garlande, 'with all the efficiency he has just outlined to you, we have captured them.'

Garlande had the satisfaction of seeing all eyes turned towards him.

'We have them and, if I may be permitted, My Lord, my dear brethren, they have lost theirs. I believe that their eyes have been gouged out as well, just for good measure. I can assure those sensitive souls (he turned towards Suger) that we have taken care to verify—and we don't need God's judgement, or the water torture or any other terrible ordeal for that—that they were guilty.'

'And Fulbert?' asked Abelard.

'Now there, my dear Peter, the canon is under the jurisdiction of the chapterhouse, and the chapterhouse comes under the bishop. You know how it goes: render to Caesar . . . I know it won't give you back . . . Forgive me.'

'My Lord?' said Abelard, walking over to the bishop in an almost threatening manner.

'We shall find him,' said Gerbert, 'we have already punished him and we shall punish him still further.'

Abelard glanced fleetingly towards me; I knew that he had sought vengeance more from an awareness of his own position than out of any strong concern. He could sense the despondency and pointlessness of this waiting. He sighed.

'I am personally instructed by Abbot Adam,' Suger intervened in a voice that was so low it forced everyone to strain their hearing, 'to confirm that the royal abbey'—he never stops talking about his royal abbey—is honoured to receive you, and to offer you its peaceful shelter for the sake of your teaching and so that you may rest.'

'Suger, you sound like an abbot,' said Garlande. 'And you,' he continued, turning to Abelard, 'you should listen to him. Revenge will get you nowhere. And failing God's justice, allow me to see that right is carried out . . . in my own way. Have I not already given you proof that I knew what to do?'

'We have to be done with this, my son,' said Gerbert.

'Done with me?'

'I didn't say that. I only . . .'

'You only . . .'

My friend had gone from anger to dejection in a flash. He looked at me again—without seeing me. He was alone. Eventually, he addressed Suger.

'Are you quite sure you want me to stay with you? You have

heard that I'm cumbersome, fractious, arrogant and disagreeable, and that I don't suffer fools gladly . . .'

'You're not going to persuade me that you're frightened of the company of kings Pépin and Hugh Capet, Dagobert and Henry I . . .'

He was obliged to stop there: in its monumental undertaking to unite the French dynasties, Saint-Denis had just experienced its first—and stinging—failure: the blow that Louis VI's father, Philip I, had inflicted on the abbey by preferring to be buried at Saint-Benoît-sur-Loire was still very recent.

'The fact is they're all kings,' said Abelard, 'but they're all dead—whereas I'm merely a minor king as far as my logic is concerned—but very much alive . . .'

'During the construction of the church of our holy abbot Fulrad,' said Suger courteously, 'in order to assist the monks, the men would harness themselves to ropes to help the cattle pull the columns up from the quarry. It is a place that is greater than those who reside there.'

'I know of nothing greater than the spirit of man.'

'Divine power?'

Abelard sighed.

'But yes, of course . . . You see how we could share the same cloister . . .'

Peter paused over the last word. Our lives and his teaching had, up until a few days ago, been so far removed from the cloister that the thought of it must have struck him as strangely new. It was true that the community at Saint-Denis did not have a reputation for being very strict.

'You would be initiated there by others, not by me, Master. You have no doubt heard that our temporal lives do not exactly match our spiritual ones. It is, alas, true. Abbot Adam is sending me to our provostship at Toury to instil a little order there. God willing . . .'

'I have gone,' said Garlande. 'Call on me if you need me. And above all, don't thank me . . .'

'I ask your forgiveness, Stephen. Thank you for having . . . and thank you for everything.'

Garlande laid his long, lean hand on Peter's shoulder. Without any warning, Heloise's words began buzzing about in my head: *my heart is not with me . . .*

The bishop's apartments were separated from the rest of the canonical buildings by the length of the nave—I felt at home at last in this old cathedral whose walls were falling down and which let in the rain.

'What does it matter?' said Abelard—and his voice echoed through the empty church. 'The master of schools has been castrated, the master of schools has been cloistered . . .'

It was the first time I had heard him refer directly to his mutilation. And instead of moaning about it, he sang a song.

As he walked among the ruins of Saint-Étienne, passing by Saint-Christophe and across the Pallu market, he was still singing joylessly, like an old lunatic with an ill-kempt tonsure, and people turned round as he passed by, muttering: 'It's him, it's Abelard . . .' and he would look round at them, continuing his singing, as if to say: 'Yes, it's actually me . . .' He quietened down once we had crossed the Pont and we began to wander about among the vineyards—Laas, Mauvoisin, Chardonnet. Our sandals were wearing out, and so we stopped outside a shoemaker's shop in the little village of Saint-Médard, where the cobbler repaired them while we waited and, when he had finished, he smeared them with some grease or ointment which we wished we could have applied to our souls.

'How do you find them, my friends?'

We left his little workshop feeling much better. I didn't reply —I didn't know what to say. These men of God made me want to vomit.

'The little fellow is great,' Peter said dreamily. 'As for the rest . . .'

He gestured as if he were sweeping the floor.

✦ ✦ ✦

I believe that Heloise escaped from the convent at Argenteuil that night and met her lover, Peter Abelard, in secret at the house where he was staying. I believe that she made her getaway with all the ease of a character in a dream, while the convent slept, and she rode to Paris wearing her midnight blue cloak over the habit which, in another flight, he had had made for her; the habit she would wear the next day when she took the veil, and for the rest of her life—if the dreary succession of days that lay ahead can be so described. I believe she left her horse at the entrance to the Close and, not stopping, she passed her uncle's house before slipping into the one where the master now resided. I believe he was awake: she found him and clasped him to her.

I wrote: I believe. That is not supposition, but Faith.

I believe: I have Faith in their love.

I believe that they spoke in words that could never be divulged and that they were like angels, all the fear and all the horrors of the past dissolving into the secrecy of the night; not only did they not suffer, but their love even earned them an eternal light, and though they did not know it, they were part of that light. I believe that that night was a perfect night of love—a love such as they had never known and would never know again—a night when all they heard was the throbbing of their heartbeats, when they touched each other's faces in the candlelight like blind people, like shy lovers. I believe that they kept their tears for the days that lay ahead, days of loneliness, days of despair—and that those tears were a work of art created for them alone, destined to evaporate with the dawn, when the bells would ring for Prime.

I believe that if I peered into my heart I even knew some of the words they said to one another—I believe that these words, these precise words they used—a man's words, a woman's words, words of desire and betrayal, words of passion and redemption, words of anger and words of forgiveness—were the first words of love that we were able to understand, and that therefore, after them, it was up to every man and every woman to make their own way and rediscover the paths into the labyrinth of their hearts again.

I believe that they occasionally fell asleep for a few moments — sometimes the one, sometimes the other — and that they awoke with a start — 'where were you, my love? Without you the path I tread is a tangle of brambles' — and, as in the fairy tales, their only dread throughout this vigil was the first glimmer of daylight.

I believe that at dawn she set out for Argenteuil without looking back, without further tears, and that she was greeted in silence by the prioress and the abbess, who took her by the hand and led her to a cell where she remained alone in prayer until the time came.

I believe that at the moment the veil fell over her forehead she clenched the parchment on which, according to the Rule, she had written her vows and held it so tightly that the knuckles of her fingers turned white. As she walked past us on her way to the altar, she slowed her pace and spoke the words of the *Pharsalia*:

> *O noble husband,*
> *Too great for me to wed, was it my fate*
> *To bend that lofty head? What prompted me*
> *To marry you and bring about your fall?*
> *Now claim your due, and see me gladly pay . . .*

We had mentioned these words the previous day and she had spoken them as a challenge and as a joke between us: the words Cornelia had spoken to Pompey, Heloise addressed to Abelard. There were no tears — she was superb and she was gone before he could say goodbye. She made a sign to him, as if she were stroking his cheek or his neck (these very simple gestures which they had been able to make freely, even up until the last night, and which from then on would only be made in dreams). Then she went on her way as the singing of the choir soared.

Three day later, in the basilica of Saint-Denis, I thought of this moment as I listened to Peter Abelard, who was on his knees in front of the magnificent cross of Saint-Éloi, surrounded by the glitter of gold and precious stones that were meant to suggest the shimmer of paradise, recite in his strong voice, the voice of a teacher, a passage of text that for once had not been written by him and in which he could not allow himself the slightest authorial affectation: 'Before God and the holy martyrs Denis, Rusticus and Eleutherius, in the presence of my father Adam, I promise stability, a religious life and obedience according to the rule of St Benedict.' Then he repeated three times the verse: 'Raise me up, Lord, according to your word and I shall have life. Grant that I may not be confounded in your expectation.'

It seemed to me that on the third utterance (although I was already far away, walking backwards, through the darkness of a side chapel at the back of the church, and I was hearing instead the words of Heloise, *my heart is not with me . . .*) he paused before saying 'in your expectation', but it no longer mattered, for I was already pushing open the little door that opened onto the cathedral square, where I could hear the blare from the great market at the Saint-Denis fair. I had once and for all entered my state of solitude and turmoil, and what bound me to my master and to the woman he loved seemed — without my having been allowed to bid them one word of farewell — to have been destroyed for ever.

Part III

The Beauty of Thy House

17

EVERY MORNING when we awoke, it raised our spirits to see that Christian was already at work.

However early I bestirred myself, he had already left our hut and could be found in the church. At first, it was to supervise the clearing away of rubble, and later the cleaning. Then he would prepare his plaster and try out the pigments in a rather strange way: when he liked a colour, he put a little on the tip of his index finger and tasted it.

Before our work began, the archbishop arrived from Bourges — and, of course, there were also the Bishop of Orléans, priests and abbots, knights from all over the Orléanais and the Berry, village people from Brinay, all squeezed into the little church consecrated to St Aignan and admiring the reliquary containing a few threads from the saint's tunic as if it housed the blessed sacrament. After the consecration, all these fine people set off for home and it felt as if we were taking possession of our domain: the church was ours.

It was neither Cluny nor Saint-Denis: it was a little country church in which the choir was separated from the nave by a simple arch and where the flat chevet was adorned by a single window: here there was no need for subtle calculations to discover where God's light entered.

I don't think the peasants cared for us very much: it's not that they did anything hostile or made dismissive remarks—but there was a silence when we arrived at a farm to buy eggs, and mutterings behind our backs. People around there didn't like to be disturbed, and the common view was that artists, who never stay put, lie somewhere between minstrels and beggars, and very much below pilgrims. I didn't complain, and neither did Christian or Gislebert, and I even enjoyed the beauty of this newly-found freedom.

It is true that our freedom was dependant upon certain obligations to Archbishop Léger of Bourges: Christian was entrusted with the decoration of the church at Brinay (together with a list of items, a note of the quality of the pigments used, timing etc.) in return for a fee of eighty Orléanais livres on completion of the chevet and the north and south walls. I excluded the arch from the contract in one of those absurd displays of obstinacy that one sometimes adopts in these kinds of discussions in order to achieve an interest-free agreement. On the other hand, I did obtain an early advance payment.

To tell the truth, I negotiated with pleasure despite my groans, increasing our imaginary requirements so as to obtain what I really wanted. There still remained the schedule of payments. Amid the roars of laughter that accompanied the signing of the contract, I heard old Léger say in jest that the signing of a contract was the beginning of a long negotiation—but I knew that it was not a joke and could foresee journeys to Bourges, days spent waiting, our work being delayed, threats and flattery. That did not bother me either—and after what I saw in Italy, there was nothing here that could surprise me.

Ever since our first meeting, I'd wondered whether he remembered that I'd seen him with Abbess Petronilla, standing behind the bed of branches upon which Robert of Arbrissel died. I didn't think so—I'm never dismayed when people don't remember me—I'd even say I find it reassuring and comforting. I said that Christian woke up before dawn. In actual fact I don't even know when he woke up, nor how he managed not to step on a single branch and slip out of the shelter with the lightness of the breeze. He told us that the further the work progressed the earlier he would rise.

Gislebert used to disappear for entire days on end — nights too — and return without offering any explanation; a short while ago, he simply opened his hands and they were covered in a rich, brown clay.

'I found some ochre,' was all he said.

In his characteristic way, Christian looked, tasted it and smiled.

'It's good,' he said, rather like a cook who is trying out a sauce.

Gislebert and I helped Christian to prepare his plaster, his undercoats and his colours: red or yellow ochre, copper green, charcoal black, green or white clay, and minium.

When he climbed up on to his scaffolding (something else Gislebert had made) and sketched crowds and horses by hand, we stayed behind; he drew for hours, without saying a word, and then he began talking, and so did Gislebert and I, and we related these stories to one another as we saw them. Frequently, Gislebert scarcely knew them, and in this way Christian taught us that pictures have to be drawn with the eyes of a child. Then he showed us his sketches, and Gislebert, whom he nevertheless invited to speak freely, merely permitted himself some trifling comments — a hand, a hairstyle. Since Christian pressed him, our beanpole pulled back his long locks, fixed his bulbous eyes on him and said in a menacing voice that sounded almost funny:

'You're the artist here.'

It was Gislebert who built our huts and who worked miracles with his hands, but he was also the one who did the heavy work, where his strength — which was a mystery to us, for his bony body resembled a burned tree — never failed to impress us, as did his natural grace.

Christian had begun by painting three background layers — a

yellow ochre, a green and a red ochre—which would give the facial expressions in his story a sense of undulating motion. Then he put in the friezes which would separate the two tiers of the scenes. I didn't have the intimate knowledge he did (for he knew exactly which way the ass that is carrying Jesus would point his ear), but I was already familiar with the space that he was demarcating and colouring.

'We must do,' he often said simply, his face lit up by an inner light, 'what we have to do. But we must do it now . . .'

I admired this simplicity and determination—and above all I admired what was not yet completely revealed to us, as if he had already actually painted it but was waiting for our eyes to be ready before releasing the wall coverings that concealed the fresco.

In the evening, when we lit our fire before falling asleep to the babble of the stream, he and Gislebert described that magical moment when none of the work has yet been done, when everything is at planning stage in the mind, but when the different component parts that are already perfectly in tune with each other, come together and harmonise. If they close their eyes, they can see the whole project completed, and with even greater clarity than when it has become a fresco or a sculpture: for one man's vision can never encompass the full richness of the scenes, or detect the harmonies and rejoice in them, as at that moment when a perfect mental equilibrium is realised between a man's sensibility and a much older symbolism that is more powerful than him, but which reveals its uniqueness through him. A mind with the potential for dreaming: this is the complete man.

Gislebert was more of a fatalist, and Christian had the more decisive mind; the former had a more innocent, childlike and stronger faith, and the latter had the gift of perfect intuition; but in both cases their work was the art of submission.

The weather grew colder; the damper air meant there were no longer butterflies in the church. Gislebert's huts may have been solidly built, and their roofs made of branches and leaves kept out the rain, but we observed the approach of winter with slight anxiety. After all, we were not hermits: we were quite happy to 'return to the desert', but it was in order to find men there. Then there was a worry that Christian didn't talk to us about, a reservation that he did not wish to share with us and about which it was therefore pointless to question him.

When the first heavy rains of autumn arrived, a skinny, hirsute child came running up to inform us that his father was offering us his barn 'on condition that you don't set fire to it'. The remark indicated the sort of man his father was: warm and gruff, and he had a little squashed tomato in place of a nose; Claude had left his sparse native homeland in Marciac, 200 leagues further south, to set up as a blacksmith here. Why? How? He said nothing and didn't want to say anything: his blue eyes shone with honesty, and humour occasionally, but they were clouded by a suffering that he preferred to keep to himself.

Without any fuss or formality, there was an immediate sense of kinship between Christian and him, an attentiveness that was apparent in the smallest things: the smithy and the painter had experienced similar storms beneath different skies.

Thanks to Claude, we spent the first winter feeling less anxious. And what a winter it was—the ice froze the trees deeper than an axe could cut and so we had to give up making fires in the church. Christian could hardly hold his brushes and only Gislebert seemed unconcerned by the cold, dashing about the countryside and the frost-covered woods as he did when they were in bloom.

At around Christmas time, Léger sent one of his sub-deacons to enquire about how the works were progressing. The man arrived looking like a snow statue and to warm him up we needed to beat his frozen feet with a mallet—to say nothing of a few good swigs of a marc brandy that Christian kept for better days. After that we had to feed him—and, of course, there was no question of watering down his wine.

The ass wasn't even grateful for the meal. However much we

explained to him that it was impossible to start work *al fresco* when it was cold, he peered at the layers of colour and the friezes suspiciously. All of a sudden, Christian's credentials appeared questionable, and it transpired that I had been the pupil of a dangerous master and that Gislebert had no cathedral tympanum to his credit, but only small churches which no one knew anything about . . . if they existed at all. Calmly, Christian told him how, for the past four springs, he had worked with the master of Berzé at the Chapelle des Moines, above Cluny—in particular he showed him his sketches for the Annunciation, the Magi, Herod, the Flight into Egypt and the Wedding Feast, in which he brought all these scenes to life. The sub-deacon raised an eyebrow and said:

'I know it has nothing to do with me, since you have agreed to it all with Monseigneur the Archbishop, but why the Massacre? It's a . . . an unexpected subject.'

Herod ordering the Massacre of the Innocents, and the massacre itself, were to go above the Presentation in the Temple and the Flight into Egypt, separated by a geometrical pattern in which only white would be added to the ochres and the green.

'It's to show that Jesus is one of these children,' said Christian with a smile, 'and that his mother, instead of clasping him to her and escaping on a donkey, led by Joseph—here (he pointed to a blank space below)—could also be another mother—there—distraught with sorrow (and he indicated another equally blank space above).

'I see,' said the sub-deacon, who saw nothing.

'I am relieved and honoured that you understand us,' said Christian without the least irony—and Gislebert and I had to stop ourselves from laughing.

The idiot droned on and it was a relief to see him leave the following morning, when the weather was slightly warmer. I admired Christian and his angelic patience.

'I know what I'm doing,' he said. 'Did you think I was going to get myself in trouble for some little sub-deacon?'

Opposite the barn, Gislebert had left an enormous block of stone — discovered I know not where, and he had a way of looking at you which discourages questions — which was the height of a man and which watched over us at night. Something about its shape made one think of a pagan cult. One evening, carved into a niche, we discovered the body of a woman and a face that stood in relief in the stone — just the oval shape that extended from the chin to the cheeks, a smooth line. Day after day (and hardly ever in our presence, as if he wished to apprise us of a secret we knew nothing about), Gislebert applied the cheekbones, the veil over the hair, the gash of the lips, the eyes that grew rounder and more surprised, and the curve of the shoulder where a child would nestle.

We might call her the Virgin Mary — but we could call her by the names of all women, and suddenly, as I gazed at her, I was shocked by the memory of Heloise.

The words of love that I had kept secret rose to my lips, and since the words would not tumble out quickly enough for me to say what I wanted, I was silent, and as I watched all this light gleam in the cold of a winter lunchtime, I dedicated it to Heloise in the secrecy of my heart.

After that, my nights were again disturbed.

A year passed, which I consider to have been a happy one, in which we gradually stopped pretending we were living in exile and allowed ourselves to be invited to other people's gatherings and musical soirées, celebrating their marriages, mourning their dead, even joining in some night-time pagan ceremonies which the peasants continued to dedicate to a spring or a tree.

Whether or not Bourges paid, we needed additional funds, and I did my best to protect Christian from these concerns. He escaped into a world we found increasingly difficult to follow. The answers to the questions that he asked himself came not so much from us as from the images that came to him in his troubled dreams from which he awoke in a sweat. When we urged him to rest and relax, he replied that his master, the one from Berzé whose name he never mentioned, always quoted Ovid: *it is not enough to want; to succeed one needs to desire.*

He therefore set to work every day—and when the springtime came, every night too—first putting his red ochre design in place with his well-sharpened stylet, applying it quickly to the still damp plaster—and then, later, repeating every detail, tirelessly until it was dry.

I remember that he spent a long time gazing at the still blank faces of the women whose children had been massacred, their hunched, perfectly parallel figures and their long hands already expressing suffering.

'That's not enough,' he would say, his mind preoccupied—and if this suffering was not plain to see, it would never be enough.

Finally, he used a splash of green clay to depict quite simply the great pain on these impenetrable gazes—and the effect was startling, so much so that Gislebert and I cried out in amazement.

'Christian, it's splendid!' said the stonemason, who was normally sparing with his compliments.

He had lit some torches and, while the nave was in shadow, the choir was gleaming in the procession of lights, lending movement and life to all the figures. The philosophers and the writers of the *lectio divina* used to speak to us about mystery and grace, and of man's tragedy and the hope of salvation: their words had never affected me as this family had.

'Do you think so?' asked Christian wearily. 'I no longer know, I can no longer see. It seems to me that I've taken it all from an old evangelistary. Yesterday, I felt confident—let us call it God's inspiration. Today, there's an empty space in front of me in which the lines and colours float.'

'Look at your women,' said Gislebert, 'look how they weep.'

'Look at them, my friend, and remember Jeremiah: *A voice is heard in Ramah, lamentation and bitter weeping. Rachel is weeping for her children; she refuses to be comforted for her children, because they are not.'*

'Perhaps it's just that I'm tired.'

'You climbed up the ladder, with the angels . . .'

'And now I am lying on the ground and I find the stone very hard for my old bones.'

He was able to laugh, a cracked laugh accompanied by a cough I had never heard before.

That evening we made him drink some wine and made him promise that he would not work the next day, but that he would roam the woods with us and bathe in the streams.

After that he painted horses and men, and mainly the face of Christ, with greater affection and freedom, and with a manual dexterity that we had seen nowhere else before, and which I — in my ignorance and Gislebert with all his knowledge — admired greatly.

Christ is both man and God, so the scriptures, the Fathers of the Church and the councils tell us. Christian depicted him very much as a man — and therefore our brother, to whom we could confide our troubles — yet he showed him equally in his divine state, endowed with that life of the Father through which our sins might be forgiven.

The blacksmith never asked what we were going to do next; when we ate at his house (which we did often and increasingly as the work advanced), he would place his big hands on the table and, after grace, he would close his eyes for a second and recover his breath; his wife patted his forehead gently with her tiny hand, which he held by the wrist before taking it in his with all the delicate roughness of the meek in heart.

We were nearing the end; Gislebert had carved figures which ran the length of the barn. Claude did not object, and he would sometimes stop and contemplate the statue of a holy martyr. The only thing he asked, after deliberating for several nights, was that we remove a devil with a gaping mouth, whose presence prevented him from sleeping. Gislebert and I went and drowned the devil.

Christian was now ill and feeble. He had asked me to cut his hair and his beard—ever since he had painted my body there was an inexplicable physical intimacy between us, a closeness of the flesh which had nothing to do with desire or possession; I felt frightened the first time I looked into his feverish eyes in the middle of his pale, naked face. He was no longer the blond prophet who could see more clearly than men—he was more a man who could feel life slipping away between his fingers faster than a fistful of sand.

Inside the church it was midday and he had been harmed by the light—he had lost his balance and I had had to hold him in my arms.

I now asked him daily when I could go to Bourges to tell the archbishop that his church was ready and that he could come and consecrate it (there was no longer any question of more money, for we had spent every last centime). Every day he told me that I must wait—and that the work was a long way from being completed. The time came when, knowing as I did the fresco and all its details perfectly, I was able to see that he had not done a thing, not retouched a colour for a whole week. But I said nothing to him because he was my brother and I loved him.

Then he noticed the arch.

His face lit up and he asked me for his stylet and his wax tablets.

'But I've fought so that you wouldn't have to paint it! And there's no more money coming in, not a thing . . .'

'I've left it out . . .'

'I can always discuss a last additional payment.'

'Go and discuss it, my friend. But just leave me to my own devices . . . And I promise you that when it's painted that will be the end of it and we can leave.'

He worked away, sketching daily life and work as he knew

them. He said that when he drew his models he thought of Claude, and of his hands, and that he was this peasant who bent down to reap and sow, striving to make the earth yield its fruit, and to domesticate the animals. He said that all of this was beautiful and that it was good that Jesus should see it and tell his father about it, so that he might remember that it was sometimes the same men who worked the land and who said their prayers.

The work progressed quickly and smoothly, without any revisions or regrets; it was not the time for further hesitations or rejections. Slowly but surely, the arch became filled up with humble-looking figures: Christian needed just a few weeks for work that would normally have taken him almost a year to complete — and he was growing ever weaker, refusing medicinal plants and doctors, refusing wine and beer, eating scarcely any meat, and pretending to be satisfied with some very black bread and bean soup.

Lastly, he filled the space representing the month of February: it was a peasant (and, again, I could not help thinking of Claude, with his weariness that resembled grief) warming his hands by a fire, an exhausted man who needed rest.

Another spring beckoned. Christian asked Gislebert to remove from the church the scaffolding platform he had used. As they returned from the fields before nightfall, the peasants strolled past this curious construction of planks which Christian, as he tried out his experiments, had covered almost entirely with paint, and where angels' and devils' wings, saints' halos and delicate horses' harnesses were all mingled together.

All that day and the following one, we cleaned the church after these years and months of work, and the pots, the colours, the scrapers, the brushes, the stylets and the cloths all disappeared. We eagerly burned anything that could be burned. Only the scaffolding remained. Gislebert refused to put it in the fire and I was of the same view; it remained standing in front of the church, like a crucifix bearing the painter's dreams and regrets.

Christian could hardly walk; and yet at dawn the next day, it was once again he who woke us up. Kneeling down on the cold stone, we said the first prayers in our church. Very soon men would come here to hear Mass, to confess their crimes and to warm themselves when it was cold.

Having touched hands, we took one another's and gave each other the kiss of peace, weeping like children as we did so—and it was wonderful to behold the smile and the joy on the face of our friend who was soon to die.

While we were sharing our joy, we had not heard the door open. Throughout this time, the local people had seldom opened it; to begin with I had thought it was from lack of interest, even mistrust, and I now realised it was through shyness.

It was not the Massacre of the Innocents or the Wedding Feast at Cana that Claude admired: it was his arch, in which he could decipher each month with a pride that made his eyes open wide. He studied each panel solemnly—and in his mind a year was unfurled, complete with its harvests and winter, and with the old customs reproduced—and when he'd finished he looked very moved and he took Christian's hands in his.

Afterwards, he glanced round the little church and in his own way he read there everything there was to know about human destiny and Christ's teaching. He did not know Herod's name, but he had seen powerful men giving orders—out of spite, and with total lack of concern—to do evil; he was aware of the dignity of Joseph guiding the donkey upon which his wife and his child were escaping from persecution; he had seen demons tempting him in nightmares, and he recognised their faces for the first time.

From time to time, he turned to Christian, Gislebert or me, and nodded his head as he said:

'All that, it's ours.'

He paused finally at the women upon whose faces Christian had depicted suffering with a single streak of green; his eyes closed and, with a lump in our throats, we could see a tear well up on that rough face.

'You haven't worked at all badly,' he said to Christian. 'I don't regret lending my barn to you, you and your knavish friends.'

It was the longest sentence that we had ever heard him speak. He took our hands in the same way he had clasped Christian's, then he walked towards the door. In front of the church porch he noticed the scaffolding platform.

'What's that?'

'It's what I use to work,' said Christian.

'Will you give it to me?'

Christian replied with a smile and the smithy heaved the structure onto his shoulder. Occasionally, he would stop on the road, put it down and look at it before setting off again.

The three of us remained in the church for a while, enjoying the silence, the peace and the light. I thought to myself that there couldn't be many such moments in life and that there must be an art in prolonging them, even if it were just for the time it takes to say a prayer. Rejoice, I told myself, in the perfect stability in which your strength has played its part but which, unlike these thrusts that hold up the vault, may collapse at the first breath of wind — leaving only the memory and the nostalgia.

'Aren't you going to put your signature to it?' asked Gislebert.

Christian was lying on the ground, looking up at the wooden ceiling.

'I've finished,' he said. 'I am resting in front of the fire that does not warm me — which will never warm me again — and my hands are frozen.'

'One day, I'll sign my work,' said Gislebert.

He stretched his spidery body and I helped him lift Christian to his feet. He had become like a small child who couldn't walk, but we had now lost any hope of teaching him. The short walk to the stream therefore took a long time.

For our last night, Christian had wanted us to sleep beside the little river, the noise of which had lulled us to sleep up until our first winter. Gislebert cut us a bed from branches and leaves, lit a fire, and wrapped Christian in a blanket that did not warm him.

We gazed at the stars and Gislebert drank wine with me. We let a few drops slip through our friend's lips, but he almost choked.

He tried to laugh it off.

'Can't manage any more,' he said. 'Even if I wanted to sin, I wouldn't be able to.'

I remembered the images he had painted on my body; I had always wanted to ask him about something that ought to remain a mystery, but the words kept refusing to leave my lips. Eventually, I made up my mind.

'The image?' he said with difficulty. 'Didn't the image wear off a long time ago?'

'Yes, brother—but you can't leave me with that.'

'Why not? It will give you something to ponder on for the rest of your life.'

He made out my face in the vague light of the flames flickering in the breeze.

'No, I wouldn't do that to you. Don't be sad, my friend. Nothing is ever sad, and tonight is less sad than any other . . . I wrote: In the beginning . . .'

St John, again . . . And now I knew what lay at the beginning when the end came: the letter Omega had been painted upside down on Jesus's forehead. There was nothing he disclosed that made my destiny different from that of any other man; and yet I felt deeply moved within myself. Christian's message had been wiped away—the path my heart and my soul were to take was still to be found.

Christian died that night after confessing in our presence the sins of a man who had led a very innocent life. As in the church, the noise of the animals, the sounds of the wind and the stream, blended with our grief and the certainty of what must be, to give us a sense of presence and reality. A man died while the earth lived, breathed and murmured—everything led towards the same place.

'Lord,' he mumbled at last in a voice that was still gentle, still strong, 'Lord, I have loved the beauty of thy house.'

His last breath passed with the breeze and our tears flowed with the stream.

On the next day, I took the road to Bourges in order to tell them that the work was completed. Gislebert accompanied me for several leagues and then left me. Claude, who gazed at flames every day of his life, had watched us leave, leaning against the scaffolding, one hand held over his eyes to protect himself from the burning sun.

There's a haze in my mind: I who see certain things—some of them very ancient, which may not even belong to my own life—so clearly that they are before my eyes on even the mistiest nights. I can recall nothing of how we parted—neither the words (perhaps there were none, just silence), nor the movements, nor the shadow of a tree.

No, I see nothing: a little dust has blown up, and that is all.

18

ALL I could see at first was a pair of naked legs with bulging veins, and a hand scratching them.

'Cervelle! What are you doing there?'

We are in Paris, beside the Seine, on the morning of Palm Sunday, 1122, and more or less everybody—ordinary people as well as grandees, butchers and money-changers—is at Mass, except for Jews and cripples, and I'm not even sure about the latter.

'I'm washing my arse, see. Remember how we used to go around with all our wooden letters tied to a string so that we wouldn't lose them . . . My first master—peace to his soul—used to beat us with it when we learned our lessons badly. He called that drumming in the alphabet through the skin on our backs . . .'

He shook his thin, ugly little face and smiled in amusement. He had that look of a child who was an old man.

'Why are you telling me this?' I asked.

'Because he used to come out with remarks that made us laugh. Such as: "Better to have a wet arse than an uneasy conscience." What brings you to Babylon?'

'I hoped I would find Sion . . .'

'You can always dream—this is a hellish place. There are as many whores as there are priests. Apparently, they all clubbed together to pay for a stained-glass window in Notre-Dame. The bishop does not approve . . .'

'You haven't mentioned Abelard . . .'

'I thought you were speaking on his behalf . . .'

'You know very well I've been away these past three years!'

'Do you really not know anything?'

Cervelle looked at me in surprise. He wiped his legs with the folds of his somewhat dirty coat.

'Come, I'll take you to Samuel's house. Bishops, popes, masters of the schools come and go — but Samuel is still there.'

We climbed up the bank towards the Petit Pont. Everything was familiar, yet everything had changed: it seemed to me that the excitement and bustle in the city had increased even more, and that houses had sprouted like mushrooms and were already driving away the fields and vineyards. They were repairing the ruins of the ramparts, rebuilding the royal palace, and the work on the Grand Pont had been completed; further off, towards the Grève, soared the new tower of the Butchers' church. Cervelle told me that the tolls had increased, as well as the taxes on market stallholders. He told me that at the last Lendit Fair there were more merchants than ever, from all over Europe and the Levant; he told me that on the right bank of the river, in the direction of Saint-Denis, hamlets were taking root around the religious foundations, and that new houses were also being built, as well as cemeteries and new markets. This village liked to think of itself as a town; it had become one, expanding by the day on the expectation of a few future wealthy men and many newly impoverished ones.

Samuel welcomed me as if I had been there only yesterday, drinking his ale. He made his comic bow and gave his familiar greeting.

'Speak, Lord, your servant Samuel is listening . . .'

The room, furnished like the dungeon of a crusader's castle, was unchanged. But whereas bishops and kings paid a great deal for their precious relics, Samuel had acquired a damaged shield or some coward's sword for nothing. We sipped his tepid beer.

'Abelard had scarcely been at Saint-Denis a few weeks,' said Cervelle, 'before he caused an almighty commotion, proclaiming that they were not living like monks, making them feel ashamed of their debauchery, and treating Abbot Adam as if he were a thief, a hypocrite and a corrupt pervert . . .'

I couldn't help laughing. This could be none other than Peter Abelard, our Breton champion, charging off into his tournament.

'When he had calmed down a little, they were happy to allow him to continue teaching in one of their priories, hoping that concerns of theology would keep him sufficiently busy, and it's true that his mind was at ease for a few months, or seemingly so at least. He was working on his treatise . . .'

'On unity and the divine Trinity?'

'The very same. Frankly, I don't always know what's come over him. What's more, he doesn't either . . .'

'What do you mean?'

'To cut a long story short, let us say that there were rumours circulating about him. As you know, people have never liked him much and he does have a talent for making himself unpopular. His accident didn't help matters — quite the contrary. He sees himself as a man of God who has been punished but purified; others see him as a strange, slightly gruesome creature. Hearing him giving lectures on morality is one thing; but to see him tackle the Mystery, Love, the very Subject itself — I think that even if he had copied out the whole of the Council of Nicaea and *The City of God*, whatever he said would have been scandalous. The fact remains that in this climate of insinuation he thought it was clever to attack his former master Roscelin, who had sent him an abusive letter, which circulated all over Paris and delighted his enemies, for all its absurd excesses. But then Peter summoned a council at Soissons, where he imagined he would easily prevail, in the presence of the papal legate. The result was that it was our Peter who found himself reading the Athanasian Creed in tears, while the crowd insulted him and his books were burned. His enemies had succeeded in having him condemned on generalities, without a single one of his propositions being seriously examined—his audacity, his personality . . .'

'His own worst enemy . . .'

'Look, I wasn't there, but I think it must have been appalling. I saw him when he was put under surveillance at Saint-Médard for a while and he told me that it was a greater humiliation than any he had experienced.'

'He knows what he's talking about . . .'

'And his humiliation was not made any easier by the fact that the matter was settled in less time than it takes to utter the words. The legate admitted that the situation was beyond him, the condemnation was not even brought to the attention of the pope (by the way, did you know that he, too, had died?), and our man was set free. Three months later, he started all over again, basing his argument on some text or other of Bede's in order to pour doubt on the famous document written by St Denys which Abbot Hilduin had constituted at the time of Emperor Charlemagne.'

'Did he tell them that everything they based their facts upon were fabrications created by their own abbot?'

'Not just tell them; he wrote it down. The scandal was so terrible that he was obliged to write a letter of retraction to Abbot Adam.'

'He wrote a retraction?'

'Well, a retraction which, if you read it carefully, retracted nothing, and apologised without making any apologies. An "Abelardism". And now he's floating on a sea of hatred and reprobation. And since Adam has just died and an unknown, or virtually unknown, fellow has been elected abbot . . .'

'What's his name?'

'He's the son of peasants who presented him as an oblate at Saint-Denis. He was educated at Estrée where the king was his fellow pupil—if you please! He's called Suger.'

I could not contain a cry of surprise.

'Do you know him?'

'I've seen him . . .'

A familiar shudder went through me. There. I was back—and everything was as if I had never left town.

Eventually, I dared raise the question that had been on the tip of my tongue ever since we'd been together:

'And Heloise?'

'I know nothing about Heloise,' said Cervelle.

The abbot's lodgings opened onto the rue de la Chevalerie on one side, and the Cour du Trésor on the other. Through the window, above the extension of the guest house, the buttresses on the south side of the abbey and the shadow of the tower could be seen.

You sensed that hardly had little Suger been elected than he found himself quite at home. Saint-Denis was where he had been brought up as a child. Were each one of us to design in our imagination a city within a city, then this would be precisely his concept of such a place, with its ramparts and its churches, its cemetery, its fortifications and its market-place . . . He had learned to read here—and everything there is to know about life, apart from how to catch trout with one's hands, he acquired in the shadow of kings. This durability and this faith in a future that would soon work wonders derived from this constant communion with the past.

'You grew up in their shadow too,' he said with a smile.

He had that rare ability of apparently dispelling any distance between himself and the person he was talking to and making you feel immediately that you were the most important person ever to visit him and that no business—even the complicated matter of the king's displeasure over his election—could be more urgent than this meeting.

'You escaped.'

'*There went up a smoke out of our nostrils* . . . Now tell me, to what do I owe the honour of this visit?'

Excessive compliments—what honour could the Abbot of Saint-Denis possibly glean from receiving a poor, unknown clerk?—gave the hierarchy a reputation for rather cruel subtlety.

'Although I haven't seen him for three years, I believe I may be able to settle the difficulties you are experiencing with one of your residents to everybody's satisfaction . . .'

'Our Christ-like philosopher?'

He said this somewhat sadly.

'You're right, he does cause me great concern. And I don't know where it's all going to end. I'll speak to you frankly, since you're his friend. I've seen him; he won't hear a word about it; he's convinced he's the greatest man in the world and that everyone is persecuting him.'

'Soissons . . .'

'Yes, indeed, Soissons . . . He really should have thought about Soissons. Was he not looking for trouble? Anyway, I despair of reforming him when our dear father Adam, in his goodness, has failed completely.'

'Allow him to leave.'

Suger did not even blink an eyelash.

'Never,' he said softly.

'You yourself say that there's nothing you will be able to do with him.'

'You don't understand: he's impossible, but he's famous and he belongs to us, at Saint-Denis. I cannot permit him to leave. It would be as if I were breaking up . . . let's say, a piece of the shrine . . .'

He smiled at his blasphemous comparison.

'Then keep him. But let him leave.'

'You're speaking in riddles, young man, and without obliging you to go, time marches on . . .'

'Let me take him away to a place of solitude, a desert where you won't hear anyone talk about him again, where he will set up a hermitage which will belong to Saint-Denis.'

'Him, in a hermitage? He's incapable of spending a day on his own. And without speaking? To humiliate him properly you would have to cut out his tongue!'

'You don't know him . . .'

'I know him only too well. But I might approve of your idea —even if I don't like your reasons. Let me think about it.'

'May I also . . .'

'No, my child. Another time, perhaps. But come back. And stay with us. We have . . .'

He appeared to hesitate—he was laying on the charm.

'We have wonderful plans for this place. And I need people like you to carry them out. In the meantime, may you be successful in this mission you have undertaken. Farewell.'

I left Abbot Suger feeling astonished with myself: I still wanted to rescue my master.

Women frighten them.

They pray to the Virgin Mary, but they're thinking about Eve —and it's Eve whom they see in every female shape or form. Those who are most chaste they accuse of concealing their charms; those who are brazen they stone. Those who keep silent they accuse of harbouring shameful desires; those who talk too much have their tongues cut out. They make fun of the ignorant ones; the clever ones make them fear impiety. The ugliest make them laugh; the most beautiful make them want to kill.

They are hideous.

I am like them.

I began trembling at the very notion that it might be possible to see her again.

As long as I was far away from her, distance and time came together and the idea of not being with her, of not speaking to her or seeing her again, was almost endurable as long as these things were not recalled too specifically—and as long as that one word was not mentioned: *never*.

As I was approaching Argenteuil, I thought about what was wrong with this renunciation I had imposed upon myself, and from which I derived a sense of heroism, whereas in actual fact it was probably due to cowardice, a battle in which I had not taken part. I remembered the circumstances of this humbling experience I had taken such pleasure in. I was worse than the poltroons who had fled during the fighting in Jerusalem: I had gloried in my retreat. I had managed to glimpse grandeur in this rejection . . . I no longer understood the elation that sometimes gripped my heart when I was persuaded to serve a cause greater than mine.

I thought of Christian every day and night, without sadness, sensing his presence and transforming him into an angel who watched over me and spoke words which I did not necessarily want to hear: *to want is not enough; to succeed you must desire . . .* With him I never allowed myself to regret words that had not been exchanged, or gestures that had not been made. When I had doubts, I remembered the faces of the weeping women and the outstretched hand of Jesus; and above all, I saw Claude walking away, that strange piece of paint-covered scaffolding on his back. In this way, I came to accept everything — starting with Christian's death. St Augustine would have told me that this consolation was a grace that could come to me only from God. Abelard, a master of language, would say that for want of another word, this was indeed how we should refer to it. But whether it was a gift from God or the art of language, I felt unable to extend the enjoyment of this consolation beyond my friend — to Heloise and — should I say it? — to myself. I was dithering on the brink of my own destiny, concerned with my own troubles, and my feelings, at the height of the most violent emotion, always seemed to belong to people other than me.

Naturally, I said nothing to you, my love.

St Benedict tells us of the rungs on the ladder of humility and I believe him, but they are steps that descend into the darkest part of ourselves, to the place where we want to cry out, where we are nothing any longer, where no light—neither the sunlight nor that of the spirit—brightens our path any more, where all that remains is an abject terror.

I could have discussed these fears with Christian; with Arnold they would have disappeared in the sound of his laughter, and Gislebert would have made stone dreams of them. With Cervelle, who had become my enforced companion, I could say nothing, nor could I let him see this struggle, this wretched purity that clouded my soul.

I said that I was approaching Argenteuil . . . 'approaching' is a big word: I was going there as slowly as I could, as if it had been one of my longest journeys, in a land of exile. I walked as slowly as I could, refusing all offers to ride in a cart and ignoring any horses. Born under the sign of the scorpion, I amused myself by drawing shapes in the dust with my feet. When I caught sight of the church spire from the banks of the Seine, I thought I'd made a mistake: already? I sat down beneath an oak tree, panting for breath, and I thought about turning round and returning to Paris. I closed my eyes: I taught my fear a lesson.

It would be enough for me to catch a glimpse of you, for our eyes to meet, to hear the echo of your voice, and I would be filled with an inexplicable joy, a happiness that is forlorn, but which is sometimes enough to give us a reason to go on living.

I climbed the hill in the way an old man would. For a while, I leaned against the little chapel of St John the Baptist and surveyed the convent. The guest-house faced the same direction as the church, at right angles to the building containing the dormitory and the refectory.

Unlike Peter Abelard, I was not the sort who could walk into a convent and storm it with a barrage of words, upsetting everything in my path. Had I the choice, I would have waited until nightfall for the shadow of the enclosure to engulf me before arriving at dawn in the guise of a lay brother bent over by his load, or a priest going to say his office. I believed (but there again it was clear that weakness was my faithful ally) that the very act of waiting would provide a glimmer of hope in which dreams might be realised. So I wandered around the convent, staying close to the walls, and moving closer to the door whenever the bell for the canonical hours rang. I watched visitors come and go and I was jealous of the soles on their sandals.

As the day drew to a close I was filled with a kind of despair. I knocked at the door and, feeling momentarily inspired, asked to see the abbess. After all, had I not been in discussion with the Abbot of Saint-Denis himself? Was some minor convent abbess of questionable morality going to deter me? All of a sudden, and for no good reason, my heart was lifted by an irrational surge of courage.

I recognised her.

Three years ago — but she was then only the prioress — it had been she who had stood stock-still before me in the Close.

She knew who I was too — and that she had the choice between denying that she had ever seen me before and acknowledging the extraordinary intimacy that there was between us — because of Heloise and because of what she had confided in us, which I had not forgotten, and that incurable torment that she had admitted to. If sinning, as Jerome tells us, is merely 'to aim and miss', then this woman had not sinned: she was justified even in her faults.

There was a feigned severity in her expression that could deceive only those who were absent-minded. Only the experience of suffering could make someone look so wholly human.

'I am not worthy to be their servant,' she said, 'but they have chosen me to be their mother in spite of my protests. Three times they elected me and three times I refused, and it needed their sweet persistence — Heloise's especially — for me tearfully to accept. Yet every morning I wake up worn down by my weaknesses and doubts. People tell me that I should know myself better in order to become closer to God; the better I know myself the less I feel worthy of him.'

She paused: there was such a distraught expression in her eyes that I was unable simply to mumble trite words of consolation.

'I don't know how to help you, sister. If you doubt, then I am crushed by doubt; if you are a sinner, then I wallow in sin; if you feel weak, then I am already destroyed. All I can say is that, in the eyes of the Lord, such trials are necessary for all creatures who pass along the way . . .'

She smiled and pushed back a lock of hair that was protruding from her veil; it was with such gestures as this that she allowed one to see that she had once belonged to this world and that she occasionally returned to it for a brief moment.

'I don't want to talk about myself any more. And you haven't come on my account . . .'

I held up my hands in protest. She stopped me without further ado.

'Don't be mistaken, my friend. Let me tell you something: you have just heard these words from my heart as a stranger, as a pilgrim whom I encountered on the long journey and to whom, in a moment of weakness or absurd trust, I chose to tell a story that had nothing at all to do with him . . .'

'You didn't tell me anything . . .'

'I showed you the bleeding wound in my side.'

'I asked you for nothing.'

'Do not be afraid.'

It was a curious exchange in which I seemed to hear echoes of an old love affair and, despite myself, I was forced to recall feelings that bothered me. But who was talking to whom? Whose ghost was I? And why did I see the shadow of Heloise behind her? We gazed at one another with a friendliness that was mixed with an inexplicable violence, a curiosity that prompted a desire to touch — even to do harm.

'You want to see her,' she said at last.

'Yes.'

'Although the Rule forbids us ever to be alone with someone else, it was I who took her in three years ago, with the permission of the abbess who did not wish her to succumb to despair.

She no longer used to weep, you know, she was like a block of stone at all hours of the day, during the office, at Mass, at prayer and even in the middle of the night when I woke her to murmur some consoling words. How I loved her . . .'

Again she surprised me. After all, she had spoken like a nun, yet when she uttered those final words her sigh was almost that of a lover's.

'With every week and month that passed, I was delighted to see her come back to life and recover. She still cried out in the night and sometimes, during the offices, I would catch an unwary glance; but just when I thought she was going to die, I believe she decided to live. She was never subjected to an unpleasant word or a spiteful look here, or if she was, it was in the secrecy of the night, and she concealed it in the depths of her heart. The others love and respect her—I would almost say they fear her. They know that the price of her dignity has been bought at great cost. When I was elected abbess I wanted her to be my prioress and no one objected: when I die, shortly, she will be abbess . . .'

'I understand.'

'Do you really understand? Then you must see that your visit will upset the peace that has returned to her.'

'I realise that.'

'Did he send you?'

'I haven't seen him for three years.'

'Why have you come?'

I was unable to reply. I couldn't say: 'I love her.' I merely stared at her.

'I need her,' I said at last. 'But not for myself.'

'Stop talking to me in riddles.'

'It's for him.'

'You need her for him? Yet he did not send you . . . William, I don't know what you're talking about. I only know one thing: what she has told . . .'

'Well?' I asked, rather too keenly.

She smiled.

'I can see that it's not only for him that you need her.'

'Is it only on her account that you have agreed to speak to me?'

She looked confused, and hesitated.

'I don't see . . .'

'Did I make any secret of the fact that I loved her?'

'You tried. She told me that you were her only friend on this earth.'

'I would like to see her.'

She sighed.

'This conversation ought not to have happened and should not even have begun. It is happening: therefore it is as if your discussion had already taken place. You will see her, but . . .'

'But?'

'Nothing. You will see her, but you will not see her again. Farewell.'

She left after she had taken my hand in hers — another gesture that a virgin would not have made and which, having spoken severely as she did, could have several meanings.

I waited for Heloise in the little garden that divided the abbess's quarters from the convent buildings. Peach trees and herbal plants grew there. I was trembling.

Heloise was not good at disguising the fact that she had a body and did not even attempt to do so. Whether she was wearing the starry blue cloak she wore as a girl, or her black nun's habit, it was impossible to forget that you were in the presence of a woman. Nothing was exposed — there was no impropriety, nothing immodest — yet there was something about the texture of her skin and the inflexions of her voice that showed that she would never be totally released from the flesh; not because she was unable to detach herself, but because she did not wish to do so.

'I've missed you,' she said as she plucked a leaf from a tree.

With these lover's words she drew close to me and surrendered herself. To feel her body so close to mine took my breath away and aroused needs and desires that I thought were reserved for the darkness of nights on one's own—and yet at the same time she was so remote that had I moved my hand she would immediately have withdrawn and would have glared at me with contempt. The image of the abbess was before my eyes: the mystery of a woman who does not desire you is as great as that of a woman who does.

A dog accepts whatever it is given and a dog slobbers with gratitude. I drooled and my lust surged; the moisture came from her tears.

I knew the salty taste of a woman's belly; I had not been afraid to drink thereof, and I had known the liqueur of life—at first I thought that, having tasted the fruit of the tree, I would be punished—then I simply felt I was being smothered by this urge. Once more I had this strange sense of drinking straight from the earth, with my hands full, with my mouth full, and the earth heaving with the wild impulses that took possession of me: a little man burdened by forces stronger than myself and which could crush me if I did not yield to their control.

I kissed the tears on Heloise's face, to dry them, to rob him of a little of the pleasure he'd had.

We were in the *scriptorium*, in the very place where, three years earlier, Peter Abelard had mapped out her destiny in such a way that every day, until the day she died, was fixed, every word already said.

'I lied to them. I lied to Him. I lied to everyone; only in the secrecy of my heart is it known that I suffer and think of him every day. I have no regrets, I do not repent, and deep within me there is this desire, this anger too . . .'

Each word was spoken and enunciated with a rage that had long been contained. In her pale blue eyes there was a will and determination that would not diminish because time had no hold over them.

'My arrogance is boundless and my duplicity knows no limits.

I am able to recall these pleasures that are already long past without my body stirring, without my moving an eyelid. I have composed a liturgy to conceal the liturgy—an orgasm with each psalm, a surge of pleasure with each prayer. I find the source of fresh desire even in his abandoning me, and it still stirs me. I am —for ever—the Bride who waits, perfumed, oiled, apparelled.'

'His abandoning . . .'

'What else would you call it?'

'You know the calamities that befell him.'

'He will endure his calamities without me until he endures them with me. Only then will he find consolation.'

Such assurance amid this confusion. I was jealous of her— and of him, of course.

'Have you seen him?'

'Not yet. I came first to you.'

She shrugged disdainfully.

'I'm not the one who needs help . . .'

'Forgive me for my friendship.'

'I didn't mean to hurt you. But you know how his enemies pursue him—how they all want to destroy him . . .'

'I almost persuaded Suger to release him . . .'

'Really?'

'I still need to convince him that he must distance himself from the world . . .'

'Always saving him from himself . . .'

She could not help smiling.

'I want to help you do this.'

Parchment, pens and ink were kept in a chest by the fireplace. She made a sign for me to open it. She scribbled a few words very hurriedly, folded the sheet, and handed it to me.

'Give it to him with love from me.'

'I will. And as for us, we shall not see each other again.'

'Not see each other again? Is this what you want? What about your promise . . .'

'It's not me, it's your abbess . . .'

'Leave Alette to her grief. I am weak, but I am also strong. Nobody shall prevent me living life.'

She took my arm and we walked round the cloister in silence before returning to the garden through an archway between the refectory and the church. Nuns passed us, looking surprised. Heloise kept her arm in mine. We approached the gatekeeper's lodge.

'And you?' she said suddenly. 'You haven't told me anything...'

Her hold over me was so firm that I dared not even reply that one doesn't say anything to someone who has not asked. I told her about the church, about the Massacre of the Innocents, and the death of my friend.

'It sounds very beautiful,' she said, 'but you haven't answered me. What about you?'

I had a lump in my throat. Should I tell her that I, too, had this thought every night of my life: *for my heart is not with me ...*

'Nothing very much... It's a long and endless path.'

'William, I've thought about you all this time and I'm annoyed with myself for being so self-absorbed that I've only seen you through my own eyes and not much through yours...'

'But it's for you, for him...'

'William, you yourself don't believe that. Listen to me: you'll find this path—and it will be your own.'

She slipped the leaf she had picked from the peach tree into the sleeve of my coat. I scarcely had time to feel the caress of her fingers and only a burning sensation remained.

19

PUFFING AND PANTING, we laid two stones down among some large trees. An almighty wind was blowing and amid the scene of devastation our two stones were the only things that remained motionless.

We gazed at them as we caught our breath, astonished that we had been able to lift and carry them, and surprised by the sudden heat emanating from them. With my pick-axe, I saw myself as Gislebert for a fleeting second. Abelard's attention was elsewhere as I tried, very clumsily, to smooth down the hard stone without injuring myself. I didn't dare consider that I would then have to use a finer chisel and cut some facings . . . I ran the palm of my hand over the stone.

I was sweating; I gazed up at the windswept canopy of the trees and then down at the stones. Now, or later? I really didn't know. Just in case, I tugged at Peter's sleeve: very carefully, we both laid down the flat slab on top of the thickest of the two blocks. The two stones were now one: an altar.

Peter was tired but, for the first time since we had begun our wandering, I saw an expression of relief on his face.

Bearing a scar upon my shoulder like the mark of the strap which, for so many years, bore the weight of my sack, I am a lifelong brother to those who wander — those tramps, pilgrims, merchants, clerks in search of a school, monks fleeing from an order that doesn't suit them . . . To be a wanderer in a wandering world seems to me to be a natural way of surviving in it, if not of being in harmony with it.

For Peter (who had nevertheless led this kind of life — and for longer than I had — during his years of apprenticeship) not to have a house was the beginning of death. Even though he had left when he was young, he came from a manor house, he was the lord of an estate.

Our flight from Saint-Denis, seeking shelter with Comte Thibaut de Champagne, the weeks of waiting, the final comings and goings of Abbot Suger's messengers — all this had worn him down, possibly also the thought of Heloise, whose message he had read, without flinching, in my presence, before tossing it in the fire.

Even if he didn't say so, it seemed to him that his learning, ennobled through suffering, should have earned him considerable respect. The privileges that the largest of the abbeys claimed — starting with Cluny, the foremost among them — whereby they paid no heed to bishops and archbishops and dealt directly with the pope — even that meant nothing to him. In this abbey of his soul which he constructed with his words and blood, he needed to talk to God in private. Other men had cut themselves off through their own stupidity, their pretentiousness, their malice; when he turned round there was nobody left and he found himself face to face with Him. Of course, there were no people to follow him and it wasn't the tables of the Law that had been entrusted to him — it was, more awesome still, the gift of knowing how to make sense of all the mysteries and to clarify them in men's minds.

In this wind it was impossible to light a fire; even though we were shivering from the cold, we remained standing, facing our altar, in the nave formed by the storm-tossed trees, and wide open to the blue-black, cloud-strewn sky, a sky that spelled the beginning, or the end.

I could see words forming on his lips but I couldn't hear them. Eventually he cried out.

'This is our house!'

And his hand encompassed this land, these woods, this wind and the entire universe. Then he leaned over the stone and kissed it too, with his lips, with his bear's arms. It was as if he were lying over a woman and pressing down on her to make her keep still. Then he stood up and spoke again, though more softly, once the wind had died down a little:

'It's my house.'

Quite honestly, I don't know how they got there. But every day, almost, I saw a newcomer arrive, or else a small group. Some of them scarcely spoke French or Latin, but they all knew who Peter Abelard was, the greatest master in the world. They waited on his every word. He said nothing.

He watched as the cabins and huts were constructed higgledy-piggledy along the river bank; he said a few words here and there, and if asked when the lectures were to begin, he didn't reply. And yet they all waited.

I set off on my own to discover the wide, curving horizon that filled the entire expanse of sky in this sad landscape once I emerged from its thick forests (with this sadness comes the smell of damp earth which must follow anyone who has been exiled here throughout his life). A road pitted by storms, a rounded hill, a church spire in the distance—was that the parish church of Saint-Aubin? But above all this, the sky that hung over the land, and enveloped everything. I couldn't stop myself walking towards the horizon that I'd never reach and which filled me with joy as it receded: when I reached the top of the hill I walked towards the wood, from the wood to the village—and thus my absurd hopes always preceded me. I returned slowly, with a pain in the knee, but with increased vigour. I entered our wood (for this land has been given to us with full possession by the Comte de Champagne, together with some fields and a windmill), I crossed over the stones that form a bridge over our straggling Arduzon brook—and I knew that I was at our home. Well, his home.

I don't have time to be nostalgic about those first nights when two peasants (for we were completely incapable ourselves—and the time when Gislebert was in charge seemed to belong to another life) built us our first cabins beside the stream. Peter came with a trunk full of books and a copy of the treatise that had been burnt. He kept the ashes, he told me, in a silver box. I remembered Luke: I have nothing.

'There will be barns and windmills here, a farm over there and an entire hamlet . . . From this altar will come a light born in the east that will shine as far as the Mount Sainte-Geneviève . . .'

Oh, him and his Mount and his Cité! Even now he never stops talking about them, and you feel he would welcome the first student who arrives from his Lutetia with open arms.

Student—that's the word now. Three times he was asked to start his lectures again; three times he refused, assuring them he would never teach again and that he came to the desert to pray. So why didn't he send them away, then? Peter, I know you as if you had created me.

Nothing disheartened them, quite the contrary. They came from Troyes, Sens and Provins, and some came from Lorraine and Germany. I had got on well with three young Jews, grandchildren of Rabbi Rachi, who had taught them to prune vines and to understand the Law and its 613 commandments. Shy and dark of skin, they were always together, and they spoke in low voices in their raucous sounding tongue.

When there were several groups of ten or more he started to speak to them about St Paul. The wild winds that had blown on the first day had abated and a gentle breeze wafted a scent of flowers to this lonely place.

'I love Paul,' he began, 'like a father and a brother, and if he torments me it is as if he were a shadow of myself . . .'

I had not heard him teach for a long time and from the very

first words I rediscovered my respect and admiration for him—rather as one recognises a woman's faded beauty in her smile. I watched them watching him, I listened to them listening to him. They didn't cough, they were not restless, they were scarcely aware that they were breathing. He had no need to raise his voice, and I was wondering why he had paused for so long before I realised that he may have merely wanted the wind to die down.

'In order to understand Paul, we need to be inside him, to make his crimes our own (and God knows that ours are greater than his), to make his sufferings ours as well, and to make his strict admonitions those we address to ourselves with prayers and tears on those evenings when we have sinned. We cannot be Jesus—nor even any of his first disciples—but we can be Paul. Peter is the rock upon which the church is founded; but Paul is its voice, its gentleness and its thunder, Paul is the spirit that lives within us still. He has said: *for what man knoweth the things of a man, save the spirit of man which is in him* . . . By that we know that he knows us, by that we realise that he is within us like none of our brethren before us.'

It was not a lecture and not a sermon—we were a long way from the sublime articulations of logic and the grammatical erudition that made him famous. His words flowed out of him like the wind and they refreshed and warmed us, and when he stopped speaking there was only silence.

In the evening, when everyone had retired and the chatter of the young had abated (their shouting too, and their games), I took him to watch the sunset; the breeze had subsided and only a breath of air—a caress on the surface of the water—ruffled the tops of the beeches and the oak trees. For a while we said nothing.

'What peace . . .' I said at last.

'A gale has blown and the Spirit has comforted me. This place shall be called Paraclete.'

✦ ✦ ✦

During the weeks and months that followed, Peter could scarcely contain his delight at the success of his school. Students now came from all over Europe, a merry band who sought truth in the words he spoke.

He had a way of interpreting the Bible that warmed the cockles of our hearts, for he explained it in simple words before extracting meanings that made your mind soar; Rachi's grandsons became friendly with him and in the evening he liked to sit with them alone by the fireside discussing the origin of a word. He threw into their pot some Greek and Latin, Hebrew and Aramaic—and even some French, for they were proud that their grandfather had been the first to use words from the language of daily life with all its problems to explain the ancient mysteries. They read the Canticles together, comparing the traditions. They uttered their comments with modesty and humility—and it was here that I admired my wrestler, my Jacob, because he made himself more childlike than them in order to encourage them to speak and to question them about the history of their people and its laws.

Quarrymen, stonemasons and carpenters arrived from the east; they had built churches in Germany and they spoke of cathedrals that were being constructed there. They set down their tools only at lecture time. A building site was opened, and I became the foreman, not because I wanted to or was especially competent, but because Peter was curiously indifferent about it. I thought of the light in Suger's eyes when he talked about his abbey, I thought of Gislebert, and I realised more than ever that my master's life was lived in the mind.

Scholars are delicately built and their arms, which are accustomed to carrying wax tablets, are not designed to carry blocks of stone or to handle beams. At night, workers frequently come away from this noisy and badly run building site where the church (being built on the very spot where we had erected the altar on the first day) would be constructed one day and would collapse the next.

Confusion arose too, due to the simple fact that there were many people, and a real village had grown up around us. None of this mattered to Abelard as long as people were quiet during his lectures; he would accept money as the mood took him; he appeared cheerful when he was angry and he pretended to be annoyed when he was affectionate.

He had changed.

I had not realised this to begin with, always seeing the 'old man' in him. There was more generosity, more selflessness, more honesty, and a kind of new simplicity about him which set him apart from the exercises in which he had so excelled. A light shone from him which was no longer just that of an astonishingly agile mind, but may perhaps have been the Spirit under whose protection he now placed himself. I would discover soon enough why, at the same time, he had not changed.

One day he flew into a real rage.

Some of Comte Thibaut's men had come to complain about a theft that had taken place in the neighbourhood—a chicken, some logs . . . It was nothing much and it wasn't even certain that a student was responsible. What is more, with the crowd that we had now, as well as the whores and the peddlers, it was not surprising that we should have a few thieves.

He took it as a personal insult.

When it was time for his lecture, he stood up and cursed the multitude as if he were Yahweh himself. There was a rumbling of surprise; people were trying to understand, some of them had misheard. He fell silent, turned his back upon them and walked off towards the Arduzon brook. I followed him.

'I shall say no more,' he said. 'I left Saint-Denis because corruption and vice were rampant there . . . And now a community has grown up around me and I find the seeds of the same corruption and the same vices. Let them resort to this! I shall say nothing.'

Students came up to us in tears, tugging at his coat. People were moaning and appealing to him and calling out 'Master!' from all sides.

So the day wore on — and I could not imagine that his mood would alter the next day. At supper time, coming from the building site where everyone had tried with varying degrees of success to move him with the strength of their zeal, we heard their songs, and some laughter.

At first, he paid no attention.

'What is it?' he asked me eventually.

'I'll go and see.'

Gathered around a red-haired student, a recently arrived Englishman who stood out because of his limp and slightly boisterous good humour, a group of them were chanting some verses in unison that comically and impudently criticised the master for giving up his teaching. I was obliged to smile and signal them to continue for I was known to be his disciple. I laughed along with them — and I sang.

When I looked round, Peter Abelard had joined us and he, too, was laughing and singing and dancing rather like a bear that had discovered it was springtime. There were no lectures that day, but he began singing some old songs he had written, and even those who didn't know them felt they were sharing in emotions that were sacred when he uttered the name of Heloise — that name I had not heard him mention since finding him again.

In the glow of the flames you could see how surprised everyone was — and above all how they had been moved by the memory of his story — for each of them was filling in the missing words and extending the words of love with words of sorrow and grief. Each of them may also have been thinking privately about a particular woman he had known or been close to, and may perhaps have touched and lost . . . As for the women, they were in tears because they themselves were Heloise, and Heloise was a sister or a mother for them.

Under the starlit sky this shipload of men and women pitched and tossed, filled with a joy that was akin to pain, and carried along by tears in which all human emotions were fused. When a hundred chests are swelling and do not burst, when hands are held and pain and pleasure mingle, men's nights are filled with stars.

That night, while everyone slept (though scarcely anyone was really asleep, to judge by the whispers of dawning memories), he spoke to me at last about her.

That night, I told him for the first time that I had loved the woman he had loved.

I told him that I still loved her.

With a lump in my throat, I told him that I would always love her.

I told him that all this made no sense, that I begged him to forget it all—and that my words would not survive the dawn.

I was not afraid—even though I had fought for so long to hide my feelings from him—and it suddenly became obvious to me (so obvious that it made me want to smile) that he had known this from the start and did not care in the least.

He didn't answer me—had he heard me? He spoke of her with respect and he sensibly blamed himself for having treated her so badly, from the moment he had forced her to submit to the pleasures of the flesh, up until the time he had compelled her to forsake the world. He said that Christ alone had protected him from despair and that only Christ could now show him the way: that he must not forget this love and tell himself that it had never taken place, but, on the contrary, he must experience it fully at last, through Christ and in Christ.

I couldn't see his face.

I told him how, from the very first moment, she had opened a cleft in my heart that nothing—neither time nor the quiet certainty that it was clear it was he whom she loved, and would do so for ever—would ever heal. I asked his forgiveness for this silent treachery and for being with him—not for his sake, but for hers, not for their sake, but for mine.

He said that he sometimes woke up sweating, filled with shame for having taken her when she meant nothing to him, simply for the sake of stealing her from me, for the sake of taking her and making her the instrument of his desires. He said that later, when what he called 'love' was merely lust—when he tried to forget the simplest of the commandments he had transgressed—the memory of his crimes lingered in his body and would never fade away.

I watched you by the river and saw how you looked at one another and how your hands came together without touching . . .

I have done wrong to her and done wrong to her uncle and, above all, I have done wrong in the eyes of God . . .

I was jealous of your love and in my heart I felt hatred for you, and I wanted you to die and for the greatest evil to befall you—I would have taken her myself had I been capable of it, and it was not a matter of strength, but cowardice . . .

May God come to my aid, may his love be granted to me, to me a sinner who has only repentance in his heart . . .

In the little room that now served as our lodgings, there was still no roof and the moon was our candlelight.

We were talking about the same woman and we sometimes used the same words; we had lived through the same life and drunk at the same fountain; and yet we were like two deaf men trying to understand one another with their backs turned.

'It's absurd,' I said eventually.

'What is absurd?'

'You regret what you have had and I what I haven't had . . . You repent for what you have done and I for what I haven't done . . . Are we not human brothers who are struggling with this emotion called love in order to try to understand it? And yet we are alone, in the midst of the desert. Let us speak no more. Sing something else . . .'

It wasn't a love song that he sang, but a solemn and terrible howl, intoned in a low voice that rose up from the depths of the earth.

> O, *How bounteous are the Sabbaths,*
> *And how beautiful,*
> *That the court of heaven*
> *Everlastingly keep.*
> *They give peace to weary men,*
> *As reward for their strength,*
> *While God in whom all things are*
> *Remains all things to men.*

While God remains all things to men . . . I fell asleep to the echo of his voice, feeling soothed: my heart was freed of this open secret, of this confession he did not want to hear and which was a burden only to me.

After that night a new sense of freedom flowed through my veins, one I didn't expect and which I didn't remember having tried to conquer. I had participated in all Peter's struggles and I had shared all his blows. It hurt me when he was struck low and I detested his enemies more than he himself did; my desire to be him had made me blindly happy, and even being parted from him had not separated me from him — it was as if a secret bond, a prisoner's code, had continued being constructed in our absence and was binding me tightly.

He only had eyes for those who served him; so in order to be noticed by him I had to wait on him with the devotion of a slave or a dog. When I awoke, I was surprised to find I was still human. Talking to him (those few, pitiful words and that confession which he had not listened to) achieved in a matter of minutes what years of reflection and tortured nights had failed to do. I remembered who I was, and however wretched, insignificant and poor I might be, I had to find a destiny that was mine and not his. I could see just how much my fits of anger against him were also linked to this unfortunate attachment.

And then I saw him as he was.

Haughty yet vain, powerful yet weak, ridiculous, magnificent, courageous, cowardly, insufferable, generous, so stupid you could weep, a master of words but so incapable of mastering himself.

It became impossible to say no to him without quaking.

It became easy for me to understand him without judging him.

At last I could respect him without loving him.

Within a few months, the community had grown and prospered as if by magic. Comte Thibaut continued to be as generous as he had been at the beginning: not a season passed without some gift or other, a new barn, a new parcel of land, the revenue from a mill, a wood, a church . . .

Our yard was still a mess, but the buildings were going up, and I often thought, in the midst of the bustle, of our first stormy evening, which was already so long ago, however recent.

Peter made our lives difficult. Every fine lecture (and his words were frequently very fine, so much so that you wanted to cling to them, like the flight of a bird at the end of summer) was accompanied by fits of temper or constant demands. He would talk to me about Paris, about the Cité, the bishop or the school, and I wanted to tell him that time had gone by and that it was he, ultimately, who had put an end to all that. But Peter did not want to hear anyone say that he'd made mistakes of any kind. Confessing his sin — with abundant tears and repentance — seemed to him sacrifice enough, and it had been made once and for all. Let's not hark back to it, his dark eyes and the lines on his cheeks and forehead seemed to say, let me not be asked about it any more! Quite the contrary, the entire universe, moved by his ordeal, should bend to his will.

Even his castration was no longer a barbarous assault perpetrated by men for certain reasons, but a punishment from God, a sign that had been sent to him—he referred with increasing frequency to Origen, whom he had always admired, and who, to liberate himself from the flesh, had voluntarily castrated himself.

And so we continued from tantrum to tantrum and we had to put up with the fact that he might call out for no reason, because there wasn't enough wine, or because the stream was flowing too slowly.

He had been a master because he had been able to inspire dreams in men's minds with his golden words; in a little while, I thought to myself, he would merely be master out of routine or habit—that *usum* that he once abhorred—a tyrant who would call out in dreadful solitude.

One morning some peasants brought us a wounded man who, they told us, had murmured his name and mine before passing out. Mine? I was incredulous. He was in the infirmary. I set off slowly, not feeling any real curiosity, convinced I was about to meet a corpse. Seeing the stout figure stretched out on a makeshift stretcher, I was still wondering who could possibly have been thinking about me before he died.

'Are you still looking for a master?'

'Arnold!'

I embraced my gaunt giant, with his cheeks hollowed from one hardship or another, with his feverish eyes and strangely broken voice, but who jumped up the moment I entered.

'Where have you come from? What are you doing?'

'I'm on the run . . .'

It was unlike him to talk with such sadness in his voice—and there were those burning eyes, that anxiousness that was akin to panic—when, ten years previously, I had been jealous of his blunt confidence in life.

'Rebelliousness wears you out, my friend, and in the end I'm not going to believe anything or anyone . . .'

'You!'

'The moment they see me they dismiss me before allowing me to speak . . . My name fills them with horror . . . If I read the Epistle to the Corinthians to them, they make the way I speak an excuse to throw me into prison . . .'

'It's almost as if you'd been given some lessons by a master we know.'

'Almost, yes.'

He laughed joylessly, and what upset me, apart from his weakened body, was this grief of a man who was bleeding from too many wounds. What cruelty and what tortures, which he stubbornly kept to himself, could have been inflicted on him that this happy crusader, this cheerful trooper, should be turned into a soldier of fortune who no longer had any faith in mankind?

Abelard put on an excessive display of delight at seeing Arnold. It was as if time had stood still and we were meeting again many years ago, in the Paris of everyone's dreams. But all those dreams had passed away—whatever was to have happened had happened and it only made for further bitterness to recall our vanished friends, or Samuel's inn, the lectures on the Seine, and our priory where we prayed so little.

After that they fell over themselves trying to be purer than the other: they confessed their sins to one another (there was no need for Heloise's name to be mentioned) and their failure to keep the commandments, and they moaned about a world that had forgotten evangelical simplicity. Even though they were so dissimilar—the subtle logician and the disappointed preacher, the man who had read everything and the man who knew only the Gospels—the intense admiration of the pupil for the master sealed a relationship in which each of them consolidated their worst shortcomings.

Peter told him about Saint-Denis and spoke of the false disciples influenced by the dreadful Bernard of Clairvaux; Arnold described Rome and how, on the pretext of fighting the Germanic emperors' abuses of earthly power, the popes had drifted into a love of power which was no less grand and equally despicable. The time when Gregory had initiated the reform which was meant to restore the Church to moral purity was long past.

I listened to them in disbelief, on the verge of anger: their zeal frightened me and their frail memories made me sad. In what or who's name did they preach this purity that had never existed? Was it the wisdom of their own lives that authorised them to set themselves up as Judges, to appoint kings and depose them? Did they speak like this to God, every morning and evening, in a burning bush that concealed them from men? Each of my questions annoyed them a little more, but I did not relent; I silenced them while failing to convince them that they should be a little more modest. Men cannot be changed.

When Peter had left us, I asked Arnold what he had come in search of.

'Thunder,' he said, 'and lightning so as to fill my hands with them and make them ring out.'

'Vanity . . .'

'You don't understand us . . .'

'I love you, Arnold, you're my brother, my giant . . . That's the reason I don't understand you . . .'

'You've changed.'

I sighed. I had changed: what did it matter . . . I reckoned I had changed for the better. And I was pleased that I wasn't always repeating the same things and always having to battle with the same phantoms.

'Come and watch the night fall over Champagne. It's not Paris, but . . .'

'I'd rather remain here.'

I was astonished by his hesitation. I went over to him and raised my candle to his face. His eyes did not blink.

'I'm going blind, William, and the world is becoming a frightening shadow theatre in which voices that I know and whose falseness I detest keep ringing out . . . You don't know what it's been like on my way here, getting lost, bumping into things, having to beg favours. You don't know the anger I feel at people's malice.'

'There's no end to malice, brother. Yet there's goodness too . . .'

'Never enough goodness, always too much malice! Never enough justice to make up for the filth and oppression of men, for the doors that are closed, the crust of bread and the alms that are refused you while these swine wallow in their revelry . . .'

'Stay alive.'

'What life?'

I took him along with me, nevertheless, walking with difficulty, guiding him through stones, helping him avoid the roots and broken branches, and the holes dug up by moles. I could feel his hand grip my arm when he stumbled. He told me that he saw the light of the stars as a white halo out of which monstrous figures emerged: architectural capitals rose out of the sky, constructed by a bad master builder obsessed with creating debased humans and outrageous looking animals.

When one sees evil detached from good, like a world of its own, it's no longer man one sees but a deformation, an excrescence, an anomaly. You have to get used to the evil within yourself, not to give into it or to confuse it with good, of course, but precisely in order to correct yourself gently and find the right road again when you had gone astray. It's not just that a world without evil is a world without God—it's also a world without men and therefore a world that is impossible—at least by the only measures we know, those of our own lives.

I have read that the philosophers of old believed in the existence of worlds parallel to ours—or that the worlds repeated themselves—or even that there was an end and beyond this end another universe. These pagan notions did not bother me as long as in each of these worlds I discovered my fellow men again, the hideous and the sublime, the reprehensible and the heroic.

It upset me that my friend, my giant so full of energy and simple faith (and I was aware that I was committing the same sin that I had accused Abelard of: I was not looking at the man who was before my eyes, but at the person who had helped me years ago when I arrived in Paris) should have been transformed into this blue flame in which gibbets and stakes shone. He believed he was burning with the Spirit, just as the prophets did, but very soon he would be branded as a heretic, a trouble-maker and an enemy of God in every town he entered, and he would walk resolutely to his death in a state of fury—an idol perhaps, but an idol of the poor who would not even have his corpse to share among them, and nothing, neither hope nor a symbol, except a blast of cold ashes on the morning of a calamity.

By what strange route would the path of the pupil join that of the master, I did not yet know; but so long as I could hear Arnold of Brescia staggering about in the starlight, insulting the Curia, all the popes, all the kings, all the bishops, all the priests as well as the entire universe, I felt that my impression that morning may not have been wrong: it was not a living creature whom I had with me, but a ghost, someone living on borrowed time.

The messenger arrived at dinner-time. He had a prince-like beauty despite the dried mud on his coat tails. You could imagine him positioned to the right of the angel on the tympanum of a church, wearing that self-congratulatory air that the elect always have, with their gaze raised to the Lord, and their well-groomed beards—I did it, eh? I succeeded. With such a physique you might have expected the voice of a prophet or the sound of a trumpet: he said nothing. He dismounted and held out the reins to the first person who would take them. I made a sign to the red-headed Englishman.

I led him, in silence, to the room in which Peter Abelard studied and kept his books. He glanced up at the tall trees and followed me at a slow pace. This man—it was obvious—had not spent his life in a monastery. You don't walk like that if you haven't killed someone or held women in your arms.

Peter looked up from his book—Boethius's commentary on

the Hexameron—and the man held out a sealed scroll to him. 'Saint-Denis', my master murmured when he saw the seal—but it didn't sound anything like a war cry or a shout of joy.

While he was reading the scroll I looked at the man who was standing there stock-still and smug, and his solemnity made me want to smile. Who was he? Certainly not a man who wins battles or fathoms mysteries: he was a messenger, that is to say a man whose life is dependent on the lives of others. My smile froze: I might have been talking about myself.

'When?' Peter asked, turning towards him as he handed me the parchment.

'As soon as possible. Abbot Suger says that a reformer like you is needed to instil some order. But he also says that there is some urgency . . .'

'I can read . . .' muttered Abelard, but a smile he could not manage to conceal flashed across his face.

The missive announced that Peter had been elected abbot of the monastery of Saint-Gildas-de-Rhuys, in Brittany, an institution belonging to Saint-Denis, and that the abbot entreated him to stop everything he was doing and follow the call of the Lord. All the newly achieved self-respect that I thought I'd acquired dissolved in my belly and I felt like an abandoned child, prey to the most ancient of fears.

The man left without staying for prayers, having just enough time to eat some vegetable soup and a little boiled meat. He didn't say thank you when the Redhead brought him his clean cloak and a fresh horse.

The autumn was growing colder and there were somewhat fewer students and rather less disorder. 'We'll talk about it after Mass,' Peter whispered to me, and during the service I could sense that he was worried. He was already elsewhere. I felt emotionally overwhelmed, and each surge was stronger than the last: I was furious with him; yet I knew the pointlessness of any resistance.

We were walking towards the Arduzon brook.

'We shall leave someone here to look after the altar,' he announced suddenly.

'Don't go. It's a trap.'

'If I fail, it is one. But I'll succeed.'

'You underestimate Suger.'

'Who's underestimating whom? None of you knows who I am ...'

His self-satisfied air infuriated me.

'But what do you think happened? That these semi-civilised monks, who speak in a dialect you would barely understand, woke up one morning, informed in a dream by the Angel of Yahweh, and saw the letters ABAILARDUS glittering in the sky among the clouds?'

'I'm not sure I care for your way of speaking to me.'

'And I don't care for your way of talking nonsense.'

He raised his powerful hands towards me to seize me by the neck. He would have picked me up and thrown me like a rag. My heart was thumping away but I held his gaze. After a moment, his fingers withdrew into the palms of his hands and he dropped his arms.

'What's come over you?'

'You're an extraordinary man, Peter, and there's no one I admire more. But you've never heard what was being said behind your back ...'

'Is that a fault?'

'Not in itself, as long as you allow people to say it to your face ...'

He dismissed the argument.

'Suger is in charge of Saint-Denis. That hypocrite Bernard has got rid of the timid Robert of Molesmes in order to make Clairvaux, under the pretext of a return to solitude and the desert, the spearhead of his conquest; his friend Norbert of Xanten is doing the same with the Premonstratensians, as is my old enemy Champeaux with the Victorines. Even my dear Robert of Arbrissel, after years of wandering, had settled down at

Fontevrault. And I haven't mentioned our Child, who is now running Cluny, the biggest order of them all . . . And as for me — look where I am. You're nothing but a knight without soldiers if you haven't an order of your own, monks to obey you, a position in the Church, and a bishop who may loathe you, but fears you. And the popes don't know anyone's names — just those of the abbeys.'

'Why not the Paraclete?'

'They'll never accept the Paraclete as long as I'm here . . .'

'And they'll accept you at Saint-Gildas?'

'Because they're suggesting it . . .'

He was silent and so was I. There was no logic to his argument — or rather there was one, but it was not the logic of men. In his anger and confusion, he would not see the truth that was burning my lips: he was a master without equal, a philosopher of the first rank, a theologian (this word that he had coined was beginning to spread) who was unique — but as a mediocre monk he would be in charge of monks who were more mediocre still.

As we drew near to our little church, he spoke to me in a softer voice.

'Will you come with me, this time? You shall be my prior.'

I smiled. Master of schools, prior, soon an abbot . . . When Peter Abelard needed me, he made handsome promises . . .

'You forget that I haven't even taken my vows.'

'Your vows?'

He looked seriously surprised at my concern.

'You'll take them with me.'

'I don't want to, Peter.'

Wisely, he didn't ask me what it was I did not want — to become a monk or to set off with him.

'I understand. But what will you do, then?'

There was a touch of disdain in this question. If you stay with me, then, because of me, you're something; if you leave me, you're nothing. I caught my breath.

'Didn't you say that someone would be needed to look after the altar?'

He looked at me in astonishment.

'Is that what you really want?'

I stifled my laughter: are you so small then, so wretched . . .

'I carried these stones with you when they were very heavy and you had no students to listen to you, no peasants, no workmen . . . With you gone, I doubt whether the Paraclete wind would continue to blow here. And I don't want you to find these stones overturned when you come back . . .'

I had spoken the last sentence humorously, for I knew it would touch him. What appeared to be betrayal was a deeper dedication.

'So you love me a little, then?'

'Love you? I love you even when I hate you . . .'

The question was childish, and so was the reply. I smiled as he placed those hands, which a few minutes earlier had wanted to smash me to pieces, tenderly on my shoulders.

He gestured towards the huts and towards the students who were walking along, talking, carrying wood or eating blackberries as they waited for the next lecture.

'We'll have to talk to them . . .'

'When the beekeeper dies, the new one taps the hives with a stick and says to them:

'"Bees, your master is dead; bees, you have a new master."'

'The master is not dead, he's leaving.'

'Do you want us to say to them: "Bees, your master is deserting you"?'

'The master is not dead, William,' he repeated inscrutably, 'and there is no new master.'

His last lecture was the saddest of all—not because it was moving, but because it wasn't. I looked at them, these young men who had come in search of the truth and still remained here with the approach of winter; these vagabonds, the red-haired

Englishman whose outrageous jokes shook the woods with laughter, young Berengar, who was frail as a child and who was attached to him by an invisible thread, these monks who had fled, these young clerics so full of hope, the Jews from Rachi, the Poles, the Germans . . . He maintained that he was persecuted and misunderstood—and it was true to a certain degree. But the first desertion was his, almost as if he had loved not the people themselves (their life stories and their peculiarities, their sufferings), but whatever it was—this link with the man himself . . . I knew each one of these men, I had delved into their joys and grief, I had shed tears over those childhoods in which too many blows had rained down, I had shared those nights of hunger, I had been robbed and too little loved, I—too—had stolen from people, betrayed and deserted them, and yet, with all that, I had not surrendered the ambition to be totally human and tolerable to God if not actually loved by him; I had always come back, I had never given up.

Like Peter Abelard, I knew that there was a human truth concealed within God's truth; I did not have his powerful mind, nor did I have the terrible blessing that Heloise's love had caused him to bear, but I had conquered the humiliation that made me acknowledge others as my brothers. I wanted to die like my brother Christian, praising the beauty of the house of the Lord.

On the second night, as they were leaving one by one, each with his bag and his stick, how many hearts burned with ardour inside the huts, how many tears flowed, how many farewells were exchanged, everyone realising at that moment that this would never happen again, that each of them would have to seek his own destiny on the dangerous roads. A young poet by the name of Hilary, who hardly ever spoke, took a reed-flute from his bag and played—I was going to say the sad tune of the nightingale, out of the habit we have acquired from our Latin Fathers of comparing ourselves to animals—but I ought to say, more simply, that it was like the song of a sad man singing at night. This melody brought about a wonderful silence, and tears that had been shed in silence, even bitterness, were suddenly being shed in joy—and the feelings of loneliness that were beginning to take root at the thought of exile were for a time, for a very last time, all fused together—and the idea that all this was over, that it would all fade away became a wordless elegy in everyone's heart—all the more poignant since nothing else would remain.

During one of the performances, a light began to shine within me that suddenly engulfed everything—this music, the time, the night, Heloise's face, the wind on the first day, the presence of the Spirit, the fear and the inevitability of death, my master's quest, all the feelings that had swirled through my life—a light in which nothing was judged and everything was present, in which opposing feelings were brought together, in which sensations were no longer excluded, in which the Presence was total, in which Unity was formed, and in which, finally, from the dust of the earth to that of the stars, from misery to joy, from nothingness to Eternity, I felt myself to be at the very heart of the soul of Creation.

When silence returned, this state of being continued and I felt as if I, too, were able to sing, with closed lips, to the tune of Hilary's flute.

I was awake until dawn, a new sense of elation in my heart—for in that state of being, in the midst of my mud-swamp, I had noticed a piece of treasure gleaming and I had gathered it up.

And now that the singing had ceased and dawn had come, it was still glittering in the hollow of my hand.

20

MEN COMPLAIN of servitude, but they do not know that solitude can be a terrible and dreadful freedom. The law that governs our nature no doubt exists and will be discovered; perhaps we will then be permitted to contemplate without fear these violent impulses of our souls, these fits of melancholy, these belligerent rages that flash through us and afflict us—as well as that urge we sometimes have to lie down in the moonlight and weep like crazed beasts, irrationally, solely out of concern for our condition—never leaving us in peace.

I survived, initially, through a routine that I imagined was similar to that which hermits impose on themselves so as not to go mad. Peter had not taken all his books with him and so I nourished myself on the Desert Fathers, I continuously re-read the conversion and dream of St Jerome, and I warded off temptations by chewing roots even though the peasants brought me vegetables, fruit and salted meat.

It was as if I had never known myself and this fear of facing myself had made me simultaneously take action and run away.

I received letters from him in which, despite his efforts to describe the lines of rocks beneath the waves and the sweetness of the woods, I could detect a situation that was closer to the one I had imagined. Whatever the purpose of Suger's mysterious scheming, it was not out of enthusiasm, nor on the strength of books they had not read and would not have understood a word of, that the monks of Saint-Gildas had elected him. From the moment he arrived, he exasperated them by pretending at first to be a poor pilgrim and allowing himself to be treated badly. The following day, he returned wearing his abbot's habit, with his servants and horses, and he lectured them about their morals and their vices, without listening to them, without understanding them, determined not to be attracted in any way to their ignorance, their anti-social behaviour and their rough language.

What could they have comprehended of his refined Latin, honed on the *Georgics* and the Vulgate, and sharpened by years of verbal jousting with the finest minds of his age? For them Latin was a foreign language which they mumbled with plums in their mouths. He, who controlled everything with the power of words, who believed that men could be enlightened by a single word, realised that he had nothing left, and that he would need to go and search among the darkest and most secret emotions, among the granite of stones, in the depths of the woods, by the fury of the sea in order to begin to understand again.

Yes, I do believe—although perhaps I am being unfair to him —that I would have gazed at the sea and listened on winter nights to its doleful moan before forming an opinion of these men.

Peter Abelard was performing in a Passion play that he wrote on his own for himself alone—but only he knew this. Therefore he loathed those monks, just as they loathed him.

Before the first threats were uttered, he had felt the hostility in this landscape and climate which he refused to think about. This was what Brittany was really like, not the mild countryside he knew around Nantes, with its good monks rolling casks of wine down to the quay on the River Sèvre, but a barbarity that was scarcely credible, squalling winds, seas that crashed against the coast, a wilderness that howled and protested and tormented the soul like some devil. In addition to all this, there was this language of which he understood not a word—and this violent hostility, this refusal to submit to any authority, be it rational or divine. *A ship secretly eaten away by worms, a rock attacked and hollowed by the salt of the sea . . .* he was already comparing his exile to that of Ovid, forgetting that the poet had not chosen his.

It was not long, he wrote to me, before the first signs of shiftiness, whispering and sniggering began. Very soon a substantial ring of mistrust had formed around him in which what masqueraded as fear (bowed heads, muffled voices) only served to conceal shameful plans.

He told me about an attempt to poison him that I could scarcely believe, so much did it appear to come out of that dreadful *Life* of Abelard which he was writing for his own sorrow and, at the same time, his glory. A young monk who had just taken his vows (and Peter had kept this man to himself in order to preserve the purity of his vocation; he did not steal from the monastery stores, nor did he have a mistress in the local town) had accidentally tasted a little food that was meant for the abbot; he died after a few hours of vomiting and appalling suffering. In his usual way, Peter did not enlarge upon the loss of the young man and his terrible fate, but on the fact that he was now certain that his monks had turned from disobedience to a plan to murder him.

He confided to me that he was thinking of becoming a Muslim, writing jokingly that at least the Saracens accorded a place for Jews and Christians . . . Abelard as a Muslim? The notion made me smile, but I understood him without believing him. Memories of Soissons came back to me: it was the Christians, his own brothers—and among them those who were closest to him —who had dealt him the harshest blows. He cared little about individuals; this made him unusually tolerant of the most bizarre ideas.

Since his castration, he had formed a tendency to complain about all sorts of illnesses, and his persecution mania had developed to extremes. I knew very well that he had enemies, but as

Peter the Child, now abbot of Cluny, had once said, he was his own worst enemy and his struggle with himself would have been enough to exhaust anyone.

There were passages in his letters, nevertheless, in which I rediscovered all my old admiration for my master: they were those in which he forgot about himself at last, and forgot about the threats, real or imaginary, that hung over him, and freed himself, letting his mind soar on the wings of the Spirit. I felt as if I were hearing him speak—and now that he was not confining himself to grammar and logic, his intelligence swirled with all the mysteries of mankind and its history. Whether one was reading him or listening to him, it was as if you were imagining a vast *Summa* in which he, with the sort of sudden impulse he was capable of, had gathered together all his knowledge—and I included in his knowledge not just his wealth of learning, his reading, his infinite capacity to link Scripture and all its exegesis, his familiarity with all the masters of philosophy, be they pagans or Christians, but also the knowledge that comes with the suffering that had been meted out to him by the castrators of the body as well as of the mind.

It was true that he had recognised the punishment and not the grace; the time when his soul would be reconciled would come too late.

I lived in a ghost village from which the students had departed as quickly as they had come. For visitors I had wounded birds, stray dogs, a few tramps—and the wind, the constant wind, my friendly wind, the wind of the Spirit which consoled me most when it blew at its fiercest.

The unfinished buildings, the church that was open to the sky and the deserted huts which caved in according to the vagaries of the weather never made me doubt the protective strength of this Paraclete whom he had called upon—just as he had on me.

A hermit, by the very gesture of retiring from society, has to reveal himself to the world if he does not want to die in vain. What's the point of a hermit whom no one knows, whom no one has ever heard about? He's a heap of bones hiding behind a pile of stones that have been swept up by the wind. For a time I was tempted to let myself rot on my feet beside my altar, waiting for my stinking corpse to be discovered by a lost pilgrim. I could spend whole days fixating on a point on the horizon, watching the play of the wind in the leaves of a tree, letting the dust sift through my fingers. Hunger, thirst and the will to live had deserted me.

I remembered (as one does an already distant dream) the certainty that took hold of me the night before Peter left for Brittany. It made me smile. Fear of living? Come now, brother, look up at the sky, look at the stars, let yourself be smothered by the beauty of Creation and consider it a privilege to be invited to die here and to be food for the ants. Peter understood the Muslims? Well, I understood those men who, in countries at the other end of the world, fed on the bodies of other men.

And yet there was something that held me back. It was not the thought of God (who had not disappeared, but from whom I was separated and who shone like a kind of distant star . . .), it was in the very depths of the physical deterioration and moral acedia into which I had foundered, a certain capacity to go on living — not to be nothing when I was no longer anything, not to disappear entirely when I was wiped out. In my nightmares (for I was wide awake when I went to bed and never slept any more) there was a source of light and heat that still stirred — and the lower I fell, the brighter this light was, and the more the heat warmed my limbs, before a sudden start left me blind and frozen. I searched for them however, and they were never refused me — as if this ultimate and unique favour had to be accorded to me — and in abundance — once everything had been taken from me.

There was a night of sheet lightning without thunder when I was surrounded by this mute anger of the skies, which caused terrifying figures, demons, childhood terrors — those that reside in men's memories — to burst forth. No, there was no thunder and no rain. I was expecting them — they would release me — but they did not come; there was only this silence striated by white flashes. Like a supplicant, I sought shelter at the altar stone and, gradually, I could feel myself slipping between life and death, making no distinction between one or the other, indifferent to pain or comfort alike, when a drop of rain, heavy and ready to burst, erupted on my neck.

I stood up and opened my eyes: there, in front of me, was the light whose source I had spent so many days searching for. In this hellish place, a monk, who had returned from illness after enduring terrible struggles with Satan, had told me, there were *a few traces of love*. And in this world where all human experience and human opinion meant nothing, there was still, in the midst of the desert, this dew of love, which I had not seen but which meant that life was not all pointless.

At dawn a child with a dog came to bring me food and I did not reject it, as I had done before, with a hard and stony look. As I took the bread that he gave me and thanked him, I saw an angel above his shoulder, smiling at me. I remembered Tobias: *the child went away with the angel, and the dog followed behind.*

The seasons passed. People alluded to me as: 'The man who looks after Peter's house.' They said: 'The madman who talks to the Spirit'. The donations continued to trickle in: the Paraclete.

I shaved off my beard and rediscovered a gentleness I knew in my youth: sit yourself by the side of the road, wait, a traveller will come by, perhaps a leper, perhaps Jesus, it matters little. Talk to him. Be with him. Open your heart to him in simplicity. Don't be afraid of him. If he is armed and wishes to rob you, your empty hands will disarm him; and if you die notwithstanding, it is because your time has come. Accept. Cease to struggle.

I prayed when the Spirit took me and called me.

After the bread, after the fruit, came the men. When the first one came and stayed with me, I was surprised: I was neither a priest nor a master, neither an abbot nor a monk; I was the incumbent of a forgotten altar and my friend was a Breton eunuch who spoke wrongly about the unity of the divine Trinity—it was enough to make anyone laugh! The man with a heroic face shared my meals and put wood on my fire; we talked about the roads we had journeyed along and he told me that he had been to Jerusalem, that he had fled from the terror of the fighting and that he wished to become a man again, however, before returning to his own land. We prayed together.

And so they came one by one, orphan children (in each of them I saw Astrolabe's face, exiled in his own country—and perhaps my own, too, so little and so poorly loved), cast out women, aimless pilgrims, untutored clerks—God's forgotten ones, who did not belong to any order and followed no rule, but who—and I could not fail to notice this—made me confident of finding some hope in living.

The seasons passed. People said: 'The man who lives with the poor'. They said: 'The monk with no rule'.

Comte Thibaut arrived in person, with a small retinue. You could see in his face the fierce spirit of his grandfather, William the Conqueror—but also all the political shrewdness, and perhaps the wisdom, of his mother, Adèle of Blois. I was told that he wept after his battles, asking himself where justice lay—and yet he knew there was a time for talking and a time for fighting. He used to correspond with Bernard of Clairvaux, and I am not sure what his feelings were about us.

'Where are we?' he asked. 'Is this an abbey, a priory? To whom does this house belong?'

'This house is the one you gave to my master, the philosopher Peter Abelard, and which I am looking after for him. It's a house of the poor—not splendid like Cluny or its mother house, Saint-Denis, nor one with the sublime strictness of Cîteaux and its nuns—a house that is open to those who have nothing.'

Thibaut looked at me, considered the half-finished buildings, the canal that had been half dug, the piles of rotting wood and the walls that were collapsing before they had been completed.

'You need money, labourers . . . Why did you not say anything?'

'Would you believe me if I said that I was waiting for you?'

He paused. Powerful men cannot cope with time.

'I believe you. And I'm here now. Next time, don't wait.'

After his visit, the gifts arrived in ever growing quantity, and a team of labourers from the other side of the Rhine, whose eyes were still dazzled by the stained-glass windows which they were installing in the cathedrals there. We did not require as much: some solid walls, a roof for the church, a fishpond . . .

The seasons passed. People said: 'The house of the Paraclete'. They said: 'The comfort of the afflicted'.

Some traces of love. I saw your face, Heloise, my love.

She came on a morning of rain, when greyness covered the earth and the sky. They were a pitiful lot, this community from Argenteuil, with its abbess, old women on foot, shivering novices, a few mules to carry their wretched belongings. You sensed that they had been met with suspicion at every hostelry they arrived at, and that food, even the blackest bread, had been distributed to them with that particular kind of disdain that is reserved for the poorest.

I had been warned of their arrival ever since I had received a message informing me at the same time that they had been expelled from Argenteuil and that Heloise, without further ado, had set out on the road to the Paraclete. I don't know whether she believed she would find him, but she knew that there would be shelter for her here. For the time being, that was enough.

As I had done on that first morning with Peter, she gazed up at the tops of the trees first before looking down at the ground again. She embraced me as a sister would and introduced me to each of the women who accompanied her; despite the fine rain that was falling, my own flock were scattered about the woods and the fields.

Our house was beautiful, and it was built quickly, with stones carried by the feeble arms of my wretched workers. I did not know whether it would stand up to the weather. It was not the grand things that I was most proud of so much as the minor details that resonated with my soul: the lime tree in the centre of the cloister, the altar in the chapel hidden in the woods, the fireplace in the *scriptorium* which I had made my room . . . Heloise followed me everywhere, first to the church, then to the adjoining buildings; a diversion from the river now meant that we had a supply of water. The wall that separated us from the farm, to the south, was as thick as a palm leaf, but it was built so low that it didn't feel like an enclosure. Two hundred feet to the north flowed the Arduzon, our little brook that was as dark as the woods from which it emerged.

The presence of women in a place transforms it imperceptibly and infuses it with a vitality that seemed to have been dormant among the stones. I had banished my tiny community to the farm in preparation for the arrival of the nuns: they gave the dormitory an unaccustomed order and harmony, while at the same time providing it with an intimacy which was theirs alone. I left them: they had barely arrived before they had made themselves at home in my house.

The rain soon stopped; Mass was celebrated by a priest from Saint-Aubin who had become my friend one winter evening, when he had arrived unbidden to share a meal on a frosty, solitary night. It was before the revival of the Paraclete and I was still a little mistrustful of any sympathy. In the end, as we stood huddled by the fire, I asked him why he had come to see me. 'Because I'm bored stiff,' he replied, with a huge laugh. James, who was known as the Redhead, was a small man with twinkling eyes. He spoke bad Latin and his expression lit up whenever the subject of slaughter arose; added to this, he had a big heart and told interminable stories once he had drunk a little wine. Each of us knows the God who is in his own heart: James's God, in his local village squabbles, would be the fighter who is never beaten, someone who defies the braggarts not with insults and provocation, but with the gentle smile of someone who knows his own strength. He liked me telling him stories from the Book of Kings, and about how the stiff-necked were broken.

He growled like thunder when he said Mass; but there was pity in his eyes, and Your glory was celebrated to the chanting of nuns.

When all was quiet, I lit a fire in the *scriptorium* where I spent all my life now, with my narrow bed, my chest, my books and my prayers. Despite the leaping flames, I was shivering uncontrollably from the cold: the fact was, I had finally found some peace and quiet in this life and other people had accepted my solitude, but now everything was thrown into confusion and upheaval once again. Under this grey rain, and in the light of these women's lost expressions, the happiness that I had thought was enviable had become pitiful.

Heloise came in and saw me in this dejected state; she placed her hands on my back, on my shoulders, over my stomach — the gestures of a mother for a child. After a moment, I drew back, feeling embarrassed. I was not really any warmer, but I managed to control my shivering.

'You haven't deserted me.'

'Was there not a certain promise we made that you should remind me of . . .'

'. . . whereas you have never forgotten it, I know.'

She smiled.

'Had Peter not left me here, the altar would have been the preserve of birds, the huts would have rotted, the walls would have collapsed . . . and you wouldn't have found a roof.'

'Does he know?'

'I made sure. I sent him a message. He replied that the house was yours . . .'

Even if it were true that I had sent Peter a message, I had not yet had a reply — and I did not expect one.

'I know how generous-hearted he is.'

I continued in this light-hearted vein, which was the product of white lies.

'He also said that, if he survives, he will come as quickly as he can.'

'If he survives?'

It was the cry of a young girl—but the question still echoed all the sincerity of her love.

'His monks are more creatures of the devil than of God and, if we are to believe him, they will not rest until they have murdered him . . .'

'If we are to believe him?'

'You know how I sometimes suspect him of exaggeration . . .'

'I know.'

While I put a few logs on the fire, she picked up a manuscript and leafed through it absent-mindedly.

'I've been very lonely, William.'

'What has been happening?'

'It's quite simple: your friend Suger conveniently discovered some forged documents which clearly established that Argenteuil belonged to Saint-Denis . . .'

'You don't seem at all angry.'

'None of what is happening can be worse than what has already happened. And I am responsible for my little sisters, some of them quite elderly and not at all well—you have seen them. Where this wretched Suger has surprised me—although on reflection I ought not to have been—is that, sensing the flimsiness of his documents, he spread rumours that vice and debauchery were rampant at our convent, that our wall was not an enclosure—and similar sorts of nonsense . . .'

'Suger?'

'You know him as poorly as I did: instead of a heart he has a royal abbey. And he crushes anything that stands in the way of his extraordinary ambition—oh, not violently and with impassioned speeches, like Bernard of Clairvaux, but with little remarks and rumours that he casts about . . . Not content with expelling us, he obtained a condemnation against us from the pope. Be careful, you're harbouring scandalous women, my dear William.'

Again, she was not angry, nor even excessively sad. I remembered the cautious young Suger, standing in the shadow of Bishop Gerbert. It was impossible for me to abhor him totally, and I could detect a sort of respect in Heloise's casual account.

'He's a strange man. I have a feeling that he won't persecute us now that he's got what he wants. The scandal will die down, as if miraculously. And he's even capable of scheming so that the pope drops his condemnation.'

'I approve of him, you know, more than he may imagine . . . For if I am honest, there's a far greater scandal than anything Suger, the pope and his legates can conceive of . . .'

She left her last sentence unfinished.

'. . . it's the scandal of my heart.'

She closed her eyes.

'I think of him. I think of him every day. And don't imagine that I think of him sensibly, in the way that the widows who are with me sometimes recall the memory of a husband killed in battle who afforded them great happiness . . . No, I burn when I think of him, I desire him as I used to desire him, and that which I used to be ashamed of I want more than anything. My obsession is so great that I cherish him, I cherish him in secret and when the words of hymns pass my lips. It is he whom I see and he whom I want, as I pretend that time has not passed by, and that the horror that he has dared to call God's justice has not taken place. Yes, Suger is right.'

'Will the scandal abate here?'

'At least it will be apparent to everyone in the full light of day and I shall no longer be able to reproach myself for my own hypocrisy. And when he comes, I want to smother him with words of love and laments.'

'Take care that such honesty does not destroy you.'

'I have a horror of lying, William. I remember our conversation about marriage, and if I blame myself for one thing, it is having yielded to the false appeal of an arranged marriage . . . Yes, I was happier with the cries and the shame, and my uncle's beatings, with men's envious looks . . . I know that most men will tell you that lying is a necessary compromise, and I am quite willing to understand their reasons as long as they don't try to convert me to their practices, which for me are worse than all the vices they denounce. In my distress I found that truth was the servant of my love, and a friend that never lets you down. What upsets me most is that Peter should have thought that I could betray him, and time does nothing to heal the scars. It's as if he never loved me, or loved somebody else.'

'He was driven mad by his suffering.'

She looked at me and said nothing. She had no need to tell me that there was no separation in her heart between her own suffering and that of the man she loved—the man she loves. A moment passed. Then:

'Now will you tell me when he is coming?'

I had forgotten my lie, and my cheeks flushed . . . But her anger vanished like a shifting wind; only her sweet impatience remained.

'Soon, Heloise, soon . . .'

She turned towards me; her eyes shone in the firelight and her hair was dishevelled. She had perfect dignity and she was totally desirable; she was untouchable and so delicate that if a finger were laid on her breast her body would come to life. Her soul was pure and her body burned. She was man's dream and man's fear—Eve and Mary, Magdalene and Judith. She was an abbess. She was a lover.

Time was of no relevance.

21

PETER ABELARD arrived having broken some bones in a bad fall from his horse. As he constantly suspected, it may have been one of his murderous monks who had cut the straps of his saddle; or it may have been that being a poor horseman, and being too heavy and getting on in years, he had fallen off.

Three, almost four, years had passed since he had left the Paraclete; living among brutes, he had acquired something brutish himself. There was a hunted look about the proud gleam in his dark eyes.

The women scattered in fear when he arrived. Only Heloise stayed behind to embrace him: she looked important, whereas he looked small. They were both dressed in black. They went away to pray together in the little chapel I had built, which was set apart, and in which I had placed the altar that was buffeted by the wind, with its poorly hewn stones and all our hopes of consolation.

They were no longer parted lovers, but the distance was just as great: they were alone in the world as they had never stopped being, perhaps. They too had made time an irrelevance, and in the silence of their separation a murmuring continued, fleeting over the streams and mountain tops. My heart sank once more. It is something that never stops and that never goes away — and that which is unfulfilled remains in our hearts throughout our lives and, no doubt, at the hour of our death, regret will still consume us — with vanity.

When they came out of the chapel they looked as though they were dazzled by the light; they did not touch each other, but I could sense her watchfulness and her concern. He walked as if he might fall at every step, stumbling heavily and almost falling, and holding out his arms like a blind man without a guide, anxious about every stone in his path.

The church's single bell chimed. They walked into the small porch — and in my mind there was the inevitable memory of their marriage, and suddenly the years weighed down once more, the burden of our lined faces, our aging bones — and we followed them in procession. James the Redhead, who was alongside me, was the only one not prey to the emotion that gripped us.

'Is he a priest, that oaf of yours?'

I indicated that he was not; then, with all the speed his little legs could carry him, he forced his way through a group of nuns, pushed past Heloise and Abelard and took his place in front of the altar.

He signalled to them to separate and they did as they were told: women to the left and men, that is to say, Peter Abelard and I, to the right.

I looked about me: none of those who had sought shelter with us at the Paraclete was there. They, the lost ones, had left during the night.

Spirit of God, light their way. Spirit of God, protect them.

An arm's length separated Heloise and Abelard. At midday, during the offertory, a ray of sunlight beamed down between them. She reached out her arm to him and touched him; his eyes did not flicker. Then she took his hand and he allowed her to do so.

They remained like that, holding hands, with the sun shining on them, throughout the rest of the Mass.

The suffering returned at night—I mean the suffering that rends the soul, the wound that always closes and always opens up again.

I did not sleep.

I heard the murmuring of their voices and then the words that grew louder, the stream that swells in the storm, and the banging, the shuffling, the blows perhaps.

I did not move.

We like to fathom other people's secrets, to decipher their thoughts and the most secret stirrings of their hearts. This wish to discover more is limitless, but the day that, by some unlikely chance, we find out what we want to know, we recoil in fear at this beating heart, this palpitating blood. And the old bitterness re-surfaces: cursed be the heart that understands.

My hand was on my stomach to calm myself: my body which I did not much care for, my plump thighs, and my face which I myself did not recognise. I remembered the night when the frail barrier that had kept me from intruding on their privacy had given way—when the self-control imposed by my fear was swept away. 'Do not think,' an Arab seer had once told me, 'that there can be any happiness to be gained from seeing the fate that lies in store for others.'

Nevertheless, it is impossible to do otherwise.

I left my bedroom and stood outside Peter's door—scarcely surprised that she should have joined him, as she did in the past, in the happy times of their clandestine nights together at Fulbert's house. I walked with the stealth of a thief, smiling in the night: so this was how they used to love.

'You entrusted me to God so that you wouldn't have to admit you were abandoning me, I whom you had married before Him and before man. You desired me, you took me and you discarded me. You had all that you wanted and more. Speak to me honestly, imagine that I'm your friend . . .'

'You are my friend . . .'

'Did you only want that—your pleasure?'

'When I was far away from you, that's what I thought, yes.'

'Say it: you did not love me.'

'When I was far away, I thought that what I called love was concupiscence.'

'And now?'

'God . . .'

'That's enough of your God! When it's a question of grasping men's minds you put him to one side. But when it's a question of love . . .'

'Love without God?'

'Look at me, master, look, touch and understand! How poor your memory is, how frightened you are . . .'

'I remember everything.'

'Do you remember the women you desired and which my love proffered to what you call your "concupiscence"? And the prostitute we visited with whom I watched you fornicate while I held your hand and told you "I love you"?'

'I remember.'

'Do you remember that my love was filled with every kind of desire and that you referred to me as "all women"?'

'I know.'

'Do you know that it meant nothing to me to be the wife of the greatest philosopher in the world—and less than nothing had you been king or emperor of the world—as long as I could call myself your girl, your whore?'

'I know that too.'

'And yet, do you remember the words your lips uttered when you put me in prison?'

'I do not forget them.'

'Don't forget: I am your friend, your sweet friend to whom

you can confide your sorrows, and your head can rest upon my shoulder . . .'

'I do not forget.'

Their voices echoed in the night like a pagan mass with the responses—Peter's solemn, monotone and sad, Heloise's violent and tender in turn.

'Why, Peter? What or whom were you afraid of? William?'

'William . . .'

'Your little Englishman, as you call him . . . Did you see us leaving together hand in hand? My poor Peter . . . Tell me—you a man of God—tell me wherein lies the sin: is it in the intention you think you have discerned in two quite innocent creatures? Or is it in your own deeds, your own barbarity?'

'Is it to me you are speaking of barbarity?'

For the first time it was he who raised his voice.

'To you, my love. You have refused to be angry with God, you're not going to be angry with me?'

'I'm not angry. I love you as I used not to love you—but I do not love you as you wish me to love you . . .'

'I don't understand any of that, Peter. I've read books and I've talked to these women who are with me—the widows who have experienced love, women who have been rejected by it, virgins who have dreamed of it, those who have been loved too much and those who have been badly loved—and everywhere I have found only one way to love.'

I was feeling cold again. There was a long silence; then I could hear their arms searching for each other and their intermittent breath. *I have found only one way to love.*

'Do you remember my body,' she said in a voice so low that I may have been dreaming it, 'my body which you touched in all its most intimate recesses, my body which you never stopped exploring and on which you saw imaginary countries, my body over which you said your pagan prayers . . .'

'Heloise . . .'

'Is it blasphemous simply to ask you whether you remember?'

'Heloise . . .'

'That's what you said to me when you taught me that I existed not just with words any longer, but with the caresses that we particularly liked—and those cries and the laughter that we had to stifle so that my uncle should not hear us . . .'

As she spoke in that soft, alluring tone, not allowing him to leave, murmuring her desire and making her voice echo with memories, I could hear the sound of clothes crumpling and being removed. Through the crack in the door, it was not her naked body that I saw, but its shadow.

'Heloise . . .'

'Call me by that name once more; if you cannot touch me with your hands, your slender hands so strong and gentle, touch me with that sweet name of Heloise that so many girls in Paris sang for your sake—a song which I confess I sang, too, on the nights we were apart, not out of love for myself, but out of love for you. Peter, give me your hand again. Do not be frightened, I implore you. It's nothing, my love, it doesn't exist, it's a dream, let time forget us for this night, let suffering pay us no heed—I beg you, the dawn shall not know, nor shall anyone, all that will be left is a trace of the old sweetness on your skin, where you can press your lips when you feel lonely, and a perfume which perhaps only you can smell . . .'

'Heloise, I can't.'

His voice came out in a breath, a sob, and she cried with him, weeping the tears she had not wept—all anger spent, wretched in his own wretchedness, bitter in his bitterness . . .

'God . . .'

This time she said nothing, allowing the name of the Lord to take its place in the midst of the silence and the night.

'You may not want to hear it,' Peter began softly, 'but our master has taken us back with a firm hand, and he now summons us together to love, to love of him . . .'

'It was not he whom I obeyed, but you.'

'Do you still wish to obey me?'

'Yes, I believe so.'

'If I ask you to obey me in God, would you do so?'

'Is there another way to be loved by you now?'

'There is no other.'

I withdrew softly. In my bedroom, I lit the candle that had gone out and I remained on my feet for a long time until my legs began to ache. I thought of the shadow of Heloise naked as I gazed at my own shadow on the cold stone. I murmured her name and, as I moved, my body's shadow moved with the breath that lit the flame. I was—though only in my dreams—someone other than myself, perhaps two people, I was a dance.

That was what my life was: a shadow in their shadow.

The following day, Peter Abelard gave Heloise the monastery of the Paraclete, with all its buildings and dependencies, all its lands, barns and mills, the revenue from four woods, a fishery, five bread ovens—and he made her abbess.

They were happy months—as far as I could tell.

After years of looking after myself in my own strange way, I would not have endured Peter taking control and making me put up with his whims and his changes of mood. But as abbess Heloise had a firm and gentle authority and I was quite content to remain in the background behind her.

She had a private room built inside the nuns' dormitory. Peter and I lived in the brand new hostelry and we took our meals with the pilgrims and travellers. Otherwise, we joined the nuns for the offices and for Mass.

They spent many hours alone together, either in the *scriptorium* which had been my refuge, or else walking beside the river, preparing what was to become the convent's Rule, organising the prayers—and even correcting them—and composing hymns. I went back to my old job of copyist, happy to be dictated to by these two fine minds—and during the offices, I let myself be immersed in the beauty of this very special liturgy they had written. For although it is true that Peter was responsible for the overall structure and the harmonies, Heloise helped him choose the subjects and, in particular, brought to the writing her femininity and her humanity, not to mention her close familiarity with all the Latin poets.

> *With his right arm,*
> *the Husband clasps*
> *the Bride,*
> *she sleeps, obedient.*
> *Her heart watches*
> *while her body sleeps*
> *and lies in the rounded arm*
> *of her graceful spouse.*

As I heard this singing echo through the nave, I couldn't help thinking of what someone like Bernard of Clairvaux, or his friend, the pure and redoubtable William of Saint-Thierry, would say. Nothing more than a modest evocation of The Song of Songs, the two lovers would have said, innocently and in unison, now that they had become, as Abelard had wished, spouses in Christ. But even if it appeared in a song sung by virgins, could this 'rounded arm' conjure up anything else when sung by them other than that joyful peace that comes after love, that surrender of the flesh? I sensed strongly that every word they uttered until the end of their lives would be listened to by people who knew their story and who would pledge them their hatred or their compassion, their admiration or their repulsion.

Peace did not last for long.

There were messages from Saint-Denis, an emissary from Comte Thibaut. Above all, there were the rumours that were rife, which my friend the Redhead related to me in sad and mocking tones. He no longer regarded Abelard suspiciously as he had in the early days, but with the amused curiosity with which you observe a hybrid animal—the kind you see on chapiters in cloisters.

'Why are they being persecuted like this?' he asked me one

morning. 'If some are to be believed, I'm risking the salvation of my soul by celebrating Mass with them. You know me—whatever they say is of no account . . . I don't like them, these hypocrites and scandalmongers . . .'

'They're telling us a very old story that conceals a very old fear.'

'As far as I'm concerned, they've been foolish, they've been punished and they've repented. I've not got that much imagination . . . Or else they've got too much!'

I knew that intelligent smile in his eyes: it's comforting to appear simpler than one really is, not to mention the pleasure of being an idiot in the eyes of idiots.

'I don't like God making too much of a fuss,' the Redhead continued . . .

'Your notion of fuss is not theirs.'

'It doesn't matter to me—as long as they can love. I'm not like the bishop, who sees fault in their very names . . .'

'They need peace.'

The Redhead scratched his forehead.

'I know what people are like, my friend. They won't find it here.'

She was sitting by the river-bank, amusing herself by tossing pebbles into the water, as children do; she was also plaiting autumn leaves together before tearing them up. If she heard my approach, she didn't turn round. My legs were heavy with the weariness of all these years.

'We're leaving tonight,' I said.

'Are you going with him this time?'

'No. He is returning to Saint-Gildas and I'm going to Cluny.'

'Our friend Peter the Child . . . That's where he ought to go. I fear for him in this dreadful Brittany and I know he's frightened too.'

'He insists on going back there. I can't see what he wants to salvage, what he hopes for or what he fears . . .'

'Is it you who is driving him away from here?'

I recognised that terrible way she had, so soft in tone, but so unexpected, of asking questions that could hurt.

'You know very well I'm not. All I did was to state what is being said. If he doesn't leave, he will be driven out . . .'

'I know that too, William. Forgive me. It's just that once again I'm feeling sad, as I always shall.'

She laughed wearily. Their suffering was meaningless and the Redhead was right: there was no peace. Their dream of a dual monastery was nothing but a fantasy—yet another. He was not Robert of Arbrissel—the saint who never would be a saint, despite Andrew's efforts—and she was not Petronilla. They carried their fate with them.

'How you've changed . . .'

'Me?'

I laughed too. As soon as I believed in something, I discovered the contrary: our revolutions bring us back to our point of departure. The world itself changes—and yet it doesn't change. An order is established which contains the seed of disorder. These stones which we heaved and carved, these stones that became an altar, will they return to stone and dust? All the same, these buildings, the church, the chapel, the wall and the farm— and that one, on the other side of the river, and the men who mend their tools and work, and the women who pray and sing, and the pilgrims who pass by . . . Stone and dust. Life: a wandering path. All these noble feelings: nothing. Exile in a strange land. What had I found, deep in that starlit night? *A few traces of love* . . . Those were the very words I had mumbled. But confronted by the woman who did not love me, the traces were marks on a wax tablet, which faded away.

'Were you to ask me for my blood itself,' I murmured, 'I would give it to you . . .'

'Your blood?'

She stood up, dropped her garland of leaves, and took both my hands which she placed together in hers.

'Who is asking for your blood?'

I suddenly felt ashamed of myself. I had thought of myself as Ovid and Job and Solomon from Ecclesiastes — as if a gust of despair had swept over me and left nothing behind.

'Forgive me, Heloise. You are the life I live and the love through which I love, the air that I breathe and the blood that flows through my veins. And you say that I have changed . . .'

'Your eyes are full of tears, William.'

'Sometimes I allow myself to be pitied.'

'Weep with me, if you wish.'

'I haven't even the right to call you "mother".'

'Call me what you will.'

'My love . . .'

'Not that . . .'

'Now you see. I would like to exchange our sorrows — and to suffer as you suffer if I could — just for one night — to be loved by you as you love him.'

'I would not wish it on you,' she said sadly.

She paused and looked at me; she was already making her way towards the convent. I took her wrist and led her towards the Arduzon brook. Above the dark woods the stormy sky grew more intense. The gaps in the clearing offered neither hope nor shelter; and yet it was impossible not to see beauty in this world and not to be affected by it — however reluctantly.

'My dreams,' she said, 'were identical to those of my classical heroines and I used to dread the fate of the biblical ones such as Dinah or the daughter of Jephthah . . . It seems to me that I'm one of them now and that some young girl, hundreds of years from now, will weep over my fate as I wept over those of Dido and Cornelia.'

'Who will write it?'

The question had shot from my mouth unwittingly.

'What do you mean?' she asked as a way of gaining time.

'You know very well. He thinks he will live on with his *Theologia*, his *Sic et Non*, his Commentaries, and I don't know what else . . . But everything has been burned and everything will be burned again — and all that will remain will be these pebbles you were tossing into the river, the leaves, even the bag of ashes that he takes with him will be scattered.'

'You're wrong. He's greater than you say he is, and even greater than his pride and this fixation with persecution that continues to tear him apart nowadays. And if his philosophical works are burned, there are still his songs . . .'

'Food for the wind.'

'You're jealous, William.'

'I probably am jealous, but am I wrong because of that?'

'Probably.'

'Anyway, I didn't ask you whether his books would be read, I asked you how — upon what stone, in which poem — your story would be told . . .'

'Who cares about a woman?'

'All those who care about love.'

The first drops of rain had begun to fall and the nearest shelter was a barn about half a league from the convent. We ran there.

'You're leaving tonight, in the storm . . .'

'We'll leave whatever the weather — but it will be a star-filled night, you'll see.'

The sound of the rain on the thatched roof was like the crackle of twigs in a fire. The barn was dry and dark; Heloise was certainly frightened. Her hand did not leave mine.

'Do you remember your promise?'

I could not help thinking of that night when I had spied on them — and how she had asked him whether he remembered her body . . .

'So, could you ever have loved me?'

The question hung in the darkness for a few seconds. She continued to hold my hand — I had nothing further to ask her.

'Allow me not to answer you.'

I trembled as I took her in my arms. Don't be frightened, I

said, I know of your love, but let me tell you of mine while the storm rages, let me love you until the rain stops, just hold you in my arms, run my hand through your hair, simply to exorcise my regrets. Imagine that this barn caught fire and that nothing remained, think of my love while this rain and this fire last, let it blaze and reduce itself to ashes (I told you that there would be nothing left of his books, but what shall I say of myself, my love? Not a thing, nothing, not a trace, not a single ash or speck of dust, I would not have to ask to be buried in the mud before it swallowed me up and filled my mouth and my nostrils, not giving me time to bid farewell to the world), I promise you that nothing shall remain—no trace of a kiss, nothing even in your memory, it will be like a dream, a wisp that you blow from your hand.

When the rain stopped I helped her to her feet and, in the dampness, bathed by the moonlight which could already be seen through the clouds, I brushed the straw from her habit.

When the time came for our departure, the nuns rose from their beds and Matins was sung in the darkened nave, as the wind blew through the tall trees.

> *Now I see what I have desired,*
> *now I hold what I have loved,*
> *now I laugh whereas then I cried,*
> *I rejoice more than I have suffered:*
> *I laughed in the morning, I cried at night,*
> *in the morning I laughed, at night I cried.*

There was no leave-taking, no embracing or wringing of hands—yet she would not see him again, even as the wind took him away—surrounded by her sisters, she was singing the nuptial hymn of the wedding that had never been theirs.

As the voices faded beneath a star-drenched sky, we were already on our way. He was travelling westwards and I was going south; we walked together for a league, sharing the coolness of the night air, our horses beside us, he accompanied by two men and I by myself.

At the crossroads I bade him farewell and he said nothing, I watched him pass out of sight, this strange man, my master, the man whom Heloise loved with a love that was unconfined.

Now I am alone—more alone than I have ever been.

Now I am alone and I know.

Many a time I thought I was on the right road and I was in a desert. But now's the time.

You shall be the first, Heloise. You shall be the first woman whom men can love and your lover will be the first man. Yes, of course there was Adam and Eve—but you shall be the Adam and Eve of love.

And I, William of Oxford, the man who loved you and whom you did not love, I shall keep your story in my heart until I die, until I become dust and ashes, mud and decay.

Part IV

Come the Storm

22

Come the storm, I shall not be shaken,
the winds may blow but I shall not be disturbed,
for my roots are in solid ground.

Peter Abelard, *Profession of Faith*

T HE SOUND of 400 monks intoning psalms at the Mass
that follows Terce, together with the chanting and the
hymns, can be powerfully affecting, for they swell the
chest and make one long to be a monk in order to belong to this
family of Christ, to be a tiny voice in this liturgy — this perpetual song — a footstep in this ambulatory, a shadow beneath this
figure of Christ who reigns wholly and indivisibly from the
vault of the choir.

But I am not a monk.

My friend, Abbot Peter of Montboissier — who was known as
Peter the Child many years ago — suggested it early on and I was
tempted by that dream that was not for me. I tried to imagine
myself walking slowly up to the altar, handing over my promis-
sory note and pronouncing my vows; but it is the image of
Abelard's sad profession of faith, and that of Heloise's tears that
stand out, and not that of the very beautiful ceremony at Cluny.

Given my obstinate determination to remain a simple cleric, Peter left me to be enlightened by God's grace.

Over the years, my strangeness has become something normal. I am dressed like a monk — apart from a cowl — my tonsure is the same as a monk's, I wash and drink like a monk. I am chaste like a monk.

I proclaimed my vows alone on the dusty road on which I travelled down from Troyes to Auxerre, Avallon and Autun. I pronounced them, with closed lips, in front of the tympana of churches, in the cloisters of priories that received me, I spoke them when I was spattered with mud from horses' hoofs, whenever I had been insulted or robbed, when I was asleep and when I was awake.

I love you.

Without you I cannot live.

I went away from you, my love, and I could see clearly that it was pointless hoping to see you again, knowing that you did not love me and never would love me. But curiously, the further away I went, the greater the distance between us, the more my resolve grew firmer. *My heart is not mine* . . . I have vowed to love you in the secrecy of my heart, to honour you in everything, to serve you and to sing your praises. When you took the veil you were obeying Peter, not God, and I was obeying nothing but the certainty that was in my heart. I could not love you? I could love only you.

I thought of Peter, condemned because of the audacity of his treatise on the Holy Trinity and his blasphemous comparisons. It was not my book they would have burned, but me, had I suggested that we were three and one simultaneously, appallingly immured by our loneliness, and secretly united in love.

Of course, there would still be days when I was angry, days when bitterness rose in the back of my throat and made me utter wicked words, and of course there were still tears and bouts of rage, and unfulfilled solace. But my determination was unfailing, and an irrevocable decision had been made — which I had no need to share with anyone except you in the secrecy of my heart. *My secret rests with me ...*

To have made any other vows than those: that, in fact, is when I would have been blasphemous.

At night, I wake up for the vigils, I light my candle and I write; I sleep, if I can, until Matins and I rise at Prime. I cross the already bustling streets of the town and I enter the monastery walls through the door next to the stables, above which is the dormitory for impoverished pilgrims. Then I enter the enclosure by the door to the south of the church. In the inner courtyard, I walk alongside the columns of the unfinished narthex, and here I am at the guesthouse where, throughout the year, the chamberlain keeps a bed free for me, in which I hardly ever sleep.

I walk into the cloister as if I was at home. In almost ten years, I have seen monks arrive and monks die; a special bond links me to them, even if a world of difference still divides us.

For several months now I have been teaching the novices grammar, taking a certain malicious pleasure in confronting the purity of their souls with that of their Latin. After all, if we can read The Song of Songs as allegory, why should it not be the same with the *Ars amatoria* or the *Aeneid*? This is what I claim, a trifle disingenuously, knowing that with the intricacies of the optative I am introducing those delicate souls to fresh torments.

I love them, these young men with their bright, shining eyes, whether or not they have elected to be here. I love the oblates, the younger brothers who have no hope of inheritance, whose expectations of life have never strayed beyond the Choir Belfry, the Bisants Belfry, or the Clock Tower, and whose absent-minded gaze I can sometimes sense reaching out to the gentle hills, escaping from the narrow valley of the River Grosne in search of somewhere else, a different destiny. I also love those who are impatient to make their vows, those young souls who are inflamed with God's zeal, who love Christ as one loves a woman, who want both to serve and pray. I love those who doubt even as they are transported, those who are affeared in the midst of prayer, those who while chanting suddenly understand the perspective of their lives, tremble and shed tears. I love their thoughtfulness, their occasional lack of concern, and the inept words that sometimes escape from their lips which will abide by the virtues of silence soon enough. I love the fact that they yearn, that they believe, that they have doubts, and, in church, I love to see them raise their eyes to the chapiters and follow the flights of the arcatures. So high and so immense! You need to break your neck in order to understand that men have built something that is not a work of man but a work of God.

I also love—though I cannot say this to Peter, or to the prior, or to the priory master—those who give up and leave, at dusk, to confront solitude and reprobation. Being a free man and not a monk, I sometimes accompany them through the streets of the town and I may offer a few friendly words to them in their confusion, or else I say nothing, just silence, a hand on their scrawny shoulder, a smile for their eyes that are hollow from worry and sleeplessness.

It's rare for them not to speak to me, or not to confide their troubles in me or their expectations. They regard the professed monks with a strange mixture of admiration and fear: for they are not allowed to speak to them, and they appear to them, far away in the church choir-stalls, like a breed apart; not like gods, of course (that's for extinct beliefs), but not quite men either (for they know what it's like to be men, they've suffered and grieved already, they've wept, they've torn their nails out and their hearts have bled)—but angels perhaps. Is it possible that by some miraculous ceremony, which they have dreamed about more often than they have witnessed, they will join them one day? That would be wonderful, though it seems to them that they will always lack something of the necessary dignity. The uncertainty as to the moment when they will be considered ready adds to the mystery and deepens it.

I know them so well, though, that the prior, Gérard, often

consults me: we talk about one, whose impenetrable expression reveals some inner torment, and we discuss another who is quite the reverse, and whose ardent zeal and whose tears that flow constantly whenever he is praying may conceal the remnants of earthly ambition. We drink some good red wine and I feel fully at ease: I give my opinion, I make decisions, I inform . . . Sometimes I reckon Gérard is cruel, but he's the one who has to decide — I must be even more perverted, for there I am lurking in the shadows, blessed with their trust and their innocence, urging them on or restraining them, helping or hindering them.

Abbot Peter of Montboissier frequently summons me — he questions me, consults me or simply talks to me. He likes the fact that for me he is still the Peter the Child whom I knew on the Île de la Cité, when we attended Peter Abelard's lectures. Here he is the object of admiration and this stifles him, for his simplicity of heart and manner is ill-suited to it — yet this only serves to increase it. And then there's his constant activity, his travelling, his political role, his involvement (and he shares his growing anxieties about this with me) in the Cluny communities all over Europe, his concern with the renewal of the liturgy, the letters he writes endlessly, his battles with enemies within and without — all these give him little peace.

When we are together, I often allow moments of silence so that he can rest. He closes his eyes and I know he appreciates those brief pauses when there is no singing, no reading, no quarrelling — perhaps even no meditation or prayer, just a short time given over to the pure grace of God. He knows that because of his wisdom, and in spite of his still being young, he is called the Venerable. He doesn't care for this — he does not like any gesture of excessive reverence and he makes fun of the letters that Bernard of Clairvaux sends him — 'What is it to be this time,' he sighs as he breaks the seal, 'insults or declarations of divine love?'

I have mentioned his simplicity; I also love his humanity, which allows him to view each man present equally — not in the manner of Suger, who considers them only according to whatever grandiose project is on his mind—but as if he were looking at them from within their own soul, as if he knew them better than they know themselves. In this way, with a few words, they come to discover themselves, to unburden themselves without shame or fear, and his kindliness is thus their reward.

Yet as he grows older, this same man (with his still rosy cheeks, and his eyes that are blue as a child's) is becoming obsessed with heretics, obsessed with blasphemers, obsessed with the Saracens, obsessed with the Jews—and is driven by a cold and fierce hatred. Over the passing months and years, I watched as his curiosity became transformed into a crusading zeal. He questioned me about Rachid and about the Arabs I encountered in Spain. He claims to know the *Talmud* and plans—an insane undertaking—to have the *Koran* translated. He says he will approach the Saracens if necessary in order to do so.

I remember my master Abelard and his friendship with Rachi's grandsons—I can hear his voice telling me that if he continued to be humiliated by Christians, he would become a Muslim. But in Peter of Montboissier I have a formidable warrior for the faith alongside me, who does not wish to *know* but to destroy. *Against the Pétrobusiens, Against the Jews, Against the Saracens* . . . His mind teems with any number of treatises that reveal an awesome determination behind his gentle appearance. Worse: he does not want to kill by the sword, but by employing that same gentleness, by what he calls love. I admit—and I tell him so without, of course, convincing him—that that kind of love frightens me.

He wants to take me on some of his travels—to Rome, and to Spain where King Alfonso has given so much to Cluny, and to the abbeys that are subject to the order. I nearly always refuse: it's as if my migratory spirit has deserted me forever. My living space lies here, all I want is to see the tiles on the towers and the beams on the ceiling of my bedroom, and the gemel-windows that open onto the street. I only want to see the faces of the people of Cluny, the monks and artisans, the priests and the wine-makers. My peace of God, my peace of love are here.

I wish to die here, like the last man lost amongst the angels.

I returned to the Paraclete with fear in my belly, on a stormy day heavy with thunder, skirting the pools of black water where the devils and the phantoms I most feared slumbered. I wanted and yet did not want to go—I had obeyed the Venerable's request to pay a visit on his behalf. I had to preserve an impassive expression on my face while my heart pounded. Love—the serpent's head that sprouts forth when you cut it off. Love—the heartstring of the lonely, the poison that makes you live.

Driven away from Argenteuil and outlawed, within a few years Heloise had re-gained her standing and her honour. The counts, the bishops, the king, the pope himself (the very one who had supported Suger by repeating his slanderous accusations of debauchery against her) had gone from disapproval to admiration while failing to provide the pardon she did not ask for.

The gifts and the lands had increased, as had the tithes and emoluments, the ovens and the woods, and the Paraclete was no longer home to a collection of exiled and humiliated women, but an organised community where it was considered fashionable for well-born widows to come to die.

I arrived during Mass—and I recognised one of the hymns written for her by Abelard. This church, I recalled, had been *my church*—just as the earth and the trees and the wind had been— and yet it gave me an odd feeling, as if I had belonged there only in my dreams. I left during the office and went to gather my thoughts alone in the chapel, worried about whether I would find the two stones that had made up my altar. They were there.

She caught me by surprise while I was praying and knelt down beside me without saying a word. When we stood up, she took me in her arms, in that particular way she had, with that joyful abandon of the body which troubled me so much, and which, every time, regardless of the years and the sadness, left me foolishly hoping.

'I've missed you,' she said.

'So have I.'

We set off to walk by the river and she showed me how well the buildings had been completed, and told me about the Rule which Abelard had given them, his liturgy and his prayers . . .

'Do you have anything else of his?'

'Do you think that's nothing?'

'I didn't say that. I thought . . .'

She smiled—but I could immediately recognise that temper which she probably kept under tight control.

'You imagined that he would write to me, that he would comfort me and help me with his advice. No, none of this, my friend: his songs and his prayers. And the fact that, thanks to his kindness, we are able to eat meat a little more often than the others . . . His gentle Rule . . . You remember his words ten years ago: brother and sister in Christ. This is what we are.'

'He hasn't written to me either. All I know of him is what travellers tell me.'

'It's the same for me: his presence is a passing cloud blown by the wind. And you know how the wind can blow, in these parts.'

'What have you heard?'

'That his monks did not kill him, after all . . .'

'. . . and that he is now back in Paris, where he teaches on the Mount, where the students rush to listen to his words more than ever . . . and where his enemies gather together in the shadows more than ever and vow to ruin him.'

'Do you know that?'

It was she who let slip this exclamation of concern.

'And, of course, he ignores them.'

'Of course.'

'Garlande is dead, his family in disgrace. They say that Suger is the rising star in the eyes of Louis VII.'

'Suger . . .'

272

The monastery buildings stood out in the twilight and the stones glinted ochre in the setting sun. Rain still threatened; to the west, the sun could be seen through one small clearing in the heavy clouds.

Through the clearing, we could see a dark shape running towards us. Heloise stopped speaking.

'What's going on?' I asked.

She didn't answer. The girl—a novice, probably—was breathless.

'Mother, mother,' she whispered, panting heavily, but she was unable to say anything else . . .

'Calm yourself,' Heloise said gently.

'Mother, he's here.'

My heart was thumping too.

'Very well, who is it?' she asked.

But already her face had lit up with a kind of smile—the extraordinary coincidence of his visit had made her forget mine.

'The Abbot of Clairvaux,' the novice at last replied.

'Who did you say?'

Both of us stared in amazement.

'Bernard, Mother, the Abbot of Clairvaux.'

'Come,' Heloise said to me.

Bernard of Clairvaux travelled on his own with his secretary Nicolas, a small man with dark, alert eyes, who smiled as much as his master looked gloomy, as if he wanted to ask forgiveness on his behalf for the gloom that constantly emanated from him. The time would come when this man would betray him: each of us has the Judas he deserves—but this fellow would not hang himself, he would make sure his talents were appreciated elsewhere.

That evening, the white shadow of the Abbot of Clairvaux attended Compline and Vespers and refused to take supper. I knew that he was often racked by stomach pains and that days could pass without him consuming any food whatsoever, preferring the pain of fasting to that of indigestion.

The following day, he declined the offer to say Mass, claiming that he was a pilgrim among pilgrims, and he attended prayers, almost silently to begin with, in the chapterhouse. I watched him looking at Heloise with an almost loving intensity. When the service was over (and even though I had not, until then, seen Heloise in her role as abbess, it was not hard to see that particular solemnity had been given that morning to the reading of the Rule and the confessions of minor omissions), she signalled to her nuns to leave. With a quick glance, Bernard indicated to Nicolas that he should do the same. I was about to follow them, but she restrained me. He looked at me for the first time, in the way that one looks at a beetle, before turning to Heloise.

'Your fervour has touched me, most dear Sister, and I have been able to see with my own eyes the rumours that have been reaching me for a long time concerning your piety . . .'

He raised his hand.

'The finger of God,' he said, enunciating his syllables, 'the finger of God has made its trace in my heart . . . He has prepared a place for you there, Sister. I was with you in spirit before I was with you in body.'

I could not believe my ears. Abelard, at the time of his great passion, would not have expressed himself more ardently. I did not know what I should do: leave? I made as if to go, but Heloise's gaze rooted me to the stone bench.

'The words you utter flow straight to my soul, Brother. Although my unworthiness is great, my heart is beholden to you.'

Their dialogue continued in this caressing, loving way, employing sensual imagery that was exalted in his case, circumspect in hers. No, she never lowered her guard. She was right, for the attack soon came.

'There is only one thing that—I say this as a brother questioning his sister—surprised me, and it is the curious way you have of saying the Our Father . . .'

The prayer used at the Paraclete is not the usual *Give me this day our daily bread*, but a strange *Give us this day our super-*

substantial bread . . . I was almost reassured: these were no longer the words of the lover, but those of the inquisitor — those that made him famous and feared throughout Christendom.

'Our master Peter Abelard took this manner of praying from the evangelist . . .'

'Matthew, I know, of course — but all the same, the tradition of our church . . .'

'Did the Lord not say: "I am the truth" and not "I am the custom"?'

She spoke these words gently, her eyes lowered, and Bernard bowed graciously. Only the name of Peter Abelard, which she mentioned deliberately, had brought a slight frown to his face. He knew what he wished to know: the wretch was still at work.

He stood up and we followed him into the cloister; in front of us, the nuns stepped to one side. Suddenly he grimaced and had to stop — he leaned against a column and we hurried over to hold him up.

'It's nothing,' he said. 'It's a long time now since I've known any pleasure and that bitterness has consumed me . . . I live in accordance with the inner man . . .'

As he waited for the inner man, the outer man was obliged to sit down on a bench, his body riven in two by vomiting that produced nothing but a yellowish bile.

'It's nothing,' he repeated, when the attack had abated a little. 'When everything that evolves from the body has left you or is nothing but pain, it is then that you belong to the Spirit, it is then that you live truly in God.'

The strangest thing about him were his eyes: there was a humanity within them, or should I say a light that comes from God, not from man, and a strength that cannot actually come from his ravaged body. Nicolas helped him to his feet.

'Let us go and dictate,' he murmured.

Heloise led them to the *scriptorium*.

'I should like my heart to unwind in your presence, like a parchment . . .'

'Your friendship . . .'

'Enter into your heart, my friend and my sister, and you shall see mine. I want to love you, to serve you, and to take you away with me.'

'My weakness . . .'

He took her hands and clasped them, kissing them with the ardour of a lover; she did not protect herself, but I could sense that she'd been taken captive.

'Heloise, Heloise, my sister, my friend, my dove, Heloise, I so long for you to take care . . .'

'Care?'

'Did you not tell me that a man was your master?'

'He is the master of my little flock — though if you prefer — the founder, the friend, the man who never stops thinking about us.'

'Heloise, my sister, my beauteous one, my sweetness, but you know that you have only one master.'

Heloise was no longer afraid. She looked him in the eye.

'I have only one master, and it is love.'

Bernard de Clairvaux had nothing to say. *If I speak in the tongues of men and of angels, but have not love . . .*

I stayed at the Paraclete for a few more days following the departure of the master of the Cistercians. I sensed a vague menace in the air, but I would have been incapable of saying what it was.

Heloise, merely by her expressions, and without uttering a single harsh word, had created the sort of distance between us that women know how to impose in order to protect themselves, whenever they wish to do so. She also imposed silence on me.

I delayed my departure in vain, waiting for some change, some knock of fate, which of course did not occur. Heaven never concerns itself with our fantasies and our vanities.

I went to Saint-Aubin on foot; they were windy days, when everything swayed and blew away, except for the steeple on the other side of the hill. My friend James the Redhead was at home in bed, in the small room next to the church, short of breath still and now unable to say a word. His eyes lit up and I could see his intelligence, but also his helplessness and his anger when the old woman who fed him a little soup and cleaned him (for he had become like a small child) made a sudden movement. I went to see him several times, and I stayed with him and held his scrawny little hand. Sometimes one of those great bouts of laughter that used to possess him would pass over his face—but it was now a frown that deformed his features horribly—as if he had to bring across the memory of the world's follies from the other side. I said goodbye to him in a way that I would never have dared to do: by kissing him on the forehead; on his wrinkled skin which no longer possessed that marvellous moistness that life endows. He looked at me, but already he could no longer see me. I should like to think that the dying have a better understanding—but this knowledge that is soundless, without the flicker of a look, without any movement, without a breath, is a science that men cannot learn.

Without saying anything, Heloise had found a simple way of showing me the futility of my waiting: she left before I did. Her prioress—I remember that her name was Monica, like Augustine's mother—told me that she had been obliged to pay a long-deferred visit to the Count of Champagne. A long-deferred visit . . . these words had an immediate effect on me: it was the action of grace that helped me remember better who I was and what my purpose was.

Straightaway, I saddled my horse and set off with my few belongings. I was two leagues away from the abbey when a pain streaked through my skull, a pain that was brief, excruciating and baffling, and which almost caused me to fall off my horse. I stopped by the foot of an oak tree. The blood was still throbbing through my head. I wanted to turn around and, quite illogically, an image of Heloise waiting for me with open arms formed in my mind. Then, as I gathered my breath and the pain abated, I could visualise the look in James the Redhead's eyes and his inscrutable wisdom.

I stood up, brushed off the dust, and continued on my way.

The Venerable asked me for a detailed account and I gave it him freely. I believe he knew my feelings without my having to open my heart to him; I preferred not to know whether he respected them or whether—as was more likely—they were of no interest to him.

We were alone in the upper chapel of the Château des Moines, at Berzé—a place I never visit without an odd feeling, knowing that my friend Christian had worked there.

'He's in danger,' he said.

'Who is?'

'Abelard, of course.'

'Why?'

'Can't you guess?'

So that was the threat, but I had refused to face up to the obvious.

'Here he is without a protector, wearied by a story that everyone loathes, a courageous philosopher, a true Christian, but often tactless rather than blasphemous in his innovative ideas . . . And I know Bernard, believe me! He did not come to the Paraclete just by chance.'

'Why should he bother about this old master?'

'Because he wants to be the only shining light of Christianity. Because his friend William of Saint-Thierry has circulated a letter full of accusations of heresy against Peter . . . who furthermore, as both you and I know, is often his own first and worst enemy.'

'William of Saint-Thierry, you say? Did I not see him attending Peter's lectures, at Notre-Dame?'

'Indeed! He, and so many others . . . But in the long run, who among them will remember?'

'You.'

'Listen, William. I have to leave Cluny and France on one of those journeys which exhaust me but which I cannot abandon if I am to keep our order going. If anything at all should happen, I want you to write to me, to get a message through to me by whatever means you can. Watch over him, my friend.'

The figure of Christ in majesty at Berzé looked down upon me from high above. I looked into his enigmatic gaze and at his long Byzantine hand for reasons not to smile. Peter, whom nothing escaped, noticed.

'Does my mission make you laugh?'

'It's not that, my friend. It's just that through one of life's ironies it seems to be my fate to find myself constantly—even when I think I'm rid of him—trying to save this man from himself.'

'I'm not asking you to do that.'

'I know, but I realise that I have cherished this conceit . . .'

'Help him, be with him.'

Not a word was spoken as we made our way back to Cluny, at our horses' own gentle pace, on that beautiful spring day in the year that would see the death of Peter Abelard.

23

A S SOON AS I heard the news that a Council had been
called at Sens, at Abelard's request, to pronounce on his
propositions and verify whether they were heretical or
whether they conformed to the teaching of the Bible and the Fathers of the Church, I could see that the worst had happened.
Whatever I might have said to the Venerable, I knew that nobody could convince my master that he had made another mistake and that he was walking straight into another disaster, although this one would be the last.

Accounts of it reached me daily, through pilgrims, through
travellers, through letters — and none of them reassured me.

On the 2nd of June there was a solemn display of relics at
Sens, where, at the behest of Archbishop Henri Sanglier, a great
many churchmen and nobles were expected. Attacked by William of Saint-Thierry and violently accused by Bernard of
Clairvaux in a letter to Pope Innocent II, Abelard had allowed
himself to be ruled by his anger and by his arrogance: he himself
had written to the Archbishop of Sens to ask him to summon
Bernard to a debate in order to establish whether or not his writings were genuinely heretical.

I had no difficulty imagining Peter, pacing up and down his

Mount, spurred on in his dispute by his young students, sure of the strength of his own mind, and misled by the failure of the meetings of reconciliation with Bernard, during which his intellectual superiority had been obvious. He was elated by words, whereas Bernard—who did not under-estimate his opponent—had prepared for the meeting with belligerent care, complaining loudly that he was weak and ill-equipped compared to this Goliath of philosophy, while in a low voice, and particularly in his letters, he mobilised the formidable support he had gathered and the fear that he inspired everywhere. This established bonds that were more powerful than theology.

Since the Venerable had been detained, I set off to Sens in the May sunshine, with a sense of foreboding. I had written to Heloise, but no reply—assuming she wished to send me one—had reached me.

I arrived as night was falling, just before the city gates were closed, and I went to pray on my own in the cathedral where, a couple of days later, the highest Christian dignitaries in France would gather for a battle over words.

There was an atmosphere of trouble brewing in the town—for they had come from all over France and from more distant parts of Europe, the mighty and the rest of them, those for whom there would be no room inside and who would assemble in front of the cathedral, shouting and waving their arms about, and calling for the death penalty. They were not mulling over Peter's treatises in order to compare arguments quietly: they wanted blows to be traded, they wanted to see blood spilled.

A few years earlier, I had met Abbot Guibert of Nogent, and he had described the events that had taken place in Laon. He told me about the ferment that had taken over the city, which had led the people to seize hold of the bishop, who had hidden in a barrel, and eventually to kill him ignominiously; I myself remembered my arrival in Paris and my first meeting with the terrible Germain. That was the kind of mood that prowled the backstreets of Sens and lay dormant in the taverns, the longing to cross swords that brought rich and poor together. I thought sadly that each of us obtains the crusade he deserves.

I wandered through the city, consumed with sorrow, half-heartedly looking for Peter. Whichever inn I set foot in, I came across faces I knew, students who had become bishops and would soon be popes, too few of whom struck me as friendly or even reasonable. Their eyes shone with frenzied drunkenness, and I realised to what extent Peter Abelard—just by the mere fact of his existence all these years, by his stubborn determination to go on living and speaking, to continue teaching—must have generated wretched jealousy among these mediocre, unambitious little minds, and among the faint-hearted who constitute the greater part of mankind. Whatever his other faults, whatever the nature of his celebrated propositions (about which not one of these fine minds was able to talk to me except in terms that were so vague they became ridiculous), it was through the extent of the hatred he aroused that I was able to judge the strange love I bore him.

No sooner have we raised to the skies these magnificent stone naves built to the glory of God, than we are led to commit a murder there—just in order to remind ourselves of who we are.

Over twenty years—a generation of men—had passed since I first came to Paris, in search of my master. I experienced no joy or affection seeing familiar faces at street corners, or happening to meet them in hostelries—my friends had changed, and those I loved were either dead, elsewhere, or had disappeared—unless they had hidden away from the crowds in order not to have to say that they loved that man, with his faults, his great weaknesses and his absurd arrogance.

I took the message that the Venerable had written on Peter's behalf to Archbishop Henri Sanglier. He read it, stony-faced. I stood there in front of him, waiting for a word that never came. He dismissed me in a fury.

Among his former pupils, there were only a few Italians who said openly that they supported him and denounced Bernard of Clairvaux's false wisdom. They were surrounded by waves of hostility.

While I was walking around the town, I felt a tug at my sleeve. My defensive reflex was parried by a laugh: it was Cervelle.

'Well,' he shouted in his shrill, unpleasant voice, 'are we not friends any more?'

He hadn't changed. He was one of those men whom you come across throughout your life and never much care for, but whom, by dint of constantly seeing them, you adopt almost despite yourself.

'Where is he?'

'I'll take you to him.'

It was at a remote inn ('his writings do not care for the daylight', said Bernard of Clairvaux in one of his letters to Innocent —and it was with remarks of that kind that one killed a man, rather than by appealing to St Jerome) that his friends met and drank together—and one might have thought (had not the mood of the whole town got to you beforehand) that the man they were celebrating was a hero who would emerge with greater stature from the onslaught.

I saw Gilbert de la Porrée, the young man from Chartres whose quick mind had so impressed Abelard, and Hilary, the poet and musician whose flute had cast a spell one night in Champagne, and Berengar of Poitiers, both rowdy students at the Paraclete, and Hyacinth and Guy of Castello, the Italians. I saw Arnold of Brescia, who was drinking alone at a table and holding forth vociferously, though no one was listening. I put my hand in front of his eyes and he flicked it away like a fly, without recognising me.

There was no sign of Abelard. There were some young men I had never seen before—those who had been drawn in recent years to his teaching on the Mount. Cervelle made me sit down next to one of them ('an Englishman, like you', he whispered mischievously), who was observing what was going on without really taking part, with a smile that was full of goodness, but slightly perplexed.

John of Salisbury confided in me quite openly, without any obvious restraint, but with a wisdom beyond his years. I admired his prudence, which I had never acquired, and his spirit of adventure which would take him further than me. He described Paris with enthusiasm, speaking mockingly about the new masters who were hurrying to the Île de la Cité, clustering around the Petit Pont and the slopes of the Mount—and sparing only Abelard because of his genuine profundity.

It was not easy to talk in such a din, but I liked this young man and, after a couple of beers, we were like two long-lost brothers who would lose touch with one another the following day.

'There he is! There he is!' Cervelle yelled as loudly as he could in his shrill voice, pointing with his finger.

Abelard swept everything aside in order to clasp me in his arms—lifting me up from my bench and hugging me till he almost smothered me.

'You old devil,' he said, punching me playfully, 'you've come back, you false friend whom I love . . .' and he was almost in tears.

'I hadn't gone away . . . How could I leave a master like you?'

'Come outside—I can't stand any more of them. I want to hear about everything you've been doing . . .'

'No, no, let's speak about you.'

'Me?'

His dark eyes lit up in a comical expression of astonishment. Another three slaps on the shoulder and we were in the street. His physical presence was just as impressive, but he walked with greater difficulty—with the passing of time his unchanging face and his still black hair gave him the aspect of an emperor, but one sensed the frailty and the weariness of the legs that carried him.

'Come on, we'll go into the countryside.'

I followed him at his own pace, stopping with him whenever he spoke to me, or recounted a chapter about his own life, or told me how much we would enjoy ourselves the next day, in the cathedral, or when he described the monks who tried to poison him, and said how happy he was to be back on the Mount.

He led me into a walled garden that was surrounded with lime trees and presided over by stone animals—lions, unicorns and elephants. In the distance, in the fine Sunday weather, a procession passed by, with relics, bishops and the king. There was a scent of crucifixion in the air. He stopped beside a rhinoceros.

'You know this is my animal,' he said dreamily.

'Why?'

'That's what they call me, those who want to kill me, and that's the word they use to plan a hunt so that they can have my hide and my horns.'

My heart was beating. So there was some lucidity after all in his playfulness.

'It was you who summoned the throng.'

'The moment I did so I knew I'd made a mistake. But it was too late.'

'You're a Breton knight . . .'

'I've jousted with children.'

'Peter—tell me what's going on. I, too, think you've made a mistake—but I can't believe you don't want to fight any more.'

'I've just discovered how Bernard was going to obtain my condemnation without a single word of mine making any difference . . .'

'How?'

'This evening, in the archbishop's lodgings, there is to be a meeting where the prelates who are due to try me tomorrow will make their judgement.'

'I don't understand.'

'And yet it's simple. Bernard will address them, he'll deliver a few words of abuse against me, some well-chosen insults and some strong words about the love of Christ; being a man of such moderation himself, he will have taken the trouble to provide them with good food and drink, and in this way I shall be condemned outright. Even those who have defended me in the past won't dare open their mouths.'

'Geoffrey?'

Geoffrey of Lèves, the Bishop of Chartres, was one of the few people who had spoken out in his favour at Soissons; furthermore, as papal legate he had tried to help him re-establish some sort of order at Saint-Gildas.

'Geoffrey won't do anything. No one will do anything.'

'Why are you going?'

'Why did Christ undergo his agony?'

He made this last remark without any pomposity. Standing there with his hand resting on the sculpture and his head among the leaves, he was simply making the most of the life that remained to him.

'I've changed, William, I've really changed. I no longer want to be Aristotle. I read a passage from my *Dialogue* the other day and it made me want to laugh. Do you know my *Dialogue*?'

'I haven't actually held a copy in my hands.'

'And Peter, the Venerable Child, claims there is a library at Cluny! My *Dialogue* portrays a philosopher (you'll have guessed, of course, that I have given myself that role—who else?), a Jew and a Christian, and it compares the sources of their wisdom . . . All very well. But look at what I have read, put into the mouths of the Jew and the Christian, when they speak to the philosopher: *everyone knows the subtlety of your intelligence, and it is common knowledge that the treasure-house of your memory is richly stored with philosophical and religious knowledge, far transcending all other teachers . . .*'

I could not help chuckling a little.

'That goes too far, William, and I don't know whether I should laugh or cry for having written anything so appalling.'

'Well, that's enough to condemn you, had they but read it!'

He laughed with me, then he stopped suddenly.

'You think so too, don't you?'

'What?'

'That I'm ridiculous, arrogant, vain . . .'

'Brilliant, unbearable, generous, forgetful . . .'

'. . . the greatest philosopher in the world?'

'I do think so, Peter, we all do.'

He sighed.

'I know very well that I think so too. But even if it's true, look where it's got me . . . Will you go on my behalf?'

'Where?'

'To the prelates' meeting.'

'I'm not part of it, as far as I know . . .'

'I'm told all sorts of people are going . . .'

'Why not you?'

'Now that would be amusing. But Bernard would be up to another of his tricks . . .'

'Was it so difficult to give way to him . . . Did he not come to see you?'

'I listened to him. Or rather, I listened to myself. The result is the same, isn't it? William, I want to ask you something, and it's that you should not leave me again. Will you agree?'

I put my hand on his shoulder and drew him to me.

'You're impossible.'

'Will you?'

'I won't leave you. But you have to promise me that you'll sometimes do what I ask you.'

'I promise,' he replied instinctively, before giving me an anxious look.

'I said "sometimes". I know you.'

'I promise all the same. Come now, let us go and drink and let us die afterwards, so that it should be a merry affair.'

He was never normally very prescient, but on this occasion the certainty of his fate enabled him to judge correctly.

Henri of Sens, Atton of Troyes, Geoffrey of Chartres, Élie of

Orléans, Manassès of Meaux, Samson of Les Prés—they were all there, nineteen in total, as many bishops as there were propositions of heresy—together with a troupe of secretaries and subdeacons, past whom Berengar, John of Salisbury and I made our way. Bernard of Clairvaux was like Jesus in the midst of a band of half-drunken disciples, their stoles awry—while the clerks drained their goblets and polished off the remains of the chickens. With a gesture of his hand, he commanded silence.

'The time has come, my friends,' he said in a deliberately low voice that was intended to stop the murmuring, 'for this scandal to cease. You have all known, for a long time already, what has been going on every day in your house. You know that an unclean spirit has gone forth and that, if you are not careful, if you do not expose it, it will return with seven spirits more evil still . . .'

There was a clamour of approbation; I have never seen a man exercise a fascination so devoid of reason; it was reflected in their gleaming eyes, it ran through their vinous blood.

'You know the man of whom I speak: Abelard. Many among you have been his pupils and were seduced by his honeyed words, by his apparent wisdom. "I once loved him and I should like to love him still," our brother, William of Saint-Thierry, wrote to me. He had a mind fit to serve the Spirit, he had the words with which to sing God's glory. What has this man whom we should like to love done with them? He has served his own vainglory, he has expressed the wisdom of the insane. He has attained the degrees of humility, but in the wrong way, searching the depths of hell to poison men's souls, refusing to see through a glass darkly, but wanting to see everything face to face. He has shown us, in the way he lives and through his books—which are now exposed to the light of day—that he is a persecutor of the Catholic faith and an enemy of the Cross of Christ. He has the appearance of a monk but, within, he is a heretic. The time has come to impose silence on his lips that are so full of evil, bitterness and treachery.'

Berengar and I looked at one another; the young man was on the brink of tears. John's expression was more reserved, but his eyes were darker. We had known that we were not going to take part in a sensible theological discussion; yet I had suspected Abelard of his customary exaggeration when he told me about the trial. 'You'll see my friend, my brother prosecutor Bernard,' he had said softly, and it was prosecutor Bernard that I saw.

'The bride of Christ cries to you, my friends, amid a forest of heresies and a crop of errors that threaten to suffocate her. Will you leave her on her own, at the mercy of one who seeks to prostitute her? The bee of France has buzzed for the bee of Italy: master Abelard and his accomplice Arnold are together again. They are vile and corrupt. We must rid ourselves of them as we would the plague. We have escaped the roars of the anti-pope Peter Léon who usurped the throne of Peter; but now it is Peter the Dragon who is attacking the faith of Peter. The former persecutes the church of God like a ravaging lion; the latter like a lurking dragon waits in ambush to kill the innocent. But thou, Lord God, will humble the eyes of the haughty and you will trample the lion and the dragon underfoot!'

His eyes literally flashed. No Christian in the gathering could ignore the crucial part he played in supporting Pope Innocent II against the anti-pope Anaclete, who had just died. It was a further sign: Bernard of Clairvaux's enemies are the enemies of God and they die horribly in the fires of Gehenna.

'I am troubled, appallingly troubled, and my weakness causes me to groan—I am a child, a lamb, frailty itself. As God is my witness, it is Goliath who has brought me out from amongst the ranks of the Jews to confront him, so small compared to him, with my sling. As God is my witness it is this man—the master of language, the perverter of words—who has dared to summon me here, for a duel in which I may be defeated . . .'

I could see the Archbishop of Sens's head drop: it was he who had consented to Peter's request, perhaps because he was secretly hostile to Bernard, who had heaped abuse on him a few years previously. But none of that mattered now: he was like anyone else, gripped by the Spirit of vengeance.

'"Everyone thinks like this, but not I." That was the phrase—proud, arrogant and insufferable—of our Aristotle. Will you let him go unpunished?'

Confused mutterings of 'no' echoed round the hall.

'Do you accept that there should be a fifth gospel, that of Peter?'

'No! No!'

'Do you believe in these revelations that have been made to him in secret, yet which have never been imparted to so many saints and wise men?'

'No! Never!'

'Will you let him to go on fathoming the most sublime mysteries and claiming to explain them to us with his lies?'

'No! We shall not let him! We shall condemn him!'

Bernard wiped the sweat from his brow; he looked as if he was about to faint. His lips opened and closed without any words issuing forth and in his eyes there were angels and demons. He had achieved his triumph but he derived no pleasure from it; pain, like a serpent, was devouring him from within. He held a scroll which he handed to Nicolas before sitting down on the bench that had been brought to him. His secretary unrolled the parchment.

'We condemn him!' a voice cried.

'You could at least allow me to read,' said Nicolas with amusement.

The hall burst into laughter.

'First proposition: "That the Father is All-Powerful, that the Son has some power and the Spirit has no power."' Cries, laughter and exclamations burst out from all sides. There was no point saying that Peter had never written this sentence and that it couldn't even be extrapolated from his most ill-considered writings.

'We condemn him!'

The propositions were read out one after the other. Some were genuinely written by him, others were pure and simple invention, and others still reconstructions of sentences taken from several books. It took a long time, in any case, for his case to be heard: it was not the propositions that were being condemned, it was a man.

Throughout the evening I tried to catch the eye of Geoffrey, Bishop of Chartres, and I failed. Oh, of course, we did not hear his voice among the chorus: but I could see the words forming on his lips, timid and dreadful: 'We condemn him.' When at last he caught sight of me, his expression froze, then he turned away.

John vanished without my seeing him. I took Berengar, my pale and distraught young friend, by the arm and indicated to him that it was time to leave. Just as I was helping him to stand up, I could feel someone gazing at me, gazing with malicious intensity. I looked up.

Germain.

He was wearing a linen cloak woven with gold thread and his stole was stained with wine. I made a sign to Berengar that he should leave without me and he stopped, not comprehending, before shrugging despondently and leaving me.

Germain, a bishop.

It could have been comic. My heart was thumping and the blood had drained from my face. I was unable to speak. But I did not want to move. He came towards me—and I remembered how repelled I had felt by his evil eyes, and by the dried scorpion that adorned his skull—close enough to touch me.

'We condemn him,' he hissed.

I spat in his face.

Outside, I came across John, the young Englishman whom nothing upset, leaning against a milepost, vomiting.

24

ONE NEVER wearies of the sight of powerful people
congregating, of the ballet that surrounds them and
the non-entities who wait upon them in the sweet
name of respect. Fear is squalid, especially when it is dressed up.

The crowd had come to see King Louis VII and Count Thibaut of Champagne—that time we were under his protection
seemed so long ago—and William II of Nevers, the pious old
nobleman who spent his life in prayer and would ultimately
become a Carthusian monk, as well as the bishops and the
famous scholars; for a time, there was a rumour that Pope Innocent II would come in person.

Everything that I had felt the previous day had now been
sensed by this crowd, which knew even less than the bishops did
about the omnipotence of God and about the Trinity, but which
recognised the smell of blood.

Parents were dragging along children, who held slings and
stones in their hands. 'We're off to see the heretic,' said some
grubby, snot-nosed lads.

Shouts rang out: 'He must be hanged.'

And further off: 'Let's burn him.'

Abelard seemed strangely indifferent as we forced our way

through the hostile throng to enter the cathedral, protected by his few friends and supporters.

He could see the faces distorted by hatred or simply curious, he could hear the insults. With a slow and heavy pace, he slipped through the crowd. Sometimes, I could see a question forming on his lips: 'Why all this?'

The mood was no calmer when we passed the gateway to the cathedral; the summer light illuminated the altar, but it was not a day for peace and radiance. I kept turning round. I was holding Arnold by the arm, my old friend Arnold who was almost blind, whom I'd kept close to me throughout the night, and who was appalled by this justice which never came. I recognised many of these faces; very few of them noticed me.

Gilbert de la Porrée was sitting next to Geoffrey of Lèves: Abelard stopped beside the men from Chartres and gave them a friendly greeting. They stared at him apologetically, without re-acting.

'How is it with you, Geoffrey?'

The man averted his gaze, trying to hide his tears and his shame.

'And you, Gilbert?'

He did not answer but continued to look at him.

'Listen to me, Gilbert,' said Abelard in a voice that was calm and solemn, with a slight smile even, 'and remember: watch out for your house when the wall next door is on fire.'

He stood up and, without waiting for answer, he made his way towards Henry, the Archbishop of Sens, who was standing in front of the altar surrounded by bishops. But it was not he who spoke when the lone figure of Abelard reached the altar, while we huddled together, as close to him as was possible.

'We are gathered together here,' said Bernard of Clairvaux in a steady voice, 'to try and to condemn the propositions of Master Peter Abelard.'

Everyone turned to look at Peter. He did not move, he did not flinch, he did not attempt to speak. He seemed to be thinking of something else.

'Peter,' continued the Abbot of Clairvaux, 'we are going to read your propositions to you one by one and ask you if you recognise that they are heretical. Do you hear me?'

He had raised his voice as he asked this question. Peter still did not reply—and he showed no sign of having understood. The sound of murmuring rose from the assembled gathering. The more devout bowed their heads and prayed.

Peter raised his hand, as if he meant to speak. He looked at them from one to another, the prelates, the abbots, the counts and the kings—and he, the century's great debater, did this extraordinary thing.

He said nothing.

His silence confused them more than his words had ever done; his silence was a more thorough triumph than his treatises. His silence achieved what a million words had failed to do. His gaze was directed behind them, beyond them, to the tormented figure that hung above the choir. He called upon him and spoke to him in silence.

He began to walk, at the same slow pace at which he had arrived, towards the exit from the cathedral. In disarray, we followed him. The rumble of noise grew louder and half muffled the voice of Bernard of Clairvaux, who followed him, breathing hard.

'Peter Abelard, do you recognise these heretical propositions drawn from your own writings, of which the first is: "That the Father is All-Powerful . . ."'

What followed was drowned in a hubbub of noise. Peter halted by the narthex and turned towards Bernard. Quiet was suddenly restored.

'I do not recognise your justice, false disciple, but God's. We shall meet again in Rome.'

We departed.

The crowd neither knew nor understood what was happening

—and I was urging our little group and Peter himself forward. Arnold asked what was going on and I didn't answer except to make him hurry along. When the wretches discovered that they were being robbed of their trial, deprived of their condemnation and the tears of the culprit, they would burst in in a fury and want to hang him. Let them console themselves by burning his books — we would be far away.

There was no time lost in pointless hugs and embraces at the hostelry. I took young John of Salisbury in my arms and made him promise not to forget his English elder brother. He maintained his solemn expression, but I knew that he was moved.

'You haven't forgotten?' Peter asked me, as he thanked his few loyal friends with a word or clasp of the hand, while our horses were being prepared at the stable.

'I'm coming with you.'

'As far as Rome?'

'First let us be on our way.'

'As far as Rome?'

'As far as Jerusalem, if you wish. That's not the problem. Hurry up, Peter.'

As we mounted our horses and the dust rose from their hoofs, I seemed to hear intimations of his death ringing out from every street corner, and I thought I could smell the smoke from his books that they no longer took pleasure in burning. It was I who guided him to the road south, the one along which we fled knowing that we would not escape them.

In the evening, we called at the inns, the priories and the abbeys — and everywhere the doors were closed.

News of his condemnation and his certain excommunication had travelled across Champagne and France, and had reached Burgundy — and soon, throughout Christendom, there would be no place where he could find sanctuary.

On the first day we followed the River Yonne as far as Joigny — the following day we reached a wood near Auxerre — and he was as obedient as a child, but I felt that he needed to travel slowly, not more than fifteen leagues or so each day. At that pace, we would reach Rome by the autumn . . .

That suited my plan.

To begin with, we exchanged very few words. Even though his face appeared calm, I knew that in his heart he was endlessly re-living the scene in the cathedral—he turned to Christ, just as Christ had called upon the Father, and gradually his torment soothed and liberated him.

On the third day, however, having slept in the woods and washed ourselves in the river, we came across some elderly monks in a priory; they were watching over one of their number who was dying. Away from the roads and cut off from temporal things, these men didn't know that a philosopher existed by the name of Peter Abelard, and they were not in the least concerned. In silence they welcomed two weary pilgrims and they invited us to pray with them for the salvation of the departing soul.

After Vespers, Peter asked for writing material and we looked at one another: people did not copy in this part of the countryside, where all they had was a book of psalms and an old gospel-book. Then he led me into the cloister and he knelt down by the well where, with an unsteady finger, he traced in the earth the first indications of a prayer. After a few seconds, he stood up, his back bent and with tears streaming down his face.

'I can't manage it,' he said, 'they've even taken that from me . . .'

'Ask me, brother.'

'I'm thinking of her,' he said.

He gathered his breath.

'I turn to her in my woe just as she turned to me, and I want to address these words to her that she will not receive . . .'

Oh, how this grief of his descends upon me; oh, this pitiful-ness he bequeaths to me . . .

'Tell it to me, Peter, tell me this prayer that you want to address to her and I promise to preserve every word of it in my memory so that I can convey it to her.'

He spoke softly, enunciating each word:

'Heloise, my sister, once so dear to me in the world, now even dearer to me in Jesus Christ, logic has made me hated in the eyes of the world . . .'

He stopped occasionally to search for a word and to look into my eyes for a sign that I had understood and that he could continue.

'I do not wish to be a philosopher if it means rebelling against Paul. I have no wish to be Aristotle if it means detaching myself from Christ, for there is no other name under heaven whereby I may find my salvation . . .'

The mental strain brought about by my promise to learn by heart—even though I am used to memorising—prevented me from yielding to the emotion that knotted my guts.

'And so that any concern and uncertainty may be banished from the heart that beats in your breast, I want to assure you myself: my conscience is founded upon that rock whereon Christ built his Church . . .'

It was dusk and some drops of rain fell from the leaden sky as the words of his profession of faith trickled out in this way—and the logician, the grammarian, the dialectician made way for the man who opened his heart.

'This is the faith to which I adhere and from which my hope draws its strength. Safe in this refuge, I do not fear the bark of Scylla, I laugh at the whirlpool of Charybdis and I do not dread the Sirens' deadly songs. Come the storm, I shall not be shaken, for my foundations stand firm.'

Night had fallen and we could hear some murmurings: perhaps the dying man expired during the prayer. I rolled those final words around my lips: 'Come the storm . . .'

I led him to our cell and I lay down beside him. I whispered in his ear: 'Heloise, my sister, once so dear to me in the world . . .'

And it was to the sound of his own prayer that peace came to him, and he closed his eyes and slept like a child.

We arrived at the hill of Autun on a fine day. Peter Abelard was exhausted and perspiring, and every step we took towards the church of Saint-Lazare was painful. Without complaining, he asked for drink. Burghers, artisans and clerks turned round to look at this weary man who, at cattle's pace, was persisting in trying to climb a slope that was too steep for him.

When the spire came into view — a light in the light of the sky — Peter stopped and leant against me.

'Was it to see this that you brought me here?' he grumbled, but he smiled as he spoke.

The houses and the churches converged as we climbed the rock of Autun and, as at Vézelay, it was impossible to forget that at the summit it was Christ who was waiting for us.

The cathedral church of Saint-Nazaire was in a poor state and the sunlight clung to the more recent church beside it, which was sparkling with colour and had been built barely twenty years beforehand at the initiative of the bishop, Stephen de Bagé, to house the miraculously rediscovered relics of St Lazarus. While one of them seemed to be sunk into the earth, the other — in spite of its smaller dimensions — seemed to go on soaring. All around it there was an atmosphere of an unfinished building site — quarrymen, carpenters, stonemasons . . .

Peter stopped by the open door in the transept, opposite Saint-Nazaire.

'Look,' he said.

On the lintel, a paradisal vegetation was coiling itself around an Eve whose breasts were the shape of apples.

'You can see what's so good about evil,' said Peter, with a smile, 'and it's true we can understand Adam.'

While he entered the church, I stayed behind with Eve, experiencing a familiar sensation behind my desire, yet one that I was unable to identify.

I wandered around the church on my own, walking behind the apse and along the north wall. When I found myself in front of the main door—the porch was not nearly complete and you could hear the men chipping on the stone with their tools—I stopped to admire the tympanum. The Christ of the Last Judgement dominated a scene of majestic clarity in which the Just were received while the damned burned. As I was admiring each detail—and the simple phrases carved in the stone, denoting that light was promised to some and abomination to others—I noticed the words written on the centre of the lintel: GISLEBERTUS HOC FECIT. It was Gislebert who had created this.

I stopped a stonemason.

'Gislebert? Is he your master?'

'Yes.'

'Is he here?'

He made a vague gesture.

'At his home, over there, by the hill.'

He pointed northwards.

I set off running.

The house was on the side of the hill. When you turned around you were within the shadow of the great church and as if protected by it; but if you looked ahead you could see the escarpment of the Morvan mountains, and the Brisecou and Montjeu woods.

Gislebert was surrounded by his tools—hammer, chisel, scissors—immersed in an extraordinary forest of chapiters from which his head emerged, shaped like that of a wading bird. I held my breath as I watched him work. It was the Flight into Egypt, the very same scene that our friend Christian had described, the other day, so long ago . . .

'You said you would create it, and you have.'

At first, he did not move—he was rounding off Mary's cheeks as if caressing them. Then his tools fell to the earthen floor. He stood up, turned and stared at me.

'Where were you?'

It was twenty years since we had taken leave of one another that sad morning at dawn when the dust was rising, and he was asking me where I had been. I began to laugh. So did he. We could not stop.

He embraced me.

Gislebert accompanied me into the church to look for Abelard. Apart from a few streaks of silver in his hair, he was the man he had always been—laconic, precise in his movements, and with a childlike mystery about him. I told him about the years I had spent wandering and waiting; he had nothing to relate, not even the journey that had taken him to Cluny and then to Vézelay: the story of his life was all around him, with his name in the midst of it all.

We ate our meal in virtual silence and it was a relief for each of us when it was time to set off again.

'Where are you going now?' asked Gislebert as we mounted our horses.

'To Cluny.'

'Good.'

We waited for a few moments for a comment that never came.

'It's time to go,' I said, still not stirring.

Abelard set off at a slow pace. Gislebert looked at me, his hand protecting his eyes from the bright sunshine. Reluctantly, I prepared to follow him.

'William?' said Gislebert.

'Yes, my friend.'

'Now do what you must do.'

I did not reply. There was nothing to reply to. I don't believe I understood.

I rode on a hundred feet or so. At the first bend in the road, I turned in the direction of the town. I caught my last sight of the church and, at the foot of the hill, I could see my friend. He had not moved, and his hand was still shading his eyes from the sun.

25

W E ARRIVED at Cluny around Midsummer's Day. Peter the Venerable welcomed Abelard to the monastery, comforted him and looked after him. After the humiliation of his condemnation and the strain of the journey, Abelard seemed to be alone in some sort of foggy land of his own. He, who had earned the hatred of the world because of his words, had scarcely opened his mouth since he had dictated his profession of faith, which I had now re-copied onto parchment to take to Heloise.

Peter the Venerable had written a skilful letter to the pope which was intended to pave the way for a reconciliation that was difficult and perhaps impossible. Innocent II would emulate Bernard of Clairvaux, the man who had probably done most to ensure his victory—he would condemn the notorious propositions, and he would support the 'brother prosecutor' in all his conclusions.

Each day, I deserted my novices for a while in order to spend some time with my master. He liked to sit beneath a lime tree which, it was said, dated from the abbacy of Bernon; that is to say from the abbey's earliest days. He still talked very infrequently, preferring to listen to sounds that were new to him— birdsong, and the wind passing through the valley. He blinked as he took a few steps on my arm in the sunshine. He was discovering a world he had never imagined, a world in which words were not everything.

One day he took my hand and made me touch the rough palms of his hands, which were like those of an artisan, a blacksmith, a jeweller or a saddler.

'A long time ago,' he said — then he stopped.

The summer days were drawing in and behind the apse of the immense abbey shadows were gradually lengthening over the garden.

'A long time ago,' he began again, 'each of us used to keep a stone with which we made our hands bleed . . .'

I remembered that: she had told me. A long time ago . . .

'Just now, I rubbed my finger on one of the scars made by that stone and it was as if an arrow had pierced my heart.'

He paused and smiled.

'I can talk about the past now.'

The pope's letters of condemnation reached the Venerable; they had been despatched from Rome very shortly after the Council of Sens — yet another sign of the Abbot of Clairvaux's speed and efficiency. They were worse than anything we might have feared, amounting to virtual excommunication.

'Should we tell him?' the Venerable asked me.

'I don't think so.'

Yet he knew. Or else our silence taught him more than we were willing to tell him. Eventually, he gently insisted that Peter the Venerable should read the letter to him.

Before doing so, Peter chose his words very carefully: the condemnation was not a reply to the letter that he had sent, and one had to be patient and not become discouraged. Abelard dismissed this with a smile.

With a sigh, the Abbot of Cluny began to read. 'Having taken the advice of our brother bishops and cardinals, in accordance with the authority of the holy canons, we condemn the articles by your good offices and all the perverse doctrines of Peter Abelard, as well as the author himself, and we sentence him, as a heretic, to perpetual silence.'

Peter was silent, impassive. I had thought, with bitter irony, that he had followed the injunction without knowing about the condemnation. Then, in a voice that was calm and steady, he asked:

'Is that all?'

'There is a second one,' said the Venerable.

'Well?'

'It ordains that Arnold and you be confined separately in religious houses and that your books be burned wherever they may be found. It also informs me that this is what has been done at St Peter's in Rome.'

'And is that all now?'

'Yes.'

Peter Abelard let out a sigh; once again he gazed out towards the hills, the clouds and the sky.

'Am I confined here?'

'Anyway, they can't say that you're not in a religious house . . . And I've not seen Arnold anywhere.'

'That's not enough.'

'What do you mean?'

Abelard remained silent, then he made a sign for us to leave him. Pensive and anxious, I walked away with Peter.

It was just before Vespers on the 6th of August, a day that was dear to the Venerable's heart, for he had specially written the office for the liturgy of the Transfiguration.

> *Hail morning star,*
> *Remedy for our sins,*
> *Queen and sovereign of the world,*
> *Who alone merits the name of Virgin.*

It was still light when we left the church, our hearts filled with magnificent chanting and yet, at the same time, with an inexplicable sadness. Abelard was no longer in the garden. I searched for him in the cloister before hurrying off, in a sudden burst of inspiration, to the *scriptorium*.

He was alone, standing in front of the only fireplace, and throwing parchments into it.

'Stop!' I cried.

He turned towards me. His face was pale despite the reflections of the fire.

'Haven't we been ordered to burn his books wherever we find them?'

'Stop, Peter.'

'Am I not the very obedient child of our holy mother the Church—am I not Peter the lost one, who is humbly appealing to the successor of Peter?'

He tore up the scrolls as he threw them in, and he ripped out the pages of the books.

'*Theologia Christiana . . . Sic et Non . . . Dialogue . . . Commentary on the Epistle to the Romans . . . Logic . . . Scito te ipsum . . .*'

I tried to stop him.

'Nothing shall remain,' he said, 'but I shall have this last source of wretched pride—this last measure of vainglory, this final bit of arrogance—that none shall have burned as many books as I have. Help me, William.'

I went to sit down on the bench beside him and, without lifting a hand, I watched the words burning, those words I had admired, which had led my mind to heights that I never believed were attainable. Gazing at the bindings, memories of his lessons came back to me—in the Close of Notre-Dame, in the boats on the Seine, at the Paraclete . . . I saw my life go past in the smoke of these sentences which might be about to disappear for ever.

'Come the storm,' I began timidly.

'It's too late,' he said. 'The storm has come and it has swept me away. I used to say that I was built on firm ground: but the wind is my foundation, I go, I fly away, I am already dying. That must be destroyed too.'

'I can't.'

'Didn't you copy it?'

'You can destroy the parchment, if you wish. But you can't destroy my memory.'

'Forget it, William, forget all that . . .'

'I promised you I'd stay with you. Not that I'd forget you.'

'The story concludes without me . . .'

'Why, when you cease to be a giant, must you make yourself a midget? Why can't you accept your stature as a man at last?'

For the first time he abandoned his expression of grim despondency and looked at me curiously.

'I hadn't thought of that,' he said simply. 'You may be right, after all . . .'

At least he stopped throwing his books into the fire.

In the weeks that followed, a gradual change came over him, which secretly gladdened us, the Venerable and me. He acquired a certain liking for talking once more: long conversations with one or the other of us, to begin with, or with the principal prior Guibert, or with Gérard, the prior in charge of the novices, in the fading autumn sunshine. Then the monks themselves grew less afraid of him and, at permitted times, they began to break down the barrier of solitude and silence that he himself had erected.

He did not start teaching again, for the days of lectures, demonstrations and logical development had long passed. But he returned—with a new perspective—to certain subjects that had preoccupied him recently. He spoke about sin with a certain freedom, saying that it lay not in the act but in the intention and that it followed—as in other fields—that God's justice was not, and could not be, that of men. In particular, he told stories from the Old Testament without resorting to that display of strength, that show of virtuosity, that had been his hallmark: he spoke of the loneliness of Joseph deserted by his brothers and that stern goodness that had always been in his heart, and about the passionate friendship between David and Jonathan . . . These marvellous figures took on a human frailty.

I also brought my novices to see him and he treated them sensitively, smiling as he told stories about his youth, when he wandered the lengths of the Loire and the Seine in search of masters, about the madman Roscelin, and Anselm, whom he had mistreated badly . . . At moments such as these, I could see the old fighter return, the man who was endlessly persecuted, the tireless reasoner, and I could see that changed as he was he had not changed . . .

One evening, he asked me to stay with him so that he could dictate—for at the same time that his mind began to fail, his body stiffened and stopped, and seemed to be filled with torments that he did not complain about but which impeded him a little more each day. His arms hung heavily by the side of his body, and to raise a hand was an effort, a journey.

Ah, wretch that I am
By mine own self betrayed . . .

In one night alone, he dictated six *planctae* which wrung the heart-strings like nothing he had ever written before. Dinah, the daughter of Jacob, the daughter of Jephthah . . . he often referred to the fate of women, as if in extolling them he had to shed the tears that he had not shed with Heloise, and show that after all these years he had become her brother in sorrow.

At dawn he fell silent and slept, exhausted, on the cold stone floor, in front of the embers which had now turned to ashes.

Bernard of Clairvaux arrived with the snow, wrapped in a white cloak over his white cowl.

He had insisted on staying at the hospice, with the other pilgrims, and Peter the Venerable himself had to go and find him and beg him to lodge with him, for the love of God if not for love of him.

Abelard was in the infirmary, prey to one of those attacks of aphasia which sometimes left him open-mouthed, like a fish gasping for air. He recovered each time, but in the process some words would get lost, which he then searched for in a sort of dumb fury, trying in vain to move his hands, as his dark eyes rolled in their sockets.

Bernard saw me and greeted me, before sitting down beside Peter, who was dozing. The last time I had seen this man, divine invective was on his lips and bile was filling his hollow cheeks . . . now, he was mumbling prayers, now, he was very holy.

After what seemed a fairly long time to me, Abelard opened his eyes — he saw me, he saw him. Bernard continued to pray.

'My brother prosecutor,' Peter whispered . . .

'My brother . . .'

Bernard took his hand and Abelard allowed him to do so; Bernard raised it to his lips and kissed it.

'We should not die with this hatred in our hearts, my brother . . .'

'So you hated me . . .'

'When anger is in our hearts, how are we to know whether it is divine or human anger?'

'Was I not your brother, closer than those of your own blood?'

'Yes, but you — was it not God's role that you wanted?'

'Look at me in my present state, look at where I am going and tell me if I know what I am and what my fate is to be.'

'I know and I am with you.'

These two men, old now, gazed at one another, the one who was soon to die, exhausted and breathing with difficulty, his hands shaking and his speech indistinct, and the one who would live on, still fired with boundless energy, and who had found the path of forgiveness — though not without having brought death in the process.

'It was all necessary, Bernard.'

'It was all necessary, Peter.'

They asked each other questions, they started sentences: they knew each other so well, they had followed each other so closely throughout their lives that one could answer for the other and finish his sentences—one could be the other. Brothers in God, human brothers. Peter smiled with difficulty. How lined and furrowed were his cheeks, his forehead . . .

'Nevertheless, brother prosecutor . . .'

'But you were attacking my sweet Lord, and his mysteries!'

'You know very well that men never partake of them. Did I not have the right to give them a hint?'

'Let them live in his mystery, behind the veil . . .'

'But there's nothing behind this veil except another veil—and once you have a notion of the mystery, there's still the miracle—faith—the mystery itself . . .'

'I know.'

'And there's still love.'

This time Bernard said nothing. However much our brother Abelard professed his love of God, even though her name was not mentioned, how could one not hear the echo of Heloise's voice and her suffering, and her loneliness at the wind-blown Paraclete? Bernard knew this and he now respected it.

'I have come to bring you forgiveness,' he said.

'Everything I have written that was heretical has been retracted. I have burned all my books myself.'

'Peter, there is a time for everything . . . I have also come to ask you forgiveness.'

'Ask me? You? God's champion asks forgiveness from a wretch, from a heretic?'

Bernard said nothing, he merely gazed at him with an almost pleading intensity.

'Peter: God has removed my heart of rock and given me one of flesh. Will your heart be harder than mine? Will you be like Pharoah, who was unwilling to listen and was cruelly smitten?'

'Do you have new punishments in store for me?'

There was a look of foreboding in Abelard's eyes.

'Forgive me as I forgive you, Bernard . . . anxiety has become my daily subsistence and you have brought me a new dish. I shall not have time to accustom myself to the taste even if I were eating roots from the earth . . .'

Bernard lay his head on Peter's breast and surrendered himself. When he sat up again his face was wet with tears.

'Farewell, brother . . .'

'Farewell.'

When Bernard of Clairvaux had left, Abelard remained silent, his eyes closed; he had set off into that curious state, between sleep and wakefulness, in which he spent increasingly more time.

'I don't know,' he said at last, as if to himself.

'What don't you know?'

'I don't know whether I believe him. I don't know whether I understand him. And I don't know whether I forgive him.'

Getting around Cluny had become too difficult for him and he was worn out by fatigue. He had been granted pardon by the master of the Cistercians and the master of the Clunisians — but from Rome there came nothing but silence.

'You are to go and rest for a short while at a priory of ours near Chalon, beside the River Saône,' said the Venerable.

'A short while . . . Isn't that what I promised Heloise when I sent her to Argenteuil? A short while can last a long time . . . Shall William come with me?'

'William will not leave you.'

I don't know why I should have come to symbolise the gentleness and the security in his life that this old man, who was becoming a child again, needed. That is the way of things: the time comes when we become our fathers' fathers — and when we realise that there is not much more time before we are our sons' sons.

We made our way along the road as if in a procession. He could no longer ride a horse and four monks carried him on a solid stretcher with a bed of leaves and straw that was changed daily. The approach of death provides us with comforts we had not considered and which we shall not enjoy for long. I walked beside him, leading my horse, so that he could see me when he moved his face.

Even in the depths of winter, Burgundy was beautiful, with its hills and villages, and its unpretentious, dependable churches; it was a country you could live and die in.

I have mentioned that he stumbled over words. I would hear them escaping into the night as in his dreams he grew delirious. He lost those words that described things, but he caught their reflections and he was familiar with their echoes, their shadows. The sunshine was a cascade of broom and the road twisted joyfully like a snake. These were not the images of a poet, but the babblings of a man who in his end was returning to his beginning.

Never was he so well received as on this road where, less than a year beforehand, all doors had been closed to him. The kindliness of the Venerable, Cluny's prestige—and perhaps, too, the simple piety that the nearness of death releases—earned him gentle attentiveness and words of comfort from everybody. Not in anger, but without any illusions, I considered how easy it was to welcome him now. Yet, when he had been the stranger . . .

He asked for nothing, and perhaps he saw nothing. Occasionally he uttered a name: 'Arnold . . .' and he repeated it, amused by the sound of the word, making it sound sad or triumphant.

The priory of Saint-Marcel-lès-Chalon was a small house surrounded by greenery. A fresh vine climbed over the arched entrance and the cloister had the gaiety of a garden. The majority of the twelve monks who lived there had seen the splendours of Cluny only once in their lives, when they had taken their vows there. They stared at us with undue respect, like travellers from another world. Their dormitory was full and too cramped, so they made a bedroom for him in a small chapel.

He did not utter another word and he existed only in his dark, intense gaze. I had seen his anger, his disdain, his laughter, his impatience and his indifference; he was now bathed in light.

Spring had come early and I had left him to enjoy a little of the countryside. I walked unhurriedly towards the Saône; without being conscious of the fact, I was growing calmer, and I was enjoying being on my own without putting words to the feelings that unsettled my soul. At midday, I started back on the road to the priory.

A monk was waiting for me along the wayside.

'Come quickly,' he said in a low voice, 'he's worse.'

They were all gathered round him and were praying. The prior whispered in my ear that he had received extreme unction, but that he did not seem to be at peace. He was moving about a lot and his face, which had been so calm for several days, was disfigured with violent motions and twisted in silent pain. I made a sign for everyone to leave.

I knelt beside him and spoke in his ear.

'I cannot pray to the Lord for you, Peter, but I want to tell you that you are my brother and that I love you — I want to tell you that you have been greater than all your misfortunes and all mine.

'I want to tell you that you will not be forgotten, either by God or by men.

'I want to tell you that I will go to the Paraclete, on a wild and windy day, to give your sister Heloise — the woman you loved and still love, the woman I have loved in your shadow and still love — your profession of faith and your cries, so that she may know what was in your heart in your final hour.

'I do not know — for I, too, am weak — whether the grief, the humiliations, the sorrows, the wounds, can be forgotten, I do not know if life can be healed, but I know your share of eternity, I guard it between my hands and in my heart like a flame that shall burn tomorrow and forever.'

I held back the sob in my breast to feel whether there was still breath in his. He was breathing.

I stood up to look at his face.

He was calm now.

His lips scarcely moved—a tremor perhaps.

I put my ear close to him.

'Farewell,' he said in a low voice, 'my only one.'

'I will tell her,' I answered, not bothering to control my tears, 'I will tell her that your share of eternity is your share of love.'

'Farewell,' he repeated in a voice that was growing fainter, as if he were going away, 'farewell, my only one.'

'Farewell,' I said one last time as I closed Peter Abelard's eyes.

26

PETER THE VENERABLE came with me to Cluny in order to deliver Abelard's remains to Heloise. Beforehand, he had insisted on writing a letter in which he described Abelard's death to her in words that were meant to reach her heart without troubling her soul.

I could not offer her any of this divine consolation, but I took it upon myself to tell her about how he had spent his last days, and I would tell her what his final words had been. In order to do so, we needed to be alone.

Peter the Venerable celebrated the Mass. The *De Profundis* was sung in the presence of Abelard's coffin. We were all accustomed to death, we clerics, monks and nuns, and we had learned to make a friend of it; we did not weep bitterly, we did not tear at our cheeks and our clothing beside the remains of those who were dear to us. A long time ago — ever since earliest childhood — we had learned that the body was a prison and that the death of our mortal frame was the beginning of our freedom, of the pure climax (if that word can be used) of our soul. I had cried, nonetheless, and no one could expect Heloise, or Peter's younger sisters, not to weep when, at the end of Mass, each of them walked past his coffin and blessed it with the sign of the cross as they sprinkled some incense over it. They were silent tears, tears without any crying or grand gestures.

Afterwards there was a gathering at the chapterhouse, and the Venerable and I spoke to them about those months when Abelard had found peace in the face of humiliation. Peter told them how the novices and younger monks liked to go and see him and receive a lifetime's teaching from him in a few words. He spoke of his moderation and recalled how he liked to quote the psalm: *Prove me, O Lord, and try me; test my heart and my mind*—a sentence he happened to have placed at the heart of the prayer he had written for Heloise.

As he mentioned her name, Peter the Venerable looked up at her and spoke directly to her. He spoke of his longstanding affection for her, of his appreciation of her intelligence and her studiousness. He also said that he was aware how much Heloise's knowledge and her mind had influenced her husband's thinking—how much she could be said to have shared in the authorship of the finest and holiest things he had written. He said that Abelard was *the man who belonged at her side*. He called her a disciple of truth, a mistress of humility. He continued and concluded:

'*The man to whom you were united by the bonds of the flesh, and later by the stronger and more enduring bonds of divine love, with whom and at whose bidding you dedicated yourself to God's service —that man is today cherished in God's bosom, in your place, or as another you. And on the day of the coming of the Lord, when the voice of the Archangel and the trumpet-note proclaims the sovereign Judge descending from heaven, he shall restore him to you through his grace; he will keep him for you.*'

There was a hush. All the nuns bowed their heads; only Heloise looked at him, unperturbed. She thanked him, saying that in their present suffering it was a balm to her and the entire community of the Paraclete.

Suddenly she broke off, came up to him and took his hands in hers.

'But there is one question,' she said with renewed strength, 'that will prevent us from sleeping, as long as we have no answer, a question which only you can reply to, if we are to quell the bitterness and the taste of gall in our mouths: is he pardoned? Can we hang the parchment that absolves him on his tombstone, so that he may rest in peace and so that our nights may no longer be afflicted by storms of iniquity? For if his soul must roam for eternity, without a hiding-place, then we prefer to roam with him—if our house has no cornerstone, then we have no home.'

Peter brought out from beneath his cowl a sealed roll and placed it in her open hands, her palms turned skywards.

'Here it is.'

'Is it the pope's pardon?'

'It is that of his daughter's abbot, Cluny.'

'Forgive me—but you are not the pope.'

'It is the pope,' said the Venerable calmly, 'who has entrusted me with safeguarding Peter Abelard's body and soul. He has allowed me to decide whether he has lived a Christian life and has died in our faith. He has given me the right to absolve him.'

For a few seconds, she said nothing. With his customary delicacy, the Venerable was correct, but she did not want the matter to be resolved in this way, even though she had to be satisfied with what she had been told.

'I must thank you,' she said eventually, in a blank voice.

She took the roll from his hands and placed her finger on the seal—was she still thinking of the awful controversy that had surrounded the philosopher's 'blasphemous comparisons'? I don't believe she was.

'Let us accompany him now.'

It was a small procession that made its way through the countryside and I found comfort in the fact that it was a very windy day, as I had promised him it would be, when I whispered in his ear, during his final moments. It was the Paraclete wind, the consoling wind that brought what Rome had not given.

There were only a few crucifixes in the cemetery: the Paraclete was still a young house. The coffin was lowered into the ground. Nothing was said. They were in a hurry. Heloise hung the Abbot of Cluny's absolution on the cross, while the two lay brothers grunted like woodcutters as they shovelled earth over the grave. The Venerable and I looked at one another, trying not to smile. When they had completed their task, he led the monks from Cluny away, and the nuns followed behind. I hastened to go with them, but Heloise stopped me.

'Stay with me, William.'

We were alone with him. I had been with him in his final days, his last hours; even when he was dead, I had continued to follow him everywhere, from Saint-Marcel to Cluny, where Peter decided to 'restore' him to Heloise, and now here. With Heloise at my side, I realised that it was her presence that had kept him alive while he was with me—and also just how much any farewell was incomplete without her.

Now it is time to say goodbye to one another, my friend.

'Well?' she asked.

I told her everything I knew, quite simply. I drew a picture of the man she loved, his silences, his sufferings and his moments of peace. I told her about the meeting with Bernard and the attentiveness of the novices. I also told her about our terrible journey after Sens. I gave her the profession of faith that he had wanted to write in the earth before he dictated it to me.

She read it solemnly, beside the cross where the pardon fluttered in the wind. *Heloise, my dearest sister* . . . When she had finished, she closed her eyes for a moment. Then:

'I don't know how I'll get through the days now . . . I had become used to the notion that I would never see him again . . . But the thought of him was always there—as well as his prayers, his hymns, his Rule, it was a way of being together. Now, there is nothing left but silence. And this wind.'

'It's not over, Heloise.'

'What do you mean?'

I told her about the prayer that I had whispered in his ear, when his breath was already failing, and the words that had slipped from his lips.

'Farewell, my only one,' she murmured. 'He died saying that? He took me with him?'

Her face was radiant. There was an expression of joy, the joy of the girl with the bright eyes whom I had seen for the first time, many years earlier, in a procession that brought with it rain and shaped the course of my life.

'Go on, you knew that . . .'

'I knew nothing whatsoever, William, and even less with a man like him. You spend a lifetime loving someone and you know nothing until he speaks his final word, until he breathes his last . . . I shall keep this in my heart . . . And, soon, when it is my turn to go I shall say these same words to him . . .'

With a sudden movement, she took something from her sleeve and slipped it into the hollow of her hand. She kept her fist tightly closed for a second before opening it for me.

It was a small pink quartz stone, with edges that had once been sharp but had become blunted with time—it was the stone they had used to love and wound each other, and which she had worn against her bosom, the stone that had shed blood, and then tears.

'Open your hand, William.'

I looked at her uncomprehendingly; it was she who took my hand and unclasped my clenched fingers. She slipped the stone into the palm of my hand and closed my fingers.

'For a long time, I've thought that this stone would disappear with him, or with me. But it's for you, my brother, it's for you to keep—you who have never left us, you who have hidden your sorrows behind ours—you who have loved in the same breath as us.'

I did not know how to reply to her. I could feel the stone in the hollow of my hand. It could certainly not draw blood any more; but it throbbed with a life in which I had played a greater part than I had imagined, even if it was not the part I had wanted. The story begins again once it has finished: the deadened feelings in my heart are continually revived. Wisdom does not exist—it is like death. Life consists of sorrow—the pain that fills our nostrils and revives us.

'I must leave,' I said.

'Come back soon.'

'I don't know.'

We didn't really mean these words. But what was there to say? We remained, motionless, standing over the tomb of the man who had been our master, looking at each other as the wind gusted. The words were theirs—silence is my lot. One has to accept it. One has to.

Then, finally, for a brief moment, she drew me to her, held my neck in her delicate hands, and stroked my hair. I pulled away.

'I really must go now.'

'Come back soon.'

'I don't know.'

She smiled.

'Goodbye, William. Don't forget I love you.'

Epilogue

I OPENED my eyes. There was a good smell of slightly green wood and the smoke stung my eyes. I remembered that I thought I had died in Guy's arms; for some unknown reason (for I have bid my farewells a long time ago and I have finished what I had to do) God had kept me on earth to suffer a little longer—be honest: it was also to breathe in this smell that reminds you of the forest and brings back images of the past . . .

I thought I saw Guy lying not far away from me—he seemed to be in a deep sleep. Was it day or night? I couldn't say. I was alone and I was frightened. I was waiting for the right moment. I realised why I had not died from the exhaustion of completing my work: it was because God wanted me to see myself die, in my terror he wanted me to see the immensity of his power, of his glory. So many brothers before me—and now me. Men live and die, like leaves . . . And what if there were nothing? If my soul departed with my final breath, and my body remained in the mud, in the ground? Throughout our lives, we never think of such things, and we would never have imagined saying them. But now, what did it matter? I tried to move; I couldn't.

There were shadowy figures moving around Guy's bed. I

don't know whether I fell asleep. The only light came from the reflections of the fire. They were murmuring and no one was paying any attention to me. I wanted to speak to them, to attract their attention, but I was unable to do so. I felt frightened again, shamefully so: was I to die like this, without anyone to help; I who had accompanied so many others, was I going to be left to die like some tired pile of flesh and bones? I couldn't even cry. I had scarcely any body left—just this aroma of wood that I could no longer smell. Everything else was already dead, even the pain. I am spirit. What is it like? To be honest, I preferred it before; I remember my light, supple body, I remember desire, the pleasures, the caress of the wind and the touch of her hands, I remember the taste of tears, I remember beauty—and it was good. It was not without its troubles, but it was good. Yes, my brother, but it's over. I know, but you ask me what it's like, being spirit; I'm replying to you. And tell me, do you accept? What do you mean? Do you accept that it's over? Come now, you know very well I don't answer questions. Yes, but this one, you have to . . . Not even this one. The question is not to know whether I accept or not. I'm dying, that's all.

When I saw them folding Guy's hands over his chest and, one after another, making the sign of the cross on his forehead, I realised that the prior had been right. My young brother had died before me.

Throughout all these years, I have been repeating to myself that death was just a habit one got used to. My life, as it were, had begun with the passing of Robert of Arbrissel—I had seen the demise of my dear friend Christian, and that of my master Abelard. With the passing years, I had awaited news and roll-calls of deaths without any particular distress. Bernard of Clairvaux, Arnold of Brescia and Peter the Venerable had died so soon after one another that it made you wonder if their deaths were not linked by a secret pact. Bernard and Peter had left this world as saints, as champions of Christianity—whereas Arnold had been shamefully hanged, and then burned.

The only one I had not mourned was Gislebert, whom I had left, shading his eyes from the sun with his hand, fading into the sunlight.

I had left Cluny when the Venerable died and I had come here, to Fontevrault, to take my vows at last. I was like those knights who, having committed many a crime, and having caused many innocent people to suffer in the name of God's glory, as well as out of their own self-interest of course, come in the evening of their lives to give their riches (I had none) and their souls to the monastery whose abbots they have persecuted all their lives. They are welcomed with kindness and respect and they are never made to feel that it is a little late to make their peace. On the contrary—in the refectory they are read the parable of the last-minute helpers and, although they bow their heads, they are happy.

There had been no news of Heloise, who did not write, and who asked for nothing; I knew that the Paraclete continued and that she was a respected abbess: people came to her, too, to die and they redeemed their souls with countless gifts. I expected nothing. I cherished some words of hers in my heart and that constituted life for me.

I had taken some time to keep the promise I had made to myself—and, to begin with, to understand what it meant. For it is one thing to obey the impulses of the heart, and it is another to discover what it is really telling us, behind the feelings that sway and move us.

At Cluny, I had been in the habit of making notes of what each of them had said to me—I preserved the words they used to describe their sufferings and their thwarted love, and I jotted down the psalms and the poems they quoted. Without being fully aware of it, I was probably already attributing to each of them feelings that had been mine, those feverish emotions that had made me delirious. And yet I constantly encountered them again, their faces anxious or smiling, present in my heart's memory.

Gradually, our conversation (for my lips moved of their own accord and I cried out inarticulately, I wept and I laughed, and I threw my hands about on a stage that had been erected for me alone) became a dialogue between the two of them. I stepped aside. In those places where life had prompted me to intervene (how to relinquish that terrible longing to be oneself, to make a name for oneself and leave one's mark?), absence and death had allowed me to withdraw quietly. Nothing remained apart from them—and it was at that point that I began to picture their meeting again, their battles, their love affair and their being wrenched apart, and it was then that I knew that the only meaning in my life had been to have been there, beside them, and to observe them and love them more than they loved each other.

Oh, of course, it required long nights and much dreaming—for you never escape yourself completely—but from that point on I could spend days and entire weeks totally immersed in their lives. My own progressed on the surface: the routine of offices, meals and prayers.

It was a tall, pale, thin young man, who appeared to be ill at ease with his body, who came to inform me about Heloise's death—saying that it was a task she had asked him to fulfil. He did not want to give his name, but I had no difficulty in guessing who it was from his dark eyes, which shone with the same colour and elation as those of his father, but which had the shape of his mother's. Peter Astrolabe was old before being young; he was a canon at the chapterhouse in Nantes. An immense weariness came over me: I would have had to tell him so much in order to explain this story, and he had come so far, and in his own way he, too, had experienced such terrible loneliness, that I was lazy and cowardly enough to keep him in ignorance and to let him leave without even telling him I had recognised him.

I gathered my remaining strength to go to Paris, where traces of our having been there were already fading. So many new houses and churches where I had once seen vines! And that cathedral that was being constructed, those streets that were filled with students, masters and parchment makers . . . There was a draper's shop where Samuel's tavern had been and I eventually found the old prophet of our revelries in a leprosarium. Already, these were difficult times for Jews—the young king Philip Augustus, conscious of the power of his expanding kingdom, which grew larger by the day, and the support he obtained by force or by gentler methods, wanted to make them pay for the murder of Christ. Samuel recounted all this in short sentences (for he was getting very breathless), hiding his face in his coat so as to conceal his decrepit state.

'Soon we won't have the right to breathe,' he chuckled.

I protested, and I told him that I was his brother.

'Abelard loved us,' he said, 'and look what they did to him . . .'

On my return journey, I knew at last what I still had to do.

At Fontevrault, for reasons of age and infirmity, I asked to be released from heavy duties and to be allowed to use the *scriptorium* for as long as possible. The prior asked me what I was copying and I told him that they were annotations. His eyes grew bigger in his crooked, intelligent face—but he didn't question me further.

I wrote their letters.

Having such an intimate knowledge of their past, I wondered at what period this correspondence might have taken place. Without giving a precise date, I imagined that at Saint-Gildas, Abelard, shortly before returning to Paris, had written a long letter in which he described his life in the style he wrote in at that time: the extraordinary way he had of complaining—self-incrimination, self-flagellation even—without ever blaming himself. Then I imagined Heloise holding this letter in her hands, with her emotions unimpaired, in spite of the years that had passed, the feelings she had for him, the intelligence of her anger, the presence of her love . . . then I returned to Peter—then to her again—and finally to him, concluding, so as to confuse the reader, with the prayer he had written for her, at her request.

And thus the circle was closed — for in order not to be discovered I had gently to introduce the texts that he had written for the Paraclete, the Rule, the hymns, as well as the questions she had asked him on various aspects of religious history, and his replies — and finally that famous profession of faith.

As I proceeded to write, everything that might seem false about what I had undertaken became lost to view. I no longer knew the difference between what they had actually written and what I had written myself. The words that flowed from my quill were no longer mine, but theirs, and as I held back my tears (for one should never weep when one writes) I fulfilled a vow that was far greater than myself.

Throughout my life — I have often said this — I have had the sense of being absent when I was actually present. But I was now blossoming in this state of nothingness. Even my humility had nothing original about it: had I not had Brother Andrew, who hid behind his champion Robert of Arbrissel, to follow as an example? My victory was not due to me, but to them; people before me had recounted the lives of saints and of knights — the legends of Brittany and Cornwall had been told — now I would bequeath the story of a man and a woman who had loved one another. I trembled like a leaf when I copied out the last words of his prayer: *You brought us together, Lord, and separated us as it pleased you* . . . My body was so weary that I thought I was going to expire there, in front of this fire, with my manuscript in my hand, with the bag in which I shall conceal it in my cowl, my stylet, my ink . . . I began to be angry with myself. I had not gone to all this effort only to be revealed as a cheap forger.

I found Guy, the lunatic who was on the point of death, and I filled him with enough energy to provide me with some too; God alone knows how we dragged ourselves as far as the church; God knows how we managed to raise ourselves up to reach the putlog to hide the pages there . . . Now the job is accomplished and I am no longer worried about accidents that may occur. No, their letters will not disappear in a fire or in a flood, no, they will not be destroyed by some squalid, ignorant lay brother who finds them at the foot of a stall . . . By a route I do not know, they will return to the Paraclete and they will be found, they will be read, they will be copied . . . Some day, in a hundred years or more, a poet will read them and will shed tears over the souls of this man and this woman, who suffered and who loved one another.

And I, the absentee, I shall have my eternity.

They have carried Guy's body away. Soon they will come and search for me. The fire has gone out. I have a taste of ashes.

There seems to be a strange tingling sensation in my right hand. I try to move my fingers, convinced I shall be unable to do so; and yet the tip of the softest part of the middle finger manages to touch the pad of my palm. I can feel something inside it. Something, what is it? My fingers won't move any longer, they are stuck there, clenched together, and my forehead is covered in sweat. But what I have begun can no longer be stopped. Something, what is it? It's the body's, the heart's entire memory, it's the whole of the soul's labours — it's all of that set in motion, while I am unable to move. *A few traces of love* . . .

My body has become totally slack and I believe a light is passing through me. I can feel my fingers relaxing and my hand opening: there's a pink stone there, in its casket of flesh.

This is how they will find me when they come to place a candle by my mouth to see if breath still stirs in me.

If I could, I would smile.

Farewell, my only one.

Acknowledgments

This book is a love story, but also a story of many friendships.

It began to emerge afer the passing of my friend Jean-Dominique Bauby. All his life Bauby had dreamt of becoming the writer he felt—he knew—he was. He had only managed to do so when he was paralysed after a cerebral accident. Many readers of his book, *The Diving Bell and the Butterfly*, were moved by his wry voice, which concealed tenderness, and by his humour and grace. The personal 'calling' I got (Bauby would have hated that word) was: 'Don't wait.' After twenty years of not writing, I decided to take the plunge before my time came for regrets. So here's to you, my friend.

I also want to thank a few of the many historians whose wonderful works have been a source of inspiration for many characters in this novel: Georges Duby (Bernard of Clairvaux), Jacques Dalarun (Robert d'Arbrisel), Arsenio Frugoni (Arnold of Brescia), among others. I owe a special debt to Professor Peter Brown, whose masterly biography, *Augustine of Hippo* (Faber, 1967), has been (and still is, along with his other works) a constant cause of admiration and a treasure of inspiration; furthermore, Professor Brown was kind enough to provide me with the source for the epigraph to this book.

For readers who want to explore further the story of Heloise and Abelard (especially if they wish to separate fact from fiction), see Further Reading on the following page. Needless to say, anyone interested in the lives and prose style of the famous lovers should start with their (authentic) letters.

My thanks go to my friend Jean-Daniel Baltassat, with whom I shared many imaginary rides (and a couple of serious mountain hikes), who lent a helping hand in editing the first part of the book, and to Teresa Cremisi at Gallimard, who gave me a warm welcome and has been a constant source of support and enthusiasm. Jean-Marie Laclavetine was a demanding and caring editor: the final version of this book owes much to his remarks.

My gratitude also goes to my English-language editors: Eric Chinski and Jane Rosenman at Houghton Mifflin, and Jamie Byng at Canongate, who have created a friendly conspiracy around this novel.

Working with Euan Cameron on the English version of the book has been stimulating and humbling. Rereading my book in his translation has been like dicovering it anew; revising it with him has been a very *franglais* pleasure, and our *entente* — very *cordiale*, thanks to the musicality of his ear — has survived every step of the process.

Last but not least, I want to express my deep gratitude to my own only one. You helped me, you criticised me, you lent me your shoulder to lay my head upon, you soothed my nightmares, you supported me, you held my hand when I was floundering. I want to tell you that I wrote this out of love for you, for the light in your bright eyes. I love you.

Further Reading

The following books may be of interest to readers who want to know more about the lives of Abelard and Heloise.

The Letters of Abelard and Heloise, translated with an introduction by Betty Radice (Penguin, 1974)

The Lost Love Letters of Abelard and Heloise: perceptions of dialogue in 12th-century France, by Constant J. Mews (Macmillan, 1999)

Heloise and Abelard, by Régine Pernoud, translated by Peter Wiles (Collins, 1973)

Heloise and Abelard, by Étienne Gilson, translated by L.H. Shook (Hollis & Carter, 1953)

Heloise and Abelard: a 12th-century love story, by James Burge (Profile, 2003)

Abelard, a Medieval Life, by Michael Clanchy (Blackwell, 1997)

The Philosophy of Peter Abelard, by John Marenbon (Cambridge University Press, 1997)

The School of Peter Abelard: the influence of Abelard's thought in the early scholastic period, by D. Luscombe (Cambridge University Press, 1969)

Abelard and St Bernard: a study in 12th-century modernism, by A. Victor Murray (Manchester University Press, 1967)

Women Writers of the Middle Ages, by Peter Dronke (Cambridge University Press, 1984)